CAPTIVES

CAPTIVES

by

FORBES BRAMBLE

HAMISH HAMILTON
London

HAMISH HAMILTON LTD

Published by the Penguin Group
27 Wrights Lane, London W8 5TZ, England
Viking Penguin Inc, 40 West 23rd Street, New York, New York 10010, U.S.A.
Penguin Books Australia Ltd, Ringwood, Victoria, Australia
Penguin Books Canada Limited, 2801 John Street, Markham, Ontario, Canada L3R 1B4
Penguin Books (N.Z.) Ltd, 182–190 Wairau Road, Auckland 10, New Zealand

Penguin Books Ltd, Registered Offices: Harmondsworth, Middlesex, England

First published in Great Britain 1988 by
Hamish Hamilton Ltd

British Library Cataloguing in Publication Data
Bramble, Forbes, *1939-*
Captives.
I. Title
823′.914[F]

ISBN 0-241-12497-2

Typeset in 11/12pt Plantin at The Spartan Press Ltd,
Lymington, Hants
Printed and bound in Great Britain by Butler & Tanner Ltd,
Frome and London

20

CHAPTER ONE

The two boys hurtled down the lane, legs flying. They followed the central green strip of grass and clover that was bordered on each side by baked brown ruts, hard as brick. The green coating of the centre was deceptive, for the plants survived in splits and fractures and the ground beneath their shoes drummed. Hidden hoof-slots threatened to turn their ankles. One then the other staggered, flailed wildly with both arms and kept going with the impetus of liberation, for they had travelled far.

The lane ran straight for about two hundred yards and for this length was bordered high on each side by hedges that drooped inwards with the weight of leaf and bloom. Elder in flower hung low. They ran through it, starred with its white blossom, dusted with pollen.

They slowed to a fast walk, coughing and beating at their clothes, and began to pick their way forward more carefully for the track deteriorated. The younger of the two boys glanced behind him to check that their means of retreat was safe, because no one had said they could be here and the overgrowing trees frightened him.

The lane became narrower again. It had clearly been trimmed by the passage of vehicles. Broken twigs and branches stuck out like bones. Tufts of hay or straw were tangled in the upper branches of small trees. They stared in wonder, unable to imagine carts so high 'I wonder where it goes?' asked the older boy. It was a ploy to stop. They both understood that.

'Perhaps we should go back?' asked the younger boy. He was nine; sounded more cautious. His face was still round and plump although the rest of his body had begun to stretch. Dark hair flopped over his face and he was pink and sweating . 'This could be anyone's land. Farmers don't like it if you go on their land.'

'No. This must all be part of the farm. Ours, John.'

'If they buy it.' The younger boy sounded doubtful.

'Of course he will!'

The older boy was eleven and his bones were made. His hair was a dark blond, his face long. He was a full head taller than his brother. Both boys were wearing grey shirts that looked far too thick for the summer heat, grey flannel shorts that reached to their knees, collapsed stockings about their ankles and hard black shoes. The older boy's trousers had been let out and the younger's taken in. Their shirts were desperately thin at the collar. The younger boy had part of a tie protruding from a trouser pocket. They had taken them off for running.

'*They* will,' said the younger boy again.

'It doesn't matter what she thinks, William. If he wants it, he'll buy it.'

'I don't think it's like that.'

'I do. I'll be right, you'll see!'

'That's what you think!'

'Don't you want him to buy it then?'

John confronted William aggressively, folding his arms on his chest.

'I don't know. I don't know anything about farms.'

'You're a coward.'

'No, I'm not! Why am I a coward?'

'You don't like it because it's different.'

'That's just stupid. A really stupid thing to say!'

'Well, follow me then because I'm going on.'

But he only advanced a few paces before he stopped and leant back into the hedge, waiting. The lane curved round to the right so that its destination was invisible. William stuck his hands in his pockets and advanced. For all his taunting, the older boy fell in behind the younger. The first bend led on for about a hundred yards then the lane swung away towards the left. It appeared to be broader again up ahead.

'Look at that tree. It's covered in fruit!' William pointed towards the hedge on their left. They stood below it and stared.

The leaves were somewhat paler than the green of other hedgerow trees. They looked it over uncertainly. The fruit had the shape of pears with an enticing tinge of yellow, covered in a light down, a dusting of flock.

William leapt in the air and seized the whippy end of a branch. He pulled it down then carefully took hold of firmer wood, bending that too so that he could detach a fruit. He let the branch go again in a flurry of bits of leaf.

'Let me see,' said John importantly, but William would not release his prize. He rubbed at the surface of it with his shirt cuff, polishing the skin beneath the down so that it shone.

'The fluff comes away. It has a good smell.'

They both smelled it.

'Are you going to taste it?' asked William.

'You taste it,' said John. 'You wouldn't let me have it.'

'It could be poisonous.'

'Could be. But it isn't. I never heard of any poisonous fruit. Berries and fungus, but not fruit. It's a wild pear.'

'Well, I never heard of a wild pear.'

Cautiously the younger boy took a small bite, using his incisors like a rodent so that the flesh of the fruit merely rested on his lips. He mouthed it and spat it out with a grimace. John laughed.

'What's the matter with it?'

'It's bitter. It draws your mouth.'

John took it, tried the same experiment.

'It's a crab pear, like I said.'

William had never heard of a crab pear, but said nothing. He threw the fruit over the hedge.

'Anyway, if it's poisonous,' he said, 'the farmer wouldn't let it grow here in case the cows ate it.'

They moved on to the next bend. There was a gate leading into a meadow confused with buttercups among the grass. The grass was pink with seed. The boys stared at it wide-eyed. Insects moved everywhere. The field droned quietly. William pointed this out, not knowing if John had noticed. 'It makes a noise, if you listen!'

John pretended to be unimpressed, but they leaned on the gate for over two minutes, listening and watching. William stuck a finger in one ear, then the other, turning, experimenting.

'Come on,' said John. 'We have to reach the end of this lane. We have to find out where it goes to.'

'Maybe it just goes on forever.' But John had no interest in romantic speculation. He ran ahead now, and disappeared round the second bend. William heard his excited yell before he got there.

'It's a pond! Look at this. It's huge!'

A farm with a pond was almost beyond imagining but there it was. The lane divided, or rather a branch veered away to the left, for the main direction of the lane was straight on again and into a further enclosure in the distance. The branch headed straight for the water and plunged in. The tracks of animals and carts were clearly to be seen in the mud through the green water. It looked as if they had stampeded in to escape the heat and had been lost. The droppings of cows and horses lay in hardened cakes on the muddy edge or as moist islets in the water itself.

The pond was a long rectangle with the short side facing them on the only side without a bank. From these other three sides roots writhed out into the water. A fallen tree lay invitingly by the left-hand bank. A moorhen called somewhere nearby.

Peering with the eyes of hunters the boys could see the nests of either moorhen or coots. They were constructed on the outermost, most tenuous limits of fallen branches so that they were partially afloat. On two of these crannogs the boys could see birds sitting. The older boy put his finger to his lips and pointed, but he had no need to do so. They both knew it could mean a late brood of eggs. No blue lagoon, no coral atoll, no barrier reef, even if they had seen or known of such things, could have appeared more perfect and enchanting than the ponds.

'He *has* to buy it now!' John hissed in William's ear. Without further words both boys took off their shoes and socks, and stepped unhesitatingly into the mud, experiencing the astonishing pleasure of smooth coolness. Their feet sank in and it squeezed up between their toes, becoming cooler yet in the depths of the ooze. They rolled up their trousers and shirt sleeves, and waded forward, hoping and knowing that it would be too deep and that they would have to swim. That

4

they had to reach the nests was inevitable. For that suspended moment of time life had no other meaning.

In the house it was cool and dark and smelled strongly of smoke and bacon. Not cooking bacon, but curing bacon, a damp-earth smell combined with a tang like new rope.

Five people sat round an oval table in the centre of the room, four adults and one girl. It was low, with heavy beams running from side to side. The floor was of uneven stone slabs. Helen thought it looked dirty, like cracked china. She was fifteen and it was too hot to chase after her brothers. And she was too old. She was conscious of her body, her breasts. The farmer had been looking at them, his eyes sliding sideways, and she had sat hunched in her dress, pushing her shoulders forwards. He was a thin elderly man, wore a cap at the table and was seated to her right. Beyond him again was his wife. Her mother sat beside her and occasionally touched her protectively. Her father faced the farmer, the better to talk business.

They had been offered tea. It lay on the table partially consumed, a farm tea of bread and butter and jam sandwiches and dripping. There was a slab of dark cake. Jempson the farmer was pursuing the last crumbs of a piece of this round his plate by licking his dark stub of a forefinger and stabbing at them. Mostly they stuck. He concluded by licking his finger copiously and wiping it round the perimeter. Helen thought he was overdoing it. She wondered what her father was making of him and hoped he wouldn't be fooled by or patronise Jempson. Mrs Jempson had said nothing during the preliminaries of the negotiation but had glowered at Helen. It was clear she did not approve of a girl being in on grown-ups' business. She was a countrywoman who combined a thin face and neck with sturdy legs and buttocks. A woman accustomed to field labour. Helen imagined a diet that she knew only from books. Yellow cream, stiff as custard, meat with marbled fat and brown eggs. The brown eggs must be in a wicker basket lined with straw. Surely such a woman had been brought up on a diet like that. It made her feel hungry to think about it. She didn't care that Mrs Jempson disapproved of her. Mrs Jempson observed her husband's concluding wipe. She stood up and collected the plates together. Bending, her bottom stuck out more. Helen

5

repressed a smile. She was carrying a whole storehouse behind her, in case of need.

No one said anything while this went on. They listened to the clink of the plates as if it was an intelligent tongue, then when that ceased and Mrs Jempson sat down again the silence extended. A clock ticked, the pendulum palely visible.

The farmer drank tea from his white china pint mug, disdaining a tea cup. China cups had been laid for everyone else. Helen assumed he retained it as a badge of independence. His move allowed her to move. She picked up her cup and looked at it. A geometric pattern ran round the rim in a narrow band that had been edged with gilt. The pattern was worn to a faint shadow where her lip had made contact, and the gilt edge was a pale grey line. The china was so fine and clear that the level of the tea within was a defined dark layer. It would take perhaps a century of lips, she thought, to wear the pattern away. Yet lips are so soft, the softest part of the external being. She felt suddenly cold at the sense of timelessness of every-thing, – the beams, the smooth worn slabs, the round edges of the table, the cup. The place was a prison of the centuries. The clock ticked gently. It sounded well-oiled, well-fed, like farmer and wife. Jempson swallowed noisily, his Adam's apple bobbing. Her parents shifted, sipped, replaced their cups.

'Have a sandwich,' said Mrs Jempson addressing her sud-denly, so that she started.

'No, thank you!' she said it too quickly. She saw her mother frown.

'Girl isn't hungry,' said Mrs Jempson with satisfaction. If she had no business being there, then lack of hunger doubled her wanton intrusion in Mrs Jempson's eyes.

'Are you sure, Helen?' asked her mother.

Oh God, I'm sure, thought Helen, with a glance at the pile of uneaten sandwiches and bowl of scooped dripping. I can't eat with the smell of damp and bacon and mud and farm clothes and hot dust and old beams. You must know that.

'I couldn't manage anything,' she said.

'I made that bread this morning,' said the remorseless Mrs Jempson. 'It came out a beautiful loaf. That's our own wheat, you know, girl. Not like the stuff you've been accustomed to in paper bags. It can be firm when it's baked. And that jam, I made it myself. Those brambles do grow thick in the lane down to the meadow. You don't want to cut them back, I always say, and he leaves them. It's my second orchard, I say. My nature's orchard. If I could take it with me, I would! And you should see the bees!' Her eyes were very dark and glistening and she wore her hair at the back of her head in a tight bun. It was lustrous as a horse's tail and jet black. Helen imagined her tearing out the bushes by hand. She glanced at the sandwiches. The dark jam oozed from them like thick blood.

'I'll have one, Mrs Jempson,' said her mother, saving the day. The other woman sniffed as she passed the plate. Her husband took one and bit into it vigorously. Helen noticed with horror that at first his teeth stayed locked in the sandwich while his gums moved. The man made a quick motion with his free left hand, pushing and prising, and the jaws moved. Helen studied her plate. False teeth disgusted her. She felt sick.

'I will stay here, I will not be ill,' she repeated in her head. 'Think of other things. Think of why they eat the cake first and the jam sandwiches after. Think of tall trees and cool shade, of the smell of corn fields.'

'Do you have a full record of what you have planted?' asked her father. Jempson brought his head up but kept chewing until he was satisfied with his mouthful. He was in no hurry. He swallowed. His skinny neck straightened like a chicken's, tucked back again. He ran his tongue around inside his hollow cheek. Round and round the bulge chased.

'Bet I do.'

The stifled reply was full of resentment. He had every reason, Jempson was thinking. As a tenant farmer, what had he to look forward to? The place was being sold under his feet, his labour and toil put to value at auction. That labour and toil had been bought by this man across the table from him. This man had bought the ache of his bones, the skin off his hands. He thought of four o'clock starts in winter, of cold that froze milk in moments, that consumed hands and ears and brought all life to a halt. The stamping of cold horses. Frozen mangolds for the beasts, pulled from frozen clamps. Long ploughing from dawn to dusk, dead weary with the bats as companions over the ears of the horse. Deaths. Cattle, calves, geese, chickens. Herbie Goodall who had shot himself with a twelve bore because he couldn't take any more. Farmers were supposed to be the fortunate ones through the war years, but what had it done for him? He had wanted to leave the land, but they wouldn't let him. Now it was over, they wanted him out. It was an uneconomic unit. The words had consumed him like a cancer. Uneconomic to the Estate. He hated the bland groomed man across the table with his small military moustache, middle-class accent and middle-class hands, but he understood it wasn't the man's fault. 'The fields are like a machine of some sort,' he said slowly, rolling his vowels. 'They must be worked hard and at the same time cared for, or they wont't go. You leave a machine alone and it do rust, and if you leave a field alone it sets with weed. Try how you like with them weeds it will take you near a lifetime to get rid of 'em. Once you get rust on a machine it's the same. Fields and machines, the more you keep 'em turned the more they stay bright and clean. Again, if you work them too hard you can wear them out, you see. You can demand too much of them. You do see that, don't you, Mr Ellis?'

He sucked through his dentures to emphasise that he had finished. Drank some more tea.

'I understand. Quite.'

Helen wondered why her father had to say 'Quite' in that way. She was ashamed of it. She was ashamed of them all for buying the place and turning this man out. She looked sharply at Jempson, but he was staring fixedly at his plate.

'And how the fields was treated has a value,' Jempson continued in the same slow tone of instruction. 'You will see all that in the Valuation of Tenant-right. There the whole workings of the thing comes together, stack and field and dung-heap. You know about that then, Mr Ellis?'

'Yes.'

Helen could see that her father was becoming impatient at the older man's laborious lecture. She also sensed that her father only half-understood what Jempson was talking about.

'Then they have told you what you have to pay? No? Not yet?'

'I don't have a valuation yet.'

'I think of that as my money, you see, Mr Ellis. The landlord can take away my land but he can't sell my labour, nor my clover nor my mangolds nor my hay nor my dung, nor my tillage that I have ploughed into that soil without I get my due!' He lifted his eyes deliberately from his plate and fixed them on Ellis.

'That is all I get as my due. They made it all clear about that?'

'They made it clear. I understand the process.'

Ellis's voice was cool, off-putting.

'The solicitors advised me.'

'Ah, solicitors, Lord bless 'em, I don't hold out nothing for solicitors! They may be good at advising but I never seen one yet that could tell a mangold from a turnip! The valuation must be done by Valuers and Surveyors, and must be done to my approval! And no one has seen to ask me yet. My seven acre is red clover after potatoes and beet, and is in prime shape and you must pay the seed drilling and rolling. What do solicitors know about that?'

Helen saw a look of annoyance flit across her father's face. Only a momentary tightening of his cheek, a brief spasm, then gone. The other man was becoming quite red. His strangling control of himself was exacting a price. Helen felt he must be near to tears.

'For my mangolds there will be the tillage,' continued Jempson mechanically, 'the dung, the bag manure, seed, hand labour and rent on that. You don't know what hand labour is yet on mangolds, Mr Ellis. But it ought to have a value beyond gold. You'll find out, come your turn. Wait till winter when it freezes here so the ground do crack. Them mangolds will be hard as a block of ice. When you drop 'un on the ground it reminds me of a man's head the way it clonk down. Wear gloves like you may, there ain't gloves made can stop the ends of your fingers from that cold hurt. Lord, how it hurts! And the old beasts are eating the things and groaning and moaning because they're frozen and you can't put them through the crusher and they're dribbling down the sides of their mouths! You can hear their teeth crunching away like a man crunching icy puddles, and I tell you, you know what they're thinking!'

Jempson laughed. It started as a series of snorts and ended with three wheezes. The elderly man wiped each cheek in turn with the back of his cuff. Helen sniffed with embarrassment. She noted that her parents were watching him with faces devoid

9

of expression. They reminded her of a house seen by daylight with drawn curtains. Out of place, without function.

'So in a farm you buy the field, not the labour with it,' Jempson continued, more calmly. 'I say it is like buying a newspaper but not the words on it. Don't you think that's a strange thought? It ain't much good without the words, is it? They're the value, the paper's just a vehicle.'

He made it into two words, pronounced it vee-hickle. He compressed his lips and stopped. Mrs Jempson had kept silent with difficulty, looking fixedly and accusingly at Ellis all the time her husband was speaking. She as much as Jempson felt Ellis had no right to purchase these things with money even though she wanted it. She would rather have sold him a wilderness, taking with her the mangolds and the clover as she had wanted to take the blackberries. She had no problem in recognising that she disliked this man for his ability to buy what they couldn't afford, and for the humiliation that he was so easily buying their work and pain and persistence. A value would be put upon all their agonies and in the eyes of the world they would be seen as trivial. A few pounds here, a few there. The ground is a bad bank to invest in, she thought. Where was the return on old arthritic limbs, hard skin and lost youth? Surely there must be more in it than just a living? At the end of the day, there must be more to take out than tillage, than hand labour. Every vertebra of her back had creaked and groaned over the hoe at some time – the other women had said she was mad, that *they* wouldn't touch it, in their East Anglian way – but she had gone on, kept trying. Her anger surfaced.

'You're buying our life's work!' she said harshly, her eyes glittering, her face grim and unhappy. 'And the life of others before!'

They all looked at her. Her words fell like millstones. She immediately felt hot shame and embarrassment, like a child.

'Don't take on so,' said Jempson. His voice was rough but kind. She recognised the same tone that he used for animals. It quietened them down. For harnessing. Or milking. Or slaughter.

'It ain't their fault they're buying the place. Somebody had to, didn't they? We'll get a fair valuation, I'm sure.'

'Rogers and Rogers are doing it,' said Ellis, too eagerly. 'I understand they're experienced. . . .'

'Plenty of experience, plenty of experience. Fair men, I should say. They do most of that kind of work, hereabouts.'

Helen caught her mother's eye. Margaret Ellis looked sad and anxious. She was a believer in omens, and Helen knew this exchange would go badly with her. Her mother gave her an artificial smile.

'Are you all right, Helen?' she asked, averting any attention from herself. She patted Helen's arm.

'Are *you* all right?' Helen responded quietly, trying not to sound too impertinent. Her mother recognised the threat of exposure. There was a brief glance of warning, a caution between them that they would say no more. Helen thought how fragile her mother looked beside Mrs Jempson. It was difficult to believe they were both females of the same species. Even a racehorse and a cart horse were more alike.

Margaret was afraid. Afraid of the uncertainty of this venture and of the risk. She was afraid of her husband, who could not be opposed. He was Lord God in his own eyes. Men to him were clearly defined into races and classes. The leaders of men and the led.

He knew nothing about farming.

He said he had read all the right books.

He said it was an escape away from the war. A green place, a place to rebuild.

He didn't seem to care who he destroyed to prove it.

'It must seem strange to you, Mrs Ellis,' said Mrs Jempson with uncanny perceptiveness. Her voice was strong, and brooked no argument.

'It isn't the same for town girls as it is for country girls. I remember when I was a lass, I had so many ideas. So many notions and fancies. My head was full of them like a tree full of starlings! But I found out, and I was brought up for this. You will be on your own out here. So will your daughter. There is another girl over at Margishall, and that's seven mile away. I expect you can ride a bike? She's a bit older'n you, Tom Baxter's daughter, but you may find yourselves alike. Never mind, you'll find plenty of other things to do, I dare say. It's a working life you'll find, no time to worry about girls – or boys!'

Helen blushed. They were all looking at her.

'Don't hug yourself, Helen,' said her mother.

'Can I go outside?' asked Helen, aflame with annoyance at her mother's insensitivity.

'Don't you want anything else to eat?'

'No. I want to go out.'

'That could have been put more politely . . .'

'Oh, its all right,' said Mrs Jempson. 'She's bored with adult's talk.'

'I'll find the boys,' said Helen. She didn't really intend it.

'All right,' said her mother. 'If you can't find them, come back. Don't wander off.'

'How long will you be?' asked Helen.

'A good time yet, I daresay,' said Jempson. He was looking at her again, not caring if she noticed. 'After we've done in here we shall have to look at the beasts.'

'Be back in about an hour,' said her father. It was, as usual, an order. Helen rose to her feet clumsily, shoving at the chair which scraped on the flagstones and half-toppled. She left it where it was and made for the door. She heard her father's voice.

'Push your chair back!'

She pretended not to hear and opened the door by its iron thumb-latch and fled.

'Pretty girl,' said Jempson.

'Yes, isn't she. . . ' said Margaret tartly – she didn't like Jempson, or his glances. She had expected the farmer to be weather-beaten, to be rustic even, but not quite as battered as this man who looked more like a tramp with his coarseness of skin and his manner of dress.

'So Rogers and Rogers you propose,' continued Jempson. 'I dare say I could approve of them. Yes, you can tell your solicitors that they'll do. I suppose I have to write to you or something?'

Ellis shifted slightly in his seat. He gave a small embarrassed cough.

'Well, Mr Howison has agreed that already.'

'Has he now? And all along I thought I had the right to agree something! So the Landlord has the last say in that, does he? I shall have to see to that . . .'

'It's what I was told by Mr Howison, Mr Jempson. . . .'

'Oh, no doubt. I don't blame you. After all what difference is it to you, Mr Ellis, as long as it gets done. But all along I thought the condemned man had a right to say he didn't want a blindfold before they shot him, and I was wrong.'

'That Mr Howison, he might have asked!' Mrs Jempson said.

'He might, but he didn't.' Jempson tipped the large mug slowly, waiting for the residue of sugar to collect and slide towards the rim. After a pause he put his finger inside, ran it deftly round and sucked it.

'Too scarce to waste,' he said. 'It's the only thing I have it in, my tea. Beet's the coming thing they say. New mills are springing up everywhere. Huge things like power stations. But they're as much work as mangolds and in any case I shan't see it now, shall I. It should make a good crop here. Beet like sticky soil.'

He stood up slowly, each move planned, right foot to side of right chair leg, then left foot similarly, grip of both hands on the wooden arms, knotted hands on knotted wood. A grunt of exertion, then on his feet, the chair clasped to his behind as though glued. Two steps backwards, replace it on the flags with a clack! Straighten back, straighten cap, wipe mouth.

'Are you ready?'

It was a command, not a question. Margaret sensed that Jempson had made his mind up, like a man with his head on the block, he had given up arguing, given up the fight and just wanted it over and done with as quickly as possible.

'You'll want to see the stock before the sale. And you'll want the machinery too. There's nothing here the farm won't work without – except capital!'

'What do I do about that? The stock and the machinery? How do I buy it?' Robert Ellis asked too quickly. Margaret and he had discussed it on the train. It was a question he was anxious to raise.

'You must bid for that at auction,' said Jempson. There was triumph in his voice that he did not try to disguise.

'Is there no way I can buy it direct?'

Jempson scraped at the end of his nose.

'No. Can't be done. There has to be a sale. That way I get the right price. They can't be fixed proper any other way, especially not now.'

13

'But what about the main things? I shall need the tractor and ploughs and harrows. I can't farm without them.'

'You shall have to buy them then. I don't know how it's done in the town, Mr Ellis, but who would come to a sale where there weren't any harrows nor ploughs nor anything left but the wood and buckets? No, I have to get shot of everything, which means there has to be a crowd. Half of them won't buy a thing, but have only come to see what things fetch, so they can add it up at the end of the day and say to theirselves, old Jempson, he's made a bob or two out of that, let's see how much I'm worth at that rate. That's what half of it's about round here!'

Jempson laughed sourly.

'But isn't that a bit ridiculous? I shall have to pay the top price for what I have to have,' said Robert, stifling exasperation.

'It may seem ridiculous to you, but it seems like good news to me!' Jempson chuckled at this, moved his cap one way then another on his forehead.

'Anyway, devil alone knows where you'll get it all from if you don't buy it,' he continued, 'You'll have to go to Taylor and Tester, and they'll have the hide off you!'

'Who are they?'

'You'll meet them at the auction, shouldn't you worry. You'll see them all right! They do say that if a horse drops a nail round about, then Taylor and Tester picks it up. Some people reckon they're gyppos but they're not. Over at Wolling way they are. You want anything from a harvester to a used glue brush, they'll have it somewhere. If they can find it!'

Margaret saw the same hard swift look of annoyance cross Robert's face and was alarmed. She had prayed that this venture would start well. Actually knelt in church and prayed, a very special gesture for a faint believer. Nothing was ever as simple in Robert's life as he felt he was entitled to have it in a properly ordered world. As it had been in his five years in the Army. Those five years had reinforced his already rigid views. She didn't want this life, had opposed it as best she could and been ignored. If it disappointed him, God alone knew how he would take it out on her. She glanced around the dim room. These were wild and melancholy thoughts for a wife who was supposed to love her husband, but perhaps only feared him.

Did he know that in a place as remote as this she might find out? Her heart thumped with panic.

'You must see the old gas engine,' Jempson was saying. Margaret looked up to see Mrs Jempson staring intently at her. Their eyes met, held for perhaps four seconds. It was Margaret who looked away. What was Mrs Jempson saying? It seemed like a warning.

'You can't get anywhere without the old gas engine. Doesn't look much, but when she's going, she goes!'

With this profound statement Jempson walked to the door and opened it. The sun tumbled in, blinding them all so that they blinked. Robert got to his feet. The door shut behind the two men and the light went out.

In the silence that followed the flagstones seemed as cold as cemetery slabs to Margaret.

'You don't go for this farming much, Mrs Ellis, do you?' said Mrs Jempson.

'That's not true!' Margaret was too emphatic. 'Ask me when I've tried it.'

'Ah, but then it'll be too late.' Mrs Jempson in that unguarded moment allowed something to break through that was clear of envy or malice. It rang like a bell of truth, amplified by the bare stones.

'Look at you!' yelled John triumphantly. 'You're filthy black!'

'Look at yourself!' the younger boy returned. 'We're in trouble!'

'It'll dry. This sort of mud comes off easily.' John the knowing one. 'Mud is only wet dust. It is, if you think about it.'

William was a little impressed. If he could explain things as well as his older brother he might not get into so much trouble.

'What do we do?' he asked. 'We can't take them off to dry . . .'

'I'm getting to that coot's nest first,' said John. He was lanky but solid, and would be a heavy man when he grew up. His fair hair was plastered to a squarish crown that brought the long face to a strange stop.

'There won't be anything in it,' said William, anxious to divert his brother. 'It's the wrong time of the year. . . .'

'How do you know?' the elder boy demanded, hands on hips. 'You're just saying that because you want me to come out.'

'Leave it alone. Please.'

William knew as he said the words that he had done it all wrong. John laughed at him and plunged towards the island nest set firm in the crook of a fallen branch. The water stank as he stirred it up and bubbles rose ominously. John floundered towards the branch, and gripped the end of it with outstretched arm. It snapped. He flailed and gripped a stouter piece. The same thing happened. He staggered and waved his arms wildly to keep his balance. He was not a good swimmer.

'Be careful!' William yelled, frightened.

'It's deep here,' said John with calculated calm.

'Are you all right?'

'No, I'm drowning!' There was a note of triumph in the older boy's voice that made William hate the brother he loved. As he watched he saw John haul himself up. The branch dipped and slapped the water. If John fell, William knew there was no way he could get to him and pull him out. As if in response to his worst fears, John at that moment slipped from the branch. William's heart pumped wildly. He ran into the water, without thinking, stumbling and splashing. John's head surfaced first, then his shoulders, then his body as far as his waist. He was laughing, delighted with himself, standing firmly.

'Did you really think I'd fallen in? You did, didn't you? I can walk about in here. Look . . .'

'You're horrible!' shouted William ineffectually. He turned and waded towards the bank. Tears of fear and humiliation welled up. He walked steadily forward over hard ruts of mud to a dry patch of grass and plantain and sat down.

'It was empty anyway!' he heard John shout. He ignored him, staring through his tears up into the top leaves of the huge trees. Was this it then? Was he to be a farmer? Another school, another place, another uncertainty. He felt bitterly cold despite the hot sun and filled with a great sadness he could not explain. There had been so many schools during the war, so many houses. When he heard John sloshing through the water towards him, he got to his feet and ran away blindly, up the lane into unknown countryside, ignoring his brother's shouts and the jarring pain of baked earth and stones. It was a release.

Helen had walked about a quarter of a mile from the house, occasionally glancing back to see it framed by hedge or field. The pale pink wash that looked flakey and unhealthy close to seemed increasingly mellow as she left it further behind.

She followed the edge of a field of corn that was now more yellow than green, and interspersed with flowers – pools of blood-red poppies and a heavy scattering of black-eyed yellow daisies. There was a heavy scent from the corn, sweet like crushed grass, but not rank. She too wondered if this was to be the final settled existence. Her father certainly seemed to think so. He had been preparing for it earnestly for six months, and had formed the idea almost as soon as he had come home from the war.

She stared across the field, half-shutting her eyes to heighten the illusion of the heat shimmer that flickered over the corn. The crop was full of small sounds, clicks and creaks. She imagined it was the very sound of growing, of stretching in the sun.

When her father had walked through the door, they had all been well prepared for him by their mother as if for a very important visitor. She had said he would have changed, that he would be older than the photograph she had of him on the mantelpiece, that he would have a tan from Africa. Yet Helen had expected some spontaneous bond. Some magic chemical recognition and merging. There had been nothing. She had held out her hand to the figure in rough uniform. He had taken it, pulled her to him, and kissed her on the cheek. He smelled of tobacco and dry cleaning fluid and sweat. His moustache revolted her, and she had to prevent herself from pulling away from this affectionate stranger who wanted to press her to his chest, wanted to press her body on his. It should have been joy, but felt like an outrage.

It was the same man, and he was older than the photograph, but the man in the photograph had become the reality. The man in the uniform was sub-standard.

Her father was a man who treated her as a child. This man was awkward with her as a woman.

Nor was her mother as pleased to have him back as she should have been. Helen watched carefully, to see if her own views were confirmed and found an increasing accumulation of evidence. There had of course been an initial period of excitement and re-discovery. Both of them had behaved secretly, disappeared, sometimes in the house, sometimes slipping out. Doors were locked that had always been open. Bedroom doors, bathroom doors. Secrecy.

The cheap cobalt-blue eau-de-cologne in the litre bottle was part used and forgotten, the leather handbag embossed with pyramids and camels was used twice then put in the bottom drawer in the dressing table. Arab silver, dull as tin, was a curio for three weeks, then was relegated to the cardboard box on the wardrobe floor. From a position of display, her father too was relegated to one of utility. Washing up, at which he was very bad, and gardening at which he was better. There were talks about taking up his previous career in retailing. Talks cut short for 'later'. Helen had sensed the growing tension after only two months, and it had begun with farming.

'I'd really like to buy a farm,' he had said openly one evening. The words were addressed to Helen in front of her mother. The two boys had been put to bed. He was wearing his dark demob suit at the time, with a white shirt and his regimental tie. The statement seemed unreal. Margaret, who had been reading, lowered her book to her lap.

'You don't mean that seriously, Robert?'

'I certainly do. I've been to a firm of estate agents. They're sending me details as they get them.'

'When did you do that?'

'I called in this morning when I was in London.'

'I thought you were seeing about a job.'

'I did that as well!' The reply was waspish. He disliked being challenged. It was something that Margaret had confided in Helen that she hoped he would grow out of. She said it was an army legacy. It mustn't be allowed to last. Privately Helen thought it would need more trenchant opposition than that.

'Is there anywhere in particular you have in mind for this farm?' Margaret's eyes were wide with simulated indifference.

'You don't have to put on that tone!' Robert was instantly defensive.

'I'm sorry. I just think it's something we should all consider very carefully.'

'I have considered it very carefully,' said Robert, oblivious. 'I'm thinking of East Anglia.'

'And are you thinking about schools as well? Just for a start.'

'There's plenty of schools in East Anglia. It's the land that counts. Good land isn't often on the market. I think I've found some.'

Helen saw that he must have been preparing for this from the moment he returned. It was a bombshell to her, a numbing shock. She left the room and lay on her bed listening to them arguing in fits and bursts punctuated by long silences. Her mother slammed the door and went to bed first. She fell asleep before she heard her father retire.

She saw William walking round the field towards her. His pace was rapid and he looked distressed. She intercepted him at the corner, and was horrified to see he wore no shoes. His feet were scratched and cut, particularly about the ankles, in the thin, veined skin.

'Where are your shoes?'

'There's a pond back there. I took them off.'

'Why? Is John back there? Why are you coming round here? You'd better go back and get them?'

'I'm not going back.'

Helen needed no further explanation. She sighed noisily.

'I'll go. You wait here.'

'I don't want to be a farmer, Nell, do you?'

Helen looked in his dark eyes. They were filled with the full passion of a nine-year-old.

'I don't know yet.'

'Ma doesn't want to be a farmer, anyway. I know that. I've heard her say so, when she didn't know I was listening.'

'But she may like it really.'

'And we'll get beaten up at school.'

'Why should you? Don't be silly. . . .'

'Yes, we will. We've got posh south of England voices now. We got beaten up when we got to Kent because we had Scottish accents and we got beaten up in Scotland because we spoke Yorkshire. I wish we weren't on the move all the time! I don't want to move here.'

'Don't you like the countryside?'

Helen sat down on the grass bank. William sat down as well. They could see nothing but the long stems of corn before them, yellowing with ripeness from the base up. They heard the singing of larks, a sound as vacant and thoughtless as the scraping of grasshoppers. The birds jerked up and down in the blue haze of the sky as though tugged on strings.

'I like the countryside,' said William. 'But I don't know if I want us all to be stuck here.'

Helen nodded silently. The ownership of all this land of corn, of all these hedges and woods and of all the very birds that flew over it seemed incomprehensible to her. They had never owned more than a lawn, a tree, a row of bushes, a rhododendron, a gravel path, in the many wartime homes. She picked up a clod of clay, baked as though kilned. It refused to break when she bent it between both hands.

'It's funny to think that corn grows out of this, isn't it?'

William nodded.

'I suppose this will all be cut soon,' he said. 'If Pa buys this, it will all be bare. Then it will have to be ploughed.'

The boy picked up a broken piece of flint and threw it idly into the field.

'What do you think of Pa?' he asked.

'Why ask me? What do you mean?'

'You know what I mean. What do you make of him?'

'He's all right.'

'I didn't know who he was. When he came home.'

'You were young when he left. I remember him better because I was older.'

Sparse, controlled words.

'Was he like *you* remembered him?'

Helen stood up.

'Come on, let's get your shoes. . . .'

'You're not going to answer me, are you?'

The corn moved like the sea before a faint out-breathing of warm air. A long sigh, caught and echoed in a nearby spinney of elms.

'All right, he's not as I remembered him. I don't really know him yet. It's funny having a man in the house. Five years is a long time.'

'And does Ma like him? Do you really think?'

'Of course she does. She married him. She was so pleased when he came back.'

Hollow assurances, seemingly trivial in the vastness of the open field that seemed to absorb them in a fraction of a moment. The sweet and meaningless chatter of the larks filled the silence again. Helen was assailed by images. The place was hot, empty, fertile, a desert, crowded, ripe, desolate, frightening.

The two men so diversely dressed walked slowly across the dusty yard at the back of the house towards the long array of low buildings that lay parallel. All but two had tiled roofs, yellow with lichen, and had previously served as cowsheds or horse boxes – there was nothing to distinguish which. The roofs were sunken in the middle like the back of an old horse. The timbers were unsquared logs of elm and oak and the walls were of tarred weatherboard. The end two were roofed in corrugated iron, tan-coloured and pinholed. The front walls were missing, exposing the gas engine bolted to a concrete block, and an array of belts and pulleys connected to each other or dangling from the ceiling.

'This used to be the stockyard,' said Jempson, indicating the dusty arena. 'I kept a herd once. Good cows. There's no money in it now. I had three horses in those boxes.'

'Now?'

'Just one, and she's old. You'll need a new one. There's nothing left in her and no one will buy her.' Jempson had stopped walking and was staring sightlessly over the roofs. 'Nothing but horse meat.'

Robert Ellis had no idea what to say and had the sense to say nothing. As far as the farmer could be emotional, he thought, he was now on the verge of tears. It was a melancholy setting despite the blazing sun. A summer farmyard is deserted and the buildings seem without function, doors idly open. Only birds are active, pecking and preening in the dust or toying with last year's straw. An occasional starling scrabbles at the eaves, building ceaselessly, whatever the season.

The time before harvest is a period of limbo. Everything has gone into the land that it can take, and everything is yet to return. Buildings are hollow. Any filled space is a useless space.

Both men looked round, for that moment in communion.

21

They saw machinery lying idle beyond the buildings, busy machinery that belonged to late autumn and spring. Now it lay stranded in green ponds of nettles, resting, apparently unregarded. But even Robert Ellis knew that nothing in a farmyard is unregarded. Each piece of chain, each belt, each rusting indeterminate piece of metal has a function. Jempson walked forward. In the second open shed beside the gas engine the binder-reaper crouched ready. A large number of giant balls of twine were stacked one on another in the corner. They smelled of tar and brine and were yellow and bright.

'Ready for harvest,' he said. 'I do like the smell of that twine. Had the devil's own job getting it – as usual. It was worse during the war. In forty-two we got none at all because of shipping being sunk. We had to go back to tying the sheaves with a twist of straw. Lor', that was hard work! You forget how it used to be. First of all we had to have all the old chaps from the village come out and show us how it was done.' He slapped the perforated iron seat of the machine. 'She's in good order and you'll need her. The blades are good and I have a stack of spares. Chain was new two years ago, and the canvas is well repaired. That's another thing you can't get – new canvas. What with things in India, I reckon we shan't see twine nor canvas next year neither. . . .'

'Surely the Ministry makes sure. . . .'

Jempson coughed with laughter.

'The Ministry makes sure of nothing! They don't tell you about all the things we can't get, do they? Farmers' troubles never make the papers. We just have to make do and mend. It's the farming way. You'll see.' They left the building and Jempson took Robert over the gas engine, explaining what every belt and drive could do. A perplexing array of shafts and pulleys were strapped to timbers let in to the roof and fastened with huge bolts. The shed was black with oil – walls, floor and timbers were pickled.

'I'll show you how she starts up . . . You'll need her for sawing timber, or for grinding metal or just for firewood or whatever else.'

Robert Ellis watched the ungainly man who could do so much that he would have to learn. The thin face beneath the cap was a study in concentration as he poured a small quantity of petrol into the primer of the machine. The gnarled hands were steady and delicate. Jempson wore a loose jacket over a collarless shirt despite the heat of the day, and he paused now to take it off and hang it from a nail in a post. He seemed extremely thin in his shirt. The cap stayed on his head.

'This is the interesting bit!' the farmer said with relish. There was a smile in the deep-set dark eyes, a twitch at the corners of his mouth. Reaching up without looking, he lifted a handle off two hooks on a beam and fitted the square socket over a projecting spindle on the engine.

'You'd better stand back a bit in case she's frisky today!'

With easy strength he cranked the handle round, once, twice, three times. The engine made sucking and gurgling noises and a smell of petrol drifted into the air. Jempson then threw himself at the handle and cranked it furiously, like a man pedalling a bicycle in low gear. There was a thump from its innards and man and handle recoiled. Smoke rose from the exhaust, a rusty pipe with a ragged lip. Jempson was grinning now, showing strong yellow teeth like a horse's.

'You see!' he said triumphantly. 'Old girl doesn't want to start. She can give you a kick like a cow!'

He flung himself at the handle again and a series of dull thumps shook the heart of the engine. These formed into a regular and quickening beat, then developed into a roar. Jempson held the disengaged handle and smiled with satisfaction.

'Let her warm up,' he shouted, 'like a woman.' He lifted and resettled his cap. Both men watched as blue smoke gathered under the roof, then seeped out beneath the eaves. After about two minutes, Jempson reached over and turned a valve, switching over to paraffin from petrol. The engine stumbled and spat, but continued, regaining strength. Ellis saw the man was for these moments entirely happy. His face had relaxed into repose. By mistake their eyes met, and the spell was broken. Jempson knew he had been watched and his pleasure noted and his face became hard. He turned off a switch and the engine faltered, misfired and then coughed to a halt.

'I'll show you the other things,' he said.

The man led the way towards the great barn that loomed at the far end of the stockyard, all but blocking it.

Part of the roof at each end of the huge building was tiled while the central section had been covered with corrugated iron painted black. The side walls began with a plinth of worn and battered red brick, then became ancient blistered weatherboard, with a surface like coke. As they approached the building the radiant heat from its surfaces gusted over them in hot waves, enhancing the impression that it was some giant kiln or oven.

'She's a great big barn,' said the man with pride. 'You wait till you see the timbers.'

He pushed open one of the pair of massive doors that occupied the centre of the side. It swung easily back to a position of repose.

Large as the building appeared from the outside, Ellis was unprepared for the size within. It soared upwards into dizzy darkness as he automatically tipped his head back to follow the line and thrust of jutting timbers. He looked down quickly, surprised by the sudden vertigo. Jempson had noticed.

'It does that to you,' he observed. 'It's like lying on your back and watching the clouds fly over on a hill. That do make you feel sick and mazed.'

Ellis was surprised and discomfited by the man's sensitivity. It was too intimate a confidence for him. He coughed and watched the dust that glittered in sunbeams here and there in the huge space. His eyes were gradually becoming accustomed to the dim interior.

'Old owl lives up there,' Jempson continued in the same gentle tone. 'Barn owl, big as a swan, white as a ghost. He does a good job, sometimes scares the living daylights out of me when I'm in here alone and forgotten about him. I was sitting here one day, stitching sacks, very peaceful. Must have been sat for about two hours when there was this almighty rush like a toppling tree and he actually clipped my head with his wings, bang!'

Jempson demonstrated by cuffing the top of his cap with the palm of his hand.

'It was like being hit with an open umbrella! He'd seen a rat, you see. Right in front of me, because I was so still. Away he went with it screaming.' The man chuckled gently. 'Lord, how I stuck myself with the old sack needle! I only noticed it then.

I'd put it right through the top of my finger! That's what the old owl done for me, but he surely didn't mean it. . . .'

Ellis took care not to look at the man, as he had done by the engine. Instead he took a pace or two forward into the barn. Stacked up in one corner was bale upon bale of hay, and to another side straw. In the central area stood a hay wain, a tumbril, a seed drill, a chaff cutter. Around them hand tools. On the walls, sacks, twine, rope, wire, chain, harness. Chickens scattered as he advanced. The floor was soft and deep with a litter of chaff and soil.

'Nests are in the bales,' said Jempson, his tone more matter-of-fact. 'Three dozen eggs a day, if you can find them. You soon get to know.' Ellis could see how much the man loved this big dark building, with its noiseless floor and calm. It was the store, the womb of the farm, and perhaps the womb that Jempson returned to for peace. The man had perched himself easily on the fat hub of a wheel of the tumbril. 'There's an old fox about. Dog fox. Hear him every night, barking by the spinney. He had one of the ducks last week, but the hens are safe enough in here. They get up on the cross-beams where he can't get at 'em. I find them there in the morning, whole row of them, because they can fly you know, if they have to. And those Americans are about at night too. I hear them shooting, and I reckon they take a farmer's duck as soon as a rabbit. They're supposed to be guarding the ammunition dumps in the woods, but they don't guard anything! Drive around with a shotgun over the windscreen hunting partridge!'

He paused, and Ellis waited. The pause extended until it was difficult to break. Jempson finally did so. His voice was businesslike, or so he hoped.

'What do you make of it then?'

Robert Ellis was caught out of position, out of words, having nowhere to sit or lean. 'I like it,' he said. This sounded ridiculously inadequate. 'It's a good farm, and just the right size for me. I couldn't manage a bigger farm. I like this part of the country. I hope I make a proper go of it. I'm still worried about the machinery. I shall need it all.'

Jempson nodded.

'You will. And a new horse, and you haven't seen the tractor yet.'

Ellis looked sharply at Jempson to see if the man was laughing at him for his naivety, but the man's face was without expression.

'I'd better look at that next. And I'll need a cow or two.'

'They'll all be there at the stock sale.'

'What will you do?'

'What do you mean?'

'Will you be there?'

'I'll be there. It's my money!' Jempson permitted himself a wry smile. 'I ain't leaving this neighbourhood anyway. You can't dig up an old tree.'

CHAPTER TWO

Heinz was flattened into the mud like a brick dropped from a height. It was instantaneous and terrifying. He tried to draw breath and failed. No airways worked, his chest and lungs cramped up. Blind fear made him scream only to find the noise was a wheeze in his chest. He pushed up with his outstretched arms. His face was buried, together with much of his upper body.

He rolled sideways with the huge violence of panic, and yelled. The sound was high and animal, air suddenly burst into his lungs. He gulped and gasped, wiping at his face, clearing the muck from his eyes.

There was a reek of explosive, yet he had never heard the percussion. His head was full of demon noises, singings and shriekings and the pumping of blood. Very faintly he made out the battering roar of a heavy machine gun. Nearby someone was screaming. It was a thin eerie noise, insistent, in short bursts like a whistle. He felt his ears, but they seemed reasonably clear, then the rest of his head and body. It seemed to take a very long time, his hands and arms refused to respond accurately. He had a momentary mad image of those tiny cranes in glass cases in seaside arcades that are lowered by spinning a small wheel. They cannot be controlled, do not obey, miss, are oblivious to the directions of the operator despite the levers.

His hands were shaking violently.

He tried to move his legs and felt them respond.

He touched his head again because it had a puzzling

27

numbness, and discovered his helmet firmly strapped on. He knew where he was.

He heard more explosions, further away, dim through the clangour in his head.

'Get up!' the penny-whistle voice was screaming. 'Get up!'

He opened his eyes and in so doing realised that he had had them clenched shut and that there was brightness around. Siegfried's upper half was making this noise. He was no more than a metre away, his bottom half buried in earth that had collapsed from the trench. The machine gun they had been operating was wedged across his chest as though he was carrying it on parade. His face was grotesque.

'Get me out of here! Jesus God, get me out of here, I can't move!'

Heinz rolled over and knelt beside the heap of earth. Men up and down the network of slit trenches were firing, ducking, paying no attention. Some were dead. Heinz wondered why Siegfried made no attempt to help himself. It made him angry. Useless bloody Saxon! There was enough going on without digging people out. He took hold of the gun and pulled at it. It was heavy and Siegfried screamed. Heinz lifted it from the earth and stood it to one side. He dug into the side of the mound of earth, scooping like a dog. His hands were wet, wet with blood.

'You've been hit. Can you feel your legs?'

'Pain!' moaned Siegfried. 'Oh Christ, oh God, oh mother of God!' His face was white as paper. Heinz realised that his legs were pulp in the mud. He looked down briefly at what he had been doing. He had excavated part of Siegfried with his fingers. He felt his stomach heave.

'I must get an orderly.'

'Get me out! I'm dying!'

Ulrich came scampering towards them on hands and knees.

'Fall back,' he ordered. 'They're advancing. We must try to stop them at the bunker.'

'Yes, *Gefreiter*. But what about Siegfried? He's hit.'

Ulrich turned his head.

'Orderly! Give this man a shot of morphine! He needs attention.'

Ulrich looked briefly and intently into Heinz's eyes.

28

'You can't do anything here. Pick up that gun and move. Fast! They're surrounding us! Give him a hand, someone.'

Obediently Heinz picked the gun up by the butt. Another man seized the barrel, cursing at the heat of the metal. There were perhaps thirty men by now, all hurrying in the same direction, crouched low. They could hear the roaring of a tank. Gasping, they lugged the gun through the sand-bagged entrance. The bunker was constructed out of anything they had been able to find – corrugated iron sheet, timbers, concrete. A lieutenant whom Heinz recognised but whose name he did not know was giving orders. He and his new comrade set up the gun. The lieutenant had managed to find a tripod from somewhere. He seemed anxious, but in control of himself. Heinz thought of Siegfried, and wiped his hands on his trousers.

'Load,' said his companion. Automatically, Heinz fed in the belt. The other man was obviously a gunner. A third soldier joined them, carrying another box of ammunition. The gunner, then Heinz, peered briefly from the gun slit. The ground sloped away below them giving an open field of fire towards a wood in the middle distance. Smoke drifted across the intervening fields. It was warm and sunny although still only about eight in the morning. There was movement in the wood. The sun shone briefly on metal. Flashes. Both men ducked. A series of explosions followed almost immediately, shaking the bunker and dislodging earth from the roof.

'Tanks,' said the other man.

Heinz could hear now, although a continuous single note trilled somewhere in his inner ear. Shock was receding. A tank shell had blown up Siegfried. Immediately before, they had been laying down a fire on small figures darting amongst the trees and then towards them across the fields from hedge to ditch. Now another group was moving along the narrow road in the centre of their view.

'Who is it?' he asked the gunner.

'British or Canadians. I don't know. It can't be Americans. Not here.'

'They're not supposed to be here! We're supposed to have pushed them back!'

The other man shrugged.

The lieutenant was in a huddle with other officers. *Gefreiter* Ulrich came over quickly.

'All right, you are to fire at will, but don't waste the stuff.'

'What's happened to the other bunkers? Where's bunkers 54 and 56?' asked Heinz.

'We don't know, we've lost contact. Just smoke. They may have withdrawn.'

Ulrich moved on. Despite trying to appear calm, his face was sweaty and he looked scared.

'Overrun, more like,' said the gunner. 'We've had it.'

'You mustn't say that.'

'Why not? At least let's hope it's the British. They're supposed to be *korrekt*. We've got nothing to stop a tank. It just has to roll up here. I should think the only thing that's stopping them is that they don't know we've no big guns.'

'Perhaps some of our tanks are on their way.'

'Don't bank on it.'

'You'd better be careful what you say,' warned Heinz. 'There are people in this unit who would shoot you.'

'So what. It looks as if we're going to get shot one way or the other.' He squinted down the barrel. 'Here they come!'

He fired a short burst and Heinz was deafened once again. The ammunition belt jumped through his fingers and cases spilled onto the floor. Other guns opened up in the bunker. The lieutenant was staring fixedly at the wood through his field glasses. The guns stopped. There was silence. Heinz thought the lieutenant looked soft. The last thing he needed was a good officer, a do-or-die, *Gott-und-Vaterland* Nazi. He wondered if they had something white to wave. Behind him he heard groans. There were wounded men in the bunker.

'There is more transport coming up the road,' said the lieutenant.

'There are two tanks.'

If he was talking to himself, it didn't matter. In that silence everyone heard.

'I think they are British.'

'Maybe we'll keep our watches,' said Heinz's companion, lowering his voice. 'You know that they say U.S. stands for?'

'No?'

Uhrensämmler. I heard it from a fellow who heard it from a friend who's a Belgian. They strip prisoners of everything.'

'I warned you you shouldn't even talk about prisoners!'

'What's your name?'

'Heinz.'

'Look, Heinz, I'm not stupid. You won't see me run. I'll sit here and plug their arses with bullets until they walk through the bloody door, but I tell you, we're stuck here like a pimple on a nun's bum and haven't a hope. We're surrounded.'

The silence was eerie. Men coughed, the wounded moaned or complained. A medical orderly moved from one to the other, efficiently, with dressings or drugs. Heinz waited for a moment when the man passed near, and touched him on the arm.

'Excuse me . . .'

'Yes?'

'My friend out there . . . the man with the earth on him . . . the gunner . . .'

'He's dead.'

'Did you see him die?'

'Look, I gave him morphine. He was finished. I'm afraid he'll be dead by now. Definitely.'

'Thank you.'

Thank you that he'll definitely be dead by now.

When the enemy made their move they did so simply and swiftly. One of the two tanks advanced straight up the slope towards them, the other stayed in the valley, its barrel swung in their direction.

'Out for a morning drive!' said the gunner, his hand reaching out for the trigger.

'No one is to fire!' ordered the lieutenant. 'We are completely cut off. Our guns can't touch a tank. It can blow this bunker to pieces.'

The tank continued steadily forward, leaving a blue trail of exhaust smoke. The barrel of its gun was an unwavering 'O' pointed directly at the bunker.

'We must fire at it, sir! Aren't you going to give the order?'

It was Ulrich who spoke.

*Watch-collectors.

31

'No. There is no point.'

'Will you surrender?'

'*Gefreiter*, be silent.'

'By my oath to my *Führer*, sir, I claim the right to try to get out.'

'We are surrounded, and you will be shot if you try to resist.'

'It is my duty to try, sir!'

'Very well. Does anyone else feel the same way?'

There was an embarrassed silence. Ulrich picked up his rifle.

'*Heil Hitler!*'

His salute was echoed by a few of the men. The lieutenant paid no attention. Ulrich slipped out of the far door, crouched, moving fast.

The tank stopped thirty yards from the bunker. It waited motionless, the deep gurgle of the engine sufficient threat. The lieutenant turned to the medical orderly.

'Have you a sling?'

'Yes, sir.'

'It will do as our white flag. Appropriate, don't you think?' There was a slight smile on his face. He looked for something to tie it to. The men watched silently as he cast around. It was a ludicrous moment. No one volunteered to become involved.

'The *Wehrmacht* forgot to issue sticks for the purpose of surrender!' said the lieutenant, still well-bred, still calm. 'Hasn't anyone got anything to tie the sling to?'

'A rifle, sir?' said Heinz. It was the most and yet least obvious choice. A soldier never parts with his rifle.

'*Hände hoch!*' called a voice in German. The tank top was slowly raised. The lieutenant tied the sling to the rifle barrel, fumbling and nearly dropping it. Still the men watched as though none of this was anything to do with them. The lieutenant poked the weapon out of a gun slit and waved it awkwardly. Heinz was aware of his thumping heart. Outside, a bird was singing noisily. Uncaring. A man sneezed, and they jumped.

'Come out!' ordered a voice in English. It was over.

In the sunlight they grouped around the tank as though they had been liberated, not captured, and the English tank commander handed out cigarettes. He flung them awkwardly, one at a time, and they tried to catch them. The tank was hot and smelled of oil. An English soldier kept his hand lightly on his machine gun. Apart from that it was all informal.

Heinz wanted to go back to look for Siegfried. The lieutenant lined them up when they had finished their cigarettes and tried to march them away. Heinz remonstrated with the lieutenant who carried his white flag on the gun barrel in the 'slope arms' position. The lieutenant looked towards the tank crew, who seemed to have understood. They leaned on the rim of the turret, the goggles perched on their foreheads giving them the appearance of strange skulls. They grinned.

Heinz crawled across the ground. It was hard as rock and he could only move slowly. Suddenly it was rock, a black freckled granite that glistened like glass. He had trouble retaining his grin and began to slide. He scrabbled and reached out his hand. He saw Siegfried's head, and heard laughter. Perhaps it was the English soldiers. Unaccountably the head was sticking from the solid rock that had closed around the man's body, enveloping him. Siegfried was screaming, mouth wide open.

'It's crushing me!'

Siegfried had no eyes. The sockets were red and wet like crushed damsons and Heinz imagined he could see white sinew like the stones. He reached out, curious and at the same time disgusted, to touch one in case these stone things were not part of Siegfried but had become lodged in his brain. Water ran from the ends of his fingers and he was terrified lest it wash away some vital flesh.

'It's all right,' whispered Siegfried soothingly. 'It really is all right.' The gaping mouth had shut.

He touched the stones and the mouth flew open and the head rolled away from him, out of reach, tumbling down the slope of the glassy rock. Where it had been, Heinz observed a smooth round hole like the mouth of the gun of a tank. The English soldiers and his own companions were all laughing at him. The hole was filled with rainwater and a beetle was swimming in it, trying to climb out but slipping and slipping. Rage welled up in him and his eyes filled with tears.

He awoke.

It was very early. Dawn light just defined outlines in the interior of the hut. It was so slight that it fell like a thin grey powder on window ledges and bunks and the outlines of sleeping men.

Heinz was sweating and at the same time shivering with bitter cold. The dream, with variations, occurred about once every two weeks. He felt down his bed for his blankets, convinced they must have slipped off, but they had not. He pulled them tight as best he could. Another day was near.

He listened to men snoring, moving. Above him Ehrich coughed and turned on the upper bunk.

The sound of thirty men, thirty prisoners, escaping for a few hours.

Then back to the humdrum, cold or warm, rain or shine. The camp. Black, grey or white, he thought, they were all as innocent as babes in their sleep.

It was the English classification for them. He remembered the screening. Kempton Park on a bright morning where they were stood in lines and made to wait. For half an hour they waited, on the platform of the station. Orders were given to various groups in a variety of languages. They were told to wait. Prisoners must learn about waiting. It is their lot, their future, their daily bread. Waiting subdues, reduces, corrects and ultimately humiliates. Ideologies are blunted by the slow drip of tedium.

A man fell down exhausted. He was sat on a wooden bench which had a cast iron plate on the back with the name of the station. Others asked permission to urinate and were guarded away to the station toilet by unsympathetic and watchful British soldiers. Heinz remembered how he had looked at them carefully, studying the men who were to be his guards. They were mostly young, with white faces, and looked just as ill-fed as the Germans.

Next to them had been a group of Russian prisoners, *Osttruppen* and *Hiwis* mixed up together. Men who had fought against their own country for whatever reason, for hatred of Communism, for food, a bellyful of kasha to sign up for the *Wehrmacht*. They were in rags, most of them without shoes: high-cheeked Slavs, broad-faced Mongols, angular Cossacks and Kalmucks and Ukrainians. The British soldiers shouted at them in English and waved at them as though driving cattle. The *Hiwis*, understanding nothing, surged aimlessly in one direction and then another. They did not bother to line up like the Germans and even tried to sit down until the guards made it plain by shouting and gesturing with their guns what would happen. Yet they had officers with them. But they kept their eyes on the ground. Heinz, towards the end of his line and near them, stared until one, an older man with a long moustache and unkempt hair, eventually sensing his attention, looked up. Their eyes met. The man instantly glanced away. Heinz continued to stare and within ten seconds the man's gaze returned. Heinz was filled with pity. These men were on the same side as he was, but were destined to be outcast. What would happen to them if they were repatriated?

He would have liked to give the man something, a cigarette, just to be able to tell him to cheer up, but a command was given over the loudspeaker system and the guards rounded up the group and moved them off. They looked like refugees not soldiers. Behind them on the platform there were, here and there, black puddles where the men had relieved themselves, unable or unwilling to communicate with the guards as the Germans were able to do. It was a sight that Heinz never forgot.

As they left, Heinz caught the older Hiwi's eyes once again. The man nodded. Very slightly. His cheeks were collapsed inwards as though he was sucking them. Heinz had inclined his head. The Hiwi immediately looked away.

At Kempton Park Heinz was questioned by a quiet middle-aged officer with a pink face and white moustache and perfect German. He remembered being asked every personal detail imaginable. Where he lived, the name of his school, the local church, the baker, names of children, names of organisations to which he belonged, did he drive? Political views. What did he think of Hitler now that Germany had lost the war?

'He has destroyed the country.'

Had he always felt like that?

'Not at first.'

When?

'Before very long.'

35

Had he heard of concentration camps?

'No.'

The Englishman wrote something in Heinz's file. Heinz was anxious. What had been written down? He didn't understand the question. The interview seemed to go on for ever, with notes added from time to time.

They were asked to fill in a questionnaire and each one was given a small stub of pencil, about six centimetres long. Heinz smiled to himself at the memory. Every single man tried to steal his pencil.

The man next to him who was called Wolfgang surreptitiously snapped off half the lead and, with laborious contortions and a wink at Heinz, inserted his hand down the back of his trousers. Heinz could not bear to watch. Wolfgang grunted and withdrew his hand. Another wink. Presumably all was well.

The English found it of course, and Heinz's stub which he tucked less painfully under his armpit, when they were deloused at the barracks. They had handed over all their personal possessions which were put in linen bags with a label attached with their name and number. Each man signed his label, and they were told to undress in a long room with an icy-cold tiled floor. Their clothes were put in wooden boxes like baker's trays for steam delousing while they filed in one at a time for what they said was an examination. Wolfgang looked worried. He made a face at Heinz and waggled his little finger.

'Put your hands on the table,' commanded a beefy Army doctor. 'Lean forward!' Heinz did as he was told. 'We've got to examine you for piles.'

Wolfgang's secret was out. Heinz heard him curse, and the doctor laughed mirthlessly. Some of the other prisoners cheered. Wolfgang was marched briskly away.

Kempton Park had been a tented camp, a place of transit, without privacy. Different from High Garrett which he now regarded as home. Many of the guards and intelligence officers at Kempton were Jewish. For some it had been their first encounter with hostility simply because they were German. It had been a shock. This was not the correctness they had expected.

36

Others described how they had been spat upon and insulted by the French as they marched to their embarkation point. They told their tales with offended innocence. The French were a civilised race. They liked the French. They were hurt by this personal affront.

Heinz must have dozed off. He awoke to the shrilling of a whistle. Kunkel had been given the job of getting them up in the morning. The man had a shaven head and was no more than one metre sixty high. They called him crazy Kunkel. He blew the whistle repeatedly, at full volume, red in the face and marching like a marionette. He walked straight down the central aisle of each hut, turned with military precision, and walked straight back out again. The men shouted at him, or groaned or called him names. Kunkel paid no attention. They seldom saw him during the day. He hid somewhere in the kitchens and prepared root vegetables. He had been seen eating them unwashed, soil around his mouth.

Seven o'clock. Heinz swung his legs out of the bunk. There would be a queue at the hut lavatory within a matter of minutes.

'Raining?' Ehrich muttered.

'No,' said Heinz. It was a question they had taken to asking each morning. This country of England seemed very wet to them, especially to the South Germans. It was also an important factor in the dismal routine of roll call. They pulled on trousers and shoes and hurried to the door. Muller, the hut boss, always wore full uniform. He disliked those who did not. Muller was a Nazi. So was the *Lagerführer* and Muller was his spy and confidant. Care was always needed. It was the same in most huts. Perhaps six amongst the thirty men were dedicated members of the Party despite the screening at Kempton Park.

Heinz kept a diary. It was no more than a record of the day-to-day routine of the place, with notes on the weather or his progress in the various courses with which they occupied their time. He had made the small book himself, the cover from flour-bag cloth stuck to cardboard, the sheets of paper from a cement bag. He knew it was 'monitored', since each morning he folded a thread from the cover between certain pages, and often it was not there again in the evening.

'*Heil Hitler*!' said Muller as they passed.

'Good morning,' said Heinz. Ehrich said nothing. They joined the queue of figures walking down the concrete path to the wash hut.

'I never know whether it's better to ignore him or be polite,' said Heinz.

'If you ignore him, he has no way of knowing what you think. I should ignore him.'

'They're busy starting a rumour of an escape attempt. So I'm told.'

'Again? It's only to keep control. That way they can order us about and claim it's for the Fatherland. It also allows them to justify beating up their opponents!'

Roll-call followed the customary breakfast of porridge and tea and bread and butter. All five hundred men were lined up in rows five deep for ease of counting. It was hot. The *Lagerführer*, Schneider, accompanied by a British major, presided from the rostrum. Guard sergeants checked off the number of men in each section. Heinz could tell by the way they stood who were the Nazis. He was astonished that the British did not appear to notice. The British major, Middleton, was lean and tanned and had obviously spent his war in the sun somewhere. He was generally liked for what little they knew about him. His manner was quiet and it was said he was fair with offenders. How he got on with Schneider was anyone's guess. Schneider carried himself like a pigeon on a roof top and had a pallid complexion with dark angry eyes. Peter Stuck, one of Heinz's comrades and a baker by trade, said he reminded him of an uncooked pastry man with raisin eyes. The description had remained with Heinz.

The counting was over. Middleton stepped forward to the edge of the rostrum. Schneider stayed where he was. An English officer who acted as interpreter stood beside the major. There was a gentle movement among the men, a sharpening of senses.

'I have an announcement,' said Middleton. His voice crackled, adding to the general impression of dryness.

'I have an announcement,' repeated the officer in correct German.

'It has been decided that German prisoners of war will in future be permitted to work outside the camps, on farms. . . .'

A pause for the German version, then more rustling. Men exchanged glances if they knew those beside them, or watched their neighbours covertly if they did not. This would be an issue. They had all debated it in the past. It had even been an issue when they made things to sell. Heinz studied the man to his right, a Nazi called Waldenburg. Waldenburg did not look his way, but perceptibly stiffened to attention, his face frozen. Heinz glanced to his left and caught the eye of a big blond man, Peter Stuck. Peter winked. The traces of a grin pulled up the corners of his mouth.

We'll get out, thought Heinz, trying the idea out again and then again. He saw Ehrich in front of him wrap two fingers together on each hand and give them a shake – a gesture of joy. Heinz found that he was smiling without knowing it. Someone gave a low cheer, then another, then Ehrich, then Heinz and Peter. It was infectious and idiotic. They cheered the thin major approvingly and he smiled quickly and gave a little nod. Behind him, Schneider's eyes were wild with alarm.

'In addition to the *lagergeld* of three shillings and fourpence, all those who work in the fields will receive three farthings an hour extra. The work will of course vary according to the farm and the season. At the moment it will mainly be lifting potatoes and turnips, as the corn harvest is largely over. . . .'

Heinz watched Peter Stuck's grin expand further. The man had big red lips, and he licked them, controlling saliva. They all had that common thought. Food. Food unlimited. Food in the ground or in hedgerows. Where there were potatoes and turnips there would be rabbits, pheasants and partridges. They knew from the guards they were plentiful. It was the war. No one had shot them. Men were away, cartridges were unavailable. Many of the Germans were countrymen who could lay a good snare. Men looked at each other with anticipation, like small boys offered the keys of the pantry.

Only the Party members stood stiffly, looking neither to left nor right, but marking who cheered, who had sold out.

'Theft will be severely punished. Taking foodstuffs will be regarded as theft. I want to make sure that is clearly understood. . . .'

The voice like the crackle of burning twigs, the sun hot on their necks. The camps seemed a good place at the moment.

Two tortoiseshell butterflies danced and cartwheeled around each other, then alighted briefly on the back of a man three rows in front of Heinz. Then they were gone quickly reeling into the sky.

What envy I have for you, thought Heinz. However brief your lives, it is so lacking in complexity.

On the rostrum Schneider looked uncharacteristically pink, his hands behind his back and his stomach stuck out. Heinz was reminded of Ehrich's description of Schneider on a previous occasion – 'a man trying to shit whole acorns'. It was obvious that Middleton had not told him of the nature of the announcement in advance.

Heinz knew he would go out to the fields, whatever the pressures they tried. There was safety in numbers, and enough of them obviously felt the same. They would keep together.

Peter and Heinz were making chessmen. It was the favoured money-maker now. Heinz, the carpenter, was expert. Peter, with what he called his baker's hands, less so. Ehrich had gone to his English class. He among this group of friends was the only one good at languages. In France he had quickly learned French.

'This could be the end of industrial growth!' said Peter, paring at a knight made from pine. The wood was a piece of flooring removed from a cupboard and the tool a chisel made from a strip of corrugated iron.

'We don't *have* to work in the fields. We can stay here if we want to.'

'I'm sick of chessmen anyway. You try to stop me! We must get wire and string.'

'We'll get that easily about a farm. Just think of all the things we'll have access to!'

'Women!'

'I don't know about that . . .'

'Oh come on, Heinz! I'm a fine figure of a man!'

'You're also big-headed, vain and German!'

'These are just a few of my attractions!'

Heinz laughed. He had been about to burn decorations on a bishop with a piece of red-hot wire which he held over a lamp. He put it down.

'I can't do this while I'm laughing.'

Peter looked up.

'Keep working, here comes Mohnke. It's propaganda time.'

Mohnke was in his early twenties – the worst age-group – and was compact, athletic and completely without a sense of humour. From the *Waffen-SS*, he had somehow managed to convince the British screening officers that he was a 'grey'.

'*Heil Hitler!*'

Peter and Heinz were seated opposite each other on wooden benches. Their carving materials, the lamp and tools were spread out between them on a well-worn timber table, that bore the names of prisoners past and present. They looked at each other first, without replying, then in a carefully studied act at the visitor. Elbow to table, fist clenched, head to fist, slightly on one side. Turn head, balancing it on thumb extended from fist. Vaudeville precision.

'You don't salute in reply!'

It was an accusation, not an observation. Mohnke could not hide his anger.

'No,' said Peter calmly, 'we don't.'

'You should. Are you Germans?'

'We've had this conversation before,' said Peter. He feigned great tolerance. 'I suppose we can put up with it again.'

'Go away, Mohnke,' said Heinz. His rage was transparent. 'We don't need to be asked if we're Germans.' With Mohnke, however, it was a case of the least said, the sooner he moved on to someone else.

The man addressing them was no caricature of a National Socialist. He wore his hair long and plastered flat with brilliantine in the style of some officers and had a distinguishing white fleck in the cornea of his right eye. It was so bright that it resembled a dash of paint. As a result it was never quite possible to meet his gaze, never possible to see the inner man for this floating flaw. He dressed immaculately and always had sharply-pressed trousers. It was said that mad Kunkel pressed them in a kitchen oven by stacking hot plates on them. Kunkel was certainly under the spell and protection of the Party members.

Mohnke's features were coarse, the nose flattened and primal, his ears large. This contrasted comically with his pressed uniform and careful accent but also gave him an air of menace.

'I want to hear you say that you will refuse to work in the fields if you are good Germans,' said Mohnke, ignoring Heinz's dismissal.

'We'll work where we like,' said Heinz hotly. The lamp flared, giving off a trail of black smoke that darkened the glass, wasting oil. Heinz automatically reached out and lowered the flame. Peter, more prudent, more phlegmatic, saw the danger of confrontation. He was also sitting facing the door where he could see Muller and Waldenberg lounging conspicuously. Other men had stopped working in the hut and a silence had fallen.

'I can't see anything against us working in the fields,' said Peter quietly. 'It will keep us healthy. We will be able to get food. The war is over now, we cannot be helping the war effort. It will give us something else to do. I have spent three years inside camps and I need a change. We all need a change. Personally I am too heavy for football or basketball or running. I am not fit.'

There was a murmur of agreement, men nodded.

'You do not understand the issue, do you!' said Waldenburg. He came forward to the centre of the hut, hands in pockets, with a characteristic casual swagger. He was a practised speaker. 'The British need your labour to help with their recovery. They are short of manpower. While Germany struggles, any man who works in the fields is assisting the enemy to rebuild. This war is not over. The military fight has for the moment stopped, but it will resume. You aren't such fools, are you, as to believe that it is all over? You don't believe that the High Command is defeated, do you? We *know*, we have positive information that the *Führer* is even now re-grouping to form the Fourth Reich. Everything that any man does to help the enemies of Germany is the act of a traitor to Germany and that Reich.'

'Come off it, Waldenberg!' shouted a man called Felder. 'The Command is finished and Hitler is dead! We all know that!'

'No, you don't!' Waldenburg climbed on to a bench. 'The propaganda machine of the British and Americans says all these things and you are stupid enough to believe them!'

There was some laughter, some silence.

'Apart from the benefits of your labour, they want to encourage fraternisation to advance the process that they call democratisation. These are all attacks upon us.'

It was very hot in the hut even though all the windows were wide open. Normally men would be playing various games outside and there would be a din of shouting and whistles, cheers, scuffling feet. Instead, today, they were sunning themselves, marvelling that in England it could really become as hot as this. As a pointed irony, the only sound was that of a tractor with some piece of farm equipment, grumbling up and down a nearby field. It was the time of day when even birds hid.

'You aren't entitled to tell us what to think,' said Heinz, quite loud. 'The war is over. I did my fighting and I have nothing to be ashamed of. Many of us want to believe that Germany can achieve democracy. We all know what they used to sing. "Through the land soldiers march, helmet and rifle at the ready." Not again. I for one believe there is life after Hitler. Germans can be civilians again. I want to work on a farm. It will be good for me, make me fit and strong for my return home, and that must be good for Germany. Perhaps we will make British friends, but what's wrong with being accepted again into the society of human beings? Besides, my home town is full of Russians. What have I to look forward to?'

Heinz had spoken sincerely and the hut was silent when he finished. The silence was one of contemplation and unity. Waldenberg, stranded on a bench, seemed a strident cypher. The sound of the tractor grew and then receded.

'Any man working in the fields is a traitor, that's all there is to it!' he declared and got down abruptly from his perch. Mohnke marched with him to the door. With Muller tagging on behind, they left the room. Peter resumed his carving. Heinz readjusted the flame of his lamp, telling himself to be calm. Despite the appearance he had so carefully preserved, he was upset by the confrontation and his hands shook a little.

'You'll have to watch out,' said Peter. 'They'll try to get their own back. Don't go about alone until this blows over.'

'I know,' said Heinz. 'But they must change. If people like Waldenburg won't change then it will be better to go back to the Russians!'

43

Peter looked at him, shocked.

'Easy, Heinz! You're going too far!'

Later in the evening, while swifts screamed and swept through the lattices of steel and wire that made the enclosures of their prison, Heinz, Ehrich and Peter sat on the verandah of their own hut. Most men were outside in groups and conversation was low. The heat had stupefied them. The evening sun was still brightly potent.

Peter raised his head and drew in a great breath of air.

'Do you smell that?' he asked. 'The smell of hay, the smell of freedom.'

'Of a sort,' said Ehrich wryly. 'It's still England out there.'

'At home they'll be cutting hay too,' said Peter. 'I wonder if they have any tractors? Will it be only scythes? All you have to do to escape is imagine that it's German hay. Just shut your eyes and think of your own meadows . . .'

'Shut up, Peter!' said Ehrich.

'Do you remember when we were in camp in France near Cherbourg? There was that whore who came each night to make a bit out of the sentries. You remember the cologne she wore? We used to sit and smell it on warm evenings, and Ehrich used to go mad . . .'

'Shut up, Peter!'

Ehrich again, this time embarrassed. Peter was breaking all their rules. There was to be no talk of freedom or women or drink or tobacco.

'What do you really think is going on back home?' asked Peter. 'Do you think it is really so much worse than here?'

Ehrich and Peter droned on. Heinz thought of Inga. He had had two brief letters from her. She was with her mother now in Hamburg where she said the city was ruined and they had nothing. Beautiful Inga who could never be trusted, even when he was at home. What was she doing now? Had she found someone to support her?

It was slow poison to think like this.

He realised with a start that the other two men had been talking to him.

'Where were you?' demanded Peter.

'I'm sorry.'

44

'You're brooding.'

'I'm not. What were you saying?'

'I was asking which you preferred,' said Peter, 'the smell of newly-planed pine or the smell of newly-baked bread. Two of the world's great smells, one particular to each of us . . .'

'To add to whores and hay,' explained Ehrich with a brief smile. He had the gaunt, weatherbeaten face that sculptors once attached to Roman patricians. He had been a plasterer in that other life.

'I'll have the smell of pine. Baking bread is overpowering. Too much of it is revolting.'

'What were you thinking about?' asked Ehrich.

'I was wondering what sort of farm we'll get,' lied Heinz.

CHAPTER THREE

It reminded Robert Ellis of an army drawn up on a reverse slope. Not the modern army that he knew with its tank spearheads, artillery and aircraft, but an army of the Napoleonic War, deployed in parallel rows, each section untidy within itself, but the squares and the rectangles themselves strongly defined. So did the ladies of Moscow look down on Borodino, he thought, smiling at this outrageous exaggeration. Yet he was very nervous. It was his first sale and vitally important. He looked again at the catalogue.

'Conditions as Usual.

Catalogue of the Live and Dead Farming Stock

Comprising

7 Cattle

(viz, 4 Milch Cows and 3 Shorthorn Heifers, 15 months)

40 Poultry.

1 Clydesdale Horse

Excellent Implements including two tractors, a binder reaper,

2 Farm Carts, McCormick grass mower, Ransome's RSLD

2 Furrow Tractor plough. . . .'

Everything was listed and every lot numbered from the Ellipse root-mincer to a roll of pig netting. He had marked with a tick every item that he had worked out he needed, leaving a sufficient space alongside to write in the price.

The stock was set out in the seven-acre stubble across the narrow road that separated this part of the farm from the house, and occupied nearly half of it. The seven-acre field sloped down to the meadow through which ran the stream. My meadow, my stream, thought Robert. My seven-acre stubble. It was a concept he had not yet been able to grasp, and probably would not until he actually occupied the place.

Margaret laid a hand on his arm.

'Nervous? Let's walk round the big items again. It might help you to relax . . .'

'I don't want to relax. I want to stay here in case anything happens. I want to keep an eye on the auctioneer.'

He felt her hand withdrawn from his arm, but he was only annoyed by it. It seemed a petty gesture.

'The auctioneer will start at two promptly,' said Margaret reasonably. 'It says two prompt in the catalogue and that's what it means. For heaven's sake, we've still a quarter of an hour. I'm going to look at the furniture and kitchen stuff again. There's some fine original things.'

'I'll stay here.'

'Get to know the neighbours,' said Margaret, indicating with a nod a group of men that included Jempson. 'They may be able to help you.'

'All right!' said Robert crossly. He objected to being told the obvious. She had a knack of it.

'But will you do it?' insisted Margaret. It had already been a very long day. They had got up at five and driven to the farm, arriving just after nine when the stock was still being laid out. Early as they were, there were already farmers there, looking, prodding, sizing things up. They disappeared early too, returning to their farms for the morning's work before coming back to the sale. The extraordinary assortment of vehicles parked in the shade of the tall hedge by the roadside attested to their presence.

'I'll do it!'

Margaret turned impatiently and left him. There were very few women at this gathering, and she felt conspicuously out of place. The men's eyes followed her everywhere, some covertly, some openly staring. Many raised their hats or caps to her, wishing her good afternoon by name. How did they know who she was? She longed to see another woman under fifty, but was defeated.

'You'll be Mrs Ellis,' said a voice beside her as she stared at a

47

collection of tin baths, scrubbing boards and mangles. She turned to find herself addressed by a brown-faced woman in her mid-fifties, wearing a man's jacket with her blouse and skirt, despite the heat. Margaret accepted the outstretched hand that was dry and hard as tree bark. 'I'm Mary Merrow. I own Cressets Farm down the road. We'll be neighbours.'

'I'm very pleased to meet you. I'm pleased to meet another woman! This seems to be a man's occasion!'

'You'll have to get used to that. Where are you from?'

'We've been living in Sussex, but I come from Leicester originally.'

'Are you new to farming?'

Margaret laughed.

'Oh, yes! Complete novices. You can tell by the way I've dressed!'

'It's a very nice dress.'

'Thank you, but I feel conspicuous. I didn't know what to expect. It would be better at a garden party, it's ridiculous here.'

'Don't worry. The men will love it. This is East Anglia and they have funny ideas about the position of women. Don't you let your husband get infected!'

Mary Merrow's eyes were twinkling but there was no doubt she was serious.

'Is your husband here?'

Mary Merrow snorted.

'I'm not married, dear! Do I look married? I run the place myself. Never had time for men when I was young, and now they have no time for me, so we have a mutual arrangement. They treat me as a man, and I condescend to mix with them when it can't be avoided!'

Margaret laughed.

'Your husband was in the army.'

It was a statement, not a question.

'Yes, he was. But not a Regular.'

'I can tell by the way he walks, his moustache. He'll have to realise that things don't go to plan in farming, and orders don't even get received, let alone obeyed. Is he from a farming background?'

'Only his grandfather.'

'Then does he know enough?'

48

Margaret looked hard at Mary Merrow. She felt this inquiry was bordering on rudeness, but it was expressed with a candour that disarmed criticism. In any case it did no more than voice her own doubts and fears. The older woman was obviously accustomed to speaking with such directness. Margaret wondered if it was the strength of being an honorary man.

'You've answered me by taking so long to reply.'

'He *has* read every book on the subject that there is. He's sure he can do it, but he has no illusions.'

As she said it, she was aware how stupid the remark must sound. Mary met her gaze calmly and made no comment.

'Well, the very best of luck,' she said. 'I hope he gets what he needs at this sale. Equipment is hard to come by these days. Has he got a good list?'

'Yes. He's got that organised.'

'Yes, I suppose he would. It's the unobvious things you mustn't forget, like a good thatching ladder, and all the harness. Tell him that tractor of Jempson's is a pig to start but is all right. The horse is done for. He's not buying the horse?'

'No. We're going to get a new horse.'

Mary Merrow nodded.

'You'll want to get on now, and I won't keep you. If there's anything you want to know about, ask me. Most of Jempson's things are no better or no worse than anyone else's. I hope you'll bump into me later on. If not make sure to pay me a visit as soon as you're in.'

'I will.'

She turned and walked sturdily off towards the line where the equipment was drawn up. Margaret, watching her, saw that the men did not lift their hats to Mary as they had done to her, but nodded instead.

Robert had strolled again round the main blocks of implements and machinery, partly to check his estimates and partly because he was not sure how he should approach Jempson or how he would be received. It was a strange position to be a new owner but to have nothing with which to work the land. It must be even stranger for Jempson to walk fields that were no longer his, to see where his cut had been good or wide in every stubble, and to realise that it had all been on loan to him and that the land endures professionals and novices alike. Now, he waited for the last act. A craftsman without his tools is utterly retired, like an officer without men, in a strange civilian world.

To delay further would be seen as cowardice. He knew he was being watched in every move. He folded his catalogue with studied finality and walked over to Jempson and his group.

'Good afternoon!' he announced firmly, holding out his hand. Jempson accepted it, shook it briefly. The men about him regarded Robert expectantly. There were five of them, as different from each other as peas from barley.

'Good afternoon, Mr Ellis,' said Jempson, his accent broader than Robert remembered, perhaps because he was among his friends. 'Good day for it. I hope you've decided what you need.'

'Yes. I've been right round.' Robert thought it prudent not to say more. He had no doubt these men would be bidding against him for some of the items.

'You had best meet two neighbours,' said Jempson. He indicated first a big man with dark hair, dark eyes and a fierce black moustache. 'This is Bill West from Pite Hall, and this is John Ingleton of Bargets.' The second man was sandy-haired with sandy sideburns and freckles and had a face of terrier sharpness. His teeth were yellowed and his eyes blue. Ellis recognised the names of both farms. They were no more than a dozen fields away. The men in turn held out their hands, and he shook them, aware of the softness of his palm in contact with theirs. Then they stood back and regarded him. Their faces were not hostile, but neither were they friendly. Robert Ellis was aware that they were taking stock of the man who had ousted Jempson.

'And this is Mr Taylor and Mr Tester,' said Jempson. 'I remember telling you that you would meet these two gentlemen at the sale, and here they are.'

Taylor and Tester inclined their heads and smiled. Both men wore ancient blue dungarees and ex-army boots. Taylor sported a trilby and had on a collarless white shirt under the dungarees; Tester a battledress jacket and a flat cap that was so black with oil and grease that it glistened. Both men were on the short side but Taylor was plump and Tester was muscular. They were unmistakably men who spent a great deal of their lives grubbing about in machines, broken nails and a missing finger down to

the first joint on Tester's left hand attested to that. Unlike the farmers, both men had pale complexions, the creases in their faces like crumples in grey cloth. Their eyes were quick and bright and missed nothing.

'How do you do,' said Ellis. He made no attempt to shake hands with Taylor and Tester. They for their part kept their thumbs stuck in their dungarees.

Ellis wondered how they were placed in the social order of things. They clearly mixed with the farmers, but on what basis was less obvious. There was an impertinence in their smiles that annoyed him, as though they distanced themselves from him and all farmers and felt themselves to be superior, to be the possessors of some special knowledge. He resented their swagger, but was determined not to show it.

'If there's something you can't get here,' said Jempson, 'these gentlemen will have it or can get it for you. And, when it comes to threshing, they have the best traction engine hereabouts, and you must book them early.'

Taylor and Tester nodded and smiled. Sharp glances struck out at him, like lizards' tongues. They still said nothing.

'I hope you aren't here to buy everything I need!' said Ellis, trying to provoke them to speech. Taylor and Tester chuckled and shifted their feet. Tester wagged his head three times in a short flicking motion, indicating he enjoyed the joke.

'Not at the prices I hope to make!' said Jempson. Taylor and Tester laughed again. Ellis wondered if in truth they were simple and if their darting alertness was no more than nervous energy given off in sparks.

Ingleton intervened.

'They don't talk much, Mr Ellis. But just you watch them, it's their sly way of doing business! Good at listening, they are, and when you make a slip they're on to it! I've been dealing with them for nigh on twenty years and I know what I'm talking about!'

The two men in dungarees chuckled again as though it really had nothing to do with them. Then Taylor spoke at last, easy in his stance, but looking towards the hot blue sky, eyes narrowed. His voice was just too sharp to be local, too nasal. An Essex man Ellis assumed.

'You'll give us'n a bad reputation,' he said slowly. 'Now, we like to *earn* that!'

The two men chuckled again. Tester scuffed at a clump of stubble as if to emphasise his glee. The rasping noise was like an unshaven man scratching.

'My name's Baxter,' said the fifth man in a southern English voice that owed nothing to East Anglia, holding out his hand, offering escape. Ellis shook it gratefully, glad to have relief from the duo.

'I farm Margishall.'

The speaker was well-dressed in a lightweight tweed jacket and open-necked shirt and flannels. His brown, gleaming shoes looked like new chestnuts, wet from the shell, and had the raised thread of hand-stitching.

Pleased to see a man with whom he could identify, Ellis took in the sandy hair and blue eyes and rather anonymous features.

'Very pleased to meet you!' he took care to infuse his reply with warmth. 'You have a daughter, almost the same age as my own. Mr Jempson told me.'

'Yes, indeed I have. Is your girl here today?'

'No. She's at school. I thought it wouldn't be a good idea.'

Baxter nodded.

'I'm sure you're right. When are you moving in? Next week?'

'That's right.'

'If there's anything you need, you can always count on me. You must come over and visit us as soon as you've settled in. My wife will be delighted to see you.'

'Thank you, I promise we will.'

They exchanged more pleasantries. Baxter was about five years younger than Ellis, and seemed determined to stress his hospitality. Despite his natural inclination towards him as a type he recognised, Ellis noticed that the others were constrained when Baxter spoke, watching him, but averting their gaze as though to make it plain that his views were not theirs. They were embarrassed by his friendliness, which even Ellis found rather too warm. He declined an invitation to visit the Baxters immediately after the sale.

'I shall have far too much to do. Thank you very much!'

Taylor and Tester mumbled something, and started to move away. Jempson, stirred by kindness, took Ellis's arm.

'Sorry, Tom,' he said to Baxter, 'Mr Ellis here had best meet

Mr Kitton before the business starts, or else he'll end up with nothing he wants, and I shan't get my prices!'

Jempson had a surprisingly firm grip on Ellis as he steered him away. Baxter smiled rather vacantly. There was a fleeting impression of annoyance on his bland face.

'I look forward to seeing you all soon!' he exclaimed, raising his right forefinger to his forehead in a flicking salute.

'Who is Kitton?' asked Ellis.

'He's the auctioneer,' said Jempson. 'You watch that man. He talks too much and he isn't much of a farmer.' Jempson released his arm. 'I don't know why I'm telling you this,' he continued. 'I don't like a man to go in blindfold, that's all. Maybe I'm too fond of this old farm to let her go down any.'

The two men were now under the shade of the hedge.

'What do you mean?'

'He doesn't make a proper go of his place,' said Jempson. 'And the time he don't put into the land seems to hang heavy on his hands. When some men get time like that, they involve others to help them waste it. I can't say any more than that, and I reckon I've said too much as it is.'

'Thank you. I understand.'

Jempson appeared to make a decision. He took a breath, straightened his cap and swallowed.

'Mr Ellis, I was born and bred in this county and my father's father was a farmer and for all I know his father before him too, except we don't know anything back that far. This farm is yours now. I wish you well, but I shall never like you for taking it from me. I don't suppose you would expect me to, would you? The old horse ain't in the sale, although she's in the catalogue, because I took her into town and had her put down proper. I did the same to the dog myself. I didn't want anything to happen to them. A horse can fall into unkind hands. I don't want this land to fall into unkind hands no more than I did the old horse, do you see? And it needs a steady man to run a steady farm. Baxter ain't a steady man. Now come and meet Kitton so you get what you want.'

Margaret was tired and hot. The rural crowd jostled and pushed in the unashamed way of people accustomed to market and animals and the contact of living things. What they wanted to see they made for. Age or sex was seemingly of little account for she had been brushed aside several times, every time with good humour as though it was part of the honour of participating, a token of comradeship. The sun was beginning to slant now. Corn camomile lay prostrate in the stubble. She wondered if she should join Robert.

During her tour of the auction lots, depression had settled upon her.

She had nothing in common with these hot and heavily clad people. She hated the sale, she hated the stubble that cut her ankles and gouged her black leather shoes and she hated their uncaring clumsiness. All their hat-raising meant nothing, she realised. It was no more than the reflex that made them tilt their hats to the changing angle of the sun, and, if asked, they would not have known they had done it. Why should they? What right had she really to be there. She was a nuisance to whom they felt obliged to twitch in response. As an animal's skin shivers when a fly alights. She was of no importance to them. After ten years of labour, after proven drudgery in the fields, after the delivery of calves, after the production of food and beer for harvest, after the fetching of ice from a winter well and the sawing of wood, she might be accepted, but they wouldn't want that. She understood instinctively that she would be expected to stay remote as an Egyptian queen. There was nothing in between for these East Anglian males. She had heard enough to know of their unyielding attitudes. She was painfully aware that she could make no distinction between carter and labourer and farmer, and from simply observing the way men grouped and talked and dressed she realised that feudal order reigned.

She saw Robert in the distance with Jempson and a man in a bowler hat. He was obviously the auctioneer.

If she joined Robert, she would be in a panic of anxiety through every purchase. Would he secure it? Was it a good buy? Did he know anything about it, for she certainly didn't.

If she didn't join him he would see it as treachery. She tried to attribute his growing petulance to anxiety, but failed, as he seldom seemed anxious. Instead she was forced to recognise it as something sprung from his war. He had become accustomed to men obeying him or being reprimanded. Wives likewise. She had been told to do as she was told.

Their love-making was not satisfactory. On his return she had found comfort and relief after so long a time and there had been the spice of rediscovery. He had told her tales she only partially believed, whispered in her ear in the night about women seen – he said not touched – in places that except for Cairo and Port Said meant nothing to her. These conjured up such visions of vice that she was excited. Inside her, in the heat of passion, he told about strange practices that were both erotic and disgusting to her. She was frightened, not knowing what he wanted, if he expected her to respond in some way that she could not simulate for him, and so fell silent. She thought he must find her dull as she listened to his gasps, wondering if she was doing enough.

The first nights, he had asked her to dab herself with the cobalt blue cologne, then had taken the huge bottle himself, pouring a small pool into the palm of his hand, massaging it into one breast then the other. It was cold on her nipples and stung slightly.

'I smell like a you-know-what!' she protested, her heart thumping.

'I know!' he said with a smile and poured a second pool of the blue liquid into her naval, then stood above her, naked, looking.

'Don't look, I'm shy,' she had protested and he had lowered himself upon her and into her, the cologne trickling between them and smelling rank as gin. She hoped he had no diseases, but never dared ask, never approached him on the subject of other women. It seemed wrong to her that she should, and she knew he would react fiercely to the question and that there would be no answer. But as time passed and nothing unusual occurred she assumed everything was all right. She resented the unnecessary fear he had given her, that trust and talking would have avoided. She longed for tenderness as well as lust.

Perhaps that had been the first reminder of the distance that had existed between them before he went away. Other irritations appeared, forgotten habits like stains through layers of whitewash. His familiarity became domination, and she had done without it for four years.

Margaret sat on one of the straw bales that had been placed at intervals beside the lots. She felt alien for good reason. Her own childhood had been a London upbringing, surburban, leafy and easy in days when the middle class prospered and there were servants, and poverty and strife happened far away to men in Northern towns with cloth caps and jerky walks on newsreel film.

Her father had owned a successful multiple store that served these north London roads. Her mother Judith was stunning, dark and Jewish – and still lived in the same house, although Margaret's father had died twenty-three years before. Margaret had never seen Judith badly dressed. It was a running battle but a joke between her parents. He complained to her about the clothes she took from the store.

'Just put it on my account.'

He had had a business card printed for her for one of their wedding anniversaries, which had on it her name, address, telephone number and that phrase beautifully printed in an elaborate copperplate script: *Just put it on my account*.

She had been angry and full of laughter, all at the same time. He told her to use it, it was his present, and she did. They had been happy and unhappy in a turbulent way but always full of emotion and verve, living every minute of everything, but he had suddenly died from a heart attack when Margaret was only ten. The house was full of girls for she had three sisters and one brother. She had gone out into the world knowing very little about men, with only the half-remembered images of her father to judge by.

She remembered how her mother had responded when she first introduced Robert. He was a pale, thin, handsome thing then, dapper and neatly dressed. She was not in love with him; was desperately and unhappily in love with another man, Peter. Robert was only a companion. When he had left, Judith said, 'I hope everything about him isn't so pale and thin!' and Margaret had blushed and protested and giggled and for a moment forgotten Peter and her aching heart. But only for a moment.

'Lost in thought?' It was Robert. 'It's just about to start. I hope you're going to mark the prices on your copy of the catalogue like I told you. I won't have time to get it all down if I'm bidding. I hope you've got that.'

'Is that what you want me to do?' answered Margaret tartly. Robert frowned.

'We went through that this morning.'

'I know, but I'm tired. Do you really need me to go round every lot? It's going to take hours.'

'Why did you come?' Robert's face was suddenly angry. 'What is the point if you won't help? You're a farmer's wife now, part and parcel of it, we discussed all that. There's no room on a farm for job distinctions. I *have* to have the machinery and tools. The farm can't exist without it. Don't you think you could show some interest in that!'

'I'm sorry, I'm just tired. It's very hot and this stubble is really hurting my ankles.'

'You wore those damned silly shoes!'

Robert stamped away. She could hear the auctioneer making opening noises, drumming up custom. She was caught, whether or not to follow him. It would be such a colossal act of disloyalty not to, but at the same time she feared for her future. Seeing no way out, she did as she was told.

Much earlier that morning Wolfgang had pulled a turnip by its leafy top, swung it sideways in his left hand and, with his right, expertly cut the top from the flesh. The root fell on the clay like a bald purple head. It was the first turnip of the day and the mist had not yet lifted from the low meadow below.

He had volunteered for agricultural work, not amongst the very first, but after seeing the numbers that put their names forward. Always careful to look after himself, he watched the growing mutual support between working prisoners and the lessening control of the camp Nazis. Eventually they had given up and tried to turn the inevitable to their own advantage, claiming the men were keeping fit for Germany.

He was in the same gang as Heinz. The two men had remained acquaintances since Kempton Park, Wolfgang now rueful and amusing about the episode of the pencil. Peter, the baker, completed their group.

The three men were working over a field that rose gently to a brow, then sloped down towards the water-meadow. Days before, they had noted its sparkling stream and bobbing cress, and they had all taken great bunches of it, packed inside their

57

shirts. Heinz had caught a freshwater crayfish, big enough to eat, but had put it back, saying one was no use. He had grander plans.

When they had started on turnips, none of them had any idea what they were to do, or how to spare themselves. They had been provided with two English ancients as overseers called Tom and George. Both these men had faces like the knots in an elm and hands like dead branches, yet they handled the knives with ease and looked at each other slyly as they demonstrated how easy it was to pull, top and throw the obese roots. They did not pretend to like the Germans.

'I fought against you beggars in the first war,' George had observed, topping a turnip. 'You beggars killed a lot of my friends.'

Swish. He topped another turnip.

'I killed a lot of Germans too.'

Swish.

'Nothing personal of course.'

Neither Heinz nor Peter understood what he was saying. Peter's understanding of English was slight and Heinz's not up to George's accent. Wolfgang, who spoke and understood English perfectly, was able to master their thick dialect.

'Then perhaps we are all equal,' he said, 'and should just get on with the work.'

'All right,' George had said and he and the silent Tom had swung down the field easily, arms dangling like monkeys' while turnips flew sideways at astonishing speed. That first day had been comical. The three Germans tried everything to keep up with the loping ancients and had fallen further and further behind. They hacked the turnips. They pulled off the leaves and left them in the ground. They developed huge blisters in the palms of their right hands where the heel of the knife rested.

On the second day they worked better but were hampered by their wounds.

On the third day they wore pads of sticking plaster on their palms and woollen mittens made from socks stitched together with the toes cut away.

On the fourth day, when they sat down at ten for what George called their 'bate' of brown bread and tea, George said, 'You lads seem to be getting the hang of it,' and showed his yellow teeth.

On the fifth day they were swinging down the field with their knives as sweetly as a troop of dragoons. They had got the knack.

'What's that?' Wolfgang asked as they reached the brow and looked down towards the meadow for the first time that day. 'Is it a fair?' The three men paused.

It was early and the first items were being moved into place by tractor and trailer, with five men helping.

'No,' said Heinz, 'It looks like there is going to be a market.'

'In a field?'

Heinz shrugged.

As they swung back the second, third, fourth times they observed the increasing assembly of machinery and chattels.

'Now it looks like a military camp,' said Wolfgang.

'It's a farm sale,' said Heinz. 'Just like it is at home. They put it all out in the field.'

'We shan't get our cress,' said Peter. 'Not with all those people about.'

'Oh yes, we will,' said Wolfgang. 'We can easily slip down to the stream.'

'What about the Walnuts?'

It was the name they had given the ancients.

'I bet they go over to have a look.'

The morning wore on and the day got hotter. Each row took the men to the hedge bordering the meadow then away again. They disturbed rabbits and a covey of young partridge. Peter found an adder sunning itself and they poked at it cautiously with a long twig while George and Tom looked on. The creature escaped lazily, even reluctantly into a hedge.

'You should stamp on it,' said George. 'That's the way you kill them!' and he demonstrated with his heavy steel-toed boots, stamping in the clay.

Wolfgang translated for the others.

'Ask him why we should kill it?' said Peter. When Wolfgang did so, Tom shook his head in pity and, as they moved back to their working positions, they saw George tap his head with his finger. Peter was angry, but Heinz calmed him quickly.

'What would old countrymen do back home?'

★

59

Heinz found in this ritual labour a kind of serenity now that arms and legs moved in unison, without thought of blistered skin. In a field each man was able to be alone as he could never be in the camp. Separated by only a few yards they were nevertheless quite self-contained. Chopping his way rhythmically down the field he pulled up a strange turnip, cut off the leaves before he had time to think, then picked it up to examine it. It was a curious misshapen thing with two plump legs like thighs and a developed vulva tucked away and hidden in earth. Checking he was unobserved, he lifted up the vegetable and spat upon its private parts, wiping them clean with his sleeve. The flesh was quite pink, and it was this that reminded him of Inga.

Hot with embarrassment and sexual excitement, he was alarmed that he might be seen. He carefully laid the thing aside. Now it reminded him of the crude stone images made by the ancient peoples, the earth mothers he had seen in museums. He moved his goddess out of the line of the harvested row, not sure what he intended, but knowing he did not want her flung in the tumbril with the others, and consigned to an earthen clump. He knew his behaviour was ridiculous. He knew that, if he was able, he intended to take her home to the camp as a talisman, a charm, a house god. He knew she would provoke only ribaldry if he did, and felt immediately that he could not expose her to such treatment. He left her sitting there, pink and naked. He felt foolish, confused and aroused.

Later, all five men stood in the shade of an elm. The great trunk had so sapped the hedge of nourishment that it was stunted and sickly for a stretch on each side, affording them a view across the water-meadow to the reverse slope on which the sale was in full swing. The staccato patter of the auctioneer floated over to them from time to time, then was obscured by the shifting rustles of the great tree. A din of larks overhead lent their confusion to understanding.

'There's a good old turn-out,' said George.

'Aye,' replied Tom in a rare moment of speech. 'Reckon we could slip away for a moment or two. Those Jerries have nowhere to go.'

'If you wish to go,' said Wolfgang formally and politely, 'then you must feel free. We will get on with our work. When the truck comes, we go back to camp.'

George and Tom exchanged glances.

'Do you know,' said Peter in German, not understanding the conversation, 'they say that if you lie on your back in a meadow and watch the clouds, that and the song of skylarks will make you mad.'

'They're tempted,' said Wolfgang also in German.

'What was that?' growled Tom truculently.

'I said to him, "We work",' said Wolfgang blandly.

'You work, Jerry. You work good, and don't you forget it.' He turned to Tom. 'Reckon we could be quick. One look, then back. We can keep an eye on 'em from the fields.'

Tom nodded.

'Reckon.'

'You stay here, work in this parcel o' the field where we can see you, understand?' said George. 'We have to report on you to the master, and he reports to your boss man, see, so don't you be getting any notions!'

Wolfgang nodded solemnly.

'Yes, I understand. We will behave.'

'Right, boy,' said George. He inclined his head briefly to Tom and the two old men moved off, making for a gap in the hedge they obviously knew well. Every few paces they looked back, as though they expected the Germans to flee.

'Work,' said Wolfgang. 'Pull turnips. Look active.'

'What's going on?' asked Peter, doing as he was told. 'What was that about?'

'They've gone over to have a look. We're to stay in sight and work in this bit of field, I think. Their English is terrible.'

'How are we to get the cress?' asked Peter. 'The Walnuts will be watching us.'

'As long as two are working and in sight, I should think they'll be satisfied,' said Heinz. 'We can slip away one at a time.'

'I'm first!' said Peter.

'It's all right by me,' said Wolfgang.

Heinz smiled. 'I thought prison camp was supposed to develop patience,' he said.

'We will all make our way down, then come back slowly,' said the alert Wolfgang. 'You slip into the cover of the hedge, and we'll stay in sight, changing rows to confuse anyone watching.'

'Don't get caught!' said Heinz. 'You'll get solitary and we'll lose the Walnuts. They won't let us out into the fields again if they feel nasty.'

'Don't worry!'

'God, it's hot!'

Heinz and Wolfgang toiled slowly up the slope. Heinz was still brooding on thoughts of Inga. A despair had settled upon him that slowed his legs and slowed his arms so that he lost his easy, acquired rhythm and kicked clods of earth, stumbling. The soil had set now like potter's clay. Time and again the leaves were unequal to the pull of withdrawing the root and snapped like old rope. Then the knife had to be put down and the purple-pink bulk lifted two-handed. His back ached.

He thought of Magdeburg and the Russians that now occupied it. There had been fields of turnips around Magdeburg before the war started, but he could not imagine they would have lasted long, and certainly not after the Russians. He had been briefly on the Eastern front and had fought against them. He remembered seeing the remains of a camp kitchen they had overrun in an advance. There were dead men spread out amongst the cooking fires and equipment as though they were part of the larder. An unregarded soldier was burning in a fire, giving off bright orange flames and black smoke. A collection of slave cooks from some distant part of Russian Asia sat helplessly on the ground. One man was clutching a large ladle, perhaps as a badge of office. The pots were still on the fires. They had been cooking two dogs and rotting potatoes. At first they had not understood what the meat was. Heinz remembered a soldier, a tall blond lad from the south, fishing in one of the pots with a long perforated enamel spoon and raising an animal's skull to the surface before it toppled back in. The boy had turned to the slave cooks, who watched him tensely.

'Baaah?' he had enquired.

'Woof!' the cooks said, smiling. 'Woof, woof, woof!'

'Shit!' The lad dropped the spoon back into the pot. 'Smell the potatoes too. They're rotten.' He picked one and grasped it in both hands, splitting it. It was the thing a farm boy would do.

The potato burst disgustingly. The centre was soft and brown and slime ran out. White things wriggled. The lad flung down the potato.

'Maggots! Jesus!'

'Jesus,' said one of the cooks earnestly. He smiled encouragingly at the soldier, crinkled Mongol eyes in a brown corrugated face with a drooping moustache. Two men crossed themselves as though to demonstrate their faith. They began a low incantation, half words, half a song, strange and mournful. Perhaps it was a prayer, but their Lord was deaf for they were all taken away and shot. Heinz never knew or understood why. The men were slaves and they had liberated them. It seemed rather better to Heinz that they had been left in slavery. He said so to the blond lad when they heard the fusillade of the firing party and saw the drifting smoke. They had tied each one to a birch tree.

'They were animals,' the blond lad said. 'Animals eat animals.'

'Where does that put us if we shoot them?'

He was reprimanded for that. The blond soldier had reported him, secretly. A lieutenant had asked him the next day what he had meant. He was standing very much to attention, terrified. A *Gefreiter* took notes in shorthand on one side of him. On the other a *Feldwebel* doodled on an army notepad.

'I think the slave cooks should not have been shot, sir,' he had said when asked.

'Why not?'

'They were captives, sir. We had liberated them. They were not fighting against the Reich.'

'They were worthless specimens of the lowest order, and we have no food for them. Remember that, soldier.' The lieutenant looked at him sharply. 'You have a good record. Remember in future to hold your tongue. You are reprimanded. You are lucky you are not being transferred to another unit. Do you understand?'

'Yes, sir.'

Heinz had saluted and left. He had escaped another six months on the Eastern front. His unit had been pulled back to France.

Magdeburg he hardly dared to think about. At moments like

63

this he could manage it, stooping over some physical task that kept him occupied. At night, in loneliness, the unhappiness overwhelmed him so that it became a physical ill. His stomach burned with indigestion, his heart raced and he belched and sweated.

They said much of Magdeburg had been flattened.

Had Inga been raped? How would he know? Would she tell him if she had? Was she with another man? How was she living?

'Here comes Peter!'

At first Heinz had not responded and Wolfgang had to call three times. They looked back to the hedge. Peter, under cover, waved, then picked up his knife from where he had concealed it. He worked towards them briefly, then stood up and walked openly up the field. He was grinning.

'It's all right!' he said. 'I've got the cress. Pockets of it. There's women in that field! I saw them!'

'Your turn, Heinz,' said Wolfgang.

'What, more cress?' asked Heinz.

'You're the crayfish expert,' said Peter.

'I can't promise anything. There may be two or three. You don't get the things in shoals like herring.'

'Don't talk about herring!' Wolfgang made an urgent gesture. 'Get a move on before it gets too late. And don't get seen!'

'Don't touch those women!' called Peter. 'And, if you can't get anything else, look for hazel-nuts.'

The auctioneer had nearly finished and he was tiring. Although his patter was becoming less profuse he still held his crowd, the words still washed over them, they attended him, he was their witch-doctor and they followed him from lot to lot, laughing at his tired jokes, silent at a gesture. They listened with respect still as he assured them, referring to his catalogue, his catechism, that there was nothing here that was not of the best, that was not an excellent bargain, was not perfect in every way – except for the minor defects that were obvious to anyone.

In this way he conferred wisdom and skill upon them and enrolled them into the knowledgeable brotherhood from which he sprang. They *knew* they couldn't be fooled. He praised them when they bought, admiring their eye for a bargain, reluctant always to let things slip so cheap. He flattered, pandered, hypnotised, and above all he talked.

The day was tiring, the sun becoming yellow. Gorged pigeons flew heavily overhead and watched from trees, sated with corn and elderberries. Taylor and Tester saw them and looked at each other. Time would come for those fat birds. A farm with a new master would be rich shooting and who better to clear it? This master looked raw as split potato. Yet he had got what he needed. They had noted that. He might have paid over the odds for essentials, but he hadn't bought anything flashy or stupid.

What was left to buy now was more their business. Uncared-for things of value, if a man knew how to use them. Ladders, paint, engine grease, timber, field drains, the miscellany that always started a well-planned sale and always seemed to end it. They moved in close to Kitton as the crowd thinned. Farmers had drifted away, leaving only a few dealers and sharp-faced gypsies. They would want the iron. Scrap, bedsteads, broken shares and thin cart-rims. Worn-out things.

Robert was pleased, and Margaret felt an enormous sense of relief, a lifting of her heart, that it had gone so well. Now that it was over she was aware what an ordeal it had been to her and felt exhausted. At the same time the unquiet enemies in her mind told her that this was only a beginning.

'I'll have to settle up with Kitton's man,' Robert said. He looked at her, seeming to see her for the first time that day. 'You must be tired. It's been a long day.'

'Yes.'

'You should have sat down somewhere. There was no need to follow round every lot.'

'You asked me to. You asked me to mark down all the prices.' Her heart started to beat angrily.

'Did I?'

'Yes, you certainly did. This morning. You were very angry about it.'

'I don't think that's true . . .'

Margaret turned away with irritation and pain.

'I'm sorry,' said Robert, 'maybe I did.' He reached out, taking her by the shoulders, and turned her to him. Her eyes

65

were full of tears that had welled up so immediately that they had caught even Margaret unawares.

'Don't cry . . .'

'I'm not crying. I'm tired.'

'This is no way to celebrate. We'll go off and have a drink in a moment. Find a really nice pub.'

'We have to get back to the children . . .'

A look of annoyance crossed his face.

'They can wait, can't they? Why raise that? We'll have to go to the house and pass a few words with Jempson. Don't you want another look round?'

Margaret shook her head.

'It isn't fair to leave them so long. We'll be very late.'

A stubborn look came across his face. It made him expressionless, wooden. Margaret described it to herself as his doltish ox impression.

'This is an important day!' he said. 'We've bought a farm, we've bought all this equipment, surely to God you can see that it doesn't matter if they have an hour or two more. Helen's *fifteen*.'

Of course he was right. Margaret knew her desire to get back to the children was a more fundamental and feeble desire to escape from what she had already allowed to happen. She asked herself again why she had not protested earlier, but in the same moment knew that it would never be within her capability to divert Robert. Or perhaps any man. A wave of misery overtook her.

'Well, as we own it, I'll have a look over it while you settle up. There's a stream down in the meadow. I'll take a walk down there. I'll see you back here . . . when?'

'In about an hour.'

'In about an hour.'

Margaret's ankles were scraped to bleeding now in several places, so she walked in a peculiar high-stepping way, lifting each foot and putting it down with a vertical crushing motion. She bent down when she felt no one could see her, spat on the fingers of her left hand and wiped at the scratches, but they stung and an itch developed.

She moved from one phalanx of farmware to the next, hoping to be inconspicuous, until she was at the bottom of the field.

66

Here only three men lingered, casting curious glances at her, then joining one another in conversation. She decided to strike out towards the stream.

The watercourse itself was about twenty feet across. Small mud cliffs covered with grass marked the maximum rage of winter floods. The stream ran fast over clean gravel. On the far side stood an ancient hedge, back from the water.

The sense of beauty and peace that assailed her was immediate. Although she had been quite unconscious of noise throughout the afternoon, she had noticed the pummelling glances of curious people. Kitton had certainly kept up a din, but he had almost become part of the natural landscape. It was the intrusion of people that she felt most, the summings-up, the unashamed stares.

Now crows were her companions, and the flapping pigeons. The sun was yellow as yolk. The grass was soft after the stubble. Her attention was caught by the ragwort, here and there alive with black-and-yellow-striped caterpillars in their hundreds. She stooped beside one plant to watch them, disgusted by their voracity, but delighted nevertheless.

She stopped to look into the water. Cress grew from the fast stream, a black dragonfly with sheen of electric blue danced and darted before alighting on a leaf. Margaret held her knees and sighed. The place was beautiful beyond content. For company she put into words the thought that had become repetitive.

'That is not the problem.'

A hunt of swallows shot down the stream, skimming, bickering, wheeling overhead.

Margaret thought of the choice that she now had had thrust upon her, between these fields, the swallows, the yellow-and-black caterpillars, the vagaries of the seasons, and her previous life of shopping, walks and school. It was to the death now. The thought shocked her. Why should this beauty bring intimations of mortality? Immediately she realised it was nothing to do with the perceived world. It was to do with feeling trapped.

Tom and George were working their way back towards the turnip field by a route that took in whole fields of hedge as they looked for hazels. Their pockets bulged. George pulled down each branch with a crook of stick he had cut, then they both stripped it.

'We'll be late back. Hope those buggers don't run away,' muttered George.

'They won't.'

'They might.'

'Nowhere to go.'

'They seem all right.'

'You can't help feeling sorry for them, can you?'

'I don't. Them buggers deserve all they get!' George did not sound as adamant as his words.

'They work well enough. . . .'

George let go another branch that whipped up with a shower of leaf fragments. They moved on, shoving the frilly nuts into jacket pockets.

'Look at old squirrel!' said George. They watched the red animal shelling acorns on a small oak, contemptuous of those so far below.

'Could knock him out of there with a gun!' said George.

Tom nudged him.

'Look!'

Beyond was an elder tree like a black and shining waterfall, bent to the ground by its burden.

'We can't take them!'

'Go on. If we don't the pigeons will.'

'How do we carry 'em?' asked George. 'Have to be a coat . . .'

He took off his ancient jacket and laid it on the ground, tweed side up. He expertly tied the arms together, felt in his pocket for the twine that all countrymen carry, and tied up each corner of the tails like the ears on a sack. He joined these to the arms so the whole thing formed an ample pannier. Without discussion or the need for suggestion Tom meanwhile plucked dock leaves. With a handful he lined their basket thoroughly against the juice of the berries. George held it and Tom began to pick, his hands soon blood-red. The bunches snapped at a touch, from their own luxuriant weight. A pigeon thrashed out of the tree, making them jump, then grin.

'Lor, that was a fat bird! Nearly fell down and broke his neck!'

'Drunk as a Lord. Them top berries are like a pint of port!'

★

Heinz lay on his stomach on a projection of the bank where the grass was firm and dry and stared into the shaded water beneath. It was fast and sparkling; in the shade amongst the pebbles he could see his quarry, but could never reach it. The crayfish gave itself away by the movements of its antennae. The pebbles around it were clear as cheap jewels, orange and black and grey. As his eyes became accustomed to the shades and tones Heinz saw another, then another, and realised they were plentiful. He must find a place where he could slide his hand to the bed of the stream and take them. Conscious that he must not stray too far, he spotted a flat shallow area overhung by willow that could be ideal. Two cows grazed peacefully nearby, black and white Friesians. There was a herd in an adjoining field which must have strayed through a hole in the hedge. Wasps were everywhere, dipping at the edge of the water and weaving through the grass around him. They were slow in their movements, drowsy. Looking up, he saw he was being watched by a woman. He jumped to his feet. She was sitting on the other side of the stream and seemed alarmed at his sudden reaction. He wondered how long she had been watching. She would think him mad. He lifted his forage cap in salute, intending it to reassure.

'Good afternoon,' she said. Her voice was pleasant but wary. Heinz replied in his best English. They looked at each other. She could be beautiful, thought Heinz. Her body is beautiful. She has fine legs and hips and her breasts fill the dress.

Margaret guessed he must be a German prisoner by his appearance and by his accent. She knew they had recently been released for farm work but could not understand what he was doing here. Surely this was her land now? He was on her field. She was uncertain. Perhaps their land ran only to the stream, perhaps the other side belonged to the neighbouring farmer. She realised with discomfort that she had no idea where their fields were. The man was staring at her openly, with candid interest. She felt herself blush but returned his gaze.

He suddenly turned and fled, running across the grass to the tall hedge beyond. It took him some time as he wore heavy boots and he was a big man, not nimble. At the hedge he paused, raised his cap again and waved it at her. She stared. He waved again. He was waiting for her to respond. She stood up.

This seemed to be enough, for he disappeared through the hedge.

The encounter left her shaking slightly. It was both unexpected and unreal. She walked from the meadow quickly, looking back twice, but the man did not reappear.

The stubble field was still busy, but now it was the turn of the victors to cart away their spoils. Old lorries growled and groaned across the uneven ground. There were only old vehicles, the war had seen to that. Tractors and trailers were a hazard. Margaret looked in vain for Robert. She saw Kitton, but did not like to reveal she had lost him. Kitton saw her and raised his felt hat. She had a brief image again of the man with the forage cap.

Jempson appeared in front of her. There was no avoiding him. He was wearing his best cap and his best market suit and had a blue handkerchief in his hand that he used for mopping his brow. She could see and smell that he had been drinking. His clothes hung about him even more loosely than usual, his face was gaunt. He held both his arms wide as though stopping cattle.

'That's it then,' he said. 'It's all gone now, Mrs Ellis. And, do you know, I don't know how I feel!'

The arms dropped.

'I thought I would feel well rolled out. I saw a man once who fell under a roller that was trailing two pair of harrows. Well, he was the most flattened man I ever saw, and I expected I should feel like that, but I don't. I feel good!'

The drink evidently made him talkative. To Margaret's consternation a small, curious audience was quietly gathering. They stood back but within earshot, pretending they had other business but listening to the fun.

'You see, it's all turned out to be a relief. This afternoon, about half way through the sale, I realised it had truly gone, all of it. I hadn't realised it till then. So it really is all yours now, lock, stock and barrel. And I was a prisoner all the time. That was what I was.'

He mopped his face again with the blue handkerchief.

'But then I said to myself, Jempson, old son, you're out. Just like Chelmsford jail. They push them out the door and they stand there with the same bundle they came in with. The very same clothes. It don't matter if it was ten days or ten years, they gets them back, and they haven't an idea in the world what they shall do next, I know how they feel. Taking the first step away from them doors is taking a step into a new existence, and you don't want to do it. I was never a thinking sort of man but I can see why so many of them don't want to go.'

He made a circular gesture towards her.

'You see, you're the prisoner now and I'm the free man. I like you, Mrs Ellis, I don't wish you harm. I don't like your husband, but I reckon you already know that. But you're twice a prisoner, which I never was. First, of him, secondly of this place . . .'

'I think you had better let me go, Mr Jempson, before you say any more,' said Margaret, trying to project a tone of command she did not feel. Jempson lifted his cap politely, took a step towards the side and made a flamboyant courtier's gesture of bidding her pass. He replaced his cap and tapped the peak with the palm of his hand. The gesture made him wobble unsteadily.

'I apologise if I said too much. I shall feel the worse for it tomorrow. I shall see to that . . .'

Margaret strode past him, hoping she appeared dignified and untouched. His shots of truth hurt.

'And you're a third time a prisoner,' called Jempson. 'You're a prisoner to yourself, Mrs Ellis, which I never was! And that's the worst sort of prison, bor! Now I shall go and get *drunk*!'

He roared the last word in defiance at the onlookers and shambled off without any apparent direction in mind. Margaret walked blindly forward, wishing that Robert was somewhere to look after her, to pluck her from this painful field of stubble. For the second time there were tears in her eyes. She saw the man introduced as John Ingleton in front of her. His eyes caught hers. His glance was searching and comprehending, yet kindly in his sharp sandy face.

'You'll be looking for that husband of your'n?' he said in round tones. 'What a day, wouldn't you say? I should say he's done all right. I should say he's done more than a few bargains! I should say he knows more of farming than what he lets on, that's what I should say, Mrs Ellis!'

These pronouncements were made in rolling volleys that comforted her and challenged contradiction from onlookers. There were a few nods and smiles. She could have hugged this

71

ferret-faced man whose intelligence was like a stored electric charge.

'Don't you ask me where he is,' he continued, 'or I shall have to tell you he's down the pub sealing a bargain or two. That's the way of it.'

'Thank you, Mr Ingleton,' said Margaret. Her words fell clear in a sudden silence. A breath of evening and autumn caught them with a hint of mortality. 'A deal has to be sealed!'

'That is so!' rejoined Ingleton. 'There's a cold breath of wind now. Sun will be dropping soon and there's a touch of the old north wind in the air. Goes fast, this time of the year. That'll take the old leaves from the trees. Time to sow, when the beech leaves fall, Mrs Ellis. I like the winter wheat because it reminds me when the snow be thick that I have something in there that is already growing, already feeling its way for the new year and the next harvest. That way there is no barren time.'

She knew perfectly well he was only ascribing this knowledge to her to bolster her stock. She was embarrassed by his kindness and had to force herself to look him in the eye. He was looking at her gravely so that their exchange of contact presented no problem. His was a timeless face, country wise. She could imagine him talking to animals, almost able to understand.

'I'm sure we all wish you good luck for the future!' he declared. 'We'll do what we can to help if you should need it.'

'Thank you, Mr Ingleton!'

She pursued her course to their car, opened the passenger door and sat down. She had to escape the confusion of so many emotions and so many impressions. She shut the door but wound down the window slightly so that she should remain in contact with the human noises outside. The sun had begun to glow orange and the long shadows of trees were dark blue. Machines sparkled as low shafts of light rang off them. Martins appeared, dashing low over the stubble, tracing and re-tracing their paths. She waited.

The lorry was late. George and Tom were angry because they had to wait until the men were picked up.

'How much do you lot get paid for this?' asked George. All five of them reclined on a grass bank beside the road. The spot was selected because it caught the last rays of the sun. George's jacket with its contents of elderberries formed a plump bundle that had been carefully placed to one side.

'Three farthings an hour, in real money,' said Wolfgang.

George shot a glance at Tom.

'That ain't a great deal,' he blurted, trying to conceal his grin. 'Not a great deal at all!'

'It is to us, my friend,' said Wolfgang. 'We get paid three shillings and fourpence a day in *lagergeld*, but that is no good to us.'

'What's this *lagergeld*?'

'This stuff.'

Wolfgang fished in his jacket pocket and produced a number of small green notes printed on greyish paper. He gave one to George, who examined it, then passed it to Tom. Tom passed it back. They both looked enquiringly at Wolfgang.

'Camp money. We can only spend it in the camp. There is nothing to buy. Toothpaste, sometimes some soap, cigarettes, combs, shoelaces.'

'What about food?'

'We can't buy food. We get what we get.'

George nodded.

'Do you get enough food?' asked Heinz in his slow English.

'No,' said George. 'Not enough at all, and we don't ask for a great deal. It's all right for you lot in the camps, but people are hungry!'

'How can you be hungry in the country?'

'The Government takes care of that. I suppose you don't see much of rationing. We got coupons for near everything you can think of. Meat's the thing, and sugar and eggs. There ain't no meal for pigs to speak of, and hen food is the same.'

Heinz nodded.

'But there are potatoes. And turnips.'

'You can't live off potatoes and turnips! You have to have a bite o' meat!'

They relapsed into silence. It was common ground and each man had his thoughts, except Peter who asked what they had been saying. Heinz explained and he too fell silent.

'What are you going to do with the berries in your jacket?' Wolfgang asked eventually. 'Do you eat them?'

George grinned at Tom.

'You can try 'em if you like . . .'

'But are they good to eat?'

'That depends. Go on, they ain't poisonous!'

Wolfgang rolled over and inserted a hand in the bundle. He pulled out a black bunch of berries and looked at them. Taking one he put it in his mouth and chewed.

'They are good,' he said. 'And they are sweet.' He ate from the bunch, then grimaced.

Tom burst out laughing, thumping the ground with his ancient fists. Wolfgang threw the rest of the bunch down, his face suddenly angry. His lips were strained purple with the juice. He spat a mouthful of skin and seed onto the ground close to Tom.

'What is funny?' he demanded. He rose abruptly to his feet, standing over the old man. Heinz sprang up also, laying a restraining hand on his arm. 'Why do you laugh? What is wrong with them?'

Tom had stopped laughing as quickly as he began.

'Don't you try nothing!' he blustered bravely. 'You're prisoners, and I ain't afraid of you!'

'They're for making wine!' explained George, still grinning broadly. 'You can eat them if you want but they taste like sweet cat's piss!'

'Take it easy,' said Heinz in German. 'Sit down again. They've had their little joke. Stay calm. They can put in a report about us, and we don't get back out here. . . .'

'You're right.' Wolfgang still sounded angry. 'That old bastard has a laugh like a turkey!'

'Ask him about the wine!' urged Peter. 'Ask him how they make it! Strangle him later.'

Wolfgang sat down. He glanced at Heinz, who had a smirk on his face, and could not prevent himself from laughing at his own gullibility.

'Very good,' he said, 'you have played a good trick on me. Now tell us how you make the wine.'

George explained slowly, talking as if they were children. Peter, unable to understand, got up and walked some way down the hedgerow that topped the grass bank. Producing a knife, he cut himself a short length of ash and began to whittle. It was a picture of complete rural relaxation interrupted only by the dark army lorry that roared round the bend. It was uncovered and there were other prisoners standing in the back who called or waved.

'Hop in, you lot!' said the driver. He nodded to George and Tom. 'Have they been good lads?'

'They been all right,' said George, and the driver let in the clutch as soon as the men had swung up behind. They stood so that the wind whistled around them. They held on to the high sides, which were part solid, part open, scenting the air like cattle, enjoying the illusion of freedom. Occasionally the lorry passed under branches that thrashed at them and they cheered and ducked, or snatched at twigs.

'Faster! Faster!' they shouted, and the young driver grinned to his mate in the cab and put his foot down, heading for every overhanging bough on either side of the road, so that the vehicle weaved drunkenly down the narrow lanes.

'I'm looking forward to the crayfish!' shouted Wolfgang at Heinz.

'Shut up!'

'Me too!' yelled Peter.

'Shut up!'

'With watercress!' shouted Peter, lifting the flap of a bulging pocket. Heinz pushed at Peter, who pushed him back. Some of the other men were singing, snatches of this and that, a few lewd verses, singing in exultation.

'And did you see the women in the field!' said Peter. 'There definitely were! Things are looking up!'

'Down!' the men shouted as a heavy bough passed close to their heads.

'And I've got some turnips,' Peter continued, straightening up. He opened his jacket. To each side was strung a collection of small turnips, clean-washed and fleshy. They clapped Peter on the back; he looked both embarrassed and happy.

'Down!' the men shouted, playing their game.

Heinz smiled and ducked, and laughed when they laughed, but he was thinking of the woman who had spoken to him. She had returned his gaze calmly, with a hint of alarm, but with an equal hint of interest. He knew he had stared hungrily; she had coloured slightly but not looked away.

'Down!'

But Heinz was too late and a mass of foliage struck him, bowling him over. The men roared with laughter. Heinz was winded, covered with shredded leaves. The pink turnip he had been concealing rolled over the battered metal floor. Dieter, a man from another hut, picked it up and grinned broadly.

'Look!' he shouted, 'Look at this! Heinz has got a rude trophy!'

They passed it from hand to hand, touching, poking, wolf-whistling. Heinz was hot with humiliation. Wolfgang, as ever alert and intelligent, intercepted it and threw it back to Heinz. Heinz caught it and hurled it away into the darkness. The men made faces at each other and fell silent.

'Come on, Heinz!' called Peter. 'No one meant any harm.'

They were returning to their hut from the gate where the lorry had left them. The other men in the party had dispersed to their own quarters. Heinz was trailing a little behind. A large moon, nearly full shone brighter than the sparse twinkling of the camp lights. The usual noises drifted from huts, – music, voices, a burst of laughter. Nightfall had become sudden and conclusive with no lingering twilight, no continuing luminescence in the sky. They followed the hard concrete path that shone slightly in the moonlight.

Six figures stepped from the darkness. They carried sticks and had no faces and said nothing.

'Run!' shouted Peter. The men attacked them immediately, lashing out with their sticks and booted feet, trying to seize them. Wolfgang was hit on the head with a crack like snapping wood and fell to the ground. Peter punched someone in the face and the man flew backwards against the side-wall of a hut before collapsing. Heinz felt a series of blows on his back. A fist hit him in the face and warm blood poured down his face. The attackers were all masked. He could see eye slits; white hate of eyes.

'You bastards won't work in the fields again!' Heinz kicked out, hit someone, punched and grappled. He grasped a stick and wrenched it away. Swinging it hard he hit flesh. He kicked a man in the stomach. The man fell, gagging. Peter was roaring wildly. He had a man by the throat and was dragging him over to the hut wall. Heinz felt a kick in the side and his legs gave way. He heard the sound of whistles and running feet, then there was a stunning blow on the head, and then nothing.

He heard English voices and felt himself being lifted to his feet. His legs gave way and he found himself on his knees. His nose was bleeding.

'Who did it?' asked the voices. 'Did you see?'

'No.' His voice was cracked and weak. 'They wore masks. How are the others?'

'They're all right, son. Let's get you up.'

He was lifted again, half-carried and placed upon his own bed. The camp medical officer appeared, examined him, told him Peter and Wolfgang were all right but bruised. Wolfgang had been taken into hospital with a suspected fractured skull. He was washed and bandaged.

'You won't be working for a few days,' said the doctor, a small lean man with a bald head. 'Still, you're in good condition. You have a lot of bruising around the back and kidneys.'

Major Middleton, the commandant, arrived, together with Schneider, the German *Lagerführer*, and asked questions he could not answer.

Who? Who?

Asked questions he could answer.

Why? Why?

'Because we were working in the fields.'

'I see. Why would they do that?'

'Because they say we are helping England's post-war recovery.'

'I see. So your attackers will be Nazis.'

The *Lagerführer* shifted uncomfortably.

'Probably. I don't know.'

'Do you have any enemies?'

'Probably. I don't know.'

'Do you think you know these Nazis?'

'No.' But I have a good idea, thought Heinz. So has the *Lagerführer*. Mohnke, Waldenburg, Muller. Perhaps even Schneider himself?

'Do you want to go to the fields to work?'

Heinz remembered the stream, the woman, the lorry and the exhilaration of speed, the flight of the partridges. He remembered Tom and George, the elderberries, the homunculus.

'Yes, without a doubt, yes.'

He watched Schneider as he replied. The white face was immobile, looking straight ahead.

'Then you must return. We will not allow these attacks to put men off!'

'These attacks?'

'You were not the only one to be attacked tonight.' Middleton was a soldier's idea of a soldier, with his short, greying hair, tanned face and sharp eyes. Heinz had only seen him from a distance before. 'All returning men had trouble. I have my suspicions.'

The commandant touched his cap with his stick in salute.

'Good night.'

Heinz slept. At some stage Ehrich woke him to say his work party had also been set upon, but had managed to run away. Peter was all right. He dreamed of Siegfried again, Siegfried's head confused with Wolfgang's and a stick descending with a crack. Warm blood ran over his face and drenched him, drenched his whole body.

He woke again covered with sweat and listened to Ehrich snoring, men coughing, moving. He felt very lonely and tried to conjure up the image of Inga; but, whether because of tiredness or shock, he could not retrieve her picture from his mind. He lay watching the moonlight move across the floor in a cold silver slab.

Robert had gone to the Black Horse because it was a social obligation. At least that was what he told himself at the superficial level of excuse. At the slightly deeper level of self-justification he knew he had gone because he wanted a drink after a long day and above all because he wanted to delay returning to Margaret. He could not face the day being spoiled by the depression he knew she would cast over it like a gladiator's net.

He had done well. He knew he had and the other men told him so as well. He had already totalled up and settled with Kitton by cheque and knew the cost had been reasonable.

Kitton had responded to his cheque by buying two pints and two whiskies. They had talked awkwardly for a few minutes, then Kitton had moved on to join other farmers, other cronies. Ingleton had joined Robert and was looking after him, introducing him to face after face, name after name. He would never remember them all, he kept saying, as he shook hands. The large, dark West had also joined them so that they formed a small group of their own.

'A nice pub,' said Robert.

'I suppose it is,' said Ingleton, looking round appraisingly. He gave the impression that he had never examined it before. 'It's handy, in any event. After a day's harvest, it's a useful old place.'

They stood in the saloon bar, which was divided from the public bar by a dark wooden screen with three inset panels of cut glass. All that could be seen was the flicker of firelight and the fragmented reflection of dark shapes. The noise of voices and laughter burst in waves from next door when the hubbub in their own bar dropped.

The saloon was floored with linoleum, scuffed and worn through in places to the fabric backing, but still better than bare boards. The furniture was solid – leather chairs with dulled brass studs, oak tables, scrubbed until the grain stood out. The pride of the room was its fireplace, huge and open, which still contained the bread oven and original cooking array of pot hooks, swivels and chains. Within the hearth stood a fire-basket of more recent iron. This had been burned until the bars were thin in places as though stretched by enormous force. These stressed areas glowed orange-red with heat in this relentless forge. Taylor and Tester had positioned themselves with practised ease at one side of the hearth and had attracted a considerable gathering. As they talked, Robert was aware of sharp glances as the conversation flowed, of heads directed away so that he could be spoken about with studied covertness. It annoyed him but he supposed it was to be expected.

'Where's Jempson?' he asked. 'Doesn't he come here?'

'He'll be here all right,' said Ingleton, 'but he'll be next door. He doesn't hold with the saloon bar. What was good enough for his father, he says, is good enough for him!'

'What does that mean?'

'This is East Anglia,' said West. As he volunteered no more, Ellis looked to Ingleton for explanation.

'Tenants don't mix with owners round here. They feel more at home with the labourers. It's his own choice.'

Robert nodded.

'Are you from these parts?' he asked Ingleton.

'No. I'm from Norfolk and my father was from Ayrshire. On both accounts I'm a foreigner, and the first is probably the worst offence! Ain't that so, Bill?'

West smiled briefly. Robert found it difficult to sum the man up. He looked like one of Napoleon's Old Guard, yet his fierce appearance seemed to mask a gentle nature.

'Speaking as a Suffolk man born and bred, I have to say yes!' He put his pint down on the varnished bar top. 'My round . . .' The sound was slight, but a girl appeared like a gundog from the other bar. She was small with dark eyes. Her skin seemed very pale.

'Clara,' said West, 'this is Mr Ellis who has bought Pyes Farm.'

'How do you do,' said Clara gravely, extending her hand. It was unexpected, and Robert fumbled with the empty glass he was still holding, put it down to shake hands. There was silence while she filled the three glasses and West paid. Clara smiled and withdrew.

'She lost her husband,' said Ingleton. 'In France. Fourth day after the landings. It has made a sad girl of her. She casts a shadow . . .'

'What made you take this up?' asked West, placing his words rather too heavily in the silence that had fallen. The big man blushed furiously. 'I didn't mean to sound inquisitive!'

Robert felt it necessary to reassure him.

'Not at all . . . I suppose it's a question I ask myself. I wanted to get away from the war. This seemed to be the way to do it.'

Ingleton nodded.

'Where did you spend the war?'

'Here and there. In Africa mostly. In and out of the desert.'

'Was it bad?'

'I don't know. In some ways I suppose it was, in others it wasn't. Everyone will tell you they enjoyed the company.

Anyway, when I got back it seemed like a good time to make a new start.'

He drank. He didn't want them to pursue this line any further in case they probed the painful recesses of his mind: the true reasons that he kept to himself and could not even tell Margaret.

'But you weren't a Regular?'

'No.'

'I tried to join up,' said Ingleton. 'So did Bill. We knew they wouldn't take us, but we gave it a good try.'

'But still, it's a big risk taking up farming,' pursued West.

'I suppose it is.'

Memories of a country childhood. Holidays. A prolonged visit, escape from streets, escape from noise. When and where he couldn't say. How old had he been? Seven, eight, nine? Lost. He didn't know. He only knew it was an escape and liberty beyond dreaming.

Images. Himself as a young man. Moustache more sleek, skin more smooth and with the sheen of youth. Clothes neat (*very* neat), shoes polished (*very* polished), hair oiled flat (yes, *very* flat). He hoped that looking as good as this would do. His father had always told him to dress right and he had done as he was told. That was how you got on. That was how his father had got on.

Himself just married – sleek as Valentino. Happy? He wasn't sure. He wasn't even very sure what happiness felt like. Laughing and 'Congratulations' and confetti. Promotion in his job and coffee brought in a small pot with its own cup, sugar and milk, instead of a mug. A house, quite new with gate, and latch crisp and snapping, privet no more than sprigs and the woodwork unbruised inside, grain still showing. Margaret learning her job as a wife. Learning her job as a mother.

It was his round so he bought more pints. The girl appeared as magically as before. Robert smiled at her, tried to catch her eye. She ignored him. She even returned his change by standing it in a small heap upon a beer mat.

Ingleton told a dry tale about a man from the Ministry of Agriculture who had come to advise him on seed and fertilisers and who had remarked upon the outstanding quality of his crop of wheat while staring at a field of barley.

Images. Births and noise, chaos from order, distances and difficulties. The final rebuff was when order and neatness were seen as a tyranny. Chaos seeping into the brain, impinging on every activity. He knew he was not particularly tolerant, but it was more than he had ever bargained for, and as far as he could see Margaret did little to combat it. She became disordered in her dress, her body, in the way she kept the house. He felt alarmed, insecure and even agitated in a way he could neither discuss nor explain. He polished everything he could, the silver plate, the knives and forks, his shoes, glasses and the bell push, as though he could in this way restore the order that was missing.

His father had died when young; his mother had said, 'You must look tidy at the funeral. It's very important. You know how he would have wanted it.' Anguish beyond despair, beyond understanding. He had been so neat. The hole in the ground was so ragged it had to be wrong. The coffin they lowered was so smooth and gleaming. The brass on that shone. He had screamed that it was wrong and they led him away. Cold rain, hot tears, and somehow he was in the wrong.

He admitted to himself for a moment that he had run away to join up. A coward's way out, but he had to survive, even if it meant getting killed.

In the car in the field Margaret was cold and angry. The sun had dropped quickly. She was astonished how black the silhouettes of hedges and trees became against the lingering deep blue of the sky. She was worried about the children. Her anger became outrage, then tears. On this important day, for her as well as him, she was of no importance. Everyone had gone and she had felt increasingly foolish. Last away had been Taylor and Tester with a lorry on to which they loaded everything that remained. Gleaners of scrap and iron. They had driven close past her. Taylor was at the wheel and raised his trilby. He grinned. It was a knowing look, not malicious but not kind either.

'He'll be in the pub, Mrs Ellis. I'll send him back, don't fear!'
She looked at him coldly.

'Don't bother. He'll be here soon.'

Taylor had sucked in his bottom lip and inclined his head as if to acknowledge the reproof. He revved the engine of the lorry loudly and drove away, leaving derisive clouds of blue smoke that fouled the field behind him.

The moon began to rise. At first it was an increased luminescence beyond a section of dark hedge, then a rim of white appeared. Margaret climbed out of the car clutching the starting handle. She had never driven the thing before, indeed had only driven a car twice in her life, but she was going to sit there no longer. In the distance a dog or perhaps a fox was barking, a high lonely sound. She inserted the handle as she had seen Robert do, and felt it rotate, then engage in a firm slot. She stood carefully, remembering that she had to hold the thing in such a way that if it kicked it would not catch her. She pushed down hard. The handle moved very slightly. She pushed harder. The handle moved further with a slow pneumatic gulp. Now she could flick the handle up in the way that seemed to work. She tugged and succeeded in turning the engine over so that it gave a series of muted pops. She set up the handle as before, and tried again. The result was the same. She remembered the ignition switch. She had not turned it on, or the petrol. She checked everything and returned nervously to the starting handle. This time, when she swung it, it coughed and fired. The next swing brought it to life, the handle kicking once, then disengaging. She returned to the car, her heart thumping. She had no plan what to do next. She turned on the headlamps. The swathe of light was comforting. Dotted over the field she could see the straw bales that had marked the lots. She wondered whether she could put the car into gear and at least drive it onto the road. She looked carefully over the controls and felt for the pedals with her feet, testing the pressure they required.

She saw another car approaching. The trees over to her left were brilliantly lit as it came along the road. Instead of continuing past the entrance to the field, it slowed and then turned in. She was dazzled by headlights as it came straight towards her. Her anger returned. Robert had got a lift back in time to frustrate her from whatever she was going to do. She sat with her hands folded in her lap, looking straight ahead.

'What are you up to?'

It was Tom Baxter and he was alone. He was smiling.

'I don't really know. I was thinking of getting it out of this field.'

'Isn't your husband back yet?'

'No.'

Baxter raised his eyebrows, and this embarrassed her.

'I expect him any moment. He has to finish off his business . . .'

She spoke too rapidly. Why did she bother to defend him?

'Are you accustomed to driving that car?' asked Baxter. 'It's a heavy thing. Who started it?'

'I did.'

'It hasn't got a self-starter, has it?'

'No. Only a handle.'

'You did very well! You have to be careful with one of these . . .'

He had climbed out of his vehicle and stood beside her door. 'Can you drive it?'

'To tell you the truth, no.'

He smiled again, but kindly. She felt that it was the first unequivocal contact she had made that day with the possible exception of Mary Merrow.

'Do you want to learn? At least enough to get you onto the road. You can't sit in a field all night!'

'All right!'

She felt nervous but elated as he climbed into the passenger seat beside her. He pointed out each of the controls carefully, and waited until she had tried everything. He was patient, and she immediately thought how impatient Robert always was. It was impossible for him to give a lesson without belittling her.

'You *have* driven a car before?'

'Only twice. I know *what* to do, but not how to do it. I want to learn!'

'Well, a field is the place to learn!'

She moved into gear and let out the clutch. The car ground forwards, jolting over the ruts in the hard field. She drove straight ahead at first, then with Tom pulling at the wheel with his right hand she turned as they approached a looming hedge. The beam of light scanned wildly across the field of stubble, catching two rabbits which sat transfixed. Their eyes glowed a strange yellowish-green, phosphor bright, then they were gone.

'The eyes of a sheep are yellow at night, the eyes of a deer are red,' said Tom. 'The eyes of cats vary. A weasel's eyes are like rubies . . .' He watched her progress to the far end of the field, then they turned for another run.

'Steer round the bales,' he said with delight in his voice. 'Go on, you're doing fine. Speed up a bit, it makes the steering easier.'

She changed up a gear, wondering what Robert would say, what he would make of this night drive if he knew. The car rumbled forward faster. The narrow yellow road created by the headlamps accentuated speed. An owl swooshed across in front of them.

'Left, right, left, right!' called Baxter. 'Between them, that's the way!'

She steered successfully down the line.

'Now figures of eight.'

'I think I've done enough . . .'

'Nonsense. Figures of eight from one row to the next, left, right, round each one and back . . .'

She went on, more confident, faster. He was still helping her to steer when necessary, hand resting lightly on the wheel, touching hers from time to time as she struggled. His head was close to hers as they peered together through the windscreen. She concentrated fiercely, determined to show she could do it, exulting in the release from boredom. She hit a bale and pushed it with her, laughing and protesting she should stop before she hit something solid, but he only urged her on.

'Enjoy it. Learn to drive in one lesson. See if you don't!'

The hedges and the trees reeled past them as the lights swung round. She passed and re-passed his stationary car which stood like a beacon with the engine running. The moon was high over the hedges, a white watcher.

'Now you see you've learned to put your foot down a bit. You can steer better, it's less jolting . . .'

'I'm afraid to go faster . . .'

'Give it a bit more. Just get the gear changes right . . .'

His right hand was resting on her thigh. She had no time to think about how it had got there, whether it was all part of the confusion of driving and whether he had even noticed. She gripped the wheel and drove to and fro one more time, drove to the end of the field fast and turned well and hard. His hand did not come up to assist her but stayed where it was, holding fast. Her heart thumped. She had no idea what to do.

She saw Robert.

He was running like a madman towards them across the field, waving his arms frantically above his head. As they watched, he tripped and nearly fell. She braked and drew the car to a halt.

Tom's hand had gone. They waited.

Robert laboured up the white highway of light. He was shouting and was alarmed or angry.

'What the devil are you doing!' he roared. 'You'll wreck the thing!' Anger, not alarm.

He saw Baxter and his face froze into an ill-tempered scowl.

'I saw the car going round and round . . . My wife can't drive. You wouldn't know that . . .' He stopped, unable to grapple with the situation, with this unforeseeable behaviour.

'I was learning to drive,' said Margaret. 'Mr Baxter was teaching me while I waited for you to come. I can't do any damage in a field.'

'You were careering round and round! I saw it, faster and faster!'

'I was only steering between bales.'

She resented his manner in front of Tom Baxter, as if she were some idiot child incapable of any normal dexterity or skill.

She could not bring herself to look Tom Baxter in the eyes. Her thigh was still warm where his hand had rested. 'She'll be a good driver,' Baxter said. 'I'm sorry if you object.' He climbed out, not looking back towards her.

'The springs could have been damaged,' Robert persisted. 'The ground is very hard and rough.'

'It was only a bit of fun,' said Margaret, then realised immediately she had said the wrong thing. Robert's face closed down. It was the expression with which she was familiar, as if shutters slammed in his mind and behind his eyes.

'It was only a short lesson,' she heard herself pleading, 'and the field is flat really . . .'

86

Tom Baxter was leaving. His left hand was behind his back, out of sight of Robert whom he still faced. He was wriggling his fingers, waving goodbye. She felt hot and at the same time amused. It had been no accident.

'I apologise. I suppose it's my fault,' she heard him say. Robert immediately told him it was nothing of the sort.

'I'll drive us home if you don't mind.'

She moved over and Robert climbed in beside her. He smelled of beer and took off over the field at a rate that belied his concern for the springs. Glancing sideways as they passed Baxter's car, she saw the headlamps dip, ignite. A salute? Derision? Humour? Robert paid no attention but drove onto the road. He careered through the narrow lanes too fast, without speaking. Margaret wondered what wrong she was supposed to have committed. The moon seemed to chase her home.

Robert waited for the apology, nursing his hurt. The carelessness and frivolity of her behaviour shocked him. If she had damaged the car they would never have got home, and spares were almost impossible to obtain. He was completely unable to understand why she would do such a thing. His anticipation of depression had been rudely shattered. This was a serious new turn of events. What had the man Baxter to do with it? He wondered whose idea it had been in the first place but could not bring himself to ask.

'I'm sorry,' she said eventually, because she knew she had to or live in speechless torment for days.

'All right. I just have no idea why you should do such a senseless thing.'

The children were all asleep, Robert too. Margaret got up quietly and went through to the living room. Another place that had become familiar to her that she would have to leave in two days. She drew back a curtain and stared at the moon which was high above the houses, giving a magic sheen to the humdrum grey of slates. She imagined the field she had left not so many hours ago, imagined the lit stubble and dark hedges, the rabbits that would be free to graze again. She had enjoyed driving the car. She considered how much she had surprised herself. The surprise of a hand on her thigh. She should have said something, but hadn't. The surprise of the man with the forage cap, the prisoner, how he had lain, concentrating, upon the bank like some hunter-gatherer of the Stone Age. How he had jumped to his feet like an animal.

She went back to bed and lay close to Robert to find out how she felt about him. It was a deliberate test she had to make. She felt little except familiarity, but supposed her expectations had never been high once the honeymoon of his return was over. She wished this husband of hers would relax, enjoy, be human, that he would start like an animal, lay his hand on her, drive in dark fields. She had accepted despotism too far. It was easier to go with the flood of it, but it was no good for her.

She slept. Waking in the early hours she retained an image from her dreams of a smiling man with his hands on her thighs, and Robert in the headlights of a car. Her heart was beating fast and she was wet. She got up immediately, harried by guilt.

CHAPTER FOUR

Peter had tears in his eyes. He surreptitiously wiped at them, not wanting to appear unmanly. He need not have bothered. Heinz, Wolfgang and many others sat stunned or in anguish. A very few managed to raise a derisive smile.

Grey film flickered before them in the mess hall. They had no room big enough for the whole camp so they had to see it in shifts. It was compulsory. Each shift had to file in as the other filed out. Those going in were talkative, curious, joking even. The men coming out were silent, pale and introverted, some grim-faced, some rubbing at their eyes. They could not meet the enquiring glances of those going in, but stared at the ground. They seemed physically stooped.

Grey film that was grained with specks that might have been the tears of humanity. The pile of sticks that were legs, teeth heaped like road chippings. Names. Buchenwald, Belsen, Dachau, Auschwitz. Shots of one interminable trench after another filled with skeletal forms in the abandon of death. The camera panned over them, again, again, again. Is this all that is left of humans? Heinz was reminded of a mummified body in the Berlin museum. The skulls were conspicuous, like carelessly arranged ostrich eggs, eye-sockets collapsed. Upturned bodies, although pitilessly exposed, seemed to have no discernible sex. Here and there a fold of flesh on a ribcage indicated what might have once been a woman. The living were as horrific as the dead. Blank, lost eyes staring from more of those egg-domes that had replaced normal heads. Groups staring through wire. Individuals trying to stand and falling, trying to crawl and collapsing. Pictures of steel doors like the mouths of brick kilns or baker's ovens. A commentary they could not believe. Trucks and railway wagons in sidings. More pits. Lime. Hair-filled mattresses. Heaps of clothes as high as a house, some baled for use. For what? Figures that stupefied, that could not be true, except that the camera panned over the dead again and again. Soldiers trying to feed the egg people who could not keep their heads upright to receive food. One in particular filled the screen. His, her, its head fell sideways again and again, rolling, unable to swallow from a spoon that was held from vestigial lips. Egg people with limbs trailing, limbs missing. Dead tangled in wire. Capsules held by soldiers who showed them to the camera. Gas, said the commentary. A demonstration of how it was dropped into sealed chambers. More ovens. Industrial chimneys. Industrial Germany.

When the trauma ended and the lights were switched on, they filed silently out, understanding why the men they had earlier passed stared grimly at the ground. When they had regained their hut they sat silent for some time. Ehrich was the first to summon the strength to speak.

'That cannot have been propaganda. That must have been true. Maybe it was not as bad as they show it, but some of it must be. All of those bodies . . . What will this make of Germans?'

'The British radio has been talking about it for some time,' said Wolfgang. 'For months.'

'It cannot be true,' said Peter. 'No one could do a thing like that, and certainly not Germany. They say these are films taken at Katyn. These are Poles massacred by the Russians . . .'

'But we know there were *Konzentrationsläger*,' said Ehrich, 'they existed.'

'But not like that!' said Peter. 'Would we do anything like that? That's not German! I don't know what it is, but it's not German! We don't stand for that sort of thing. We are an honourable people!'

'So you do believe it, a bit,' said the observant Heinz.

'I don't know,' said Peter.

'There is no hope for us if it's true,' said Wolfgang. 'We will all be cast into outer darkness. Germany is finished. The world will dismember us, we will never be forgiven. If that film is being shown to the world, we will have no home.'

'If it is true, we have no right to one,' said Heinz. 'Perhaps they intend to keep us here forever. Perhaps we will never be repatriated. We sit in this hut and we only know part of the story. Perhaps the B.B.C. is telling the truth. We should listen to the news.'

'They will hate us,' said Wolfgang. 'We are prisoners of that film as much as we are prisoners of this camp, whether it is true or not.'

'Look out, here's crazy Kunkel!' said Heinz. 'What's he doing out at this hour?'

'I wonder what he made of the film show?' said Wolfgang. Kunkel marched briskly down the length of the hut, clomp clomp clomp clomp, and snapped to attention. He raised his hand in salute.

'*Heil Hitler*!'

There was a chorus of groans and shouts.

'Piss off, Kunkel!'

'Stick it, Kunkel!'

'Get your hair cut!'

Kunkel's head was so shaved it looked like sandpaper. He ignored them all. Mohnke entered with Muller.

'Oh God, it's them again!' said Peter.

'Bastards!' said Wolfgang. He still wore a bandage round his head. He would return to work tomorrow, the doctor said. Muller and Mohnke looked neither left nor right but marched in step to the head of the aisle. Both men were in uniform. Kunkel moved sideways, taking three precise steps. Each time his heels clicked together. He stood to attention. Muller and Mohnke stopped, turned sharply about, stood to attention with a click, then stood easy. It should have been laughable but wasn't.

'You will all have seen the film,' said Mohnke. 'I do not know by what right the British have enforced this, and I shall of course be making the strictest enquiries. I have come to impress upon you, German soldiers, that what you have seen is propaganda lies. The purpose of these lies is to demoralise you and to demoralise the German people, to make you question the righteousness of our war. We are told from a source which without question has access to the truth that the film you have just seen was made in a typhoid hospital in British India! Into this they have inserted shots of Polish dead at Stettin at the hands of the Russian animals. Review what you have seen in the light of this. Think how the film has been put together and for what purpose and you will see that nothing that they have shown you could ever have happened on German soil! You know it cannot be true. What then do you make of the British for promoting this terrible lie? Their motives are the total destruction of Germany. Remember Dresden, German soldiers. Reject these British lies for what they are! *Heil Hitler*!'

He raised his arm in salute. Muller and Kunkel aped him, a few men replied. There was an undercurrent of unease, mumbling. Mohnke and his party marched from the hut.

'If it was propaganda, why is Mohnke so shit-arse scared?' asked Wolfgang.

'The trouble is that none of us can dare to believe it, not even part of it,' said Heinz.

'Do you think that Kunkel is a queer?' asked Ehrich. 'There's something very odd about him. What about him and Mohnke?'

Wolfgang laughed briefly.

'Now who's putting round propaganda . . .?'

'No, but seriously,' protested Ehrich, 'There's a lot of it about. It's not natural the way he spends his time with them, and in the kitchen. . . .'

'Go on, put me off my food!'

Wolfgang shoved at Ehrich, who fell back on his bunk with a laugh.

It had taken their minds momentarily away from the film.

'How's the booze?' asked Peter. 'Let's have a look.'

Peter and Wolfgang got up and walked to Peter's locker, a wooden cupboard about a metre high with another on top of it. He unlocked it and they drew out a large tin marked 'Shell Motor Oil'. From the top protruded a cork and from that protruded a short length of rubber piping secured by pieces of string to a length of wire similarly bent. This formed a fermentation lock. Peter carefully withdrew the cork and lock and tilted the tin. Wolfgang picked up an enamel mug that stood beside the tin and Peter tipped some of the contents into it. Wolfgang tasted it. 'Not bad.' He offered it to Peter who stood the tin very gently upright before taking the cup. He sipped.

'It still tastes like turnips!'

'It'll always taste like turnips. The thing is, it's alcohol!'

'It's alcohol!' They shared the contents of the mug with delight, sipping as though it was a liqueur.

'It's the bread yeast,' said Peter. 'It isn't right. You need a stronger yeast, a wine yeast to get a really good fermentation going. . . .'

'Don't complain. It's wonderful.'

'We need another tin, then we can try the elderberries. . . .'

'We need a still, then we can try schnapps. . . .'

Peter replaced the cork carefully. Wolfgang gave him the mug which he also replaced. He shut and locked the door. The little key had a loop of string through it. Peter put it over his head so that it hung down inside his shirt.

'Things were looking up,' he said, 'until they showed us that film. If it's true, do you think they will keep us here forever? They can't do that, can they?'

'Of course not,' said Wolfgang.

CHAPTER FIVE

'Pump!' shouted John. 'Go on, it has to get started, has to lift the water from the bottom. . . .'

'I am pumping!' William yelled desperately. He flailed the iron handle up and down, puffing and almost falling over. At every stroke the pump clanked with a noise like a hammer beating iron. A thin trickle of water ran out of the iron spout.

'Don't put that in the bucket,' commanded John. 'Wait until there's a proper stream of water. That'll be rusty.'

'Shut up, know-all!'

Helen stood to one side, watching the two boys. She was there for encouragement. She knew that in the house their father would be waiting.

The pump was attached to a brick wall forming part of the rim of the well that stood in front of the house. From it a long iron pipe disappeared into the depths. The well had a wooden lid, one half hinged so that it could be raised. It terrified Helen, who suffered from vertigo if she even looked over the brim. Near the boys were four brand-new galvanised buckets. They were to fill these and decant the water into two five-gallon milk churns in the kitchen at the back of the house. There was no plumbing, no water tank.

There was a dew on the ground, just sufficient to glaze the grass and form small glass-beads on twigs. A leaky gutter on the house dripped quietly into a flower bed, a blackbird turned leaves for worms. It was half-past six and just light. Both boys wore gloves, for the pump-handle was cold, and William paused to blow inside his, pulling them away at the palm.

'If you do that, you idiot, all the water drops down again!'

'Shut up and do it yourself!'

'No. We each have to do at least two buckets.'

William attacked the pump again in a frenzy. There was a sucking and a gurgling and water shot out in spurts. William could not keep pumping and also move a bucket under the spout. He tried to reach with his left hand, leaning forward, while pumping with his right, but failed.

'Pass it!'

John was laughing as he watched.

'You should've thought of that!'

'Here you are,' said Helen, and placed the bucket so the water gouted in. She picked up the second bucket and had it ready.

'I'll help you carry,' she said.

'No,' said William, 'It's my job.'

'I'm stronger.'

'Do you see how we've got to have a bath?' said John. 'That big tin thing like a long bucket. We've got to sit in that. Ma says we can sit in front of the fire.'

'I'm not sitting in front of the fire!' said Helen. John laughed.

'Why not?'

'Never you mind!'

'The water takes hours to boil on the stove . . .' puffed William. 'I think we should all give up washing . . . I think we should give up school . . . I think it's your turn to pump. . . .'

They had occupied the house for two days now, camping in it from room to room with furniture interspersed with boxes and crumpled newspaper. The boys had been given a room, but had moved each night to another as there were four to choose from. Helen had taken the smallest bedroom and stayed put. The plan of the house was simple. The front door opened into a brick-floored hall that in turn gave onto the living room that had previously been the farm parlour. This was the stone-floored room where they had sat with Jempson. Now there were rugs on the flags, a sofa, three armchairs and an oil lamp on a stand. One door led to the working kitchen, formed from part of what had obviously been the dairy with a stone top and stone shelves for milk and cheese. This was a cold place where no one would linger but the kitchen section was kept at a reasonable temperature by an oil-fired range that burned day and night.

95

The other door led sideways into the back kitchen, now piled high with dining-room furniture. The floors were worn from the passage of boots over hundreds of years where men had gathered to breakfast before working in the fields, and returned in the evening to be given beer. In this room the dairymaid and cook had lived and worked. The staircase led directly to a long corridor that ran the length of the north wall of the house. In this way every bedroom faced south.

John and William had discovered that the end room looked directly into the branches of a big old tree with smooth bark and spare leaves. Their father had told them it was a walnut and they had already invented a fantasy of throwing open the window to harvest the nuts. To their disgust, Jempson had taken this year's crop. William's particular delight was the huge open fireplace. A cast-iron fireback seemed to have fused into the surrounding bricks. Whatever emblem or coat of arms it once bore, it now looked like bubbled coke. Pot swivels and chains lurked like gallows in the darkness. William had found out within half an hour that you could stand in the hearth and look straight up to a rectangle of sky and see the clouds reeling overhead. It was like being at the bottom of a well. He slipped into this retreat for a moment. The inglenook had a damp dark bacon smell, spiced with a bitter whiff of soot. William remembered the stories of small boys used as chimney sweeps and, looking up, his sharp eyes saw there were indeed ledges and pockets let into the soot-caked walls. He could hear the wind, high up, moaning with a soft, low note around the chimney. He quickly scrambled out.

'We are going to start ploughing today.'

They looked at him with numbed minds. They had supposed that it had to start some time, that farming must begin, but for it to do so now, today, with only this unit of unskilled labour seemed fantastic.

'Don't we need help?' asked Margaret, voicing the fears of them all. 'You can't plough alone.'

'The boys can help me. There's over a week until they have to go to school. So can Helen.'

'But they aren't accustomed to it. They don't know what to do.'

'They only have to help me hitch up, keep an eye on things. The tractor does the work.'

'But can you do it? Have you ever ploughed before?'

'Yes.'

'When?'

'When I was a boy. You can't forget. And it's your turn to milk the cow.'

'But I can't milk it, it won't let me!'

'Oh yes, it will, when you've shown it who's in charge. Be firm.'

There was only one milk cow but Robert had already bought six heifers that were to be delivered that day. He had begun to talk of a Friesian herd, all pedigree. Elated, he had recently begun to talk of hundreds of things. She should have been delighted to see this vigour, this happiness, but all the time she could not suppress the thought that the whole venture was fraught with recklessness. He seemed to consider so little before rushing ahead.

He seemed to take so much for granted.

The oil lamps, for example. Or feeding the chickens, or carting the water. She had known they would have no electricity until Robert managed to raise enough money to buy a generator, but had had no idea what was involved in lighting an entire house by oil. Now the lamps were lined up in the kitchen waiting for her just as the cow would be waiting for her in the stall.

The lamps were numerous. Helen had her own lamp for her room, John and William each had one. They kept them on all night, to Margaret's concern, so they needed filling every day and the wicks needed trimming. In the living room there was a large brass lamp with twin wicks on a rakish stand that smoked in any draught. In addition a Tilley pump-up lamp hung from one of the beams on an iron hook. The dining room had a lamp on the table; the kitchen had two. At the head of the stairs a further heavy brass light hung on chains. Three hurricane lamps were kept by the back door, one for the privy, one for the cow and chickens and one spare. In all there were twelve, each needing daily attention.

She laid down the paraffin can and filler funnel. Helen was polishing the body of the living-room light. Both of them were

97

black to halfway up their arms. The boys watched, awaiting instructions. The pump was their chore, not the lamps.

'I shall have to remember how to set out "lands". I shall put down ridges at twenty-two yards. That should be all right with this soil. I asked Jempson, and he agreed.'

Margaret nodded.

'He should know.'

He had dressed for the part for Ploughing Day. He wore a khaki Army shirt, open at the neck, and a pre-war tweed jacket with baggy grey trousers and leather braces. His boots were new and black. He had bought them the day after he bought the farm and had soaked them daily with acrid dubbin. It was important to make them waterproof, he declared, as if this was a pearl of wisdom. Margaret, remembering childhood warnings, thought the dubbin would rot the stitching.

He was ready, the farmer set for the plough, the tiller of the soil. He looked happy and confident. Confident as a man might be who had carefully read his copy of Watson and More on *Agriculture* the night before.

'Come on, boys. You'll see how it's done!'

The boys left with him, wearing holey jumpers and their oldest grey school shorts. This was more interesting, the excitement of unknown machines. Helen watched them with a sense of unfairness. Perhaps there was something they could do that required strength she did not possess but she doubted it. Margaret, alert to her daughter's glance and brief sigh, laid a hand on Helen's arm.

'We'll find something. Don't worry.'

Helen smiled briefly. She must not be noticed.

'What was that?'

Robert stuck his head back round the door.

'Nothing. You get on with your ploughing!'

'Now you wind the handscrew here to set the depth of furrow,' instructed Robert, showing the boys as he turned a small wheel with both hands that adjusted the height of the plough wheel. The plough was beautiful, painted bright blue for the sale. The shares shone like swords, the twin discs like axes. A machine to do battle with stubble and clay and cut the unbroken sod. Satisfied with the setting of the wheel, he turned to the tractor.

This was the boys' particular delight. They had been allowed to sit on it by turns yesterday, and of course had sneaked back to it unsupervised and climbed over its hard metal seat and pulled at the steering. It was dark green with its name in dull cream on the very front and sides of the radiator. *Fordson*.

'It's a white-spot Fordson,' their father had said knowledgeably. They also had an older tractor that was not used for ploughing. That was the orange-spot Fordson, a poor thing by comparison, with rust patches eating its mudguards and rubber tyres as smooth as an apple. No one had seen it running, for it would not start and had been bought for spares. Robert had said confidently that he would get it going again, and the boys believed him and already wanted it because they should then have a two-tractor farm and that would be a real symbol of strength.

The white-spot Fordson had only two blemishes – a tendency to kick and a rusty exhaust. The exhaust had been wired upright in two places and someone – presumably Jempson – had recently given the rusting metal a coat of aluminium paint so that it had a spurious gleam. Robert asked John to pull out the choke as he had told him yesterday and to adjust the throttle. He advanced on the starting handle that was clipped upright to the front of the machine. John sat in the driving seat, hands on the wheel, very self-important. William envied him his confidence. He was afraid of the thing. It was huge and hot and smelly and ran on massive iron tyres that crushed flints. William shuddered when he thought what it could do to bones.

Robert paused to pump at the carburettor to ensure a flow of fuel, then grasped the starting handle in both hands, holding it with a piece of rag.

'Here we go!'

He hurled himself at the handle, winding it round and round and round. Nothing happened. The boys were impressed. They had never seen him behave like this before, and were pleased. This was more like the sort of father they could admire. William longed to be upon the tractor, then perhaps he could share the smile his father exchanged with John.

Robert threw himself into it again, leaning down, then tugging the iron bar up. There was a thump and a roar. The handle spun, then it disengaged and hung swinging. Blue smoke squirted from the exhaust.

'Let the choke in. Gently!' he shouted, and John obeyed, steadily moving the toothed iron bar until the note of rage in the engine died to a workaday roar.

'Down!' Robert commanded, and John reluctantly lowered himself to the ground. Robert took his place on the driving seat.

'Fasten on the plough! Take out the pin and put it through the hitch! Come on, William, do something!'

William ran forward. He could feel the heat of the tractor now. He was afraid to do something wrong and fear made his small fingers clumsy. He dropped the pin but John picked it up quickly with a tutting noise. William did not look up. He knew his fault had been seen and could have cried. John was expertly tightening the nut and lock nut beneath the pin. That was all there was to it, there was nothing for William to do. He stood up and moved back, hands sliding to his pockets.

'Get your hands out of your pockets!' roared the man. 'How can you expect to get anything right if you have your hands in your pockets!' William said nothing. He stood still with his hands straight by his sides, looking at the ground.

'We're off!' Robert shouted, then he was waving at the boys to follow and John was running after the plough. William followed. He knew he must try to please more than John.

They followed the plough, walking to one side, watching the magic. The gleaming shares were buried in a continuous incision. They made a metallic slithering noise, audible above the roar of the tractor. The conversion from stubble to chocolate soil at the polished breast was mesmeric. The stream of earth flowed past like a river in spate and they were stunned by the beauty of it. From it flints emerged. They were in fantastic shapes and the boys picked them up, wiping at them, at first carrying them or filling their pockets. Soon they had too many, and began throwing them back.

'These might be weapons!' said John. 'Arrow heads or axes. It might dig anything up . . .'

'It might dig up pottery,' said William. 'Keep your eyes open for pottery!'

There were worms that seemed as big as snakes and disappeared down brown subterranean tubes. There were strange red pebbles as round as marbles with wrinkled skins. There were leatherjackets like small shiny dates and larvae and curled green caterpillars. Gulls began to follow, shrieking and flapping.

'I've found some pottery!' shouted William, and John was on him in a flash.

'Let me see!'

'Let me clean it!'

William spat on it to clean it, then rubbed it on the leg of his shorts.

'Let me see it . . .' commanded John.

'All right, but I found it . . .'

They peered hopefully.

'It could be anything,' said John. 'What's it doing in the middle of the field?'

'I think it's very old,' said William, defending his prize. 'There wasn't always fields here, I expect. There could be lots more. There could have been an ancient village . . .'

They looked at the piece of blue and white ware.

'It's got flowers on it,' said John. 'It can't be old. It's a bit of a plate!'

'How do you know? It could be a very old plate. I'm keeping it anyway!'

And William added it to the collection in his pocket. 'I'm going to remember where this place is so I can come back to it another time. It's beside this big tree with the broken branch and this much in . . .' He tried to remember it. Shut his eyes and saw it in his imagination, opened them and imprinted it all again. John had already gone on, and he ran to catch up.

The field was new to them, unmastered territory. As the tractor's progress outstripped theirs, they were distracted by blackberries in the hedge. The tractor became small in the distance as they picked and gorged. It turned at right angles and proceeded on the second leg of an 'L' as their father set out the headland. They found a sloe, smokey with the bloom on its berries, and fell upon it with greed, to recoil with thrilled disgust. They sucked at the green flesh and spat out the stones, grimacing. They made up tales of belly-ache and poison, imagined making jam out of it and leaving it for Helen, for Pa, especially for Pa. They discovered old birds' nests in the skeletal hedges, feeling the perfect clay bowl formed inside a blackbird's, the soft down within moss of a chaffinch's, knowing nothing of the bird that had made them. John lifted out the blackbird's nest and stood it on one of the turned furrows. They examined it with disbelief.

'Put it back!' said William.

'What for? It won't come back. They'll make a new one every year.'

'You don't know that. You don't even know what it is.'

'Neither do you.'

'No, but I'm going to put it back. Then I'll come back and watch it and see.'

'Like you're going to remember where you found the piece of plate!'

'I hate you! Put it back!'

'You put it back.'

'I will!'

And William lifted the nest carefully and pushed into the hedge with his hands, ignoring the thorns that tore at him so as to protect the shape of the nest. He placed it on the crook of the branch from which John had removed it.

'See!'

His hands were covered with scratches that were beginning to streak red.

'Hurry up, he's catching us!' commanded John. The tractor was on the third side of the field now and approaching the bottom. They moved on faster, disturbing gulls that were already ahead of them, determined to maintain the distance that had developed. The machine was producing a low steady note.

'Have you noticed earth has a smell?' said William.

'Of course I have!' John was dismissive. 'Let's make for that wood on the far side. I wonder what's in there?'

'Is that on the farm?'

'I don't know. I don't care. What does it matter?'

'We shouldn't go on other people's land. Pa told us not to.'

'So what.'

They trotted up the line of furrows to the far end of the field and stared at the wood. In the October sun the beech trees revealed a first hint of bronze in the green of their leaves. Convolvulus stood high in the hedge and honeysuckle was still in flower. Occasional leaves of bramble were scarlet. The boys saw chestnut trees, already tattered and yellowed. They looked for and found a gap in the hedge, plunging through impatiently, knowing without saying that they were looking for conkers. The sound of the tractor immediately died to a whisper. The ground underfoot was soft with mulch, spongey. They looked at each other for courage. It was dark after the reeling sky over the fields.

'He'll be angry when he sees we've gone,' said William. 'I don't think we ought to go on. Let's go back . . .'

'I'm not going back!' said John. 'You go back if you want to. By yourself!' He moved forwards. 'We only want a few.'

Their footfalls were almost inaudible. A blackbird flew up, surprised, clucking and chattering.

'This isn't our land!' insisted William in a hiss. To shout in the wood would have been like shouting in church.

'Why not?' demanded John, uncaringly.

'We haven't got a wood, just a spinney. Pa said we had a spinney. A spinney is just a few trees. He said so. He said it was a few trees with old fishponds in them. This can't be right.'

'I bet this is our spinney!' said John. He too was hushed in his reply. William was surprised that even he responded to the silence of the place. They advanced like hunters. Strange fungi grew up from the mulch or on the boles of living trees.

'I bet these are all poisonous,' said John. 'Deadly. If you made a brew of this and put it on an arrow, it would kill.'

They arrived at the chestnut trees. High above, the prickly globes of the cases were heavy. They searched for short pieces of branch and threw and threw again into the leaves, threw with great casting sweeps, watching the arc of the falling wood and waiting for the dropping reward.

Many of the cases had begun to split, revealing a slim segment of glistening brown. These they pulled apart with their fingers, pocketing the nuts. The unopened ones were broken open with a heel. The beauty of the chestnuts was overwhelming. They showed each other the best specimens, astonished by the gloss and colour and markings. Nuggets of gold would have meant no more to them. Time passed unheeded. William noticed crows flying over, calling raucously. The sound of the tractor had ceased. His pockets bulged and his hands smelled rank with the juice from the cases. They would be in trouble for running off.

'We don't need any more,' he said. 'I can't carry any more anyway.'

'Let's go further into the wood then.'

'We must go back!'

'I'm not going back. He'll just go on at us. Let's have a look. Just a bit further.'

'Please let's go back.'

'No. If we're going to get into trouble, we might as well go on.'

John plunged forward again and was almost out of sight in moments. William ran after him in panic, as intended. Both boys stopped abruptly. They had burst from the trees and found themselves on the edge of a wide break in the woodland. It stretched straight and true in each direction, forming a daunting perspective. At each end the ground sloped gently upwards, making a boxed frame of ground, wood, and sky. The open space between them and the opposite trees was about thirty yards. It was grassed and had been heavily rutted by vehicles with large tyres. It was as astonishing as discovering a main road.

The woodland opposite had been notched out with alcoves cut among the trees. The cleared spaces had been provided with concrete floors. The deepest ruts passed close to these. Within the alcoves lay stacks of bulbous grey shapes, cradled on chocks of wood. Beyond in the woodland they could see further shapes, blackish, grey, and there was a faint whiff of wood smoke.

'Come away!' hissed William.

'What is it?' said John. 'We must look.'

Caught between curiosity and fear they teetered on the edge of the chasm of openness then ran like animals across the gap. William's heart was pounding. They were close to one of the immense heaps. The grey shapes were arranged upon each other to form a pyramid, six rows wide at the bottom and six rows high, twenty-one in all as they counted.

'What *are* they?' asked William, hand cupped, mouth close to John's ear.

'Bombs,' said John confidently.

'Let's get out! They're huge . . .'

'I'm going to look. It's a dump for bombs.'

Before William could protest, John was off. Parting low branches he stood on the concrete apron. William was terrified.

'No!' he shouted. Another blackbird, chattered loudly and beat off through the undergrowth.

'Shut up!' John hissed urgently. William watched as his brother approached the fat tubes and examined one. He took his time, tipping his head to one side and reading markings that William could just perceive, then walked round the stack out of sight. William knew it was deliberate. He shivered with apprehension, suddenly very cold, but was determined to stay, to show John he was not afraid. He had to urinate, turning his back so that John should not see. The stream seemed to go on for ever.

'I see you!' said John, making him jump and wet a shoe. He could have hit out with anger.

'They're thousand-pound bombs. It says so on the side. And there's huts in the trees beyond, hundreds of them in rows, with windows. Come and look!'

'I don't want to. We must get back.'

'You always say that.'

'I don't.'

'Then come and look.'

The two boys moved cautiously forward. The dark shapes were revealed gradually to be huts of corrugated asbestos cement. In the gable end of each was a steel-faced door and two windows. They peered in. The dark interior was piled high on both sides with drab olive cases. They stared, imagining what they might contain. The smell of wood smoke drifted to them again. John gestured to William to follow him down the side of the hut. Faintly, they could hear low voices, laughter. They moved like foxes, alert but ready to flee.

Beyond the end of the hut they could see a clearing in the trees a few yards distant. It was a man-made shelter, not a mere hole in the trees, with walls of woven branches within which canvas had been stretched to form a hut circle. A roof of canvas pulled over a horizontal branch covered half of it. From the other half drifted the smoke the boys had smelled. In a circle inside the clearing sat a ring of men in uniform, but without hats. As seats they used the same steel boxes the boys had seen in the hut. Two more stood on end in front of them and formed a table. The men were playing cards. The boys could hear the sound of money rattling on the makeshift table, the slap of cards. There was an exclamation, a burst of talking. Someone lit a cigarette. The smell was sharp to their heightened senses, quite different from the wood smoke. Money rattled again. Curling winds drove downwards, enveloping the camp in the wood smoke. Men coughed. The setting, the clearing, the circumstances were so unreal that William felt strangely light-headed, as if in a walking dream. What could they be doing? Why were they hiding?

'Oh shit, man, stir that fire, for Christ's sake!'

The voice was American. John and William backed away from the corner of the hut, then moved fast back down the flank. They ran back across the rutted break and into the soft, silent woods with their mattress of leaf mould. Panting, they stared at each other, wild-eyed at so much discovery.

Robert suppressed his rage that the boys had drifted off and left him. He sat bolt upright on the tractor, enjoying the living feel of the thing, enjoying the sight of the turned furrows and the scream of the following gulls. It was intoxication to him, the realisation of remembered childhood. As a boy of eight, he had visited his grandfather's farm with his father. They lived in Manchester. The streets there were straight and red-brick with privet hedges that did not dare disobey. His memory of the place was of wet cobbles and a corner shop where the woman was kind to him. No one else had been kind, they never seemed to have time. His father and mother were grey shadows. He had tried hard to obey them, hoping that that would be the way to favour, but nothing much came of it and his school friends despised him. His father's minor job in the town hall served only further to isolate him, as his father dressed for the part and insisted upon neatness in Robert.

The day when he had been taken to the country was graven on his memory. His grandmother was ill and his mother was away from home, or he would never have been taken, he was sure. The sun had blazed. They had taken a train and been met at the station by a pony and trap. He was not told the purpose of the visit. Many years later he discovered his father was lending some money to his grandfather – money lent him by his wife. Robert was never allowed to know things of importance.

He had been stunned by the silence. Put outdoors to play, he had walked into a green field and sat down. He could not believe the fine clarity of peace. It was as if a man who had drunk from a muddied river all his life was suddenly given a glass from a clear spring. Accustomed to the din of traffic and factories, people, cars and horses, sounds to him had always been an immediate assault. The experience of listening to the thin far away noises of agriculture was as beautiful as music. He remembered vividly the sound of a church clock heard from that field. It had chimed out all four quarters before striking the hour. The sound had travelled so far that it varied on the breeze, pushed this way and that over fields and round trees, fainter then stronger. It had been towards the beginning of hay-making. Several fields away he had seen the flash of sun on steel, then heard perfectly clearly the sound of a scythe being whetted. He had decided that one day he would own a farm. He had lain down and discovered that even the grass has a sound, a faint sigh, in the slightest breeze. His father had ignored the land, never even enquired how he had spent his time. Whatever had been decided, his father was not in good humour and the journey back was wordless except for the necessities of direction and tickets. His father disliked the country. He had died not long afterwards. Perhaps he had felt the cold hand on his shoulder that day. His heart attack had been massive and unexpected.

It might have been thought that, having been subjected to this insensitivity and oppression, Robert would have been alert to it and hated it. Instead it had imbued in him a strong sense that no one was entitled to anything with less difficulty than he had encountered. It had been a fundamental shock to him to see the shape and form of his children when he returned from the war. He had not been able to visualise any real change in them despite the photographs he had twice been sent, and the short spells of leave. He had discovered that they had none of the self-contained virtues he valued in himself. Helen was the possible exception to this. The boys simply seemed undisciplined and contemptuous. He could only blame Margaret for that. He had tried to make all allowances for a woman on her own, but she was far from being the only woman left in that condition, and he could not see that other children were as disobedient as his own. The farm would be good for them. They would have to learn to do, and do right. They would have the colossal advantage of the countryside, the freedom. He sighed to rid himself of the disappointment of their disappearance, then drew in a deep breath to exhilarate himself. He leaned round and pulled the cord to operate the self-lift mechanism as he had reached the end of the furrow. With satisfaction he turned on the headland to resume the furrow in the opposite direction. As he did so he saw a figure standing by the hedge. It was Ingleton, who waved to him. Robert stopped the tractor, disengaging gear and applying the brake, but leaving the engine running. Ingleton approached.

'I didn't really mean to interrupt,' he said. 'There's nothing worse than just getting started, then having to stop. However I thought I ought to call in. The seed merchant is doing the rounds. You should expect him any day, he's just left me. A man by the name of Clutton. He's all right. You won't get anything any cheaper by going elsewhere. How's it going?'

'Very well.'

Robert felt that he was under inspection, noting the other man's keen glance over the plough and tractor and the turned furrows.

'You don't bother with setting out the lands?' asked Ingleton. Robert snorted.

'I brought the two boys with me to help do it, but they've disappeared already.'

Ingleton gave a small laugh.

'That's how lads are. Still, I think there's a lot of nonsense talked about setting out a field. That's competition talk! You've done a right good job, I see. This isn't your first go at a plough!'

'It is,' said Robert, pleased.

Ingleton raised his eyebrows in polite disbelief.

'You're having me on!'

'It's true.'

'Well, I'll be jiggered you've got it right. How deep have you got her set?'

'Nine inches.'

Ingleton nodded.

'What do you intend to sow?'

'Wheat.'

'Well, that will be right. Old Jempson used to plough too shallow in my view. He was giving up, you know, and ploughed at about seven inches. It's easier and quicker. He didn't care, latterly. But it don't give you a good root-bed and this soil will take up to ten inches with no bother.'

'Thank you,' said Robert.

'I wasn't giving you a lecture, mind,' said Ingleton quickly. 'I ain't telling you how to do it . . .'

'I know you're not. I'm very grateful.'

'Well . . .' Ingleton was made shy. He pulled back his flat tweed cap, and readjusted it. 'People never tell you things like that, and it's important. You can only find out from neighbours, and if I can help, you must ask.'

'I most certainly will.' Robert was embarrassed in turn. 'Quite.'

'And how will you get on with the drilling?' Robert looked at him blankly. 'You aren't going to sow by hand?'

'No. I bought a drill. From here.'

'Well, it's hard work on your own, and risky. I should always be worried I had a jam in the hopper and ended up with a half-bald crop. You need a man for that. You're going to need a man for a few things, I should think.'

The gulls were becoming impatient at this long stoppage. They had worked nearer and nearer along the last furrow and now most sat a few yards away, waiting and watching, white as washing. Robert climbed down from the seat of the tractor. It was much easier to hear when the two men moved away some distance. Some of the gulls took wing, settled again.

'What do you do?'

'I have a couple of old chaps. Tom and George. They live in my cottages. They're on my beet now in the field that comes down to your meadow.'

'Could I get someone?'

Ingleton lifted his cap and scratched his head with his little finger. He replaced it and straightened it again.

'There isn't anyone hereabouts. Not even an old chap. All the young fellows went off to the war and we haven't seen any of them come back again. Maybe they will one day, as long as they weren't killed, but I reckon a lot won't. Not now they've learned to do other things and learned that you can earn money by doing 'em! But you must get yourself some prisoners like I have.'

Robert was surprised.

'Prisoners?'

'I suppose you haven't come on that. The Government has released them for agricultural work because of the shortage of labour. You can get them from High Garrett at Braintree. You go and see the commandant and he will organise it.'

'Do they bring them to work?'

'Yes. And pick them up again in the evening.'

'Who pays them?'

'You pay the camp, the camp pays them. It's only three farthings an hour per man. They work well when they get accustomed to it.'

'I'll look into it. Thank you.'

'And are you going to buy a horse?'

'Yes.'

'I think you're right. You need a horse on this clay, and fuel for tractors is a real problem.'

'All the wagons are horse wagons.'

Ingleton nodded. He had known that in any case. He knew everything Jempson had possessed, had helped the man with most of it at one time or another. He could have told Robert Ellis where every weld had been made in plough or harrow or chains, every stitch in harness. He doubted he would ever have the same working relationship with this distant, middle-class man. Ellis even stood defensively. While Ingleton rested comfortably on his right leg, with his left boot balanced on the toe of his right, Ellis stood upright, almost to attention. Ingleton's hands were comfortable in the pockets of his jacket. Ellis's were straight by his sides. Tension seemed to flow from him.

'I must have some pigs,' said Robert. 'I want three at least. I'm going over to market on Wednesday. Three saddle-backs, I fancy.'

'A good pig. I have whites myself.'

'You have pigs?' Robert sounded surprised. Ingleton smiled slightly.

'I should think everyone has a pig or two! Pigs are to Suffolk what stitches are to tailors! When they brought in the Feedstuffs rationing in February of '41, it was to prevent people like us from using too much cereal on keeping beasts. The idea was to release the cereal for human consumption. No household is supposed to slaughter more than two pigs a year, you know, and you must eat it yourself or sell half a side to the butcher. You aren't allowed to give it away, they do say! The Self-Suppliers Regulations they called them. Damnfool name!'

Ingleton laughed at the expression on Robert's face. 'That is only the beginning! You do be going to have a surprise how many Regulations there are for us farmers! And, by Gor', you will have a surprise how many more of them there are that no one keeps!' The thin-faced man rubbed his sandy stubble, eyes twinkling. He was looking for some similar response in the eyes of the man facing him, some human sign of brigandage when beset by authority. Instead Robert merely looked worried.

'How do I find out about all these things?'

'Oh, don't worry, the man from the Min. of Ag. will hand you out the King's Regulations!' He inclined his head to Robert. 'Well, I'll bid you good day and let you get on with your work.' Ingleton moved off without more ado. Robert was left calling after him.

'Thanks for all your advice! I'm much obliged!'

Ingleton waved in the air, acknowledging, indicating it was nothing, and walked off through the gateway to the road. Robert heard the sound of a car door open and close. He climbed back on the tractor, straightened the machine out and proceeded on his next long furrow. The gulls flew up in a screaming plague. What Ingleton did not know was that Robert had already bought six new heifers. Staring ahead at the uncut bristle of the stubble he reviewed his finances. The farm had cost one thousand, nine hundred pounds and the equipment eight hundred and twenty. Tenant-right another three hundred and fifty. He was already two hundred and fifteen pounds in debt to the bank with the cows costing thirty pounds apiece. Pigs would cost about five pounds each. A horse? Forty, fifty pounds. Margaret knew nothing of this, did not even know he had been to see the bank manager. There was the fertiliser and seed to purchase still. A long investment for the heady days of harvest. He looked behind him at the chocolate-coloured ribbon streaming out from the plough. It would be both exhilaration and relief to see the green shoots of spring. He wished that Margaret could see it as he saw it, feel the peace, adventure, order and challenge of it. So far she had seemed either disengaged, disenchanted or frivolous. The children bored him.

The two women were polishing the brass. Helen took after her mother. The likeness was particularly heightened by their similar hair styles and similar utility dresses with simple 'V' necklines and short half-sleeves in similar prints. Helen was slim, however, where her mother was full. It was only a matter of her youth.

'What do you think of it then?' asked Margaret. Helen held out her blackened hands and wriggled her fingers in front of her mother. 'Not this, the farm. I know it's early to say.' She paused, picked up a cleaner piece of flowered cloth and rubbed at her own dirty fingers. 'What I'm trying to say is, are you all right?'

There was such earnestness in her mother's voice that Helen felt compelled to reassure her, knowing that it was just what she sought.

'It's fine, I'm fine. It's very different.'

'Is it how you imagined it at all?'

'I don't think I ever really imagined a farm. I had an idea, but it was all story books.' She picked up the tin of Brasso, placed her thumb over the top and shook it vigorously before tipping some of the yellow liquid onto a cloth. She began to repolish the side of a lamp that had already been polished.

'Farms are always clean in story books, have you noticed that? No dirt, no muck. I hate the privy, Ma! It's so smelly! Books never tell you anything like that. I'm sure there's rats in there. And fancy there being two seats. Who would do that! It's embarrassing just being in it!'

The privy was a primitive earth closet of corrugated iron situated just beyond the walnut tree. The seating arrangements consisted of a broad plank in which twin oval holes had been roughly cut and smoothed.

'Husband and wife shared, I suppose,' said Margaret. Helen made a noise of disgust.

'Do you think Mr and Mrs Jempson shared?' asked Helen. Her imagination had already sat them there side by side, Jempson so thin he might fall through, Mrs Jempson like an egg in an egg cup.

'I don't know. But people did, you know. People were more robust about these things . . .'

'I think it's revolting.'

Margaret smiled.

'So do I. It will have to go.' She changed the subject. 'Are you looking forward to going to school?'

'I don't know. In some ways. I'll get to know people. I'm afraid I won't like them or they won't like me.'

'That's natural, to begin with.'

Helen wiped off the polish she had unnecessarily applied.

'Is Pa going to be happy here?'

The directness of the question startled Margaret. She froze, cloth poised, her heart suddenly bumping.

'What do you mean?'

Helen wiped back her dark hair from her forehead.

'It's what he wants to do, isn't it? He wasn't very happy when he came back from the war. He criticises us all the time and shouts at us. He shouts at you too.'

Margaret looked carefully at her daughter, at the thin neck, the small indented triangle where neck joined body, the small, round breasts, the shoulders that were those of a young woman. Was she to share confidences with this slender creature and by the same token of embrace burden her with problems she could not solve? It was a moment that had to come, but why now, in this place, at this time? Would any other time be better? She decided it was too soon. It would be selfish to spill out her fears, and once done it could never be recalled.

'It's only his way,' she said untruthfully, 'he doesn't mean anything by it. He's been away a long time and got accustomed to men obeying him. It'll take a little time to get out of the habit, to realise we're all civilians here!'

She tried to make light of it, tried to smile at these words, but her lips froze. She knew she must look crazed, with pain in her eyes and a grin on her lips. Helen's watchful eyes observed everything. She felt disappointment that the moment had eluded her. She wanted desperately to make contact, and would try again. She felt she was old enough to be entitled to the truth. She needed it if she was to deal with the boys. William in particular. She wondered how her mother could pretend to herself that all those watchful young eyes and ears were severed from intelligence.

'We are going to be *allowed* to be civilians, aren't we?' she asked, acid with disappointment. She saw her mother's face darken with anger. The situation was saved by the sound of a motor car drawing up outside the farm house.

'I can pretend I didn't hear that,' said Margaret, going to the door. 'You mustn't be rude about your father!' What a hollow cry, she thought.

The man who stood on the step had his back turned, waiting, but she knew who he was before he faced her. Only Tom Baxter would be wearing a new-looking tweed jacket and twill trousers. His shoes today were brown brogues. He raised his cap and looked at her with mock solemnity.

'Good morning.'

His eyes moved over and around her, then past to the room beyond. Margaret felt ridiculously self-conscious about her blackened hands and arms.

'We're just cleaning the lamps . . .' she explained, but he merely nodded.

'How's the driving? Am I forgiven?'

Margaret felt herself begin to colour. Helen might be listening. She must avoid this line of banter.

'The car survived all right. My husband was not at all pleased. He thinks it was very irresponsible when spares are so hard to get.'

'You know what I mean.'

He was looking at her candidly. She returned his look with what she hoped was a glance of arctic coolness. She said nothing.

'Are you alone?'

'Helen my daughter is with me.'

'Your husband's ploughing. I saw him as I drove past. He seems to be doing all right. Can I come in?'

'I suppose so.'

'Well, you must be neighbourly. You can introduce me to Helen. I have a daughter of my own, you know, who must be almost the same age.'

'I know.'

She moved back inside and Baxter followed her, taking off his cap. Helen had got up from the table as though about to flee the room. She still had a duster in one hand.

'Hello, Helen,' said Baxter, advancing and holding out his hand. 'I'm Tom Baxter.'

'Mr Baxter has a daughter of about your age,' said Margaret.

'She's called Ann,' said Baxter. 'You'll meet her at school, I suppose.'

'I expect I will,' said Helen. She looked guardedly at this stranger who seemed to be so much at ease in their new house. He had a squarish, bland face and blue eyes. He was superficially attractive, like the heroes of women's magazines. There was no one thing about his features that was particularly memorable. What was striking was that he was looking at her in a way that had nothing to do with the fact he had a daughter her age. She was glad the man had his back turned to her mother.

'I was just going . . .' she stuttered, clutching her duster across her chest.

'Pleased to meet you!'

Helen fled to the back kitchen.

'She's a pretty girl,' said Baxter. 'Takes after her mother . . .'

'Please!'

'All right . . . I'm sorry if that embarrassed you. But it is true. I had to see you again, for a moment.'

'Please sit down.'

'Do you feel safer that way?' His voice was still teasing, uncontrite.

'Yes I do.'

'All right, I'll sit down.'

Baxter sat at the table with the oil lamps. He picked up one of the glass funnels and a clean piece of cloth, breathed down the funnel and started to polish it inside.

'This is a chore. I remember it. We have a generator now. They're going to bring an electric line out to here in about two years, they say. Of course that may mean five at the present rate of progress. I expect you'll put in a generator anyway?'

'I don't know.'

Margaret remained standing in front of the open fireplace. She could hear the faint soughing of wind in the chimney, feel a draught around her ankles from the gap beneath the door. It would be cold in winter, she thought inconsequentially. She didn't know what to say to him. She wanted him to leave.

'This place is a lot brighter without old Jempson's things,' continued Baxter, 'He made the place so dark you couldn't see your hand in front of your face. He wasn't a good farmer, you know, barely kept this place ticking over. He didn't really use the land.'

He picked up another glass funnel, blew down it, repeated the process of polishing round and round inside.

'I had to see you again, you know.'

'Shh!' Margaret raised a finger to her lips. 'Helen may hear.'

'Come to the door then. Come outside for a moment.'

'No. You must leave.'

'I'll leave if you show me out . . .'

'All right!'

Baxter put down the lamp funnel, got to his feet. He waited for her to go first, to fulfil her part of the bargain. They passed through the hall and out of the big main door.

'You enjoyed yourself, didn't you, driving round the bales. It was good fun!'

'Yes, I enjoyed myself, but that doesn't give you any right to come here like this.'

'Can I take you driving again?'

'No. Of course you can't.'

'On the road this time. You have to learn to drive. You're miles from anywhere.'

'If I learn, I'll take lessons.'

'Who from? Are you cross with me?'

'No. Yes.'

Baxter laughed. He kissed her lightly on the lips before she had time to realise what he was doing, and was gone, pausing only to replace his cap with a little flourish when he reached a safe distance.

'I'll see you again!' he called.

Margaret darted inside like a child and slammed the door. She had made a complete fool of herself, she felt like an *ingénue* at her first dance, yet she was excited as well as angry. Baxter's disarming directness made what he did seem conveniently unreal. She sat down at the table, picking up the lamp glass he had just polished. Fresh from his breath, she thought, and she fresh from his kiss. Robert must never suspect even a hint of it. Robert with his anger and vanity.

She thought of the photograph of himself that Robert had positioned on their dressing table upstairs. He had sent it from his first posting in North Africa, complete with a frame and stand, and had asked for it on his return. It showed him in Army uniform, his hat beside him on a desk. He was smiling at the camera. In his right hand he held a pipe, just short of his mouth, with no tobacco in it. The background was some photographer's drape suffused with nebulous shadows. Robert's teeth were too white, his moustache too perfectly trimmed. The whole thing was romantically out of focus, perhaps shot through gauze. She had clung to the photograph at first and had shown it regularly to the children.

'This is your dad. Isn't he handsome!'

She had continued to believe in it until his return, ignoring the reality of the leaves he had been able to obtain, the uneasy reunions. Now she loathed it. She even tried moving it to less conspicuous positions, but Robert always replaced it to the fore, treating these movements as tidying mistakes. She loathed the imposition of it and the vanity it displayed.

Yet Robert seemed to feel it was an essential part of the male principle that she keep it there. Perhaps she was confused because she had lost her father, the only man in her life, at an early stage and had sought to find in Robert those same attributes. Her natural instincts when she loved Robert had been to obey and to be subservient without much question. Perhaps her present feelings spoke for themselves. Her obedience was less because she loved him less. She wondered if he had any idea of what he had done by bringing her to this place. Did he think the photograph was some talisman that would ward off ill luck? She smiled and polished the lamp glass against her breasts.

★

Robert drove up and down in the tractor in a state of exultation. The activity was itself hypnotic, the lines of stubble in front, the lines of turned earth behind, the monotonous drone of the engine and shudder of the gouging plough. One approaching hedge was replaced by another, one cloud of displaced gulls reformed to another struggling mass. His irritation with the children seemed unimportant. This activity with its freedom and purpose was a thing that he had looked forward to all his life and had managed to achieve. He considered that not many people were able to say that of their occupations and existence. The turning of the earth and the making of it fertile must be amongst man's most creative activities.

He was concerned about Margaret. Her pleasure with the place seemed to have dwindled before they had even begun. It alarmed him, as her attitude to the farm sale had alarmed him. As her failure to discipline the children properly had alarmed him. They were strangers, grown things, unpliant. He needed their labour.

Robert recalled his visit to the bank manager. He had placed an account with him immediately before the farm sale so that he might pay by cheque and deal locally. The manager had been overtly friendly, and overplayed his part. They had sipped dry sherry together at eleven o'clock in a small office with two windows overlooking a courtyard with a mulberry tree. The fruit was ripe and throughout their discussion fat blackbirds thrashed in the leaves, gulping the berries. The windows were open so that the curtains rose and fell gently in the breeze, affected by some giant breathing. The manager was a florid man with thinning hair and a round face, too fond of the bottle, too inquisitive about Robert's military career. He had drunk over half a bottle of the sherry while Robert politely nursed his glass.

On the second occasion, his affability was reduced to jovial civility and his drink to one pale Amontillado – the difference between a depositor and a borrower. The blackbirds had made the yard white with droppings and the day was sunless. The windows were closed and so was the generosity of the bank. There was no fruit on the mulberry, no birds in the branches, no promise of an unsecured loan. Money, it was explained, was tight. Stocking farms was expensive, and Mr Ellis, when all was said and done, was new at this type of venture. Security was all.

Two hundred and fifteen pounds was a lot of money, and the sherry bottle was replaced in a walnut veneered cabinet that the manager locked with a key on his watch chain. It was secured against the tractor, against the plough, against the harvest that had not even entered the earth as seed. And he was denied the sherry.

He pulled the self-lift, swung the wheel and proceeded down the line again, noting with satisfaction the amount now turned. The furrows were drying already. It would take him part of the next day to finish it, then that would be one field done.

Prisoners. Ingleton was right that he would need help. There was a stack still standing that must be thrashed. An old stack from the year before that Jempson had left. It would be fit for feed only, the man had said. The mice had overrun it. He would thresh it for his six heifers, then he would know how much feed to buy. He wanted more chickens too, proper fowls in sheds instead of the motley bunch of the farmyard, and they would require proper feeding. Eggs were a good staple and fetching a steady price, he was told.

Prisoners. Heat. The ribbons of earth, like a desert in a way until nourished and planted. He remembered prisoners in North Africa. German, Italian. He wondered if any of them at Braintree had been in North Africa. He remembered Paterson.

The sand was surprisingly coarse and gritty, not like the soft sand of builders, and interspersed with jagged pieces of brownish stone. The perpetual wind had scoured about these intrusions until there was a sand-sculpture around each like a tailed comet. The trenches the men built filled quickly. Sand-bags were the only answer. If you can't dig down, build up. Not very far from them they could see a shimmering black line that floated above the sand. That was the enemy. They felt uncomfortably exposed without any cover except their illusory camouflage nets. As much as possible was in tents that were as hot as hell, even with side walls rolled up.

'We need a spotter plane. You can't see a thing through this haze.'

Paterson was lying across the bonnet of their staff car staring through binoculars. It was ten o'clock in the morning and hotter than standing under an arc lamp.

'I saw something then. Tanks, I think. Can't tell. There was just a glimpse, then it breaks up.'

The car was protected by an awning of camouflage netting that looked like filthy bandage dressings. It provided dappled zones of half-fierce shade. Paterson had stretched an old blanket on the bonnet of the car before he could lie on it for support. They used old blankets on the leather seats which became burn-hot. To both sides of them were tents and the camouflaged masses of guns, barrels protruding, light tanks and machine gun positions set up for defence. Perilously near stood the tented mass of the ammunition and fuel dumps. The lorries were parked in the open, some distance back, spaced out to present a difficult target. The men seemed to have disappeared in the heat. Melted, thought Robert.

From the white sky there was a roaring whine. Paterson rolled off the car and both men dived under it. Behind them, behind the lorries, perhaps half a mile away, a huge plume of sand erupted into the air. It still hung there when they heard the explosion and turned on their bellies to look. It collapsed like a slow, dull firework. The percussion had shaken the sand, even at this distance, giving a small jolt that set grains trickling into depressions. They stood up again.

'They can't see us either,' said Paterson. 'That's good! Krupp eighty-eights!'

'Just keeping us alert,' said Robert.

'When do we advance?' asked Paterson. He looked at his watch again. They were increasingly strung up and nervous. They had been waiting since dawn. To their far left their own guns replied to some command from headquarters, rocking and buffeting beneath their nets. Smoke rings shot out, expanded decoratively and rose into the blazing sky. Cartridge cases clattered. They heard orders. The guns fired again and again. Men appeared from their positions of shade, talking, swatting at flies and dusting at their weapons, some shading their eyes to try to see where the shells were falling. They all sensed the same tension.

'It's like being on the starter's block,' said Paterson. 'Exactly the same feeling. I did a lot of sprinting when I was a lad. I was quite good. Did you go in for any sports, sir?'

Paterson had gone to a public school.

'Not really. I wasn't very good at sport. I used to go swimming. With the school. Once a week.'

'Oh.'

Paterson's tone conveyed that this did not count at all.

A messenger on a sand-coloured motorbike appeared. He stopped to the right of them at the colonel's tent.

'That's it then,' said Paterson. 'Messenger from H.Q.'

'Get prepared then,' said Robert abruptly, getting his own back. 'Look to it.'

'Yes, sir.' Paterson looked momentarily annoyed.

Overhead somewhere in the sun aircraft were fighting, locked in their own private war dance. The rattle of their guns was clear.

In front of them the German machine gunners made a dancing wall of sand which leapt into the air to the height of a man's waist, daring them to cross it. Robert was scared. His heart was pounding. Lieutenant Paterson looked white but calm. Two brown-burned men with north-country accents flung themselves down nearby with a heavy machine gun and opened up. They grinned cheerfully at the two officers in the staff car, exchanged some banter, then lugged up the gun and belt between them and ran on, crouching. All around them a general advance had started. Grant tanks were roaring forwards, leaving a hot stink and clouds of sand. Men ran beside them and behind them, bayonets fixed, through and beyond the curtain of sand. The curtain faltered, changed position, stopped. Heavy guns exchanged rounds. Paterson engaged gear and they moved forward. Their objective was an insignificant outcrop of boulders on top of a sand slope that would afford cover for a further onslaught on the German positions. Robert's Company advanced at a fast trot. It was a pace that all the desert veterans had adopted. Their crouched stance was desert caution. They paused only to allow the men carrying machine guns to catch up. Explosions started to erupt around them. A man, then two men were blown into the air. A light tank was hit and burst into flame. The wounded began screaming. It was so sudden that Robert hardly had time to react. The car hit something, or dropped into a hole, lurching sideways. The two men scrambled out, lay flat.

'Get those guns up!' he shouted. 'Mortars. Between the boulders!'

He had seen movements, the characteristic drop and turn. Two of the Grant tanks had joined them now and were firing in support. The machine gunners lay flat on the sand, bracing their legs and fired short heavy bursts. A sergeant ran over, crouched but ignoring the risk.

'If we go round to the right sir, I reckon they have no line of fire.'

'How many mortars?'

'Four or five and two machine guns. They're isolated now, if we're quick.'

'Order Company to attack from the right flank. Paterson, our guns to lay down a frontal fire from here. Bring one heavy machine gun, two light with us. Where's the radio, Sergeant?'

'Just there.' The sergeant gestured to a trio of men in a huddle in a depression in the sand.

'We must keep those tanks. I'll get on to H.Q.'

He made himself get to his feet and walk, crouched but calmly, to the radio operator, giving his orders. He felt sick. Just beyond, in the sand, were bits of red meat, the body remains of his dead men. Medical orderlies stooped amongst the injured. He had been in action twice before. Each time he felt his stomach heaving, bile rising into his mouth. He swallowed, wishing he could spit into the sand. Not in front of the men. H.Q. confirmed the tanks would stay in support. They emphasised he must take the ridge. He gave the order to advance towards the right flank. Paterson was giving orders for the gunners. Paterson rejoined him. The men began the advance.

An aircraft fell out of the sky. For a suspended period of time that was like a dream within a dream they watched it. The Germans ceased firing too, and there was almost silence. They heard the engine stutter and stop and looked up to see a spiralling plume of black smoke. The engine sputtered again and the plane levelled out only to tip nose down again. Flames burst from the plume of smoke. It seemed to be dropping directly on top of them. No one jumped from it. They could hear the vicious hiss of air through its torn structure. They watched it plunge into the sand, watched the ball of flame that floated upwards like a fiery balloon. Firing re-started. The mortar shell that killed Paterson must have been fired at just that moment, the German gunner waiting with it in his hand releasing it at the moment of impact. Everything was suddenly still. Paterson was dripping on him. His hand hung down over Robert's forehead and blood ran down his middle two fingers. He was twitching, his fingers fluttering like the fins of a landed fish. Robert pulled himself free, finding he had only been knocked over and partially buried in sand. He was in the bottom of the crater left by the explosion, Paterson was on the lip, his body in the open, his head and arms hanging down. There was a hole in his back with white shattered bone exposed. He would have been screaming if his head wasn't half buried. Robert knew what he should do, but he could not move. Bullets spat overhead. He shivered violently and was sick, vomiting up quantities of burning yellowish liquid. He could not approach his lieutenant. Paterson managed the impossible and raised his head from the sand. He must have still been able to see because he formed the words, 'Help me,' and repeated them, his head nodding, but Robert could only watch. He could not explain it to himself, but all power of motion had left his limbs, all power of thought was suspended. He cowered and waited. Before long the head dropped and it was over. Flies crawled over him.

Medical orderlies found them both. They picked Robert up, examined him. They examined Paterson.

'Killed. Right away,' said Robert.

They looked curiously at him.

'Are you all right, sir?'

Perhaps they suspected concussion.

'I'm all right. He was killed right away.'

The orderlies exchanged a glance. There was a general advance and here was an officer in a shell hole. They put Paterson on a stretcher, watching Robert from the corner of their eyes. They saw he had been sick. He had failed to cover it with sand. He got up carefully and looked over the edge of the hole. The company was well ahead of him by now, at the base of the boulders. He must have been knocked out for some time. He advanced across won space, among the dead and injured. The mortars had stopped firing.

★

Robert turned the tractor again and pulled the self-lift cord. As soon as he resumed his return run he saw something was wrong. The last stretch of furrow was only half-turned, the stubble jutting untidily from the broken fold. He stopped immediately and jumped down from the tractor. He examined the plough. Lost in memories he had hit some stone and broken a share. Instead of an edge like a knife he had something the shape of a shattered tooth. He kicked at the metal in despair. The impatient gulls drew closer and scolded him for stopping, dipping and calling. He threw clods of clay at them in frustration and rage, but they bobbed effortlessly in the air. He would have to visit Taylor and Tester. So soon. He had no spares.

The men showed no surprise at his visit. He felt they might have been expecting him.

'Easy to break a share when you ain't accustomed to a plough,' said Taylor. Robert had found them behind an assortment of sheds behind their extraordinary house. It had once been a farm, but now every available part of the farm garden, stockyard and outbuildings was filled with old vehicles, drums, equipment, machinery, building materials and scrap. The predominant colour was the red-brown of rust. The ground on which they stood was uniformly stained with it and there were puddles the colour of strong tea, despite the heat. In this rusty earth were water-repellent islands of thick black oil. Both men wore their customary dungarees. Tester held a monkey wrench. They had been disembowelling an oilcake breaker and various cogs and spindles lay on the ground together with the big wheel.

'A welding job,' said Taylor, seeing Robert's eyes straying over their work. He wondered if they intended to put it together again. Other pieces of machinery had been similarly spread out and left to rust.

'Let's find you a share . . .'

Taylor led the way to a wooden-sided shed with an orange rust roof that was nevertheless watertight by the appearance of the interior. On oil-sodden shelves were rows of parts.

'It's a Ransome's plough,' said Taylor, 'Let's see . . .' Robert was clutching the broken section but Taylor clearly knew precisely what was needed. He knew what everyone owned. Tester watched without comment as his partner handed Robert a replacement spare.

'That's only a spot of rust on it. You look at the edge. It's had hardly any wear. Almost as good as new . . .'

'Have you a new one?'

Tester snorted. He smiled.

'You won't get a new share for love nor money, Mr Ellis,' said Taylor, explaining Tester's smile with a wave of one hand towards the man. 'You wait till this one polishes up in the ground. Like silver!' He handed it to Robert. 'How do you find the ploughing?'

'Fine.'

'Have you ploughed before?'

Taylor's pale-faced curiosity annoyed him, but he determined not to show it. After all, Ingleton had asked the same thing.

'No, I haven't.'

'Well, don't set her too deep, not in this soil . . .'

'I know.'

Taylor nodded his head up and down. It expressed disbelief that Robert knew anything. He felt compelled to justify himself. Tester watched silently, arms on chest, cradling the wrench like a babe.

'Driving a tractor is just the same as driving any other vehicle,' Robert said. 'I don't know what all the mystery is about. And, as for ploughing, you have to start somewhere to learn. I've read everything there is on the subject. I should think.'

'Books don't tell you everything,' volunteered Tester. 'Farming's a funny old business.'

'Well, I daresay Mr Ellis has read all the right things,' said Taylor. Robert suspected he was being mocked but there was no evidence to prove it in their faces or their manner.

'Let me pay you for this share,' he said.

'No, no!' Taylor was emphatic. 'You can't pay for that. Not when you've just arrived. Have it from us. A neighbourly gift, shall we say. We wouldn't hear of you paying!'

'I'd prefer to pay.'

'We wouldn't hear of it. I'd rather you didn't have it than pay for it!'

Robert had no choice. He thanked them and started to leave.

They watched him without saying a further word. Robert remembered the stack that needed threshing.

'Do I see you about a traction engine, and a threshing machine?'

'You do indeed,' said Taylor. 'What had you in mind?' That old stack?'

Robert was furious that the man knew so much about his business. He determined to defeat them by responding with absolute calm.

'Yes. It must be time to get it done now. Before it gets any later in the year.'

'Before the rats and mice have everything.'

'Yes.'

'We could do that?'

'Will you?'

'Just you say when. We have to order up the steam-coal, you know. We have to wait for that. You can't get it on demand. Not now.'

'Could you order it then, and tell me as soon as you can give me a date?'

'Delighted, Mr Ellis. That old thing will be a heavy job. You'll need men.'

'I shall have some prisoners,' said Robert. 'Three men at least.' He felt pleased.

'That should do,' said Taylor. 'Long as you get good workers. You won't be able to sell that corn. It'll be a mess. It ain't fit for humans, you know.'

'I know that. I want it for feed.'

'I see.'

Robert left triumphantly, knowing their curiosity was now thoroughly aroused. When he had driven off, Taylor turned to Tester.

'What do you reckon? Ploughing from books!'

Tester shrugged.

'We'll see. Better order the steam-coal.'

The boys worked their way back like Indian scouts. They had seen the abandoned tractor and plough in the field and knew they were in trouble. The house afforded more safety than anywhere else.

126

'We'll say we came back to help but he was gone,' said John hopefully.

They were pressed to the scorching wooden wall of the barn. It smelled still of tar. Their objective was the back door by way of the stockyard.

'Don't tell him where we were or what we saw!' said John.

'I won't,' said William. He was behind John. They ran across the dusty space.

The cockerel had been drowsing quietly in the sun. The intrusion was too much for him and he flew at them, wings outstretched, head stuck forward like a gargoyle, screeching. He pecked their pale legs and their knobbly knees, and they flailed at him ineffectually, yelling. The cockerel knew they were afraid and kept up the pursuit to the very door. William was sobbing, the pecks leaving pink marks. John was white. He had run faster, been pecked less. The noise brought Robert, scowling.

'I've been waiting for you two,' he said. 'Come here!'

He reached out and grabbed John and smacked him hard on his behind, holding him as he struggled. William watched and waited his turn. He hated this man, but wanted his father. He saw his mother appear for a moment in the doorway beyond, white, unsmiling and sad. She glanced and moved away. No hope.

'I did my pumping this morning!' he shouted, but Robert caught hold of him just the same.

CHAPTER SIX

The whistle sounded piercingly. Kunkel had stopped at the foot of Heinz's bunk. Heinz sat up. Kunkel avoided his look but, with eyes glazed and distant, blew another blast, before marching down the central aisle. Heinz listened to his boots. Clump clump clump. Click. Whistle. Clump clump clump.

'Go to hell, Kunkel!'

'Stick the pea up your arse, Kunkel!'

No answer.

The same each morning.

The same abuse, the same meaningless insults repeated so often they were as formal as a greeting.

Seven o'clock.

Heinz quickly swung his legs to the ground. He felt immediately that it was warm again. Ehrich was already on his feet beside the bunk, towel round his neck.

'It's sunny,' he said. 'Too good to be locked up in here. The birds are singing if that silly bastard would shut up. Let's hurry, if there's any chance of outside work I'm going to take it.'

'Well, there's no more at Bargets. There must be another farm with turnips!'

'It's getting late in the year.'

'What do we do for the winter?'

Kunkel clumped out, pausing at the door for a final shrill.

'What do farmers do in the winter? Feed stock, clear ditches. Plough. There's the whole season of ploughing and sowing.'

'Will they let us out? After that film . . .?'

Heinz shrugged. They had been protected in the turnip field with the Walnuts. Whatever they had heard or seen, they said little. Heinz doubted if they could read in any case. A new farm meant new contacts. They might get work near a village, amongst English people.

'If we don't get a job,' he said, making light of it, 'I can get back to the chessmen. I could do with the time to finish a set or two. I could do with the money.'

'But I want work outside,' said Ehrich. 'So let's move.'

At roll-call the men lined up in their customary rows, five deep. Another day in the blessed sun. Another day when Schneider was joined by Middleton. There was a buzz of curiosity amongst the men. It meant an announcement and any announcement might affect their freedom or their chances of repatriation. The guard sergeants checked them off and there was an expectant silence. Since the showing of the film there had been a series of rumours which had produced apprehension even if everyone stoutly believed they were rubbish. It was said that German prisoners were to be sent to Africa as labour, or to Australia to work mines. The Nazis in the camp were most vigorous in promoting these tales. Notices appeared on walls, were defaced, torn down. Some men had renounced Germany publicly, perhaps from shame, perhaps to unburden themselves.

Beside Middleton was his usual interpreter, the English officer with the impeccable accent. They had a microphone on the dais today, linked in to the camp tannoy.

'Good morning!'

Middleton was always polite. The officer did not translate, but waited.

'I have two items of news for you,' he said, as Middleton began. 'I hope they will both be well received. The first is that you are now to be able to receive broadcasts through the camp loudspeakers. The broadcasts will be news and current affairs, and they will undoubtedly help your grasp of English as well as keeping you all up to date with what is going on in the world.

'Secondly, in an attempt to initiate better communications between you all and your families, there will be an issue of special postcards, one to every man. Efforts will be made to ensure that these are delivered by both the civil and military authorities in Germany. These cards are for the moment in a standard form for ease, and I do urge you to use them. This is a first step, please take it.'

Middleton stopped, the translator stopped. There was a buzz of excitement. Schneider shouted at them for silence. He seemed annoyed at the announcement. Heinz thought that Middleton looked embarrassed too, but could not understand why. It was good news all round, he thought. Wolfgang caught his eye and winked. Men were smiling. Post again! Post at last! News! The Nazis did not smile. Muller looked grim. He saw Heinz observing him and scowled. Heinz looked away. There was no need to promote danger.

They filed past a table where a sergeant and a soldier handed out the precious postcards. Heinz took his eagerly and advanced, reading it. He was concerned by the printed boxes on one side, for the address and for the forwarding address in case the addressee could not be found. The forwarding address had already been filled in with a rubber stamp. He was annoyed to see the heading on the other side.

Ein Mitglied der Geschlagenen Wehrmacht sucht seinen nächsten Angehörigen.

The man in front of him was muttering. He turned to Heinz. 'This is no good. Why did they put that on it?'

A member of the defeated German army seeks his nearest relative.

'I suppose they are trying to make a point.'

'Move along,' said a young guard. Men were stopping everywhere to examine the buff cards. 'Look at them in your hut.'

'There's nowhere to write anything!' protested the man in front of Heinz.

'Saves trying to think of something to say!' said the young guard. He grinned. He did not mean to offend, Heinz saw, it was simply the insensitivity of youth.

Back in the hut they sat down and examined the cards in detail. There were two lines in which they were to delete alternatives. They were allowed to say they were in British/American/Russian hands, and that they were healthy/in hospital. Please send a card back at once.

'I see why the Commandant was embarrassed,' said Heinz. 'A postcard contrived by the military mind! Write here, delete there.'

'It's propaganda,' said Ehrich, but without anger, resigned that there would be a price to pay.

'I don't mind,' said Peter cheerfully. 'It's a start, isn't it? We may get real post. We will be able to send things and get things . . .'

'What things do you think we can get out of Germany now?'

The speaker, Walther, was in the bunk to their right. He was an older man who looked as though he should never have been sent further than the corner shop, yet had been on the Eastern front.

'We're the lucky ones here. We complain, but we're looked after, we eat, we have clothes. Back home they're starving.'

'No one must send these cards.'

Predictably it was Muller. He held his out at arm's length and carefully tore it into four pieces, dropping them on the floor.

'You are to do that with them. They are trying to humiliate us. No German can send a card with that written on it.'

No one made a move to follow Muller. The matter was too serious for precipitate gestures. Heinz put his card away thoughtfully in his breast pocket.

'I shall send mine,' said Walther. 'We are defeated. It's a matter of fact.' Many men agreed. Muller had no support.

'I shall send mine because I want to write to my mother and my girl friend and I don't care!' said Peter. 'I haven't heard anything for two years, and this is good!'

Peter got a laugh and a cheer. He flushed and looked embarrassed.

'Those of you who ignore the instructions of the Party are noted and well known to us,' said Muller. '*Heil Hitler!*'

'Don't threaten me, Muller!' said Peter.

'Don't challenge my authority, Stuck,' said Muller. 'I'll report you to Schneider!'

'Oh! Oh no!' the men groaned in mock horror. Muller turned on his heel and walked to his corner of the hut.

'He'll run off to Mohnke first, you wait and see,' said Ehrich. 'Take it easy with him, Peter. He's a dangerous shit. We'll get attacked again.'

'They don't frighten me. Who can lend me a pen for this postcard?'

*

They had got the farm work they wanted. It was much quicker than they expected. The Commandant explained briefly that he had had a visit from a farmer that morning who had agreed to take them. There was a small group of men listening. Those who had not got work elsewhere, or who were tired of hobbies and lectures. Peter, Wolfgang, Heinz and Ehrich managed for the first time to get in the same work party. There were only two others with them, a young lad of nineteen called Wilhelm and a man called Paul. The truck picked them up almost immediately. The canvas had been dropped and they enjoyed the drive. The season was on the turn. Heinz noted the colour in the beeches, a slight yellow here, a light tan there. The hedgerows were thick with old-man's-beard. Honeysuckle was still in heavy flower. Peter pointed out the apple trees. The cooking apples in back gardens were beginning to fall. He had plans.

'We're going down the same road that took us to Bargets,' said Heinz.

'How can you tell?' asked Wolfgang.

'He knows the tree that hit him!' teased Peter. The two men stared uncomprehendingly. Ehrich knew the story. They did not explain.

'If you were not so dense and unobservant,' said Heinz, 'it would be obvious. Same fields, same houses.' They were approaching a fork in the narrow leafy lane. The truck turned to the right. 'We've turned off now. If we'd gone left we'd have been back there.'

'I hope they've *got* apples,' said Peter. 'Every farm must have some apples.'

'You be careful,' said Wolfgang. 'That would be theft.'

'I wonder what we'll get?' asked Ehrich. 'I hope it's not turnips. All I seem to have got is damned turnips!'

It was mangolds. The truck stopped briefly at the farmhouse while the driver went to the door. A man who appeared to be the farmer came out and he and the driver spoke briefly. The farmer waved his arm, pointed, gave directions. The driver returned to the truck.

'He's coming with us, lads, to show you what to do.'

He waited. After a minute a tractor appeared round the farm building. It eased past the lorry on the grass verge and drove ahead. After a short drive the lorry stopped and the tractor turned left into a field.

'Down!' called the driver. The men groaned. The driver grinned. 'It's only a small field. In fact it's only half a field, you lot should knock it off in no time. See you tonight!'

'What did he say?' asked Peter.

'He's having fun,' said Wolfgang. 'He knows we love turnips.'

'My name is Robert Ellis,' said the farmer. He was standing beside his tractor, one foot on the crank case, upright. Heinz noted the remains of tan on his skin. An ex-soldier, probably from service in Africa. Was this going to be a good thing or not?

'I understand that you all know how to lift mangolds, or at least turnips. It's the same job. You pull them and top them but, whatever you do, do not touch the root. Do you understand? Each man is to take two drills apiece and lay the mangolds in the drill between so that a cart can go through. Then they will be taken to a clamp and covered. Understood?'

'Yes, sir,' said Wolfgang. 'But I will have to translate. Not all of us understand English perfectly.'

Ellis nodded. Wolfgang translated, turning to the others and winking at Heinz, Ehrich and Peter as he did so. He had no idea if Wilhelm and Paul understood English. He turned back to Ellis.

'What is your name?' asked Ellis.

'My name is Wolfgang, sir.'

'Then I will give you all the instructions.'

He had left them to it and they were working down the field in a ragged line. The ground was reasonably moist but the clay stuck. It was a temptation to hack at the earth-ball that clung to the root, but they resisted. It was clear that Wilhelm and Paul had not lied and were accustomed to this kind of work. The half field would soon be lifted.

'What do you think of him?' Peter asked Heinz.

'An officer of some sort, I should think. He's seen service in Africa. He still has a tan.'

'I noticed that. I didn't like him much. He'll keep an eye on us. I should think he'll report us if we're not careful. It won't be like working for the Walnuts.'

'I liked the Walnuts,' said Wolfgang. 'I hope we see them again.'

Heinz explained to Wilhelm and Paul about the Walnuts. Wilhelm listened and smiled. Paul listened and scowled. Paul was going to be a difficult companion. They could hear a tractor running up and down.

'That's him,' said Wolfgang. 'We shall be able to hear when he stops or when he heads this way. That's all right. It gives us warning.'

'How do we know he hasn't got a foreman?' said Peter. 'And there's chestnut woods over there.'

They looked.

'Edible chestnuts,' said Peter. 'The trees aren't big, but they're still big enough to carry nuts.'

'Coppice wood,' said Heinz the carpenter, 'for fences and posts and handles. 'I'd like some of the wood.'

'How do we know he hasn't got a foreman?' repeated Peter.

'We don't,' said Heinz, 'so be patient and don't do anything today!'

'The man is an arrogant Englishman,' said Paul, who had apparently been giving the matter some thought since Peter had addressed Heinz. 'I hope he gives us good food.'

Heinz made a face at Wolfgang. They worked on in silence for some time. The day had the particular limpid clarity of a warm October when overnight dew has lifted. Puffy white cloud moved lazily overhead, casting occasional shadows. Twice rabbits broke from cover in front of them and ran for the hedge. Peter pursued each one with loud yells, crashing through the leafy tops for a few yards before stopping, panting and returning to his work with a grin. They quickly reached the end of the field and turned to take the next rows. With six of them it would be done that day. At the head of the field they glanced over the hedge, trying to get their bearings.

'I know where we are,' said Heinz. 'There's Bargets over there. Look.' He pointed to a pink-washed farm in the distance. 'We're on the farm that had the sale. The one with the meadow.'

'The one with the watercress,' said Peter.

The one with the woman, thought Heinz.

'This farmer must be the new owner,' he said. 'That's why

there's still half a field. He's just bought the place. Out of the army and onto the land.'

He wondered who she was. He hoped this farmer wasn't married.

'These mangolds are well chewed,' said Wolfgang. 'Someone should shoot the rabbits.'

The field next to them was in grass. Six heifers stared at them, wild-eyed and glossy. They had the bold black and white of Friesians, each with a white face flash. They snorted. Remote from them, a Jersey cow lay chewing.

'Nice cows,' said Heinz. They looked as new and bright and shiny as scrubbed schoolgirls. With common accord they kicked up their heels and galloped away, leaving the strong sweet smell of their breath. They all laughed, except Paul, and returned to their work.

William sat at his desk smothering his misery. He was accustomed already to the anxieties and loneliness of new schools and had known what to expect, but it didn't make it any easier. This was his second day. His first had passed as slowly as a confused year.

The school had wooden board floors with the knots and grain raised from wear. It smelled of chalk dust. The inside of his desk smelled of ink and old varnish, a dark acrid smell that was familiar and reassuring. There were initials all over the top, with dates going back to 1928. Someone had filled in much of the carving with a pencil. It was the worst desk, for the newest boy. On the first day no one had told him where the boy's lavatory was and he had been too shy to ask until forced to by painful necessity. Then he had waited until he had seen a male teacher, rather than ask Miss Pearce, their class teacher. He was nearly fainting.

At playtime he had been approached by a few of them. Where was he from? Why did he speak with a funny voice? They were neither friendly nor unfriendly. When he told them he came from Pyes Farm they looked at him uncomprehendingly. He could not tell them where it was, because he had no idea of his own location. It was his first encounter with the strange fact that although these were country children they belonged to this large village, almost a town, that had shops, banks, a railway line, and that they regarded farm children as strange savages, as figures of fun.

They were better dressed than he was. None of them was smart, but their clothes were not so worn.

They ran out at half-past three and disappeared down familiar ways in groups. He had waited for his father to appear in their ancient car, sitting on the low wall that surrounded the playground, and standing each time a teacher passed in case it was forbidden.

Miss Pearce was kind to him, but in her efforts to introduce him to his fellows embarrassed him painfully by telling them all about him from the little she knew. The girls stared at him and smiled. Novelty provoked curiosity. The boys stared at their desks, or knocked things on the floor and giggled. They shared smirks and did not catch his eye.

John was faring slightly better. He was in the top year and they were more serious. He was also bigger than most of them, and that immediately gained him respect. He was less anxious than William and more confident. By playtime on the second day he already felt secure enough to wave to William without joining him, surrounded by his own class. William, who was alone, felt stabbed. The boys of his class were kicking a football. They had not asked him to join them and he watched hopefully, waiting to be invited. They let him wait. He knew he had to be patient.

'You talk funny,' said a girl called Sally, in broadest Suffolk. He turned to look at her. She was almost blonde, like wheat straw with very blue eyes. Her hair was in two pigtails, each with a red and black ribbon. Her face was round and inquisitive with a small mouth. She giggled. Her friend stood beside her, a dark girl, the listener. She smiled, not unkindly.

'I can't help that,' said William.

'I didn't say you could,' said Sally. 'But you do. You don't talk like a farm boy! Jimmy Bradley, he's a farm boy, and he doesn't speak like you. And you aren't big, like Jimmy Bradley, and you're all white.'

'We haven't been there long. We've come from Kent.'

'Where's that?'

'I don't know. A long way away. My mother says it's south of here. It's south of London even.'

Sally's eyes were round and knowing.

'I've heard of London. Have you a wireless?'

'No.'

'We've got a wireless. My dad bought it. We listen to it every afternoon when we get home. We listen to Dick Barton and Children's Hour.'

'I expect we shall get a wireless.'

Sally looked doubtful.

'I don't think you'll be able to get it out on a farm.'

'Of course you can!'

'How do you know! You don't know everything!'

'Nor do you!'

The dark girl giggled at this. Sally scowled at her.

'Shut up, Mary!'

The dark girl was spurred to speech.

'Have you got a football?'

'No.'

'My brother's got a football. A real leather one. You should see it.'

'I've got a bike,' said Sally. 'I can cycle it. Can you cycle a bike?'

'I'm learning,' lied William. Sally was impressed.

'You've got a bike?'

'Yes,' he lied.

'We're going down to the sweet shop after school,' said Sally.

'They've got liquorice sticks and locust beans and you don't need coupons for them. You going to come?'

'I have to wait for my Pa. He's coming to pick me up. In the car.'

'He takes you home?'

'Yes.'

The girls looked at each other, burst into giggles again and ran off. Mary looked back at him curiously. William had no money for liquorice sticks or locust beans anyway. He returned to watching the boys.

'You can put your jacket down for a post,' shouted one of them. It was the invitation he wanted. He was out of it in a flash and folded it into a heap. They passed the ball to him and he kicked it to and fro, uncertain what he was supposed to be doing or whose side if any he was on. It didn't seem to matter. Once he was knocked flying. He was sure it was deliberate and he cracked his head painfully on the tarmac. He got up saying nothing and continued with the game. He knew the rules, he knew the tests, he had done it all before, and before.

Wolfgang noticed the lorry first. It drove past the gate at the end of their field, first in one direction, then returned. The driver was clearly looking for something. They paused to watch him. The lorry stopped some distance further on, then they heard it growling and roaring as it entered the field beyond the cows. This was clearly an event of some sort and merited attention.

'What's it doing in the field?' asked Peter.

'Delivering something!' said Wolfgang. Peter threw a handful of mangold leaves at him which bounced harmlessly off his shirt. The lorry approached a long thatched stack that lay in the field. The lorry stopped, then the engine stopped. In the silence the men heard a church bell far away strike three. It was distant and sweet and painfully reminiscent to Heinz. He had vivid images of Inga and himself in a scented, sandy pine forest outside Magdeburg. They had been lying naked in a secret spot after making love. It was before the war and they had listened to the drowsy tolling hours thoughout the afternoon. He remembered that at the sound of four he had turned to her.

'If it's four o'clock, it must be time to start again. . . .' And he had kissed her, first on the mouth then all of her, as she smiled. The other men were listening too. He did not know what sights they saw, but their faces were raised, their senses alert.

The lorry restarted. There was a clang and a rattle, followed by a heavy rushing.

'It's tipping something,' said Heinz, dispelling images. He remembered the bottle of wine they had shared, passing it from mouth to mouth because he had forgotten the glasses, forgotten everything except that he wanted her body.

'It sounds like stone,' said Wilhelm.

'Or coal,' said Wolfgang.

'Let's get on,' said Heinz. 'We want to finish these things.'

It was mid-afternoon. Clumps of washed red poppies grew amongst the beet and yellow-eyed feverfew clung to the furrows between the leaves of camomile, scenting the air. Their work was quiet. A pheasant, alarmed by their presence, belled and rang somewhere in the adjoining field. Occasionally they heard the sound of men's voices on the still air, the clank of machines, the throb of a tractor. A pair of carthorses clopped past the field on the road, unhitched. They paused to watch the huge animals in full ploughing harness, necks comfortable in their collars, eyes invisible behind blinkers. They blocked the narrow road completely with their shoulders and rumps. A man sat on the right-hand horse of the pair, controlling them both with a word, murmuring to them as though to babes. The hitches dangled from the animals and swung in the sun by their sides. Buckles flashed. The man saw them, took them in carefully as he passed, and eventually nodded, before his back was turned.

'Good 'arternoon,' he said, acknowledging fellow labourers in the field, raising a hand. They answered, a ragged salvo of noise, pleased at the greeting. Peter was smiling foolishly and Heinz realised that he too had broken into a grin. It was their first casual contact with civilians. The Walnuts had been told to look after them. This passing man had judged them on their merits.

The sound of the tractor stopped in the field beyond. With accord they bent to their work, anxious to please. After a pause, while they lost the sound of it in the defile of the lane, they heard it approach along the road. It swung into the field and stopped just inside the gate. Robert Ellis climbed down and walked to them. He looked ostentatiously at the amount they had done. The men stood there, knives dangling, regarding the massacre they had achieved. Robert Ellis walked from row to row, nodding. The mangolds lay like severed heads.

'Well done,' he said. 'My wife is bringing some tea from the farm. She'll be here any moment. I see you have almost finished lifting them. The next thing is to put them into clamps and cover them with straw. They have to be earthed over.'

Robert knew all this because he had read about it. He was nervous of clamping but dare not show it. He waited until Wolfgang had rendered a translation. 'After that you are going to help to thresh the big stack over there.'

He pointed.

'The coal arrived this afternoon, and the traction engine will arrive early tomorrow. I would like all of you to come early tomorrow, and the next day. Tomorrow you can start building the clamp while the traction engine arrives and sets up, then we will thresh all day. The next day we will start early. The machine is on hire so I want to get the work done as quickly as possible.'

Wolfgang explained. He had not understood all the words himself, but the meaning was clear. He did not know what a clamp was, so missed that out.

'Here comes your tea.'

Robert pointed, Margaret walked through the gate, lopsided, carrying a large withy basket with a lid. Heinz instinctively started towards her, but a glance from Robert stopped him. Heinz recognised her.

Margaret was preoccupied with her task and was both angry and embarrassed. Robert had said that there was no way of carrying the tea to the fields on the tractor. It would certainly spill all over the place. She had intended to ride with him on the tractor, clutching it. She saw the sense in what he was saying but doubted his reason. She imagined he did not want his image tarnished by being seen as a means of transport in front of the men. Maybe he was right. She could see that his authority had to be established and maintained in front of the prisoners, but wondered why he could not say so. That would have taken her into his confidence. Instead she felt she was being treated again as though she could not comprehend, was useless, as with the cows. She was hot and the basket with its giant brown enamel teapot was heavy. She had three white clayware mugs and three tea cups and a small can of milk. Uncertain what to give them to eat and having little choice she had cut slices of her own brown bread, thinly spread with butter. She had no butter-making equipment and it was from their own meagre ration. The bread was dense and unleavened. The children complained about it, but again she had no yeast. She had bought the brown enamel teapot and the mugs at the farm sale, aware that the size of them was an advantage. Her utility dress stuck to her uncomfortably under the armpits. She was wet with sweat and uncomfortable. It was not the way she would have liked to appear in a field full of men.

She recognised Heinz immediately when she put down the basket. His eyes met hers, flicked away, immediately returned. He smiled very slightly. He looked wary. Margaret set the basket down on the body of the tractor. She was not sure what to do next. Should she serve them or was that not proper? Were they supposed to look after themselves? She opted for the latter, picked up the basket again and held it out to Peter, who happened to be nearest.

'Here you are.'

Peter smiled at her unashamedly. Heinz stepped forward and took the basket from him. Peter was playing stupid.

'Thank you very much,' he said, his eyes meeting hers for a moment before he turned away. 'May we stop now?' he asked Robert.

'Yes, you may.'

'Thank you.' He stood awkwardly, holding the basket, not knowing where to go. The mangold field offered few obvious places and he did not like to put the basket down and investigate whatever it contained in front of the man and the woman.

'Come on, we'll take it to the hedge,' he said in German. The other men were also staring at Margaret. He resented it. 'Come on!' he urged. 'Don't stare!' He had no idea if the farmer understood or not. It was more important that he usher them away. They followed him to a place where they could sit on a bank in the hedge between the dog-roses and a hawthorn. Wolfgang and Wilhelm remained standing, the others flopped down. Heinz lifted the wicker top of the basket, lifted out the teapot and canister of milk. There were six slices of bread, cut thick.

'Any sugar?' asked Peter, anxiously. Ehrich had lifted the lid of the tea pot and was sniffing.

'No sugar,' said Heinz. 'They don't have sugar any more than we have, I suppose.'

'Tea,' said Ehrich. 'It smells strong enough. Why don't they have sugar?'

'Because it comes by ship and is rationed,' said Heinz. He read the papers that were supplied to the camp.

'No jam!' said Peter.

'I can't eat bread without jam!' said Paul, but he took a piece of bread and bit into it anyway. He made a face.

'You're being watched,' warned Wolfgang. 'You had better like it or we won't get it again.'

141

'It's delicious, it's delicious!' said Peter. He smiled and pushed bread into his mouth, chewing extravagantly. Heinz poured tea into the mugs and cups. Wolfgang added milk.

'She's very pretty looking,' said Peter. 'Get an eyeful of that! Look at her tits, look at that tight dress!'

'Shut up!' Heinz was furious, trying not to show just how angry he was. 'If they hear you, we'll be in real trouble. How do you know they don't understand us?'

He was disturbed by the rage of his own feelings.

'She's all right,' said Wolfgang. 'This farm could be all right. I'd sooner have her than the Walnuts, I can tell you!'

Peter chuckled. Heinz scowled and tried to eat the dense bread. It was too fresh and would be indigestible. Wilhelm was saying the same thing, but rudely.

'What do I do with it?' he asked in a whisper. 'Can I chuck it in the hedge?'

'You do that and we'll never get any more!' muttered Heinz. 'You eat that bread or, if you can't, pretend to and take it away in your pocket! Are you some sort of fool?'

'English bread is rubbish,' said Paul.

'Ask me,' said Peter. 'I'm the baker. Ask me what I think of this bread!'

'What do you think of this bread, Peter?' It was Wilhelm again.

'I think I'm glad we never invaded England!' Paul laughed, Wilhelm joined in. Even Ehrich and Wolfgang smiled.

'What's the matter with you, Heinz?' demanded Peter. 'She's got you smitten, hasn't she! Heinz is in love with the farmer's wife, just like that!' He flicked his fingers. 'Just like that! Eat your bread and butter, lads!'

Heinz tipped some of his tea on Peter's leg. Peter leapt to his feet with a shout.

'Yell quietly!' said Heinz. 'Go on. Mustn't make a fuss!'

Peter laughed.

'They're a good-humoured lot,' said Robert.

Margaret nodded. She was examining her feelings, her reactions to the fact they were Germans. The shy man had only glanced at her, but in a serious way that haunted her. She recalled the lifted cap from the fleeting encounter in the meadow. His face worn the same grave expression. Today he was wearing grey trousers, a cap and singlet, and she could see and admire his muscular body. His arms and shoulders were strong and captivity had made him spare. She was ashamed for herself, but looked, trying to appear casual, uninterested. She became conscious of her own body, of her thin dress, of her soaked armpits and the smell of her own sweat. She felt bare and unattractive. Instinctively she tucked her hair back from her forehead, then realised the men were watching her covertly, as she watched them. She felt a sudden level of hate, not directed at the big man, but at them all, at their race.

'They work well too,' said Robert, apparently unaware. He was leaning against the large rear wheel of the tractor. It was warm from the sun and from use. He was wearing corduroy trousers today, with one of his khaki shirts and the army braces. His hands were thrust deep in his pockets. He produced his pipe and stuck it in his mouth. He sucked at it. He seldom smoked except in the evening. The gesture was one of utmost contentment with his lot in life. Margaret felt a traitor.

'Do you think the tea is all right?' she asked, to break the contented silence as much as anything. Robert made an annoyed noise, dismissive of this interruption.

'Of course it is. They'll be pleased.'

'They must get very hot. I wonder if they get fed well enough? I wish I had something more to give them . . . I should have given them jam on the bread . . .'

'For God's sake, Margaret, why?'

Robert was exasperated. He drew the pipe from his mouth to make the point, folded his arms on his chest.

'We don't have jam for ourselves, but you want to give it to them!'

Margaret shrugged. 'I feel sorry for them in a way. I can't help it. I dislike them at the same time. They don't have their homes or families. I have all sorts of feelings.'

'They're prisoners of war! They aren't here on holiday!'

He stood upright, tucked the pipe back in his pocket, his face angry. Margaret read in it petulance. Robert swung himself back onto the tractor. He looked down on her from the seat.

'You go back to the house. I'll make sure they put the things in the basket when they've finished. They've had nearly ten minutes already. I don't want them to think this is a charity!'

'Can't I collect the things . . . you'll forget them.'

'I won't.'

Margaret turned and left. She felt the eyes of the men boring into her back, almost felt their hands upon her. She hurried, stumbling over picked beet, and nearly fell. She refused to look back. In the lane she paused out of sight of Robert and the men to take stock of herself. It was cool in the shadow of the high hedges and heavy with the smells of cow parsley and moss. Convolvulus formed high banks of white trumpet flowers. She saw the quick motion of something rust-brown among the ground ivy and remained completely still, following the minute tremors that moved here and there until she saw the hunting wren. It in turn saw her and flicked away. There was peace and beauty in nature, even in the deadly nightshade that left its glossy black berries temptingly within reach. She smoothed down her dress and pulled at the front of it so that it fell more loosely and hung away from her armpits. She was cooler, able to think.

The reappearance of the man from the meadow had produced something like panic, but pleasant. Robert had been insensitive, perhaps resentful. He must have noticed how they looked at her. Even he.

She walked down the lane until she came to the five-bar gate that closed off the entrance to the grass field occupied by the new cows. They stood near the gate watching her. Looking beyond them she could just make out the movement of the prisoners through the thick far hedge, could just discern the sound of their voices. They laughed from time to time. She had never heard Robert laugh since his return.

The cows had been a complete surprise to her. Robert had told her nothing about them. Last week, early, a cattle float had turned up while they were eating breakfast. She had said nothing then, but remained at the table as Robert and the children ran out to see the new acquisitions. John and William had been arguing about the number of pump strokes each had done. It had been acrimonious and they were going to be late for school because Robert was angry with them and being slow and difficult. The arrival of the cattle would guarantee their lateness. She had automatically put the kettle on the range to make tea for the driver. She did not even bother to look from the window as she heard the tailboard drop, then heard the sound of hooves on wood and the lowing. She was wondering how they had managed to pay for them. Robert had gone with them right away to the field. The children were excited. She could hear their shouts.

Robert had come back late to the house, pleased with himself, with a smile for the driver. The children looked hot and untidy. William had torn another hole in his trousers.

'They're fine animals!' he said to the driver.

'Aye, so they are, Mr Ellis,' said the driver, who only drove animals and knew little about them, but could see and smell the possibility of a breakfast when it presented itself. 'Good morning, ma'am. They look happy in that old field, they certainly do.'

'What about taking the children to school?' she asked Robert. 'They're very late.'

'It doesn't matter!' Robert was careless. 'We don't get cows delivered every day. They can go in later.'

'Won't do them no harm,' said the driver. 'I was always happy not to go, I can tell you. They never learned me nothing anyway. Still, they say learning is more important these days. I don't know though, I ain't so sure.'

'Would you like a cup of tea?' she asked to suppress her annoyance. 'Have you had breakfast?'

'That's very civil of you, ma'am,' said the driver, reckoning that that was the best answer, to leave all his options open for whatever came. Robert had taken them to school in bad humour.

The cows were young and beautiful. They moved casually towards her, eyes wild and muzzles dripping with excitement. She could see droplets on every bristle. Their tongues flicked this way and that and their tails were half raised. They drew up in line ahead, facing her. They snorted and bobbed their heads. Margaret held out her hand. The boldest sidled closer, eyes turned back like an ogre's, and licked her hand, enveloping it in a firm grip that was wet yet fiercely abrasive. She had no idea that a tongue could be so rough and snatched her hand away with an exclamation. The heifers scattered, tails high, dropping wet dung. It was so derisive and mutinous that she was compelled to smile.

She walked back towards the farmhouse considering recent events. Her sole experience with a man since marriage had been when the butcher held her hand too long when giving her her change. The butcher knew Robert was away to the war. He asked if there was anything else she needed.

She was fascinated by Baxter's boldness and supposed she found it flattering, although she was not sure if she liked the man. There was a hint of danger about him that was exciting.

She was dismayed by the prisoner. She would have to find out his name. He looked through her gently and his eyes were like javelins. He didn't strut or hold himself to attention or pose, but stood squarely without grace or self-consciousness. He commanded respect without a word. Some men have an eloquent presence and some do not, she thought. She wanted to know more, and he had made himself plain, without words. How could she feel like this when he was German?

She had slept separately from Robert the night after he beat the boys, not daring to visit them either as she knew that would have been the ultimate disloyalty as far as Robert was concerned. She had felt a coward, but was not ready for that yet, perhaps not ever.

Two peacock butterflies supped side by side on the ripe, fermenting fruit of brambles. Their wings jerked open spasmodically, revealing jewels. Margaret brushed her hand lightly over the dry rustle of their wings but confused and drunk, they refused to move. She thought briefly of her three sisters, all married, all dispersed, two in England, one in Canada. Dispersed mentally rather than physically. They had been relegated in her life with Robert. Her brother John was still close and she longed to see him. She decided she must write and invite him to the farm, telling Robert afterwards. He was the older, wiser brother. After Father there had always been brother John. He might be able to mend things, or at least offer advice.

The butterflies took to the air chasing each other in spirals, then dipping and dropping to alight as though suddenly tired. There was a touch of mortality in their behaviour. The year would be ending before long and they would drink and play it out.

She hurried back to the house, feeling the chill of the shade.

In the field Robert let the tractor into gear so that it jerked forwards for a few yards. It was his too-obvious way of telling the men they should return to work. Heinz approached the tractor. He was carrying the basket in which he had put the teapot and the mugs. The bread had been disposed of, some of it into the hedge. He wanted a closer look at this man who must be married to the beautiful woman in the dress.

'Here is the basket,' he said awkwardly, holding it up to where Robert sat on the tractor. Robert took in the tall muscular man who stood like a horse, without affectation or apology. He had no intention of taking back the basket.

'Put it down under the hedge please. My wife will collect it later.'

Their eyes met. Heinz looked at him calmly.

'Yes,' said Heinz. He returned to the hedge and put it down carefully. The other men waited, ready to resume.

'I will return here with a cart,' Robert said, addressing them carefully. 'Do you understand?' Wolfgang nodded on behalf of them all. 'We will lift the mangolds now and start to build a clamp. Do you understand a clamp?'

'No,' said Wolfgang simply.

'It is like a haystack but we make it by piling up the mangolds and covering them to preserve them. We will make it near the gate so it is easy to get them in the winter to feed the cattle.'

Wolfgang translated. The men nodded and said they understood. Robert swung the tractor in an arc and left the field, crushing some beet. They spurted and burst.

'Fool,' said Paul when he was out of hearing. 'If he had put it in reverse he would not have done that!'

'He drives badly,' said Peter. 'I'm going for a piss.' He winked and pointed to the distant chestnut trees. 'All right?'

'Be quick,' said Heinz. 'It won't take him long to get back.'

'It won't take me long either.' He trudged off, patting his pockets. The others worked, pull slice throw, pull slice throw. Peter disappeared through the hedge. After several minutes he reappeared, trotting swiftly over the stripped rows.

'All right?' asked Wolfgang. 'Did you get chestnuts?'

'Better than all right!' Peter opened his greatcoat slightly. They caught a glimpse of grey fur. 'The chestnuts are useless – too small. But I got this!'

'It's a rabbit,' said Wolfgang.

'It certainly is. I found it in a snare. Look!'

He showed them a length of bright brass wire and a whittled stake like a small wooden tent peg.

'Surely that's stealing,' said Ehrich. 'You should put it back.'

Peter grinned.

'Not likely!'

'What about the snare?' persisted Ehrich.

'They'll just think the rabbit went off with it.'

'How are we going to cook it?' asked the practical Wolfgang. 'We can't cook it here. You'll have to get it back to camp. Why not put the snare back?'

'Because I shall use it again!' said Peter, flushing. 'I wouldn't have brought the thing if I'd known you would treat me like a thief! I don't want it now!'

He pulled the rabbit from his coat, holding it by the hind legs in his right hand, flinging his arm back to throw it into the distant hedge. Paul and Wilhelm watched silently.

'No!' said Wolfgang. 'Don't do that!'

'Ehrich called me a thief!' Peter was hurt and childish.

'I'm sorry,' said Ehrich. 'It wasn't meant to be any comment on you. It was a comment on how the English will see it.'

'This farmer isn't setting snares,' said Heinz. 'I don't believe that for a moment. The only person he's depriving is some poacher.'

Heinz's sanity penetrated to them all. Ehrich shrugged, then nodded. Wolfgang clapped Peter lightly on the back. Paul snorted and returned to his work with a derisive sneer. Peter looked relieved. He tucked the rabbit back in his coat.

'We'll find some way of cooking it,' he said. 'It will be the best rabbit you've ever tasted. A real turnip-fed fat rabbit, roast perhaps, in rich brown gravy . . .'

Heinz threw a fistful of leaves at him. They were smiling again and Peter was relieved.

Helen and Ann Baxter sat down in the dry grass of the bank. They were at a crossroads where the larger road taken by the bus veered off at right angles and their own lands separated at an angle, one to Pyes Farm, one to Margishall. A wooden signpost, bleached grey by the weather, indicated each farm. Helen was secretly impressed. She had never expected to live in a house that was marked in this way.

They lay facing the sun. It was four o'clock and the blaze was becoming tinged with yellow. Ann chewed a leaf of sorrel, offered one to Helen who accepted it, made a face.

'It fills your mouth with saliva,' said Ann. 'When you're thirsty.'

The girls had quickly got to know each other at school. Ann Baxter had seen to that immediately after Helen was introduced to the class. While the boys had no bus to get them to school, Helen was lucky. The girls' school was in the next town, served by a bus morning and afternoon to coincide with school hours.

'Well?' asked Ann.

'Well what?'

'What do you make of it? Of this place. Country life.'

'I don't know yet. I haven't had time to find out.'

Ann wore a grey skirt and short grey socks. Her white blouse was carelessly open, and she unbuttoned it further, spreading back the collars to allow the sun to fall on her neck. She lay back. Helen noted with envy her firm pointed breasts and wished she was better shaped herself. She wished she had a blouse like Ann's. She had a white shirt with the long sleeves cut off and stitched up by her mother on the sewing machine. The thread had kept breaking and the result was not professional.

'It's boring,' said Ann. 'Until you arrived there was no one out here. There's only one boy and he's useless.'

Helen did not ask what she meant.

'You've met my father,' said Ann.

'Yes.'

She remembered the way Tom Baxter had looked at her when he came to the house. She knew she was blushing and was glad the other girl was lying down and could not see her face properly.

'He quarrels all the time with my mother,' said Ann. Helen said nothing. 'They don't get on. He goes off with other women. He visits them and has sex with them. I know. I've seen him.'

Helen was appalled. She felt herself colouring even more.

149

'Do you find that shocking?' asked Ann, eyes shut, moving her face in the sun.

'I do a bit,' Helen heard herself murmur. Ann suddenly sat upright and looked into her eyes.

'Why? It isn't, you know. It's what goes on. The first time they took our cows to the bull, they wouldn't let me come. There was all this whispering in the house, and secrets and nonsense. I pretended I was going to school as usual, but I didn't and I followed them. I watched it all from behind a hedge, and all these men were leaning on the fence making jokes about it. They didn't want any women there so they could make their dirty jokes. That was what it was about. And, when the bull got tired doing it, they poked his cock with a stick and made him go on. You should see the size of a bull's cock! Have you ever seen one?'

Helen shook her head silently.

'Do you find that shocking?'

Ann was looking at Helen intently.

'No. Not shocking. I think its embarrassing. I wouldn't want to be there.' She wondered what Ann had seen her father do but at the same time was afraid to hear. Ann got to her feet.

'I'll walk along the lane with you to Pyes Farm. I haven't been along here for months. Jempson didn't mind but his wife hated me. She was fat and horrible.'

Ann Baxter's judgement. Helen thought of her own impressions of Mrs Jempson. She saw slim, blonde Ann walking ahead of her, pretty, young and swift in her judgements. She remembered the thin, lined face and sturdy buttocks of Mrs Jempson, the suppressed bitterness and rage. Ann had some of that quality too. She was trying to shock, trying to probe. She was a danger.

The two girls walked slowly along, pausing to pick a blackberry here and there where they were still ripe and firm, pausing to lean on a gate. They watched a lizard basking on a stone. It sensed them and fled.

'We could go into town together one day,' said Ann. 'I could say I've gone to visit you and you could say the same and we could go on a Saturday. That way they would agree. We could go to the cinema. Have you ever been to the cinema?'

'Only twice. Have you been often?'

'No. But more than twice. I was taken twice by Harry Beardsley. He's the boy I was talking about. He put his hand up my skirt.' Helen moved on, embarrassed.

'I might come. Let me think about it.'

'Does your mother let you go out a lot?'

'No. I don't think I've ever been out like you describe.'

'Mine does. I make up some story about what I'm doing and I don't think she believes it but as long as she can tell my father it's all right. They both just want a good story. I know why Mrs Jempson hated me. She found old Jempson on the tractor with me. We were driving the hay rake round the field. He had his arm round me because I was steering and she saw it. You should have seen her face!'

'But he wasn't *doing* anything?'

Ann laughed teasingly. 'Now that would be telling!'

Helen was horribly fascinated by the other girl's conversation. She had never talked to anyone in this way, and although she disapproved deeply of the girl's apparent obsession it gave her a frisson of pleasure. She wondered if she had been too sheltered. Having no means of comparison she was concerned that she must appear unworldly and childlike. What *did* she know about anything? Her father had gone away, she had been brought up by her mother who kept her close, kept her safe.

'You've got the German prisoners working for you, haven't you?' said Ann.

'Yes. My father was going to get them today. If they've come.'

'We had them as well. They're all ages, you know. There's some smashing young men! They go about with almost nothing on.'

'You don't look!'

'Of course I do! There's no other young men round here. If you don't count Harry Beardsley, and he's only a year older than me. Let's see what you've got!'

'Is that why you came down the lane?'

Ann grinned.

'Of course it is! You really are slow, Helen!'

'I'm not looking with you!'

'Don't be silly! We'll just walk quietly along the lane and keep out of sight. It's not spying on them or anything. We've a

151

perfect right to walk down the lane. Of course you'll have a look. You're not afraid, are you?'

'No.'

'Well, come on then!'

They tiptoed down the lane on the grass verge. They could hear the sound of voices and advanced even more slowly, Ann in the lead, Helen well behind. Ann stopped and half-crouched, half-lay in the hedge. She beckoned urgently to Helen with her left hand. Helen joined her. Through the small gap they could see the mangold rows. The Germans were no more than twenty yards from them, approaching.

'Look,' whispered Ann, 'He's young, he's smashing.' She had one hand cupped to Helen's ear. With the other she pointed to Wilhelm.

'Let's go,' said Helen. She moved cautiously away, stood on the far side of the lane out of sight. Ann continued to watch. The voices came closer. To Helen's horror, Ann bobbed to her feet.

'Hello!' she shouted over the hedge. Helen heard a startled exclamation, then a reply in fractured English. Ann laughed and ran off up the lane to the farm. Helen followed her because she could not think of anything else to do. Eventually Ann slowed down. The girls were panting.

'What did you do that for?' demanded Helen.

'I like him!' said Ann. 'Find out his name. Please find out his name! Didn't you enjoy that?'

'I don't know.'

'You didn't see him! I enjoyed it!'

William turned left out of the school gates through the two brick piers with their massive stone balls. He hovered on the pavement uncertain what to do, scuffing at the dust between the paving stones. John had already left. William had gone to find him but a master with a heavy moustache who smelled of sweat and tobacco stopped him. He was just locking up and was surprised to see anyone returning.

'You're John Ellis's small brother, are you?' the man asked. He seemed kindly enough. 'He went off with Jimmy Bradley and his father. He gave him a lift. If I'd known, I'd have asked him to take you.'

'My Pa's picking me up,' said William.

'You should learn to cycle,' said the teacher.

'I am, sir,' said William. 'I've got a bike.'

'That's good.'

The man wondered if he had. The boy before him was dark-haired and earnest-looking with expressive brown eyes. The eyes had withdrawn, had become shuttered and blank. The boy's clothes were thin and patched, not uncommon in these post-war years, but even more than was usual.

'You'd better go, I'm locking up.'

Other children passed William, mostly in groups, noisy and preoccupied. Boys were popping tar bubbles in the melting road, leaving their footprints. Sally and Mary passed him.

'Ain't your Pa waiting?' asked Sally.

'He's just late,' said William confidently. 'Expect he'll be here soon.'

'We're going swimming,' said Sally. 'You could come with us.'

'Swimming?' William was nonplussed. 'Where?'

'In the river of course. Ain't you seen it? By the town bridge where it's shallow. There's a flat bit there. Lots of us go after school when it's hot. My Mum doesn't come home till after five so there's lots of time. We often go, don't we, Mary?'

Mary nodded. Giggled.

'I can't anyway,' said William. 'I have to wait here. My Pa'll be here soon. Anyway, I haven't got a costume.'

Sally laughed mischievously.

'We don't wear costumes! We wear our knickers!'

'And vests!' said Mary virtuously. The girls ran off laughing. William waited. Before long all the children had gone. William sat down on the forbidden brick wall, hoping it was now all right. None of the teachers had passed yet. Miss Pearce appeared suddenly, clopping up to him in long black skirt and white blouse over which she wore a cardigan of faded beige. Her shoes, the origin of most of her commotion, were shiny as wet coal. Her heels were of burnished steel.

'Are you waiting for someone?'

'My Pa, miss. He's picking me up.'

'Here?'

'Yes.'

'Good night then.'

'Good night, Miss Pearce.'

It was evidently all right to sit on the wall. He waited. An occasional car passed. Children passed, on their way home after visiting shops. Some were chewing at the liquorice sticks that Sally had mentioned. Some were from his class and nodded to him, staring unashamedly.

'What you doing here?' they all asked. He replied with the monotonous answer.

'Waiting for my Pa to pick me up.'

They walked on wordlessly, not caring enough about him to ask any more. The master with the moustache left the school. He closed the door firmly then locked it with a bunch of keys he took from his pocket. It occurred to William he might be the headmaster. William slid off the wall onto his feet. He tried to look casual. The sun was dropping now and it must be well after half-past four.

'Hello, young Ellis,' said the man. William noticed that his face was a yellowy colour and that the pores of his nose were enlarged and obvious. He did not look healthy in the open air.

'Are you still here?'

William nodded.

'Your father late?'

'He told me he'd be late,' said William quickly. 'He told me to wait for him. He said he might be quite late.'

'All right then. Good night.'

'Good night, sir.'

The man walked away. William heard him begin to whistle to himself quietly. A blackbird burst into song as if in response. It was quickly answered by another. Dusk chorus was beginning. William sat down again. He wondered if he should begin to walk home. It was a long way and he was not sure if he knew the road properly. It would get dark before he made it. In any case his father would be furious if he arrived to find no one there. Far away he heard a railway train puffing. Lights began to go on in houses across the road as shadows lengthened. He heard Sally and Mary returning and was overcome by embarrassment. Before they could see him he darted back inside the school gates and hid behind one of the brick piers, pressing himself tight into the corner it made with the wall. Sally's voice approached the gateway, passed it, was gone. William waited, counting to

154

one hundred before he peered out, then emerged. He sat on the wall again.

'Are you sure you should stay here? It's beginning to get dark.' It was the man again. William hadn't noticed his approach. 'Can't you get a bus?'

'I haven't any money,' answered William truthfully.

'I can lend you some.'

'I have to stay here. I must.'

'All right. But, if your father doesn't come by seven, I shall have to do something about it. If I had a car I would take you home. Why is your father so late?'

'I don't know.' The man's voice was kindly in its enquiry, but disapproving.

'I will come back in a bit to make sure you're all right.' The thought turned William's stomach but he said nothing. The man whistled to himself again, not looking back. William began to cry. He did not know he was until he felt the wetness on his cheeks. He wiped it away fiercely. It was the same old story over again as he had known it would be. New schools, new fears, new misery. What had happened to the car? Had it broken down? Had there been some terrible accident?

When the car approached suddenly it caught him in its headlamps and he held up a hand to his eyes, partly to shield them, partly to wipe them. His relief was overwhelming.

His father climbed out of the car. His face was unkind.

'There you are!' he said. 'Get in quickly.'

'I've been waiting for hours!' said William, climbing in and making an ineffective job of shutting the door so that his father sighed and leaned across him to slam it properly. 'What happened?'

'Nothing happened.' His father's fury showed in his driving as he ground at the wrong gear. William could not see his face in the darkness but could imagine exactly how he looked. 'It's far too much having to drop everything and come all this way to collect you children. I've had to stop everything to get here. I had five men working. You'll have to learn to cycle or you'll have to walk home!'

William sat wordless as the car drove through the town. The shops were shut now and street lights here and there were alight. They crossed the bridge over the river and William had a brief glimpse of the sheet of still water and the pale patch of gravel. Two boys were still playing there, trousers rolled up. They were lifting stones for sticklebacks. William could tell by the way they were crouched. They drove up the hill and into the lanes. He felt an unhappiness that seemed to rise from the pit of his stomach, hurting every part of him up to his jaws. It made him produce too much saliva, as if he was about to be sick, so he swallowed and swallowed, eating the nausea, watching the dark trees flash past. Occasionally they rattled against the car. A barn owl swooped across in the car's headlamps. William knew his father had simply forgotten him.

'That was a late trip!' his mother said when he arrived home. That was all. Apparently she was afraid to say anything more. William wished she had more courage. She made him a big tea, but that wasn't enough.

'You should have waited for me!' he said to John later.

'You can find your own way home. I did.'

'You got a lift! Now Pa's saying he's too busy and that we'll have to walk. Or cycle.' William's face was intense in the yellow light of his hurricane lamp.

'Maybe it'll make him buy bikes. We need bikes. And a wireless. We need electricity.'

'Ma says he spent all our money on cows and things.'

'When did she say that?'

'I don't know. I heard her saying it as we were coming up here. She was complaining.'

There was a silence. Far away they could hear a dog fox barking, nearer an owl. The walnut tree shivered in a light breeze. Their window was open, the air still warm.

'They go swimming in the river after school,' said William.

'I know,' said John dismissively. He allowed the pause to extend. 'We could make ourselves canoes and go out on the pond.'

'How?' William was eager.

'Those ammunition boxes in the woods. Did you see they had lining trays? They were long. We could join two together and paddle them. They would make a canoe.'

They lay and thought about it, skimming in imagination on the limpid water of their private lake. It had to be done.

★

Ehrich made a face at Wolfgang, but he drank the contents of the mug in one.

'It isn't champagne,' he said, 'but I detect a hint of alcohol amongst the turnip.' He handed the mug to Wolfgang who poured himself a generous helping from the Shell oil can.

'There's still a hint of oil in it!' he said.

'Complaints, complaints!' said Peter. 'You have to admit it has a kick!' Wolfgang passed the mug to Heinz. The four men sat outside the hut on their chairs. The air smelled keen and there was a hint of a chill to come. Thicker dews would be followed by frosts in the next weeks.

'Autumn is really on its way,' said Heinz. He pointed to the small puffs of cloud that had caught the colour of the sun. 'That cloud is high and cold. You can feel the fingers of winter.'

'That's the wine!' said Wolfgang, to laughter. The men did not want Heinz to become reflective. In their own way each one of them sensed the sadness of a closing year. No matter how it might yet blaze with an Indian summer, another winter would come with them in captivity, another Christmas with no news, no wives, no children, no family.

'How's that rabbit?' asked Ehrich, more to break any train of thought than for any other reason. Peter leapt up.

'Christ! It'll be ready by now. How're we going to eat it?'

'Easily,' said Wolfgang. 'Out here. Why not.'

'We may be seen.'

'The Tommies won't do anything. I bet half of them have snares set out there.'

'Perhaps it's a Tommy's rabbit!' said Ehrich. The men smiled at the thought.

'I'll get it,' said Heinz. 'Where do I collect?'

'Fritz has put it in an oven for us,' said Peter, 'You know, the thin little fellow with jug ears. He's peeling potatoes. Go to the back door and knock quietly. He's expecting you . . .'

Heinz got up and moved quietly away. No one knew if what they were doing was forbidden, but it was always good to be cautious. In any case, a rabbit wasn't much between four.

The maze of wooden huts would have baffled anyone not familiar with the camp. Heinz moved easily between them, passing small groups of men talking, standing and smoking, playing chess by the light from a doorway. There was always a general hubbub at this time of night. In the huts set aside for club activities he could hear two pianos playing, rehearsing some show. There was a flourishing music society. A voice broke into song. Stopped. Argued.

To the rear of the camp, near the wire perimeter fence and the service gates, the cluster of store and cooking huts formed a distinct group. Heinz could hear the sound of washing-up – plates and cutlery clattering, water draining away. There was a smell of boiling potatoes left over from their evening meal. He made for the particular hut and tapped gently on the door. It was ajar and there was no reply so he slipped quietly inside.

There was no sign of Fritz. The row of ovens was unattended. He could smell what he was after and, looking round, found a cloth. He opened the oven. The cooked rabbit was browning on a baking tray. Heinz picked the scalding tray up carefully and turned out the gas. He wondered where Fritz had got to. He ought to thank him at least. Looking round he saw a door at the far end of the kitchen that was dimly illuminated from the other side so that light shone around it in the gloom of the kitchen. Clutching the tray in one hand he walked softly to the door and carefully turned the handle, lest there should be guards on the other side. He looked through the narrowest of openings and stopped immediately. The squat naked form of Kunkel was bent forward over a scrubbed table so that his chest was pressed flat upon it and his buttocks thrust outwards. Behind him stood Mohnke wearing the top half of his uniform, legs braced and his trousers round his ankles, thrusting rhythmically into him. Kunkel made no noise, did not move, Mohnke suddenly pulled at Kunkel's buttocks, thrusting wildly, then threw himself on him, grasping his shoulders.

Heinz moved away like a wraith. What he had just seen was dangerous. If they knew he had seen them they would kill him.

He vowed to tell no one. He wondered what Fritz knew. It must be why the man had fled the kitchen. He walked swiftly back towards their hut with the rabbit. The smell of it was rich and strong. It had been a foolish episode. He felt silly with the baking tray.

'That smells wonderful!' said Peter. 'Any trouble?'

'None.'

'Good old Fritz!'

Peter produced a home-made knife filed from a piece of corrugated iron and disjointed the meat. The men picked it up in their fingers, exclaiming at the hot fat, blowing at the pieces.

'Hurry up!' said Ehrich. 'This smell will travel everywhere!' They ate ravenously, savouring every morsel, then sucking the bones one by one. When they had finished they sauntered to a quiet part of the perimeter fence and threw the bones over.

CHAPTER SEVEN

Threshing was to be done on Saturday. The boys were the first to hear the approach of the machines. They had lain awake in a state of excitement since first light. The first sound was no more than a vibration, a feathering on the air from far away. They held their breaths and told each other to be quiet. The second noise, the true herald, was a dull rumble. The third noise was a metallic clank as iron tyres rang on the road, followed by chuffing. The two leapt from bed, tearing off their pyjamas, and pulled on their clothes in a matter of moments. They had laid them out specially the night before. Even their shoe laces were undone. They were down the stairs and out of the house before anyone else was even up and ran full tilt for the noise and the smoke. One pillar, jet black, rose from the roadway, another followed as white as snow. Then there were two hollow bursts from the whistle that made them jump.

They rushed onto the road. It trembled under their feet as the monster approached, straddling the road like an iron tortoise. Pebbles burst and screamed under its iron wheels. Brasswork shone, a white horse leapt on a crest on its prow, its funnel was bound with black hoops like an ancient bombard. As it crawled nearer they saw the dizzy violence of the fly-wheel and the hurtle of the brass regulator that spun like a carousel. Taylor and Tester stood on the monster. They saluted the boys, lifting their hats, smiling at them, at the impression they always made. They made gestures, showing they were not going to stop, shooing the boys forward. Behind the traction engine they towed the threshing machine. Its huge box-shaped bulk completely framed the lane. It had become entangled at various stages on its journey and was festooned with pieces of branch, wild hop and old-man's-beard. The boys kept running in front until they were back at the entrance to the farm. Here they stepped aside to let the monster pass. Their father appeared at the farm door, pulling on a jacket over his shirt and jumper. The boys had never noticed but the morning was cold and bright with dew. Their shoes were soaked and grey.

Taylor leaned down to them from the engine.

'Water!' he shouted. 'Tell your dad we shall need plenty of that. Fill milk churns, you see. This old girl gets thirsty when she gets going!'

He lifted his hat to Robert. It was almost an afterthought. The machines rolled by. Water meant pumping. Pumping meant them. They fought each other for the bucket, for the handle, for the churns.

The setting-up of the thresher was a wonderful show. The traction engine was parked beside the glistening heap of steam coal and its fire door was flung open to reveal astonishing flames. Tester shovelled coal onto the footplate with rapid economical motions and Taylor transferred it into the inferno with practised sweeps. They were both blackened and sweating and it was only six.

'You see, Mr Ellis, the coal has to be shot just right,' said Taylor. 'It has to be just so!' He shovelled in some more, looked into the glow and clanged the fire door shut. 'Where the coal stands, that's where the engine stands. Where the engine stands determines the position of the thresher. Now it ain't any good any o' them all being in the right place if the stack's in another!'

He chuckled at his exposition. He was in a good mood.

'You see, we got it just right.'

He looked at the stack and his positioning with pride.

'Mouldy old stack though, I should say. But we shall see!'

Tester nodded in agreement, adding more coal to the footplate then leaning on his shovel. They regarded the stack as a man might weigh up a cow at auction. Robert suppressed his feelings of annoyance. They all had a long day ahead of them.

The morning was brightening by the moment, but the heavy dew still lay on the long grasses and glazed twigs. The coal was wet with it. The engine panted contentedly and Taylor laid a hand on it, caressing it. Only a fool would doubt the need for such loving care. Robert moved away, feeling superfluous.

The boys noticed little about the rising sun. They were hot and wet and steaming slightly from their exertions. The buckets were lined up in front of them to receive the gouts of water. John flailed away and, as each was filled, William put another in its place and emptied the full one into a milk churn. He then placed the empty one at the end. In this way they had quickly filled five milk churns. Robert collected the churns, loading them on the back of a trailer and pulling them by tractor back to the engine. The boys sat on the trailer, steadying them, getting wetter still as they rocked and sloshed.

'How many men have you hired, Mr Ellis?' asked Taylor, when they returned.

'Six prisoners.'

'I hope they can work,' said Taylor. 'We shall get up a head of steam and when we do this old engine will fly! She will turn over the thresher for at least thirty hundredweight an hour, if they can keep her loaded that fast. I hope they aren't lazy beggars these Germans.'

'I think they'll do,' said Robert.

Tester picked the full churns off the back of the trailer as if they were pints of milk. Robert had struggled to load them. A deceptively strong man. A deceptive man altogether. The engine began to hiss violently, steam escaping from joints and crevices and from pipes beneath its belly. Taylor jumped down and walked to the thresher. He clambered upon it and from within its wooden sides produced a large fold of leather, hard but shiny, that he hoisted onto his shoulder with a smack.

'The belt!' he announced.

The belt was laid out on the weedy stubble of the field. It was six inches wide and glistened like a steel coil. At the joins in the leather, steel toothing made a glittering seam. The boys watched entranced as the two men performed their ritual. Tester picked up one end, Taylor the other. They pulled it out, then they shook it and slapped it. They laid it down as taut as it could be pulled, beside the machines. They stepped back and viewed the arrangement. Taylor picked up his end and placed it over the valley of the traction engine. Tester picked up his and,

162

by bracing himself and hauling violently, slipped it over the corresponding pulley of the thresher. It hung slack under its own weight. Tester nodded. He held up his two hands, palms about six inches apart. Taylor climbed silently onto the traction engine and rocked it forward. It was done skilfully so that the spade lugs of its iron wheels no more than bit the earth. He climbed down again with an air of certainty. The threshing tackle was now set up. Tester was already in position, crouched with one eye shut, sighting along the line of the belt from one pulley to the next.

'She'll do,' he said laconically.

'She'll do,' Taylor repeated to the boys. 'She'll do, Mr Ellis. Shall I give her a turn?'

Robert nodded. Taylor wiped his hands down the seams of his dungarees. Another part of the ritual, a cleansing. He climbed back onto the traction engine and pulled a lever, releasing it gently. The thresher shuddered to life. The noise and motion was terrific. Woodwork rattled and slammed. Its great hollow belly was empty but within it drums and riddles and screens shook and beat. Pulleys rattled and chains and belts strove. A cloud of white dust rose as if it was on fire. The boys knew she certainly would do and looked at each other and grinned. Taylor pulled on the whistle once, twice, five times to announce it to the world. He eased his hat back and managed a smile. Robert found that his face too was wearing a foolish grin. He was elated. It was such a moment as he had hoped for. A reward for all the worry. He wished Margaret had been there to share it.

The prisoners arrived. The timing was good. Taylor had just reached out and shut down the power to the pulley drive. The lorry pulled in to the side of the road by the field gate and six figures dressed in drab grey jumped down. Taylor opened the valve slightly so that the machinery kept moving slowly.

The prisoners advanced excitedly, except Paul who hung back and remained expressionless.

'Nice!' said Wolfgang. 'A nice steam engine! This will be fun!'

'It will be hard work!' said Ehrich, but he was smiling. They were walking fast now like boys about to break into a run. Paul was well behind.

'That stack is in a disgusting state,' said Peter the baker, casting his professional eye over it. 'I hope they don't intend to sell it for food. The wheat will be covered with fungus. Wait till you see the mice!'

They gathered round the traction engine in a half-circle, eyes full of pleasure, absorbed in watching the motions of the thing. Taylor, observing them from above, looked proud. Tester, arms akimbo, looked them over like stock.

'You like my engine, *ja*?' shouted Taylor.

'*Ja*,' said Wolfgang. 'It is beautiful. You have looked after it well.'

Robert stepped forward from where he had been standing beside the stack. He must take control. He was holding a pitchfork. The men turned towards him, said good morning.

'Today we are going to thresh this stack.' He indicated with the handle of the pitchfork. 'You see those long wooden ladders,' he said, addressing Wolfgang, but forced to shout over the engine that was still turning. 'You use those for getting onto the stack. Remove all the thatch first. This is a pitchfork. You will use these to remove the thatch, then you will use them for lifting the corn sheaves. You pass them to the threshing machine. One man stands on top, cuts the twine on each sheaf and lets the corn drop in.' He paused, waiting for Wolfgang to translate. 'These gentlemen' – he indicated Taylor and Tester – 'will keep the engine running and look after the machine.' Taylor and Tester nodded. They hadn't worked with German prisoners before. They were surprised at the motley appearance of their clothes – perhaps they had expected them to be in uniform. Tester disliked them on principle. He would make sure the beggars worked.

Paul had been put on the bagging by the others as it was the most boring and immobile job and smothered the operator in clouds of evil dust. Wilhelm and Peter were clearing straw as it cascaded from the straw board, assisted by the two boys and by Robert who joined in each operation for a time, patrolling round and round. Tester checked the corn from time to time and adjusted the blast of the blowers by moving the blower slides. He carried a large red oil can with him and was perpetually in motion, squirting it here and there onto bearings and into the innards of the thresher and the engine. He listened, he adjusted, he moved on.

Ehrich, Heinz and Wolfgang were showing off. Ehrich was on the threshing machine and Wolfgang and Heinz were throwing the sheaves. As they moved across the stack, they hurled them further and further, enjoying the challenge. Ehrich was forced to reach out to catch them with his own fork, shouting when they fell short. He had got the hang of it now. Taylor had demonstrated the easy way to pick up a sheaf, cut the twine with a knife and let the corn drop into the drum and concave. He explained that the twine must never be allowed to fall in and showed Ehrich how he himself pulled it round his leather belt. Now Ehrich wore a grass skirt of it halfway round one side and made hula-hula motions from time to time and shouted and pranced. Wolfgang and Heinz were engulfed occasionally by the steam and smoke of the engine as it tended to blow their way. They were sweating profusely and had stripped to their singlets. Chaff stuck to them, making them itch. They flung more sheaves at Ehrich every time he cavorted, until he was almost submerged by flying corn, but nudged each other and made sure they stopped when Robert appeared. There was a view from the top of the stack, over the fields and to the woodland. In the far distance they could see the spire and tower of the church that kept time for them in the mangold field. They could see other farms in the distance. They could see the meadow that ran down to the cressy stream. They could see the farmhouse. Heinz had been keeping an eye on it throughout and was the first to spot the two women. They left by the front door, carrying the tea basket. Heinz nudged Wolfgang, and pointed. Wolfgang grinned.

'It's your lady-love!' he said. Heinz gave him a shove into the corn.

Margaret and Helen approached cautiously. They knew that Robert did not want them to visit the scene, and the tea was Margaret's idea. She wanted to see Heinz. She admitted that to herself. She had not examined the strength of her compulsion. Helen wanted to see Wilhelm but of course said nothing. They backed each other in their venture.

'They can't work on like that without a break,' said Margaret. 'It's very hot work.'

'Of course they can't,' said Helen.

'Robert's been up for hours in any case. And so have Taylor and Tester.'

'It can always be a quick break.'

Nevertheless she was very nervous, especially as she knew she would be seen on their long approach. They cut straight across the fields in a straight line, using stiles. She could clearly see Heinz on the stack with Wolfgang. They could not see Robert.

'What a noise!' said Helen. 'It shakes the earth. You can feel it.' They now stood at a gable end of the stack, avoiding the clouds of grey dust and the flying chaff. 'They're all staring at us.'

'I know, don't look,' said Margaret. 'Look down.'

But she did not follow her own advice any more than Helen did. Looking up at Heinz she caught his eye briefly. Between sticking a sheaf with his fork and throwing it to Ehrich, Heinz shot her a covert glance and a smile. She smiled back, looked to her basket, moved on. Wilhelm had stopped moving straw and openly rested on his fork, eyes following Helen. Helen felt herself blush and turned her back to move away.

'Get a move-on, lover-boy!' said Peter to Wilhelm in German. 'You look as intelligent as a dead cod.'

'Like mother, like daughter,' said Wilhelm. 'You noticed as well. They're terrific! It's good working here!'

'Keep your mind on your job. She's English, you're a German prisoner and you don't need any more trouble. If you want to be repatriated, you be a good boy!'

Robert appeared from behind the traction engine and saw the two women. His face clouded with annoyance and he advanced on them quickly.

'I told you not to come out here. It will distract everyone from their work and slow things down. I thought I made that perfectly clear. The forecast is for this weather to break. We have to get on.'

Taylor, having observed the basket, craftily shut the steam power down behind Robert's back. A loud hiss accompanied Robert's protests.

The threshing machine slowed.

'No!' shouted Robert, whirling round, 'Keep it going!'

'I reckon we need a cup of tea, Mr Ellis,' said Taylor clearly. 'Some of us have been up since five. And in any case this old engine needs liquid refreshment.'

He swung himself down and dropped to the field. There was nothing to be done now, and Robert knew it.

'Pleased to meet you, ma'am,' Taylor said to Margaret, lifting his trilby. 'How are you settling in? Your husband is making a right attack upon it, isn't he? Getting on with the ploughing and now this and a whole clutch of new heifers all with calf. A right attack. How do, girl.' He nodded to Helen.

'This is my daughter Helen.' Helen shook hands, Taylor wiping his first on his dungarees. Behind him the traction engine hissed to a standstill. Robert shot it a furious glance.

'All right, we have to stop now, I suppose, but make it quick!' Margaret pretended not to notice, and calmly looked round for somewhere to set the things out.

'Tea, lads!' announced Taylor as though he was in control of the party. The men on the stack stuck their forks in the corn and slid down to join the others on the ground. Taylor took the basket easily.

'Now what you do is set it out here,' he said, opening it and laying down the huge teapot and then the mugs and slices of bread on the iron steps of the traction engine. 'It makes a rare table. We allus eats off it, don't we?'

Tester nodded.

'Sometimes we do use plates,' he added drily. Laughter was a balm to everyone except Robert who stamped off round the machinery examining this and that. Margaret filled the mugs. She had had difficulty in finding eleven and they were all shapes and sizes. The prisoners formed a polite queue and took their tea in turn, after Margaret had served Taylor and Tester. She had no intention of calling to Robert after his show of bad grace. Helen held the plate of bread and butter and offered a piece to each man in turn. No one refused it. They all stood looking at Margaret, embarrassed.

'I think they're waiting for you, before they start,' said Taylor.

'Please begin!' said Margaret. The men stood in a half-circle where they were. The tea was too hot and she saw them sip and recoil.

'I have more milk.'

She took round a white jug with blue bands around it. She had been sparing with the milk in case Robert scolded her. He often reminded them their milk was for sale. Each man held out his mug in turn and she trickled some more in.

'We sell the milk, you see . . .' she said, explaining herself unnecessarily. The boys urged her to fill their mugs right up. She did so, and they drank it all in one swallow, holding them out immediately for more. She gave them half a cup each. They looked hot and dishevelled and skinny beside these grown men. They all did, both she and Helen. When she reached Heinz with the milk her hand was shaky. Heinz introduced himself. It was a bold step to take, but he had seen Robert leave.

'Thank you. My name is Heinz.'

'How do you do?'

The greeting that was in itself a question confused Heinz. He was not sure what he was expected to say. He had opened the door for the others however. They all gave Margaret their names. All except Paul, who made a point of standing a little apart. They had hungry glances. She took the milk back and put it away in the basket. The engine was letting out long sighs. She set out after Robert.

'Robert, I'm sorry. I'm sure they'll work better after something to eat and drink! You can't expect them to go right through to lunch on nothing. They must have started very early.'

Robert had his hand thrust in the bag at the extreme end of the thresher. He had a handful of corn, and was allowing it to trickle back into the sack.

'You've undermined me and made me look a fool in front of everyone.'

'Only if you take it that way.'

Robert let the corn drop and turned to stare at her.

'You should join them for tea,' she said. 'That would be right.'

'I'm damned if I will!'

Margaret turned and walked away. She must look cheerful and smile, she told herself. Heinz collected the cups swiftly when he saw her and handed them back.

'Thank you,' he said. 'That was a good cup of tea.' He looked carefully into her eyes. She looked steadily back before turning with the mugs.

'What are you going to do now?' John asked Helen. They were sitting on the heap of straw.

'I'm going to stay and watch for a bit. It's exciting and I'm fed up with being indoors. Ma will just find me more things to do.'

John made a face at William behind her back. They had planned to slip away unseen and get the ammunition boxes they needed for a canoe. The warm weather wouldn't last forever.

Taylor wound at handles, opening valves. The thresher rattled and shuddered. The boys got up.

'I shouldn't sit there,' John said to Helen. 'That's where the straw goes. You'll get smothered. Anyway all the men are looking at you. Your skirt's too short.'

'No, it's not, and I know they're looking at me!' Helen coloured but sounded calm. 'Why shouldn't I be stared at? It's none of your business.'

Paul and Wilhelm returned to their position. Straw abruptly spewed out of the wooden mouth of the thresher, high up above their heads. Cavings blew out at low level forming a slow-mounting heap. It made Helen jump, and she moved away, standing back from the flying dust. Wilhelm smiled at her. He was not shy, and it was Helen who immediately looked away.

'It is all right,' he said in careful English. 'It will not harm you.' He was clad in grey trousers and a coarse blue singlet and was muscular and dark. He held out his pitchfork towards her.

'You want to try to use this fork?'

Helen shook her head and backed off. She felt immature, faced with this bold approach. Paul was already changing the corn bags over. Wilhelm moved some straw, leaned on his fork to watch her retreating.

'Get on with your damned work!' shouted Paul, bad-tempered as ever.

'*Ach Gott!*' He broke into a stream of German abuse. Wilhelm ran to him. They peered in the bag. Wilhelm yelled to Wolfgang to stop the machine, and Wolfgang shouted to Taylor who promptly disengaged the drive. Tester was alongside Paul in seconds.

'What's the matter?' he demanded tersely. Paul pointed in the bag. Tester looked, then plunged in both hands bringing up a cascade of corn. It was stained red. Taylor joined them, took one look and moved immediately towards the front of the thresher. Robert walked quickly round the stack.

'What's the matter? Why have you stopped?'

They all gathered in a half-circle around Taylor, who stooped beside the flanks of the thresher. He slid out the riddles from its interior one by one. The wind riddle and the capes riddle were shallow trays filled with a wet pink-and red pulp that here and there moved, revealing minute limbs. Taylor tutted and shot the contents onto the field, one after the other, turning the riddles upside down and knocking them. Perhaps two hundred tiny mice and bits of mice scattered on the ground, chopped or whole, moving feebly. The boys and Helen stared aghast. Taylor thrust the riddles back. Only Wilhelm and Paul appeared unconcerned amongst the prisoners. Taylor and Tester treated it as a matter of course and entered into a discussion with Robert about what they should do to keep the grain clean.

'Damned mice! I knew we should run into them soon. It'll get worse in the centre of the stack. That's where they have their nests, see. The adults go downwards. We shall have fun as we get near the bottom, I should say. If you have an old cat or an old dog or two I should bring them here and all the sticks and shovels you can lay hands on! Shovels are favourite!'

'What about the corn?' demanded Robert. He was disgusted by the bits of mice and the blood-soaked grain.

'Oh, it'll do well enough for feed. It's only blood, the bits don't get through. We shall have to keep a man on the riddle all the time now. The boys could do it, it's not heavy work. You must just keep looking and emptying! Give them something useful!'

The boys heard this as they stared at the carnage. Many of the baby mice were perfectly formed and apparently undamaged, although no bigger than a maggot. They were quite pink like rose petals with eyes shielded by translucent lids. They moved slowly, as if in deep sleep, their paws like hands, pulling at the membrane. Heinz was disgusted. The pulp reminded him of Siegfried. He felt sick and turned away. The boys fled to a safe distance.

'Who's going to do this?' demanded Taylor. 'One of you. You!' he pointed at Wolfgang who shook his head, at Peter, at Paul. Paul shrugged and nodded. It would be easier than lugging the sacks.

Helen joined the boys for a moment.

'I feel sick,' she said. 'That's horrible. All those tiny pink things, moving! I'm going back to the house.' She turned and walked quickly away. Robert saw her as she tried to hurry inconspicuously. He called her to stop, so that everyone turned to look.

'Take the basket with the tea things. You can't go back empty-handed.' Helen returned and did as she was told, looking away from the bleeding heap and hating her father for calling her back. She was sure it was on purpose.

'Let's go,' said John to William while attention was turned to Helen.

'Let's slip away. Now. Let's get the boxes and make a canoe.'

Mouse harvest, thought William. The words stuck.

'I'm coming.'

They walked slowly out of sight round the decapitated stack and, keeping it in line of sight between themselves and the men, retreated across the field, at first cautiously and then breaking into a run. They scrambled through the hedge oblivious of tearing thorns.

'Mouse harvest,' said William. 'They were all alive.'

'They weren't alive,' said John with certainty. William was not convinced.

They worked their way across another field and onto the lane. They passed the familiar tree with the fluffy pears. Their mother had told them they were quinces. They were a bright strong yellow now, with flecks of tobacco brown where they touched each other or rubbed the branches. William picked one and sniffed and nibbled at it as they walked. The scent was overwhelming and rich. The passed the pond, noting the rings in the water as unseen birds scrambled up the banks. Footmarks starred the water's edge. The water was clear and undisturbed. A frog jumped in lazily, belly-flopped and dived. It was irresistible. They hurried on to the end of the lane to where it died between two far fields. Beyond the largest of these lay the woods. It was ploughed now, waiting for the iron harrow and for seed. They skirted it, one foot in the furrow, one foot in the margin, one-legged boys making for the gap in the hedge. Bramble leaves were red as fire now, holly berries suddenly bright. The overwhelming impression was of yellow, with here and there the virulent green of a patch of nettles. The chestnuts in the wood were orange-brown and gold. Silver birches scattered golden guineas. The mulch rustled with the first loose leaves. They moved stealthily. William picked up an occasional chestnut that the squirrels had missed, but John frowned at him and motioned him to hurry. They paused at the break in the woodland to take stock and listened like animals, heads turned in the breeze. Hearing nothing, they ran swiftly across and into cover.

'Wait,' said John. 'Listen.'

They listened. Far away there was the drone of a vehicle, irregular, moving over heavy ground. It was not a tractor but something lighter and less powerful. Nearby there was only the silence of woods, a solemn and wary emptiness.

They moved forward, avoiding branches. The ground favoured them. It was soft as rags. They soon approached the clearing. The seat boxes and table were there but it was deserted. The boys picked up empty Camel packets from the beaten mud, looked inside, sniffed them, wondering at the rich smell, and thrust them in their pockets as treasure trove. The place felt like a house and they felt like thieves.

'Let's get into a hut,' said John. William nodded. The place was too private. They moved cautiously to one of the hexagonal huts. The door was open and restrained on its hasp with a piece of stick through it. They looked down the row. An avenue had been cut through the trees and was grassed and trim like a park vista. All the huts had their doors open for ventilation, they supposed. They slipped inside.

It was hot and dark even so. Steel boxes were piled up neatly on both sides leaving clear a central aisle which terminated in a ventilator on the end wall of the hut. This let in enough light for them to see that the boxes were of varying lengths but all in the same drab khaki with stencilled lettering in black or light olive. The hut smelled of oil and warm metal.

The cases were secured with catches that snapped fiercely up. John had to take one catch, William the other. They paused, listening, after the noise, then lifted the hinged lid. Inside were

172

shining belts of ammunition, gleaming brass in webbing straps. Bemused, they stretched out hands to lift it. This was Treasure Island, buried doubloons, unbelievable wealth and riches. It mesmerised them. The cartridges were surprisingly heavy and cold. They clattered together like the chirp of sparrows.

'Machine gun bullets,' said John. 'That's why they're joined together. Take them.'

They pulled a belt from a box. It seemed endless, like a magician's string of handkerchiefs, and John walked further and further down the hut with it over one shoulder while William fed it out. It trailed along the floor, rattling until it reached the door, then the end appeared and William grabbed it, walking towards John so that it was doubled up.

'It's empty now,' said William. John folded the belt upon itself one more time. It was heavy. He went back to the box. They peered inside. Within the metal outer case was a thin inner one. They lifted it together. It came out easily.

'This is what we need,' said John.

'I'm afraid,' said William. 'Let's go.'

'Don't be stupid.' John had already snapped the catches on another case. He picked up the belt and started off with it again. It ran out over the ammunition case as if he was dragging a chain. William dashed to it to lift it clear. The noise had been sharp, carrying. Together they emptied the second box as before, and again lifted out the tray.

They heard the noise simultaneously. It was the drone of the light vehicle, but startlingly near. William froze in panic.

'What do we do?'

'Keep quiet.' John moved to the door and peered out, looking to the left.

'Move back inside, just stay still.'

'I'm running for it.' William started off, regaining the use of his legs. John grabbed him.

'No!' They'll see you! They can't see you in here.'

'Who are they?'

'You'll see. Sh!'

They moved far back into the darkness, pressed against the cold metal of the cases. William saw that it was true, it was dark inside. They could not be seen.

A jeep moved past very slowly, droning up the grassy break.

They saw three soldiers, two in the front and one in the back. They wore uniform. The man in the back carried a shotgun and was aiming it skywards, swivelling gently. None of the men gave the hut a second glance. The boys remained where they were until the sound of the engine had died. They heard shots, voices, from the distance.

'They're out shooting,' said John. 'Get a liner. The thin thing. We'll take one of the belts of ammunition.'

'What for?'

'For fun!' John was already snapping the boxes shut again. William picked up the thin metal case. It was easy to carry. John picked one up as well and slung an ammunition belt over his shoulder. A swag of it clattered down. He tried to control it and failed.

'Carry the end,' he urged.

They set out, John first, bowed, and William behind holding on to the belt of bullets. They ran through the woods until they felt safe in cover just before their own fields. They sat down panting.

'We'll hide the ammunition here,' said John. 'Let's get back to the pond.'

They buried it between the grey roots of a beech, scooping out the soft brown mould with their hands. When they kicked leaves over the spot it was invisible. They made for the pond.

Clutton the seedsman was in the house. He was a comfortable-looking man with rosy cheeks and grey hair. He wore a tweed jacket and a yellow waistcoat and sported a gold watch chain.

'I didn't mean to drag you away from your stack!' he protested to Robert. 'I didn't know you would tackle it on a Saturday. I thought it would be a good day to introduce myself.'

'It doesn't matter,' said Robert. He was glad to get away.

'I should think the stack's a bit of a mess.'

'It's full of mice.'

'Well, harvest this year was wet, you know, and there was little enough time to deal with what there was, let alone threshing old stacks. It was fine immediately after, and it's been good since. Hot weather in between. Look at today. Anyroad, Jempson never got round to it this year, so it's stood a whole fourteen months.'

Margaret had introduced herself, asked Clutton if he would like tea.

He had accepted.

'What are you thinking of sowing, Mr Ellis?'

'Let's look at the plan.'

The plan was a yellowing piece of tracing linen that had been copied from the deeds during Jempson's tenure or earlier. On it each field was numbered and each size noted in ink. The rotations of previous years were pencilled on each field in Jempson's writing. In red pencil, the fertiliser applied had been lightly added, with quantities. Clutton nodded, he was accustomed to this and had seen the plan many times before. When Robert laid it on the table, Clutton smoothed it with a stroking movement, caressing an old friend. He relaxed visibly.

'Are we talking fertiliser as well as seed?' he asked.

'I suppose we are,' said Robert. He glanced at Margaret. Her face wore the anxious look she always had when purchases were being discussed. He hoped on the one hand that she would leave the room and let them get on with the business while on the other hand he wanted her attention and interest. His confidence in his decisions was far from absolute.

'The harvest this year gave oats and barley above average nationally and wheat a bit less,' said Clutton. 'It was in the papers a week ago, you may have seen it. The yields were all above pre-war level, but not much. It's still good. There was a lot of broken straw on the barley though, and that slowed things down. This next year I should say oats are a good bet and beans and some peas.'

He emphasised this by stabbing at selected fields on the map.

'And of course you need an acreage of wheat and mangold and potatoes. And some kale as well for those cows I see you've bought. That's what I should do if I was you.'

He ran his hand, palm flat, across the map again, soothing its wrinkles. It would be so easy, the gesture implied, if Robert simply followed his advice. They next discussed the merits of one field and another, how oats could go on a two-year ley without fertiliser but on the other fields would need a hundredweight of potassium nitrate per acre. How potatoes needed two hundredweight and three hundredweight of sulphate of ammonia, how the old mangold field needed lime to cleanse it and the wheat field nitrate of soda.

'Potash and nitrogen for potatoes and beet,' said Clutton roundly. It was a practised litany. 'That's what I say, and anyone will agree. You ask around. I understand this soil, you know, Mr Ellis. After all, I've been helping to look after it for fifteen years in this part and I've seen it come on, mark me. I've seen it come on well!'

Margaret had to leave the room to make the tea she had promised. She wanted to hear how much it would all cost, the seed and potatoes and potassium nitrate and potash, but hurry as fast as she did they were already shaking hands when she came back and put the tray on the table. She was angry but hid it. She sensed that Robert had hurried deliberately. Clutton looked immensely pleased with himself and was flattering Robert openly.

'Your husband is a rare farmer, Mrs Ellis!' he proclaimed, rising to his feet for her. 'He has a real grasp of fertiliser and seed. A lot of these old chaps round here have no idea about mineral fertilisers. If it ain't dung or lime it ain't no good to 'em and they don't know what's what. They don't move with the times. It's still soot and shoddy for some of 'em.'

'Have your tea, Mr Clutton.'

'Thank you, Mrs Ellis, I will.'

He sat down and produced a notebook from his jacket pocket. While she poured he wrote in it carefully and handed it to Robert

'Check it all through, Mr Ellis, for there's your order. If you just sign it on the bottom, that's that. It will be under way.'

She noticed that Robert hardly looked before signing it with a flourish. Clutton closed the book. It had a thick elastic strip on one side that he turned over the top to secure it with a snap. The finality annoyed and disturbed her. Clutton tucked it back in his pocket and stretched out for his tea.

The boys were balanced like acrobats. They sat on the bottom of the steel cases with their arms extended, legs pressed against the sides until they hurt. They hardly dared move. The cases rocked and wobbled treacherously. Very slowly each managed to lower his arms until they touched the water, dipping gently with one hand, then the other. The flat-bottomed craft skidded forward. William, in a panic, tried to stop himself from shooting into the green depths and instantly rolled sideways so that he fell out with a splash in the mud. John roared with laughter and nearly followed him. William trudged to the shallows, pulling the case.

'Shut up! I'm soaked! It's not funny!'

'Oh, yes it is!'

But he tried again immediately and succeeded. If they moved with the greatest care, with no violent motions, they could propel the cases right across the pond, then round and round. They held on to the branches of the willow and examined the nests of the waterfowl. They watched newts slide away as they approached, clawing their way into the green depths.

'How deep do you think it is?' asked William, trying not to sound anxious. The thinness of the cold metal on which he was sitting produced delicious fear. They could hear the sound of the threshing machine in the distance and the steady chuff of the traction engine. Men's voices drifted over from time to time. They lost all sense of the afternoon, dazed by discovery of water, of balance. Their legs trembled with strain. They were soaked from repeated sinkings. A moorhen appeared, pushing arrogantly across its territory, and they chased it wildly, falling into the water, then swimming, holding on to the boxes. The moorhen ran across the water on tiptoe and disappeared into the hedge, flicking its tail and clucking. A white butterfly alighted on William's arm, refreshing itself from a droplet of drying water. Mosquitoes danced in clouds in tree-clenched shafts of sunlight. The position of the sun alerted William. He felt cold.

'It's late!' he called to John. 'We'd better hide these and get back. What are we going to say?'

'Nothing. Don't say anything at all. Say we were walking.'

'We'd better get dry. We'll be in trouble.'

'Why should we be?'

'Because we were supposed to help.'

John snorted.

'He's got plenty of people to help!'

William knew this was not the point but said nothing. He

always felt sick at moments like these. He knew there would be confrontation and pain.

They pulled the cases to the shallow end and carried them into the adjoining field where they hid them in the hedge with a covering of tussocks.

'We'll go back to the house,' John proposed, 'then no one will know how long we've been there.'

They worked their way back towards the farmhouse by the hedgerows, concealing themselves with quite unnecessary care. Hazelnuts tempted them but they marked the spots between them and moved on. They returned by the wooden wall of the barn, listening. The noise of the machines was far away now. The barn doors creaked gently as the wood contracted in the first breaths of the evening breeze. There was coldness in it. A chicken clucked, settled. They were prepared for the attack this time, but that made it no less terrifying. The cockerel came running, more sure of itself after its first success. The boys fled, but it quickly caught up with William, beating with its wings as well, so that he stumbled and fell. It pecked his knees and thighs, holding on and tugging, its mad black eyes flicking with rage. William screamed, hit it in the body, scrambled to his feet and managed to get away. Margaret appeared, alarmed by the noise. She brushed William down, noting but not commenting on his damp pullover and trousers. The cockerel had made small red bruises wherever it had struck. There were two cuts where it had gripped his thigh. William clutched himself, sniffing.

'That bird doesn't like you,' she said. 'It will have to go. It runs at me too but I carry a broom.' She ushered them through the house and out to the front door, not allowing them to pause.

'You had better go out to the field right away and tell them its five o'clock, or almost so. The lorry will be along at half-past.' The boys looked at her, thinking they understood.

'It's all right, I shan't say you only just came in. Where have you been?'

'We were playing at the pond,' said John.

'I guessed,' said Margaret. She smiled briefly. A short flash of how she had been, before Pa.

'Did they have enough water?' asked William, hopefully, hopelessly. He knew the answer.

'Your father was angry about that. He had to come back to the house twice with one of the Germans. He wanted to know where you were. I said that you were around. You shouldn't have run off. You know it annoys him.'

'The mice were disgusting,' said William. 'They made us sick.'

'Yes. Helen said it was revolting. Were there really so many?'

'There were *millions*!'

'If you do a bit now and help with the tidying-up, he may forgive you for running off.'

She hardened her heart to them, watching the small figures plod grimly down the path. Heinz had come back with Robert each time. It must have been by his own choosing. He had pumped away while Robert filled the churns. He looked at the house whenever he felt that Robert could not see him. Margaret saw him from the house window on his first trip and knew she had been seen in turn. She fled from the window in panic, not letting him see her the second time.

Threshing had finished. The pile of waste straw stretched out like low downland and the site of the stack was no more than a brown rectangle of mud in which pale green stalks of weeds had struggled and died like worms. The prisoners sat on the straw or on the threshing machine or leaned on their forks. Taylor was cleaning and grooming the tractor engine as if it was a horse, patting it, talking to it. It hissed from valves and cylinders, the huge flywheel still.

Tester made his rounds with the oil can and an adjustable spanner, tightening here, loosening there. They all moved slowly, limbs heavy with exhaustion. Robert stood by the sacks of corn determined to show that the master could outmatch the men. No one looked at the heap of dead mice. As they reached the bottom of the stack, adult mice had fled everywhere, then rats. Paul and Wilhelm had chased them, whooping. Tester stamped those within reach with an expert boot.

'That was hard,' said Ehrich. 'I'll ache for a week.' He was lying on his back on the straw.

'Like a night with a Hamburg whore!' said Peter.

'Berlin,' said Wolfgang longingly, 'definitely Berlin!'

Heinz made the right noises but did not join in the laughter.

He could not take his mind off the farmer's wife. He watched Robert covertly, wondering what she saw in the stiff upright figure with the unsmiling face. He did not look a generous man. On the contrary there was a sharpness about his face that could be hard. Heinz had had enough experience of officers to think he was a good judge. There were plenty of Germans just the same, dictatorial, class-ridden, intolerant. If Robert had been a German, he told himself, he would probably have been a Nazi.

The boys came running to the man. Heinz saw he was angry with them.

'It's almost five!' said John, puffing. 'Ma said we were to tell you.'

'Where have you been?'

'In the house.'

'You weren't there earlier.'

'We were around.'

'You ran off when I needed you to get water. I'll talk to you both later. You can both go with the men to the lorry.'

Tester walked up to Robert, hands thrust in dungarees, very square.

'There's a belt missing.'

Robert stared at him.

'What?'

'One of the drive belts from the thresher.' Tester turned so that he was partly facing the prisoners. 'There's a belt gone. It can't have gone on its own. One of them has taken it.'

'What's up, old lad?' It was Taylor. He jumped down from the traction engine, immediately sensing the tension.

'There's a belt gone. One of those beggars has had it. It was there when I stopped the machine.'

Wolfgang had been leaning on his fork. He straightened himself. He saw that Heinz and Ehrich had got the gist of it, but Peter's face was content. Wilhelm sat up. Paul did not move but appeared to be listening.

'They steal leather for shoes,' said Tester. 'I've heard of it. Then they sell them to us.' His face was hard as a fist.

'Stand up!' commanded Robert. 'All of you!'

Wolfgang hissed at Peter. The men got up, but Paul was slow, truculent.

'Who does the bastard think he is?' he growled.

'Shut up!' snapped Heinz. 'They can make real trouble. Do you want to go home?'

'I'm not jumping for him.'

'Stand up at once!' Robert was angry and confronted Paul quickly. It was tactically and psychologically right. Paul coloured and got to his feet.

'Stand up straight. To attention!'

They made a line, Wolfgang hissing at them like a goose. Ehrich and Heinz each had straw wrapped around a leg. All of them were covered with chaff and dust. Robert walked down the line. He was in his element. Even Taylor was impressed. The boys stared from a safe distance. This was yet another dimension. Here was another stranger, but so fierce and confident that he made men afraid. John was proud of him. William felt awe. This Pa held himself upright and walked with a prowl.

'Who took the belt? Own up, and I will say nothing to your camp commandant. That belt is vital. You can't just take things. We are short of things too, do you understand?'

They stood in wooden silence. Robert stood still, looked to left and right down the row, folded his arms on his chest and waited. No one moved. Opportunist sparrows landed in the field and hopped to the threshing site, gorging themselves. The traction engine hissed ominously as though it disapproved. Taylor eased his cap back, straightened it again and propped himself against the thresher. Tester held his oil can as though it was a pistol and he would shoot someone. The silence extended.

'All right, you will stand here until someone owns up,' said Robert. 'You will not return to camp until I have that belt.'

Wolfgang was angry. Someone must have the belt. He knew he hadn't. He felt a sense of responsibility, but couldn't let his friends down. They stood. Taylor and Tester continued to dismantle the rig. They wound down the levelling gear on the thresher and Taylor rocked the engine so that the belt drive could be removed. The shadows were lengthening and the sun began to grow orange. The boys perched themselves in the straw and watched with fascination. Robert remained still, arms folded. His dignity transcended the absurdity of the situation. None of the men was inclined to treat it as a joke now. Heinz perceived that the longer this silence lasted the worse it would be for them all. He didn't have the belt. They must find out who did. He shot a sideways glance at Wolfgang, but Wolfgang was stolidly staring at the ground in front of him.

'Sir,' he said, 'if you leave us for a time we will find out if anyone has the belt.'

Robert's eyes turned to him, looked him over. Robert was thinking that he needed their labour, that they worked well. The man looked honest enough and had a plain craggy face. It was a way out and one he understood.

'All right. You have three minutes.'

He signalled to the boys and to Taylor and Tester. Taylor muttered darkly to himself but followed. Tester was inclined to stand his ground with his oil can until Taylor took his arm.

'Come on, boy. Give them a chance . . .'

'Give 'em a chance? I'll break his bloody neck . . .'

Nevertheless he allowed himself to be moved to the other side of the thresher where Robert lifted his shirt cuff and consulted his watch.

'I mean three minutes,' he said to Taylor.

'I hope they understand you,' Taylor responded with a sly grin, 'because they haven't a watch between 'em. Neither have I!' Tester snorted and gave a wolfish smile.

'All right,' said Wolfgang, 'he said three minutes, who's got it?'

'Not me,' said Heinz, 'that's sure.'

'Nor me,' said Ehrich. 'Search me, anyone. I'm not a fool.' Wilhelm was equally vehement.

'I can't work leather! What would I do with it! On my honour as a German!'

They looked at Peter. He coloured immediately.

'You're joking! You can't cook leather!' Wolfgang smiled drily. They looked at Paul. His face was angry. He stared at them challengingly.

'Why are you looking at me? I don't want this damned belt! I hope that English bastard rots!'

'So,' said Wolfgang, nodding his head eagerly. 'No one has it. This is a classic dilemma. What do we do? We don't know if everyone is telling the truth or not so we all turn out our pockets and after that we take off our clothes. I want my repatriation. I want it as soon as possible and I don't want any nonsense getting in the way. Above all I don't need another six months in England over something like this!'

Wolfgang turned his pockets inside out in front of them all, showing the others his few possessions, a box of matches, an English threepenny piece, a folded piece of paper, a bootlace. Heinz followed suit, turning his pockets out to reveal nothing but chaff and small pieces of straw, and his home-made knife.

'Oh shit, what's the matter with you!' It was Paul. 'Whose side are you on? This is pathetic. We are Germans and they are English. That man is our enemy. I have the goddamned belt. What do you want to do, turn me in? Is that all it takes to turn loyal Germans into traitors?'

Wolfgang looked at him. His monumental calm was ominous.

'Just hand it back, that's all. No one will say it was you. Just put it on the ground so that we all get home and no one gets reported. All right?'

'He's right,' said Peter.

'I don't need your advice!' snarled Paul. 'You're all in trouble. I shall report this at camp. I'll let people know.'

'Just put it down,' said Heinz.

Paul produced the belt from his trousers. He had it tucked from his waist so that it hung down his trouser leg. He flung it down on the stubble. Heinz bent down and picked it up. He placed it well away from all of them on strictly neutral ground. They waited in silence for Robert to return.

'Say nothing, don't look at anyone,' said Wolfgang.

Robert returned with Taylor and Tester. He saw the belt immediately, picked it up and handed it to Tester. Tester weighed it in his hand and looked at the line of men. His face was still angry. The machines were very personal to him.

'All right,' said Robert, 'this time I will say nothing to the camp commandant, but I do not want any repetition. If anything else at all goes missing I will report it as theft, is that understood? We are short of materials. We don't have things. It is a serious thing to steal. I know that you men make things with materials, but you must not take anything from this farm that we use. You may have wood that we do not use if you ask for it. There may be other things, but you never take anything without asking. I hope that is understood.'

The men said nothing. They stared stolidly ahead. Robert beckoned the boys.

'Take them down to the road to wait for the lorry.'

Heinz and Peter sat on the bank close to the hedge. It was dry and grassy and Heinz had taken out his knife to cut saplings. He whittled at pieces of wood. Wolfgang, Ehrich and Wilhelm stood or leaned on a gate. Paul sat apart. He had moved down the road in the opposite direction from which they expected the lorry and scraped at the dry earth by the roadside with a piece of stick, ignoring them. The boys hovered uncertainly. At first they had sat beyond Heinz and Peter but the bank was partly overwhelmed by the spread of cold shade. Now they stood up. They were supposed to wait until the lorry arrived so that the men could be officially handed over.

'You boys are in trouble?' said Heinz. He felt sorry for them. They were skinny, awkward, growing. They had the faces of children all over Europe. He had seen it worse in the East, he had seen it better in France. There wasn't a scrap of fat on them. John looked back at him sharply with hostile eyes. John reminded Heinz in some ways of Robert. It was William the younger one who glanced up quickly, with a slight smile. Heinz marvelled to himself at the situation, which could only have been possible on this island. Six men in the charge of two children. Six prisoners being herded back to camp.

'I was always in trouble when I was young,' said Heinz. Peter smiled politely, not fully understanding, but determined to be pleasant. He felt sorry for the boys as well. 'My father, he was a very *strong* man. I think the word is hard. He was always "talking to me later". Don't worry. Your Mr Ellis will be happy now that he has punished us. You will escape.'

Heinz had cut a straight piece of green ash.

'I will show you something that I did as a boy in Germany. I made them with my brothers. I was not as good as them, but good enough!' He grinned at the two boys. 'Brothers always think they are better than each other when they are only different. Right?'

William nodded, entranced. John said nothing, did nothing. Peter watched too. There was much of the child in him. Heinz cleanly cut off three lengths of ash stick, each about three inches long. He took the first one and cut one end on a curved oblique so that it tapered gracefully. He only took one cut. Next he ran the knife cleanly round the diameter of the stick an inch from the end, pressing it in firmly with his thumb. He stuck the knife in the ground when he had finished.

'This is the magic bit,' he said. He rolled the length of stick between the palms of his hands, pressing vigorously. He winked at William, stopped and slipped off the severed end of bark which formed a perfect green tube. The exposed wood was white as bone. He notched the wood carefully, looking at the result against the evening sky and slipped the bark back on. He passed the result to William.

'Blow!'

William took it eagerly and put it in his mouth, his small cheeks inflating. A shrill whistle burst from the pipe. Heinz smiled, slapped his knee. Wolfgang and Ehrich looked up from where they had been talking. Even Paul shot a covert glance.

'Make me one!' said John.

'Sure.'

'That's clever,' said Peter in German. 'Make me one too!'

'Baby!' said Heinz. 'The boy was first. I shall make myself one as well!'

He cut one for John that played two notes, then one for Peter that did the same, then another for William and finally one for himself. They peeped and whistled. Wolfgang, Ehrich and Wilheim joined them while Paul moved further away.

'I suppose you all want them?' Heinz demanded.

'Why not?' asked Wilhelm. 'They're good.'

'You watch now,' Heinz said to the two boys. 'If you watch closely you can do it for yourselves and for your friends. The angle must be right. It is not as easy as it looks. This is a German present to England, yes?'

'Yes!' William watched with care. Heinz carefully cut a longer flute for himself that played three notes. They all piped and shrilled. Peter lay on his back, laughing, making terrible sounds. Heinz played a tune, or part of it.

When the lorry arrived they trilled to a flourish and stopped, picking up their coats. The lorry driver leaned down to the boys.

'You've got a bunch of bleeding canaries here, lads!' he said. His mate laughed as if it was witty. 'What's your dad been giving them? Birdseed?'

The lorry drove off. The men hung onto the framework, playing. Heinz and Peter lifted a hand, waved to the boys. William and John waved back, cautiously. The lorry lurched down the road, the shrill piping dwindling in the evening air long after the lorry had disappeared.

'Was it all right to take things from them. And to wave?' asked William.

'I don't know,' said John. 'They *are* Germans.'

The boys sat down on the bank and blew their whistles for a bit, slipping off the bark tubes and replacing them. As the ash bark became soft with spit the shrill notes began to dwindle and the whistle became more of a fizz.

'I'm not blowing mine any more,' said William. 'I'm saving it.'

'We can make our own with a knife,' said John. 'We'll do it tomorrow.'

'I suppose we have to go back now,' said William. 'I hope Pa doesn't thrash us. I hope the canoes are hidden all right.'

'I don't care if he does thrash us,' said John defiantly. He did not fool William.

'Oh, yes you do. And I do.'

Robert hardly reprimanded them at all. He was cheerful and even elated. The stack was thrashed and the yield although of poor quality was good. He could realise his ambitions for pigs and chickens. He had brought the prisoners to heel, and as Heinz had foreseen it had delighted him. He told Margaret about it, how he had been firm and how he had kept them to attention. The boys said nothing. All in all, Robert said expansively it had been a good day, a day full of the real sort of rewards that life had to offer. He would get the chaff cutter going and what with that and chopped straw there would be plenty of cattle feed for the winter. The mangolds were more than enough. Robert sucked his empty pipe and stared at the fire that Margaret had earlier lit. Even the boys had been quiet, sitting in the inglenook toasting bread and then reading by firelight. Now they had gone to bed and there was the subdued hollow roar of draught in the chimney. Night sounds could occasionally be heard from its shaft. Owls, a far-off dog barking, even the cows not yet settled.

'This is how it should be, Margaret. Isn't it? You can't complain about it. Harvest home, a fire, a book . . .'

'It's fine, Robert.'

'Come closer.'

She moved obediently and he put his arm around her shoulder, letting it fall gradually until it cupped her breast. He stroked her while she sat motionless. With his hand he undid the buttons of her blouse and caressed her.

'What about the door?' she said. 'What about the children?'

'I'll shut it. I want to make love to you here.'

He locked the door and returned to her, taking off his trousers and then his shirt until he stood naked in front of her. Kneeling, he began to undress her impatiently, pausing to kiss her breasts fiercely before he pushed her onto the thin rug on the hard brick floor. He pushed himself into her with the same urgency, without whispering or caring, and she found it more erotic than anything he had contrived and threw her legs about him violently, clasping him as he gasped and collapsed.

William blew his whistle under the bedclothes but it would only hiss by now. He tucked it under is pillow for the morning. Helen was dreaming of Wilhelm and of Ann. They had gone to town, and they stopped to look in the window of a shop. It was a baker's but the window was full of dead mice that moved, of small pink limbs. A man walked behind the display and tipped on more from a sieve. The pile collapsed as slowly as crumbling brown sugar. She awoke and heard her mother and father going to bed. Their voices were quiet and calm. She slept again.

CHAPTER EIGHT

After the threshing the month passed quickly. The uncertain colours of late summer and early autumn made way for November in full warpaint. Ploughing gave way to harrowing and sowing. Hedges were gaunt and skeletal and the prisoners were put to cutting them with sharp hooks. The pale flesh of slashed wood shone everywhere. In the water meadow the cress died back to starveling green strands. Reeds whispered and rattled in the cold winds. They lit a fire in the evenings. The need for all six of the prisoners ceased and Robert was by now so conscious of his outgoings that he continued to employ only three to work intermittently on the fields and, increasingly, on the house. Margaret found that Robert had plans for it to which she had not been party. She was used as a sounding-board to corroborate his intentions, but did not protest too much. She was pleased to have any improvement.

As far as the boys were concerned, the big event was bikes. The problem of transport had so annoyed Robert that he had found and bought two so that he would never again have to drop everything to collect them at four o'clock. The bikes were far from new because the Government had cut production further but they were newly painted and had had new transfers applied to them. Each had a new bell, obtained perhaps from some pre-war stock, and the boys loved these and rang and rang at them. They could not have been more pleased with a Rolls-Royce.

Margaret took them out to the road early to teach them to ride. The flat straight that ran past the mangold field offered the best chance for beginners. Perhaps two cars a day passed that way, or a lorry delivering beer, or a farm cart. The hedges had been trimmed and the verges were even. Two holly trees marked the beginning and the end of the course.

'I'll hold the seat,' said Margaret. 'One of you at a time.'

'I don't need mine held,' said John. He was defiantly proud. 'I can manage.'

William said nothing, was glad to have help. He was frightened of the wobbly, oily contraption. The day was blustery and the gusts of wind were a further terror. A pale sun alternated with cold shadow that chased wildly down the straight road. Overnight rain had half-filled the ditch that ran down one side. It sparkled when the sun shone, ruffled by the wind. In the shade it looked ominous. William stood on his pedals and sat on the seat. To his alarm the bike fell sideways and he only just managed to return his feet to the ground in time.

'You can't hold it, Ma!' His cry was anguished. She had struggled with it and failed. His earlier first attempt at forward motion had already given him a skinned and bloody knee. John was managing better because he had longer legs and could reach to the ground with them when astride the crossbar. He had even managed to wobble from holly tree to holly tree like a circus performer on a tightrope.

'I can start you off,' said Margaret. 'I'll run with you as long as I can. When you're started you'll be all right. You have to learn.'

'Of course I want to learn!' William was upset. 'I just think I'll fall off!'

Margaret pondered the difference between them. John was confident and more capable, perhaps less aware of danger, while William was burdened by his anticipation. Nevertheless he continued. He seemed so small, the bike far too big. This was what she had hoped that life in the country would offer. It was real joy to her and she drew in great breaths of the fresh breeze as if it were the heady fumes of spirits.

'Come on then!'

She clasped the seat as he balanced and pushed off again. This time he started forward properly, the handlebars slewing with every effort. She watched his small legs pumping up and down and ran until she could no longer keep up, stopping with hands on hips to see him fly down the road.

'Not so fast!' she cried after him, panting for breath. But William could only maintain his equilibrium by pushing. He knew if he slowed he was gone. The faster he pedalled the better chance he had of survival. The dimension of speed he had achieved was undreamed-of and terrifying. Road and hedgerow hurtled past but he dared not brake, dared not do anything but push and push and hold the handlebars rigid. When a boisterous gust caught him unawares he could do nothing but hang on as the machine keeled suddenly sideways and he crashed head foremost into the ditch, flying over the handlebars into the water. The bicycle landed on top of him, hitting him on the head. He lay still for a few seconds, out of surprise more than anything else. The water was cold and he was soaked. He heard his mother shouting, coming nearer. Her voice was high and concerned. Nearer he heard John laughing. He lifted himself up. Margaret was pulling at the bike, pulling it from the ditch. He climbed out, covered with mud and water.

'Are you all right?' Margaret's face was anxious. Her hands ran over his knees, face, hands, over his head. He winced, and she felt again, examined the lump that was rising.

'You gave me such a fright!' she said. 'You were going too fast!' William felt proud at this. She was holding him. It was like old times. B.P. Before Pa.

'Is the *bike* all right?' he asked. They examined it together while John showed them *he* could manage by cycling up and down. At the next attempt William managed to cycle as well. He pounded backwards and forwards from holly tree to holly tree, knobbly knees flying, while Margaret smiled and turned her face to catch sun whenever it appeared. He knew how it must feel to fly, and he was fledged.

'We are going to build a bathroom,' Robert had announced, 'with hot and cold water.'

'Will it have an inside toilet?' asked Helen. Robert had laughed.

'Of course it will!' It made Helen feel stupid. She felt she was not to know what he meant. Margaret and Helen were delighted by the prospect but had no idea what it involved in a house which obtained its water from a well by pump and had no electricity. To Helen in particular, anything that would obliterate the disgusting privy would be an unbelievable joy. She was particularly embarrassed because the men also used it now they were working on the house. She was in it when one of them had come and rattled on the door. The door was solid enough and had a sound bolt, but she could see the feet and knew it was the one called Peter. She had been horrified and had shouted at him to go away. There had been an embarrassed mumble in German and the feet disappeared. Now she did not use it during the men's working hours, and was sometimes forced into the fields.

Robert had employed Heinz, Peter and Wolfgang to begin with. Heinz was an obvious choice as a carpenter was essential. Peter had lied and said he was a painter, insisting Wolfgang repeat the fiction when Robert asked if he had building experience. Wolfgang had had several jobs. He could claim to have been a motor mechanic, electrician and plumber at varying times. He said he could lay bricks. They all enjoyed the fiction of their enormous building skills. Robert was not entirely deluded. He guessed they were probably competent in some of what they claimed and as they worked well together he saw no reason to change them for other men. He still needed them on the fields occasionally as well.

'We'll be working up in the roof space today,' he announced to Margaret. The boys were outside in the yard, running the bikes surreptitiously through puddles to watch the water split under their wheels.

'We're going to try to strengthen the joists and get the tank up.'

'Are you going to work with them?'

'Yes.'

'What about the harrowing?'

A look of annoyance flashed across his face.

'I know about the harrowing.'

'You said it wouldn't wait, that's all. I thought I'd remind you.'

'Perhaps you could do it.'

He looked at her without expression. She was intended to retreat defeated.

'All right.'

Robert studied her face.

'You know you couldn't.'

'I think I could. I could drive the tractor. It doesn't need to be straight, not with the harrows. You don't drive it straight. I have to learn sometime. You've always said you want me to help.'

Outside she could hear sounds of sawing and hammering. The workforce had begun on their task, sorting and cannibalising old timbers from behind barns, from the stack of assorted wood that lay amongst nettles and dead willow-herb. Heinz was going to cut it to size and work it. There was no chance of obtaining new timber.

'You're serious?'

'Yes, I am.'

'I suppose this is because that fellow Baxter said you would be a good driver.'

She felt herself colour. She was surprised by her anger that he should throw that in her face. She wished she knew what to do. She felt like striking him across his wooden, stupid mouth. Instead she did nothing but continued to stare at him defiantly.

'All right then!' Robert clearly intended to teach her a lesson, 'You can get on with the harrowing. I'll set it up for you. Be ready in ten minutes. I hope you know what you're doing.'

He started up the tractor, watched by Margaret and the men. In the spirit of the occasion it refused to start until he had laboured the handle wildly. Sweat stood out on his forehead despite the blustery day and Robert grimly maintained a cheerful smile for the Germans. Heinz watched Margaret. She glanced at him, and he smiled at her covertly while Robert was stooped. She smiled briefly back. When the tractor finally fired Robert asked her if she wanted to drive it to the field, hoping to shame her in front of them, but she declined loudly. He drove off at speed leaving her to follow. The harrows had been left ready in the five-acre behind the stockyard and sheds. It was not far, but she was angry that he had not asked her if she wanted a lift on the tractor. She walked after him, seething but determined not to show it. She smiled again, at all the men, who stood looking at her not sure what to do or say.

'Good morning. I'm going to try the tractor.'

Wolfgang and Heinz replied in English. Peter, always rather awkward, touched the top of his head as though he was searching for a hat to lift, snatched it away and looked embarrassed. Margaret walked out of the yard by the back gate, her skirt flying in the boisterous wind. The boys chased her on their bikes, asking where she was going and then following, pushing them.

'Mr Ellis is not so kind to your lady-love!' said Wolfgang to Heinz. 'He should have given her a lift. She has to trail behind him.'

'She has such good legs!' said Peter. 'I like these windy days! I remember when we were in Lyons, the girls stood on the street corners so that the breeze would catch their skirts and we could see their knickers and garters! Those girls were something! But so quick!'

'Shut up, Peter!'

It was both Heinz and Wolfgang simultaneously. Peter grinned at them oafishly.

'He treats her badly,' concluded Wolfgang. 'She was keeping up a good face in front of us. And his boys are afraid of him. There's nothing much to him. Can't they see?'

'It's not our business,' said Heinz sharply. Peter gave a short roar.

'I don't believe *that*!'

They heard the tractor stop, then the clinking of chains. It started again, just beyond the sheds. They could see the puff of blue smoke.

'Easy on the pedal!' said Wolfgang. They heard it start, falter, regain strength, then proceed on an even note.

'I'd better get the saw going,' said Heinz. He wanted Margaret to succeed and was pleased. He hoped she flew up and down the field like a Valkyrie.

Robert, Peter and Wolfgang were stooped in the roof void where they had just hacked out a hole through the ceiling. It was warm beneath the tiles despite the cold wind and they could hear the drone of the tractor and the popping of the gas engine as though beside them. The hole was to form the access hatch for the tank. It had been the first visible manifestation of the new bathroom. The slightly rusty object had been purchased from Taylor and Tester complete with ball valve. This time they had not refused payment but had struck what Robert had thought was quite a hard bargain, asking a pound. Tanks, like everything else, were unobtainable so he had no choice, but it irritated him. Taylor and Tester both knew as did Robert that he would be back so he paid with a pretence of affability.

'A bathroom, eh?' said Taylor, lifting his cap and resettling it. He had agreed to deliver the tank as a sweetener. 'There aren't many of them hereabouts. I think Mr Ingleton and Mr Baxter are the only people I know with bathrooms. You'll be very modern, as they say. Next thing, you'll be needing copper piping and all the fittings, I expect. And a cylinder, and a pump and a generator for electricity and all that.'

'Yes, I will.'

'That's difficult. You can't get new copper or brass, you know. Not for love nor money.'

'Not for fish nor fowl neither.' It was almost the first time Tester had spoken during their transactions. He was blackened with oil as usual and wore his customary dungarees. He cradled the spindle and cogs from some machine in his arms. It still dripped oil.

'I thought you might have some . . .'

'Happen we have. I daresay we can look out what you want . . .'

'Thank you very much.' Robert started to make his escape. Something about the two men felt claustrophobic. Their buildings and yard were an entangled mesh, a web.

'It must be expensive, this internal sanitation,' said Taylor walking with him back to his car. 'Still, the ladies have to have these things, I dare say.'

Robert said nothing.

'The first thing you have to do is put something up there . . .' He pointed to the sky. 'And then you have to put a bigger thing there to hold it!' He pointed to the ground.

'A septic tank.'

'Aye, one of those. I suppose you are getting those Germans to dig it. I should say that will take a long time.'

Robert had not thought it out. He had been more concerned with supporting the weight of a tank in the roof and getting the thing.

'I can hire you a shovel attachment for your tractor. That will shift the muck a bit sharply. Make it into a bulldozer.'

And so it was. Bit by bit Taylor and Tester had become appointed as suppliers of everything except the bath, w.c. and pump. Taylor and Tester's terms were cash. Taylor told him so when Robert offered a cheque for the tank.

'Sorry, Mr Ellis, but we don't hold with cheques. We don't have an account, you see. That makes it no more than paper to us.'

Squatting in the roof space hammering a trimmer into place while Peter wedged up the other end, he thought how tight cash was becoming. He wondered how Margaret was getting on in the field but was damned if he was going to look until she had finished. She said she could do it, so let her. She had driven off steadily enough, but he wondered how well she managed to turn. He had bought two pigs, both saddlebacks, and he wondered if Margaret ever considered how he managed to pay for them. She did not know about the chicken houses and runs he had ordered or about the extent of his indebtedness. He had calculated everything out exactly. With a reasonable harvest next year they would clear their debts and make a modest profit. He had checked it again and again, sitting in the big barn in a shaft of sunlight. He wished he could tell her his plans so that she would admire his skill and organisation. He wished he had a little more money. He needed to be encouraged. He hammered violently at the large nails while Peter watched him, wondering what possessed the man. He only succeeded in bruising the wood.

The gas engine popped rapidly, stuttered and blew an occasional perfect blue smoke ring. The breeze snapped them up immediately. There was no pattern or rhythm to it although Heinz had tried to detect one. A belt from the drive wheel of the engine ran to a circular saw set in a worn wooden bench. The teeth glittered in the light, giving it a silver rim. Heinz picked up a rough section of wood, complete with its bark as felled. He could not tell what species it was, but it looked like elm and would be hard. He fed it carefully forward through the guides until the blade rang and sawdust jetted sideways. The transformation of the wood thrilled him as it always had. The blackened crust of bark fell away from one side, leaving the creamy white timber. The smell was slightly peppery and warm. It was elm. He turned the baulk over and ran through the other side. Sawdust had begun to form a fine fume in the air. He finished the remaining two sides and looked at the squared wood before adjusting the saw and splitting it into two joist sections. It was an irony in time of shortage to use elm for joist timbers. He set aside the finished lengths and picked up another rough length, turning it and looking down it for the best cut. This was work he understood and it brought a pang of recall of similar occasions in another place. As a lad he had worked just such a saw in his father's yard before he learned his craft. Hot, dusty work followed by plenty of beer, eyeing the girls. He recalled Margaret's smile. Brief but warm. What else could she do with her husband stooped there in front of her. This was all a dangerous game, but he knew he could not give it up. She enchanted him. God knows, he was sex-starved enough to fancy anything, but it wasn't just that, or her legs or breasts, although he wanted them. She was lonely and she was unappreciated, she was nervous. He finished sawing down the lengths and turned off the gas engine. It stuttered to a halt. He picked up a hand-saw and began to trim the ends. In his pocket he had the measurements for the timbers of the opening. He would work them in the shed and take them up prepared. He looked forward to cutting the tenons, to using chisels. He even had a short piece of familiar triangular carpenter's pencil that he had found on a ledge. It had been made in Germany, years, a lifetime ago, before the war. He drew on the wood with a square. With the engine and saw quiet he noticed the sound of the tractor, very close. The field in which Margaret was working was divided from the shed by only an elder hedge at this point. There were reassuring noises from the roof of the house. He laid down the square and pencil, determined to see how she was doing. The hedge was easily parted. He stepped into the heart of it, where it was dark. The elder leaves, red and green and brown at the same time, afforded perfect cover.

He watched the tractor approach and turn at the headland. Great drifts of leaves were flowing across the field and the harrows turned up a cloud of brown dust. It was at this point, as they drew away from him again and the dust cleared, that William slipped.

At first John and William had watched the tractor moving up and down, filled with admiration. John had become bored first and had cycled off, saying he might go down to the village. William had stayed on, putting his bike down by the gate. As the tractor and harrows turned away from him, he ran up behind and sat upon one of them. There were five zig-zags to the set, three in front and two behind. He sprawled on one of the rear pair, lying sideways at first, then on his front, watching the earth flow beneath him in a juddering stream. Then he tried lying on his back, holding on tight with both hands and with feet wedged in the frame. This way he travelled the whole length of the field while every fibre of his body shook and jarred and the clouds and sky reeled overhead. His mother didn't see him until she turned at the headland and glanced behind her to be sure the set had all taken up their places. She had immediately stopped the tractor, and climbed down white with alarm. William sat up.

'What do you think you're doing? I wondered what on earth it was! I looked round and saw this shape. I thought it was a sack! God, William, you gave me a fright when I saw it was you!'

'I just sat on them for the ride! They move very slowly.'

'Get off, it's dangerous.'

'It isn't really. You move off and you watch. Nothing can happen. Let me sit there!'

Margaret smiled. She came to him and put her arm around his shoulders, squeezing him.

'Where's John?'

'He's gone off somewhere on his bike.'

'All right then, but don't tell your father. Hang on tight!' And so he had ridden up and down in a trance of movement and vibration and dust until, careless with practice, his left foot slipped off the frame. In a second his leg was beneath the harrow, hauled along the harsh earth. In a second his shoe was torn off and stones ground into his leg. He screamed piercingly. Margaret turned immediately, yanked the tractor out of gear, and in two strides was beside the harrow, horrified. He had slid further so that most of his small leg up to the crotch had passed through a gap in the frame. She had no idea how Heinz got there, but he appeared beside her almost as quickly as she reached the harrow. She bent down over William, tugging at the harrow.

'No,' said Heinz. He carefully lifted the harrow from the free end, tipping it gently so that it was just clear of the ground. 'Can you move your leg?' he asked.

'Yes,' said William, 'I'm all right.' He looked green and frightened but to their astonishment he withdrew his leg without assistance and stood up. Heinz replaced the harrow on the ground.

'Do not move. You may have broken something . . .' But William stepped between the sections of the zig-zag and stood before them on his right foot. Margaret knelt beside him, examining his pale leg, starting at the foot and moving tenderly up to his thigh. Heinz turned and walked back up the field. He found and returned the missing shoe. He knocked out the dirt and undid the laces as he returned.

'There's absolutely nothing wrong with him,' Margaret said to Heinz. 'He's very lucky!'

'He should not have been on there.'

'I know. It was my fault. I let him ride on it.'

'It wasn't your fault! I slipped. It was mine.' William was quick to defend. Heinz smiled wryly and handed the boy his shoe. William's socks were smeared with mud. The clearance of the harrow was enough so that William had been bumped, not crushed. Margaret felt sick.

'Don't say anything to Pa!' begged William. He put on his shoe, struggled with the laces.

'We won't say anything to Pa,' said Margaret.

'I'll get back to my bike,' said William. 'Then he'll never know.'

'Are you *sure* you're all right?' Margaret's panic was abating.

'Certain.' William stamped his left foot, held up his leg and bent it to prove the point. Margaret nodded and smiled at him weakly. William walked off across the turned field. He felt shaky from shock although he would not have admitted it in front of the man. The two adults watched his retreat.

'I had better get back,' said Heinz, 'or people will want to know why I am here and they will ask.'

'Thank you.' She turned to him. He looked into her eyes carefully.

'Are you really so afraid of your husband? Is he such a dictator?' The directness of the question flustered Margaret. She stared at him in confusion.

'What do you mean?'

'The first thing that you worry about, you and the boy, is that he shall not know. I have seen that.'

'You had better go back,' said Margaret to avoid any further questioning. 'Thank you very much for helping. I couldn't have lifted the harrow.'

'He should not have been there.' He continued to regard her carefully. She found his concentration alarming. 'I was watching you driving the tractor. That is how I saw it happen.'

'You should be doing your work.' Margaret was painfully aware of her own emotions. She was aware of the old shirt she was wearing and the old skirt and shoes. She was dusty and dishevelled and without poise. She felt at a disadvantage in everything. When Heinz stooped and kissed her it was scarcely a surprise and for a moment she allowed him before turning away.

'You mustn't do that!' she shouted.

'I know,' he said. 'But I wanted to, and you wanted me to.'

He smiled at her, walking backwards away from her for several paces, a slow retreat. Then he turned and strode quickly to the hedge. He paused briefly at the gap and waved to her and was gone. Margaret climbed back onto the tractor seat. She felt suddenly cold and the muscles in her legs shook. She had not at once turned away. She had for a moment allowed a German prisoner to kiss her, had wanted it. She let the tractor into gear, roaring off too fast so that the harrows bounced and slewed, then moderated her pace. What would the future hold now?

When William cycled across the yard the cockerel flew after him, its ugly gargoyle head thrust forward, its beak gaping. William kicked out at it with his right foot, trying to keep his balance, and it flapped easily out of range, returning immediately to the chase. It followed him round the barn, legs pumping up and down and wings wide-stretched. William knew how he was going to deal with this. He cycled into the barn, half-fell, half-scrambled off his bike in the chaff and dust, and slammed the barn doors. The cockerel stopped in a flurry, confused. Its head darted this way and that, its wattles shook. William watched it through a gap in the timbers. He could hear the distant unsteady popping of the gas engine and the muffled peaceful drone of the tractor. From the house came the faint sound of hammering. There was no sign nor sound of John. He moved to the heap of bales and drew from a gap a length of wood that he had indentified over a week before as a useful piece. The first foot of it had been turned and then it became square in section. It had obviously formed the shaft of something before it had been broken off. He opened one of the barn doors slightly. The cockerel tilted its head and regarded him with malevolent eyes. William opened the door further, stepped forward so that he was exposed to view and hissed at the bird. He clutched the piece of wood firmly in his right hand. The cockerel dawdled uncertainly. William ran quickly along the side of the barn. The cockerel, assuming he had fled, gave chase. William shot round the corner out of sight. This was a place where tall nettles grew amongst rusting sheets of corrugated iron and tattered sheets of bird-netting. The cockerel hurtled round the corner, out of control. William hit it on the head with the piece of wood. He hit upwards, as if driving a cricket ball. There was a hard smack and the bird fell over. Its wings shivered and its legs kicked convulsively. William watched it, horrified at the plan he had executed so thoroughly. The bird's beak opened and shut. Its eyelid had closed over the one visible eye. William leaned back against the barn as if it might at any moment spring at him with renewed fury, but it was still. He leaned forward and poked at its body with the length of wood. The bird flopped. He moved its head about with the wood, up and down, side to side. The head was loose as a finger on a glove. He laid the piece of wood against the tarry side of the barn and cautiously touched the cockerel. When there was no reponse he slipped his hands under it to pick it up. It was astonishingly warm and he almost dropped it. He had somehow assumed that it would be cold. The head dangled down on the limp neck. He moved aside some nettles with his foot and pushed the body of the bird between two sheets of corrugated iron that formed a bridged hiding place. The nettles stung him as punishment. He tried to rearrange them. There was little sign of disturbance when he had finished. He walked back round the barn and replaced the piece of wood between the bales where he had first concealed it, then picked up his bike and wheeled it outside. He was elated and appalled at the same time. It was a terrible thing to do, but he could cycle round the yard in peace. He tried it, round and round, over and over. Nothing would be said about sitting on the harrows. He would say nothing, Ma would say nothing. Nothing would be said about the German kissing Ma. He would say nothing, although he had looked back and seen it through the hedge. He wondered if Ma would say nothing to him. He liked Heinz who made whistles. Nothing would be said to Pa about anything. Nothing.

He climbed on his bike and cycled across the yard past Heinz at the circular saw, wondering what Heinz would do. Heinz looked up and gave him a wave and grin. All was well. Heinz stooped again to his task, making the blade sing. William pedalled quietly out of the farm and onto the road. He saw John, in the distance, and shouted and waved. John waited for him and they both moved on, looking for unfamiliar territory. The network of lanes seemed endless and it was easy to get lost, but just as easy to return since all the lanes seemed to lead to three crossroads.

'Where have you been?' demanded William.

'Down in the meadow. And I've found a sand pit.'

'Where?'

William followed him. It wasn't much of a pit, more a digging beside the road, but it exposed pure yellow sand between vanilla slices of palest cream. They laid down their bikes and scrambled up it, making sand slides. William regarded his knees with satisfaction.

'It stains you yellow!'

Flopping down on the top of the slope, they discovered Tom and George with a bundle of snares. Tom carried the wooden pegs in one hand and George had the bright brass wires. The boys stared at the gnarled men, ready to flee.

'How do!' said George. He moved the wires slowly behind his back. John's eyes had picked out a snare set in the grass. The top of the sandy area was riddled with rabbit holes. He rightly guessed they had no right to be there.

'You'll be the Ellis boys,' said George.

'Yes,' said John, giving nothing away.

'We're setting snares. Want to see how it's done?'

John, the bold one, nodded and advanced. William more cautiously trailed behind.

'You don't want to go galloping about up here now. You see them tracks, there's a snare in near every one. You get your foot in that and you'll come down a right cropper!'

George took them from place to place, while Tom nodded, watching them suspiciously, fearing their discretion. George showed them the lethal wires tucked amongst brambles and in long grass and ferns. He showed them how he draped moss around the nooses, bent down grasses and secured them with twigs.

'Now you lads mustn't say anything, mind,' he insisted. 'We ain't supposed to be on this land even though its overrun with rabbits. It's called Coney Warren, see. Coney is the old name for rabbits.'

George sat down.

'How do you like farming?'

'It's alright,' said John.

'Your Da is making a right go of it, I hear, what with buying cows and pigs and chicken runs and doing up the house. Old Jempson never did that. Old Jempson never had the money. So he said. Some said he was just mean, some said his missus was mean. He always paid us well enough if we did summat.'

'You worked on our farm?' John was surprised.

'Oh aye, off and on when we was needed. We've worked on every farm hereabouts.'

'That's true,' assented Tom.

'The thing with farms,' said George, 'is that you mustn't plough in everything you've got, not all at once. You must take it gentle, always keeping enough back. You must always do like next year will be bad, because like as not it will. You should tell your Da that. He's running at it slap bang, I say. Now that's all right if you can afford it, but who can these days?'

The boys ignored the hanging question.

'You boys hungry?' George suddenly asked.

'Maybe,' said John cautiously. George laughed.

'You wait and see!' He felt in the pocket of the ancient jacket he was wearing and produced a penknife which he opened to reveal a long blade. To their astonishment he plunged it into the ground and began digging vigorously around the base of a fern. He quickly pulled out a brown rhizome, brushed of the earth and scraped at it with the knife blade, revealing pale flesh.

'That's a fern nut,' he said. 'Some people call them pig nuts.' He put it in his mouth and chewed it, meanwhile digging out another which he offered to John.

'They're better roasted. When I was a boy we would get a whole basketful and sit and eat them like they was roast chestnuts. We put them on a shovel over a fire.'

John bit his. The taste was earthy, nutty, but with a sharp quality and pleasant. He nodded.

'It's all right.' William held out his hand for one. It was a peace offering to say nothing about the snares. The boys fell to digging with their fingers while George told them how they might never go hungry if they knew where to look. He told them where to find the nests of snakes in dunghills, and where to find lizards in the sand behind them. He told them what fruit made the best wine and how he could find water with a hazel stick and how Tom was the best 'twitcher' for miles around, and how Stimpson's mill had blown up when he was a boy because old Stimpson had paused to light a pipe and the dust had ignited like gunpowder. This was all as it should be to the boys and they listened entranced.

Robert was pleased with the works in the roof. The opening was neatly trimmed at last and Heinz had made a frame and a hatch to fit it. It was expertly made with mortice and tenon joints. The hatch was formed of planks he had sawn and 'V'-jointed with a plane. They were manoeuvring it into place, kneeling on the new bearers they had inserted to spread the load of the tanks.

'After this, we'll get on with the bathroom itself,' he announced. The men nodded. Heinz had a mouthful of screws. Wolfgang and Robert and Peter were holding the frame in position while Heinz leaned over the hole awkwardly, inserting them overhand. The frame was large as they had to get the tank in through it. 'You are the plumber, Wolfgang . . .'

'*Ja.*'

'I'll have to get back out to the fields. There is more cultivation, manure must be spread, do you understand? You will have to manage more of the work on your own.'

'It is all right,' said Wolfgang. 'You tell us what to do and we do it.'

Heinz drove home the last screw, puffing with effort. He slapped the frame affectionately.

'Finished!'

Before anyone could move he had swung agilely down through the opening so that he was dangling by both arms from the frame. He kicked himself back and forth, grinning.

'It is strong enough, I think!' Peter laughed, Wolfgang was smiling.

'I hope you break your neck,' he said in German. 'Show off!'

'What was that?' asked Robert.

'I said he shows off!'

'Do you enjoy your work here?'

Wolfgang was solemn again.

'We do. It is good to get out of the camp. There the waiting seems very long . . .'

Heinz let himself drop to the floor below. He placed a pair of steps beneath the opening for the others. They viewed their efforts with pride from below.

'Now you must come down and have a cup of tea,' said Robert, and ushered them into the living room. He was pleased with the way they worked; the physical intimacy of working together in the loft had broken many barriers. The prisoners stood awkwardly at the entrance to the room looking at the domestic interior as though it were a museum set and they must stand beyond some rope and stare at it. It was now years since any of them had seen a room with furniture. They looked from rug to chairs to sofa, to the fireplace with its mantel decorated with plates and pewter, to the curtains at the window and the

October leaves that Margaret had arranged in a vase with sprays of green ivy. Peter's eyes filled with tears and he wiped at them hopelessly, turning away.

'Sit down,' said Robert, not noticing. Heinz swallowed, Wolfgang looked at Robert for reassurance that they could cross the invisible divide and enter this set. They were all dusty. Cobwebs from the roof space stuck to their clothes. Robert interpreted this part of their hesitation correctly

'Don't worry, the covers get more dirt than that . . .'

Wolfgang took the lead and perched on the edge of an armchair, wiping his hands on his trousers as if this would make some difference. Heinz sat on the sofa, Peter on a wooden high-backed chair.

'It was hot up there,' said Robert. 'We all need our tea.' He left the room to find Margaret already in the kitchen with a singing kettle.

'That's good,' he said, 'we all need big mugs. You'd be surprised how hot it is in the roof.' He paused, aware that he had been clumsy.

'How did you get on?'

'I got on all right.' Her manner was frosty. 'I got about half the field done. Why don't you come and see it?'

'I will. As soon as the men have gone.'

His response was too quick. She wondered why his work in the roof was suddenly so more deserving that hers in the field, but bit on her anger. She felt nervous about encountering Heinz. It overrode everything else.

'How many are there?' she asked.

'Three of course. And me.' He looked puzzled. 'How many did you expect?'

'Three.'

Robert shrugged and went back to the men. She despised his impatient gesture. Leaving the kitchen quickly and silently, she mounted the stairs and entered their bedroom. She looked at herself candidly in the dressing table mirror, turning Robert's photograph flat with a smile of satisfaction. She wanted to see what Heinz had seen of her and was amazed by her own excitement. She felt no guilt.

The woman she regarded had black, blown hair and gleaming dark eyes. Her khaki shirt was one of Robert's, loose

205

at the neck and tight round the breasts, revealing. Her skirt was old brown tweed, cinched in at the waist but full at the knees. She had become tanned with her time out of doors. On impulse she applied a touch of her jealously guarded lipstick to her forefinger, wiping it across her lips so that it was almost invisible. She could not remember when she had last put on lipstick. She could hear the men's voices rumbling in stilted fashion downstairs. She liked the extra colour she had added and felt that she must look good. There were lines of weariness below her eyes, that was all, but they added to rather than detracted from her face. She stood Robert's photograph upright again, pipe in hand, moustache on lip, teeth too white, and left the room.

In the kitchen she poured tea into four pint mugs then went to the pantry, bringing out a stoneware container which held their meagre sugar ration. She decanted some of this into a bone china bowl, stuck a teaspoon into it and loaded everything onto a tray. She was perfectly well aware as she carried the tray in front of her that her skirt was close-fitting.

The men leapt to their feet. She put the tray down on a low table.

'Here is your tea,' she said. 'Would anyone like sugar? You can have one spoonful as you've all been working hard.'

She saw an angry scowl flit across Robert's face and was glad. She saw delight in the faces of Peter and Wolfgang. Heinz watched her intently in a way she liked. He looked at her mouth as he took his mug of tea and thanked her with a smile. She thought he had noticed, and was pleased. Robert talked to the men in a determined and rather ponderous fashion.

'Where are you from?' he asked each of them.

'From Schramberg,' said Wolfgang. 'Near Freiburg.'

'From Magdeburg,' said Heinz.

'Wurzburg,' said Peter.

Margaret watched the men's faces and wished he had not asked. Each reply brought a flicker of pleasure followed by a withdrawal as memories were aroused. Magdeburg, Wurzburg, where are any of us, she thought, except within ourselves at any time trying to get by? These places might as well be craters on the moon. She wondered how cratered they were, had no idea. She wondered how Robert would answer if he was asked where he came from.

She stood holding the tray awkwardly, not knowing what to say. Robert was explaining his plans for the farm to Wolfgang, telling him he was going to build up a pedigree herd and set up egg units. He had never talked to her of his ambitions in the same lucid way. She listened, smiling now and then when one of the men glanced at her. She knew they would rather that she was involved in the conversation and were sensitive to her exclusion. They finished their tea and stood cradling their mugs. She approached them with the tray, first Peter, then Wolfgang and finally Heinz. He looked at her intently again and she was astonished by her own reaction. The tray shook and the mugs slid to one side. Heinz caught it and gravely held it with both hands. He then offered it to her. She muttered thanks and fled. It suddenly seemed improbable that she had been kissed by this German man, and had allowed him to, however briefly. First Baxter, now Heinz. She was no different in any way from what she had always been. Except that she now had Robert with her. When she had lived in anticipation of him, she had been, she supposed, both withdrawn and obsessed by him. Perhaps this had presented a formidable front, given her an aura of unapproachability that now had slipped. Was her dutifulness so obvious? If others could see it, could Robert? He never seemed to notice.

'The men are going now,' said Robert, sticking his head round the kitchen door. She was drying up the mugs and hanging them from hooks set in a shelf over the sink. 'Where are those boys? They're supposed to be here to take them down to the lorry. I have to get on. Where's Helen for that matter?'

'I don't know where the boys are. They went out on their bikes. Helen's out with Ann Baxter.'

'I don't like the Baxters.'

'She has to have friends. You don't like Tom Baxter.'

'I certainly don't. Why should I!'

He turned angrily and left.

'Come and wait outside,' he said to the men. 'The boys should be here soon. If they don't turn up, I will take you down there and you will have to wait on your own.'

Wolfgang nodded.

'We can do that.'

'I know, but I am supposed to make sure you are accompanied.'

Heinz had been waiting for a moment to ask a question.

'Mr Ellis, there are some short pieces of elm left over from the work. We can make things with them. Can I have them?'

'Yes. Of course you can.' Robert always seemed to expand when being magnanimous.

'Thank you.'

'Get them now if you like.'

Heinz walked round the side of the farmhouse under the walnut tree. To his right was the privy, which he could faintly smell, and ahead and to the left was the gas engine and saw bench. His route took him round the rear of the house, past the kitchen door. He saw Margaret, as he had also planned, and stopped in the doorway. She put down the cloth she was using and they looked at each other.

'Why are you here?' she asked.

'I am getting some pieces of wood. That is what I have told your husband. It is true that I want the wood, but I have come to say that I am sorry if I alarmed you. You are beautiful, you know. I could not help it. You will not tell your husband?'

Heinz was anxious. She considered frightening him by saying that of course she would, but dismissed it. Instead she simply replied no.

'If he reported me, I would never be allowed to come here again,' said Heinz. 'I would be locked up. They would probably not allow me out for farm work. They might keep me for longer.'

He had advanced slightly through the kitchen door in his anxiety. Margaret's heart was wrenched by his face. The man had disappeared, to be replaced by the concern and helplessness of a boy.

'I won't tell him,' she soothed.

'You are wearing lipstick,' Heinz observed. He was watching her lips. She licked them unconsciously in response. He grasped her hungrily and she responded. He crushed her briefly to him and hard, then he darted out of the door and stood outside a few feet away.

'I am going to get the wood now. I must not be too long. I will see you tomorrow!'

208

He smiled and blew her a kiss with his fingers and was gone. She closed the back door and leaned against it, defending herself from the assault of her feelings. When Heinz reappeared round the front with his pieces of wood, Robert was holding forth about the well and float switches and the need for electricity, which would arrive next year. He no more than glanced at Heinz and his pieces of wood.

John and William were coming back late out of sheer boyish uncaringness. They had been reluctant to part company with Tom and George and their heads were stuffed with marvels. They had the road to themselves and were cycling abreast, trying in short bursts to manage without handlebars. When they saw Jempson leaning on the gate and staring at the cows in the field, their first impulse was to turn and flee the other way, but that would have meant an immense detour and real trouble.

'Keep going!' urged John. 'Just go right past.'

Jempson had heard them from afar, however, and as they pushed towards him stood in the road and hailed them. They were forced to brake and stop, holding their bikes like defensive weapons.

'Hello, lads. I was admiring your Da's new cows. They're a fine bunch of animals.'

The boys watched his adam's apple slip up and down his thin throat. He looked cleaner than they remembered him and paler as though he had blanched from lack of weather. There was nothing now to mark him out as a farmer, and this was disconcerting.

'I have come back to have a look, you see, and you've caught me at it. I do, from time to time. I've seen those Germans working. I see you've had the old stack threshed. I bet that was a right one!' The boys shifted from foot to foot, moved their handlebars and scrunched gravel with their tyres. Jempson's talkativeness embarrassed them. He gestured to the fields, to his former domain.

'I can't get accustomed to it, you see. I don't suppose lads of your age would understand that. When I wake up in the morning where I am I hear old cock crow across the way and I think I'm back in that old house.' He paused, lost in his memories. 'Tell me, what has your father planted?'

The boys looked at each other. They knew only vaguely because it had not seemed important to them. There had been sacks of this and that and they had run their hands through it, watched it being sown, but had not made a record of it.

'Oats and beans,' said William. He particularly remembered the shiny white beans, hard as flint, with purple-black eyes. They had tried to chew them but found them vilely bitter.

'What else?' asked Jempson.

'Some wheat,' said John.

'But mostly oats and beans,' pursued Jempson.

'A few potatoes and some kale or something,' added William, 'but I think it was mostly oats and beans.'

'That man Clutton has no cause to do that,' said Jempson. 'Him and his beans. He has been selling the things round here like dandelion seed. It's bad. What sort of price will they fetch, eh? Just because the Ministry decides!'

The boys looked at him, uncomprehending. They shuffled again. The man seemed to have lost his power at the same time as he had found this garrulousness. The earth-strider, the farmer, had become a middling-old man who was anxious.

'Don't tell your Pa I've been looking, he won't understand and he might think I was watching him, but I ain't, I'm watching the land. You don't see what I mean, do you? It's nothing to lads. Ingleton has beans as well and so has Mary Merrow and West and Fairbrass and Merchant and half of Suffolk, but they has them in *moderation*. I expect I should have them in moderation if I was still here. Aye. Anyhow I hear your Pa has a couple of pigs.'

'Yes.'

Jempson nodded slowly.

'That's good. Can't go wrong with pigs. At least they eat better than beans. Can always feed 'em on the things. You see how I was leaning on this gate. It's a strange thing now, but I could no more put my feet on that land than I could walk into Buckingham Palace. That's how it is. It would be trespass now, and I should feel it and yet I tilled every parcel of that stuff for all my life! You boys had better go. Don't listen to me.'

Jempson returned to the gate to stare at the cows. He didn't look back. The boys pushed off as fast as they could and escaped.

Arriving at the rear of the house they noticed the saw was idle and were aware of their lateness. Heinz had neatly brushed the sawdust into a heap in a corner and the machine was clean. They walked as silently as possible round the back to the barn where they would leave their bikes.

'No cockerel,' said John. William said nothing. He would like to have told John what he had done. His guilt was enormous. He would have liked to tell John he had seen the German kissing Ma. But there was a devil in John that he did not trust. He might run to his father, enjoying the power of betrayal. William felt sick and belched. They stacked their bikes against the bales and began walking towards the house.

'You go ahead, I just want to look at the pigs.'

John shrugged.

'Afraid of Pa?'

'No!' John walked on. William went directly to the hollow place between the iron sheets. He could not account for his actions and it troubled him. He had felt a sudden anger coupled with curiosity but had never felt a desire to hurt.

There was nothing there.

He was filled with cold fear. His father must have found it and the crime was out. He put the sheets back noisily, looking around, but nothing seemed to have been disturbed, the nettles had not been flattened. He guessed, prayed, that a cat had taken it, or a fox. Then, if it was discovered, they would be blamed. He must hurry to the house.

When he entered, his mother ushered him quickly through to the front.

'He's waiting. They've been waiting some time.'

His father was angry at their lateness. John stood silent and blank-faced. William didn't care about that. Nothing was said about the cockerel. He felt enormous relief.

They sat with the men on the customary stretch of bank. The Germans seemed inclined to laugh and joke amongst themselves and it seemed that Heinz was the butt. Peter pushed at him and slapped his back. Heinz was red-faced and becoming increasingly annoyed.

'What are they talking about?' John asked, as if William would know. Heinz turned impatiently from the others, with sharp words, and came over to the boys.

'I will make you whistles again?' asked Heinz.

'Yes please!' said William. Heinz cut a stick and began. He extended them to three notes and was pleased. They worked reasonably well, and the other men seemed to have quietened.

'You will be musicians when you grow up!'

'Not likely!' said John.

'We can show you something,' said William. 'Something to eat.' It was a gift in exchange for a gift, but John was angry.

'That's a secret!' he said.

'No! Nobody said it was!'

He was angry with John because he could not tell him about the cockerel.

'You should not show me if it is a secret,' said Heinz solemnly.

'I will!' said William and seizing Heinz's home-made knife from him he plunged it into the ground and dug out the root of a fern that he had seen. He scraped at it just as George had done and offered it to Heinz.

'Here you are. You can eat it. It's better roasted.'

'Thank you,' said Heinz gravely, accepting it. John moved away angrily. The three men were all touched. It was a second kindness in their barren lives. Sugar in their tea, a shared secret. They did not underestimate either.

The lorry arrived a little late, and the driver smelled of beer, so there was no doubt why.

'Lucky bastard,' said Peter to the others as they stood in the back.

'Let's have a go at the turnip wine this evening. It has to be improved by now.'

'Why?' asked Wolfgang, laughing. 'What's the wood for, Heinz?'

'Carving. It will soon be November, then it will be Christmas. Perhaps I can carve something to send home. I thought I would also carve something for the farm boys.'

The wind was cold. They wore their coats and had the collars turned up. It was getting dark and as they passed under trees the dying leaves rattled and scattered.

'I think it is the mother you want to impress!' said Peter mischievously.

'Shut up! You said too much in front of the boys.'

'They don't understand German.'

'Just keep off the subject, understand?' Heinz was suddenly angry. He held onto the steel frame of the lorry with one hand and waved his fist in Peter's face. His eyes were blazing. Wolfgang had never seen him like this. He intervened.

'Look, we're sorry. We had no idea it was so serious. Peace! All right?' Heinz lowered his fist, relaxed by stages.

'All right. But no more.'

Wolfgang had been going to tease him about the gnarled pieces of elm, which reminded him of the episode of the turnip, but thought better of it.

They arrived to a camp that seemed vibrant with subdued excitement. The usual noises had ceased. The sound of radios was muted.

'What is it?' Peter wondered aloud. They found out as soon as they reached their hut. Post had arrived. Ehrich had it, a brown envelope each for Peter and Heinz. They took their letters and separated. Heinz sat on the edge of his bunk turning it round and round in his hands, examining the outside, savouring and prolonging the moment before he opened it. He felt both excitement and fear. The contents could be anything, exultation or destruction. He smelled the paper. It had a sharp tang, mingled with glue. He examined the stamp and the postmark. The postmark was Magdeburg, the stamp was an Allied occupation stamp, five pfennigs, a yellowy-green. He had never seen one before.

'Look like official stamps, don't they?' It was Walther, the elderly man from his bunk to the right. 'Go on, open it.'

'Did you get one?'

'Yes.'

'Good news?'

'I don't know. A bit of both. My brother is alive, my mother died.'

'I'm sorry.'

'It's all right. Things go on, wherever you are. We are to be allowed to write a postcard every month, they say.'

Still Heinz hesitated. The writing on the envelope resembled his mother's, but he had to confess to himself he could not be sure. In such a short time he had already forgotten Inga's hand. Her writing had always been immature. She even wrote with her tongue protruding, the pink tip forming the words around

213

her lips. He slit the top of the envelope gently, and extracted a single sheet of coarse brownish paper that might have been used before the war for wrapping Wurst. Glancing first at the other side, he saw that the signature was his mother's. With thumping heart he read the letter, crouching back in his bunk so that his face was invisible to others. Above him he could hear Ehrich moving, but he said nothing. Had Ehrich had a letter?

'Dearest Heinz,

I cannot tell you how relieved I was to get your postcard and to know you are alive and well. I see you are in English hands in a prisoner of war camp and I am now able to write back. You understand of course that things here are changed and not as they were. We are in the zone of occupation of Russian forces as you may know. Your father has trouble with his heart but otherwise is well. Inga is not here but has gone to Hamburg. When I write to you next, I will try to give you news, but for the moment I do not have her address. If I get it, I will ask her to write to your Camp 78 direct and then you will get two letters if you are allowed to receive them. I hope you have enough to eat. Please write as often as they let you. Let me know when next you write when you expect to come home.

All our love,
Mum and Dad.'

Heinz read it through again and stared at it with tears in his eyes. So much was unsaid! She had taken such care to get it past whatever censors the Russians used. No news of Inga! Even if they obtained Inga's address he doubted if they would send it in the post to him, because then the Russians would know it as well. How was he to answer? How could he tell them when he was coming home? How starving were they, that they asked if he had enough to eat? In every line he could read volumes. Despite himself, he sobbed.

'Easy down there,' said Ehrich. 'Are you all right?'

'I'm all right.'

'We all got our letters earlier. Those that got them. Some didn't. You aren't the only one, Heinz.'

'I'm all right! It just says so little!'

'It's only the first letter. It's a start! Was it bad news?'

'No. It was just no news.'

'I know. Mine was the same.'

214

'You won't be going back to the Russians!'

'Will you go back to Magdeburg?'

'We aren't given the choice. You go back where you came from. The Allies agreed.'

'I suppose we do.'

'And she doesn't even know where I am. All she knows is that I'm in England, in Camp 78. This is just cruelty!'

'We aren't very popular just now, you know. We are cut off from things in here but every day the War Trials go on. It is a steady drip of poison. The German people count for little more than dogs. Perhaps we are lucky to be in here for a bit. Perhaps things will improve.'

'My daughter says that people are starving,' said Walther. 'There is very little food. There is hardly any medicine. We are the lucky ones, I think.'

'Let's get out the turnip wine!'

It was Peter of course. He too was clutching a brown envelope, but being Peter he had ripped it when opening it.

'Everything all right?' asked Heinz.

'Everything is just fine!' said Peter. His voice was uncharacteristically strained. They did not question him further. 'Come on!' he said. They followed him to his locker, bringing their mugs. He unlocked it and pulled out the oil tin, took out the cork and air lock. They sat on his bunk and held out their mugs while Peter dispensed the yellowish liquid. They drank eagerly.

'God!' said Ehrich. 'I'm surprised that it doesn't strip the enamel!'

'It's improved,' said Peter. 'More alcohol.' He stood upright. 'We must get Wolfgang.'

'I'll go,' said Ehrich.

'No, I'll go,' said Peter. 'Just let me have a few.'

Peter drank one mug followed by another. Its effect was almost immediate. They all drank some more.

'What did your letter say, Peter?' asked Heinz. Peter looked at them lopsidedly.

'My brother was killed, in the last three days. And my mother. She was killed. By a horse and cart.'

The others stared at him.

'That's right. All around her there was war going on. Bombs,

215

tanks, buildings falling in. She was knocked down by the milkman's horse. It panicked when planes came over. The cart ran over her.' He poured himself yet more and drank almost without noticing. 'She was frail, you see. It wasn't even a very big cart. I remember it, quite a spindly thing with a small tank on the back for the milk and a measure hanging on brass chains. The horse was the quietest animal you have ever seen.'

'I'm very sorry,' said Ehrich. Heinz nodded in agreement. There was too much unhappiness in his heart for him to make hollow sounds.

'Now I'll go to get Wolfgang,' said Peter. 'I need the air.'

Outside it was dark. Bats were chasing low between the huts. The opera group were singing in one of the recreation huts to the accompaniment of a hearty, inaccurate piano. A cold wind felt fresh on his face and he held up his head like a dog scenting, breathing it in. The wine had made him drunk. He was slightly unsteady on his feet. He wondered what his mother's funeral had been like, without him there. Who had turned up? What was left of the town?

His route to Wolfgang's hut had become confused. The fresh wind had cleared the sky and the stars shone clear and bright in a way that he had seldom seen since imprisonment. He stared up at them, laughing slightly despite his grief because the stars seemed to reel and slide sideways so that he had to grab a fence post to support himself. He propped his back against it for a moment trying to locate the Great Bear so that he could unravel the sky as he had always done as a boy. His father had taught him the stars, always starting there. From the Great Bear to Orion. A half-moon, waxing, was hanging in distant trees beyond the perimeter fence like a Chinese lantern. Dazzled by it, he could not immediately see the stars again, only a shadowy globe. To his left in the darkness he heard voices, whispering, where shadow lay deep from a near tree. Without thinking, lost in himself, he blundered on. He was surprised and puzzled by the white forms in the grass and it took him some seconds to realise they were bodies and that they were two men locked together, while a third sat nearby. All were naked. Even in the blackness of the moonlight's shadow he realised that. The two on the ground rolled apart and he had time to see Waldenburg and Kunkel. He never saw Muller's face, but it was Muller who hit him with his boot, bringing the steel-shod heel down on his skull. Peter dropped like a stone, but the naked Muller hit him again and again. There was no other sound except the whack, whack, whack! of the boot. It stopped. The men dressed in panic. White flesh was swallowed in the dark. Soon there were only faces and then these were partly hidden by caps. The opera club sang on, bats fed unperturbed. The figures departed one by one, leaving only Peter Stuck, staring at the moon. In only ten minutes it had cleared the trees and was shining full on his white face.

There was pandemonium in the hut when Peter was eventually found. Heinz and Ehrich had waited for perhaps twenty minutes before deciding that Peter had obviously joined Wolfgang to do something. They agreed they would both drop in on Wolfgang's hut. Heinz filled his mug with the turnip wine to take it as a present. They put the oil can away and locked it up.

Wolfgang was puzzled that no one had come. It was not like Peter. He drank the turnip wine and said it tasted like petrol and horse piss. They talked for about half an hour about Wolfgang's letter, about Heinz's letter, about Ehrich's letter, showing them to each other. Heinz and Ehrich returned feeling light-headed. When Peter was still not there they were in a dilemma. If he had walked out or was trying to escape, then they must cover for him. On the other hand that was very unlikely, knowing the man. If the guards had a head count that night, he was bound to be missed. They decided to do nothing, hoping that he had slumped down somewhere under the influence of the turnip brew.

A guard found him at two and every light in the camp went on. Everyone was stood to attention at the bottom of their beds. Middleton inspected each hut, ending up at Peter's again. He inspected Peter's possessions. His face was white and grim. These things occasionally happened in camps, but Middleton had never expected it under his regime.

The locker was forced with a trenching spade and Middleton examined the contents, sniffing the oil can. It was taken away by guards. They did not know then that Peter was dead. Middleton announced only that he had been found and that he had been attacked. He interviewed each member of the hut in turn through the night. Lights were turned out in other huts, around the perimeter. The men were allowed to sit on the ends of their beds until it was their turn. They sat upright, saying nothing, under the cold and watchful eyes of two of the younger guards, both armed. The atmosphere had changed. Men were wondering. Kunkel and Mohnke and Muller sat like grey statues, staring to the front. The eyes of the other men were upon them. The previous attacks were common knowledge and suspicions were high.

Middleton got to Heinz at about four o'clock. He was direct with him.

'Heinz Geisseler. Sit down. You are no stranger to violence yourself. Who did it? Have you any idea?'

'No, sir.'

'You would tell me, Geisseler, wouldn't you? You aren't protecting anyone?'

'I am not, sir. Peter Stuck is my friend. If I . . .' He paused.

'Knew who hit him?' encouraged Middleton, leaning forward slightly. They were sitting in the small room used for interviews just inside the door. It was dusty. Middleton faced Heinz alone. An armed guard stood just inside the door.

'If I knew who hit him, I would be tempted to deal with him,' said Heinz. Middleton nodded, bit at his moustache. He had a pad before him on which he had listed all the men interviewed. There were notes beside some of them. Heinz saw nothing beside his own name. Middleton must write the notes after the interview.

'Geisseler, Peter Stuck is dead.'

'What?'

Heinz stared at him open-mouthed. He could not comprehend this new catastrophe. He was very tired and the emotional drain of the last day seemed to have slowed down his powers of thought. He had an image of Peter drinking from a mug. It was so fresh that it could not give way, but stayed like an image on the retina.

'What do you mean? I thought he was injured.'

'No. I said he had been attacked. He was hit on the head and killed. It was not an accident. It was a savage attack. Was he drunk?'

'A little bit perhaps. I could not tell. Not *very* drunk.'

'Were you drinking with him?'

'I had a small amount.'

Middleton nodded.

'You know it is against the camp rules to make alcohol?'

'Yes, sir.'

'Did Peter Stuck have any particular enemies?'

'No, sir. Peter got on with everyone.'

'Except certain National Socialists.'

Heinz looked up at him but said nothing.

'Come on, Geisseler, we know that the last attacks were because men decided to work in the fields, and we have a good idea who carried them out. We have never been able to prove it because they were masked and because there was a lot of silence from those who might have known. Is there any reason why this should be a political attack?'

'They didn't want us to send those postcards.'

'I have been told that. Personally, I agree that the wording of the cards was offensive. But would they attack Peter Stuck because of that? Did he send a card?'

'Yes, he did. He got a reply. His brother was killed, and his mother.'

'I see.' Middleton wrote on the paper. 'I'm sorry to hear that. Many men got bad news. I am afraid that was inevitable. For many it was the first mail after the end of the war. Would they attack him for sending a card?'

Heinz shrugged.

'Most men sent the cards. Why Peter?'

'Can you think of any other reason?'

'No.' Heinz remembered how Peter had been the wild man of the last attack. Was it revenge for that itself?

And so it went round and round. Heinz was trying to help, trying to put together any strands that might form a thread, and Middleton probed and prompted. Tomorrow, he said, it would be the military and civilian police. Heinz could not remember the comings and goings from the hut although Middleton pressed him. They had been paying no attention. Everyone had been going about their normal business. Heinz wondered about what Peter had witnessed in the kitchens, but said nothing.

*

'You shouldn't have shown those Germans the fern nuts,' John was complaining. 'Now they'll dig all of them up. Anyway, it was our secret.'

The two boys lay awake listening to the scraping of the dry walnut leaves outside.

'We'll take the tops off the bullets tomorrow,' he contributed when William said nothing. 'Then we can make explosions.'

'How?'

'We take out the powder and put it in a tin or a jar then put that down a rabbit burrow. You'll see.'

They planned the next raid. It was getting too cold for much more boating on the pond. The newts had disappeared and the water had become sullen with dead leaves. The case liners were well concealed under branches against the next year. It was time for other sports. William was still thinking of the cockerel. It was the worst thing he had ever done in his life and he could tell no one about it. The disappearance of the corpse was particularly upsetting. He listened to John, but could not prevent himself from crying quietly.

Margaret lay under Robert's weight, letting her arms rest round his shoulders while he pushed into her, waiting for him to stop and roll off. She had not wanted him to make love to her, but had not liked to refuse. She was not satisfied when he did finish. He fell asleep almost immediately, leaving her thinking of Heinz, she half-Jewish, he a German soldier. Each day the Nuremberg trials continued. Already the world had become numb with atrocities.

She married, he . . .? She didn't know.

She happy? No, she wasn't happy. She accepted her position. He? He had a solemn and kind directness.

She had put on lipstick for him. There could be no doubt about that if she was honest with herself.

There was no future in it, but there was a present she could not control. She wanted Heinz in the bed with her, imagined him there, not caring about Robert's snores, and she was glad and savoured her infidelity to him. She had been host to Robert's children and even now was host to his semen although she did not love him. She obeyed. She had always obeyed and ultimately she probably always would, but she had experienced

220

the thrill of disobedience and it was heady. She hugged herself, hugging Heinz, and asked Judith to understand. Judith did. Judith would have been to the point. 'Have a good time, girl. I did!' She fell asleep. She awoke to hear one of the boys running outside and, looking out of the window in the dingiest grey of dawn, she saw William chasing the cockerel. She had no idea what for and, not wanting to wake Robert by shouting, she quietly returned to her side of the bed. She felt a sense of relief as though she had made an important decision and was happy. She would not admit to herself what the decision was.

William could not at first believe the sound. It intruded on some dark dream he had forgotten until he awoke with a start and realised it was real. He pulled on his trousers and jumper (no underpants, no shirt, no socks) and ran downstairs and out into the yard. The bird stood in the doorway of the barn. As soon as it caught sight of him it backed off in alarm. As he approached, it cocked its head once, then fled, legs pumping and neck outstretched. William ran hopelessly after it, making encouraging noises, relieved and delighted, but the bird was taking no chances. It took flight and cleared a hedge into a field.

CHAPTER NINE

November brought two notable events as far as William was concerned. The first was that he was given a kitten and acquired a dog.

He had been campaigning for a cat of his own since they arrived. There was no shortage of them around — half-wild animals that stalked the barn and fields. They were of doubtful ownership, having come with the farm, and certainly there was no one of them William could call his own. When they found a litter of kittens in amongst the straw bales, all five of them were brought out and stood in a stumbling row on the brick path in front of the house.

'Which one do you want?' asked Pa. William pointed to a small tabby with a white chest that was chasing its tail.

'All right. Do you want one, John?'

'No. Not particularly.'

Pa nodded. He addressed William sternly.

'You will have to look after it if it's yours. You understand that? Not expect someone else to do it.'

'I will.'

The distraught mother had been shut in the kitchen where she had been lured by milk. Robert took one kitten from the end of the row and put it back amongst the bales. Without more ado he picked up the other three, dumped them in a swill bucket full of water and shut the lid. He had had it ready all the time. Luckily Helen was upstairs and missed the scene. William was in tears, desperate, but John was less caring. William begged, promised to look after them all, tried to seize the bucket and tip them out, but Robert was unmoved.

'It's the kindest way. There are far too many cats. They won't know a thing.'

William ran away howling, clutching his kitten.

The dog was for all of them. Like the kitten it was free. It was a gift from Ingleton.

'Children need a dog,' he had said one day. He was always solicitous to the children and to Margaret. On the next visit he produced a tan and black and white mongrel puppy with crumpled ears that he assured them would straighten out. 'It's an allsorts dog,' he said, 'they're the most intelligent.'

As children will, they called him Patch because of his piratic sooty blotch around one eye. Patch had to live outside as a farm dog should, in a kennel made by Heinz. He was a dog of prodigious enthusiasm, and chewed everything.

The second memorable event was the celebration of Guy Fawkes Day. The boys had been collecting cordite for some time now and had become familiar with its uses. They kept it stored in jam jars in the water meadow in a stricken tree. As the weather worsened the American guards at the dump spent less and less time in their woodland lair. They seemed to have given up even the feeble pretence they had made of guarding the huts and spent their time instead shooting pigeons and pheasants from the breaks in the woodland at dawn and dusk. The boys had no difficulty in stealing an enormous quantity of brass cartridges. They had begun to take boxes as well, just to store them. After school they sat and opened them with a pair of pliers each, turning and twisting the head of the bullet until it worked loose, then pouring out the shining black fragments. They were like cake decorations, minute logs.

For November the Fifth they had no money. They weren't given any pocket money on a regular basis. Robert took the view they had no use for it and anyway they were saving for a radio. John had been invited by Jimmy Bradley over to his father's farm about two miles away. He was having a bonfire and his father had bought fireworks — expensive and almost unobtainable after the war. John's pride was hurt. He told Ma about Jimmy Bradley's fireworks and nagged at her for money, not knowing where he would buy the things. Ma had no money and it was forbidden anyway. They could have a bonfire if they used only small wood and faggots. That, like cats and dogs, was free. Ma said it was traditional and fireworks weren't and was determined to make the best of it. They were feeling the pinch of Robert's stocking-up. The chicken brooders had arrived and been installed. They were soon full of small yellow chicks that died at an alarming rate. It seemed a strange time of year to raise young chickens but Robert said the time of year didn't matter provided they were big enough before the cold weather started in January.

In the meadow after school on November the Fifth they filled a cocoa tin and a jar with cordite. Both containers had lids that fitted tightly. The lid of the jar screwed on. It was a jar Ma used and treasured and they knew she would miss it.

They had punched a hole in the edge of each lid, sufficient in size to allow the cordite to run out. Letting it trickle, they pushed the containers down rabbit burrows, lying flat on the wet ground. Inside, the burrows were dry. From the mouth of each of the burrows they laid a fuse, combining both to form one. They extended this in a long trail of cordite to a retreat behind a mound. From here they lit it with a match and watched it fizz violently as it shot across the ground. As it approached the burrows they flung themselves down. They had done this before but on a small scale. Two deep explosions followed, thumping the earth like a giant fist. A scattering of soil fell on them. They had made two impressive holes in the ground, blowing turf everywhere. They gathered as much of this as they could and kicked soil into the craters and laid the turf on top. It was not much of a repair, but no one seemed to go through the meadow.

When their father remarked on the bangs, the boys said it was probably fireworks or maybe the Americans blowing up something.

The bonfire seemed a tame thing to them although Helen and Margaret were entranced by the flames that lit the field. At one stage they watched Jimmy Bradley's rockets shoot skywards in the distance and were consumed with envy. They were feeling very poor.

As far as Helen was concerned, the main event of November was the time she was seized by Wilhelm. She had talked to him on several occasions after school. Wilhelm had been putting sawn logs in a stack in the end shed. Heinz was running them through the circular saw. Helen had to admit to herself that she had strayed there deliberately. They were out of sight of anyone.

'You like me, yes?' asked Wilhelm, putting down an armful of wood. He stood so close to her that she could feel the warmth of his body, hot with work.

'Yes.'

'You would like me to kiss you?'

'No!' Helen was alarmed, but had no time to flee before he had done so. His right hand felt her breast, stroking, sliding inside her shirt before she was really aware what he was doing. She managed to push him away with difficulty. He smiled at her.

'You like that?'

'No, I didn't! How dare you touch me!' She knew she was red with embarrassment, but was determined not to flee like a child.

'Your friend Ann Baxter, she likes that!' Wilhelm smiled again.

'What do you mean!'

'Ah! She hasn't told you. Your friend Ann Baxter and me, we are like so . . .!' He linked the forefingers of his two hands and pulled at them, smiling at her in the same slow, bold way, then he returned to his work, winking at her. She walked away, straightening her shirt. 'I worked on that farm, you see!' he called after her.

CHAPTER TEN

As Christmas approached the men worked on the house. They talked of the festival very little as it heightened their isolation and loneliness. Heinz, Wolfgang, Ehrich and Wilhelm formed the usual gang, Paul came and went as required.

November had slipped perceptibly into December and the lorry was always covered and tightly laced. The rain was often studded with bursts of rattling hail and it was good to be working indoors. Ditches filled with water like milky tea that overflowed and undercut the roads. Geese sported in the nearby farms. Heinz and Wolfgang watched the lanes from the back of the lorry in the grey morning light and noted the changes. Holly was suddenly dominant as the other trees died back and only thorn and elder hung on to leaf. Summer seemed as far away as home. Around the farm in the old orchard the first tender spikes of daffodils and snowdrops had foolishly emerged.

They missed Peter Stuck a lot, they missed his cheerfulness, his perpetual hunt for food. They missed sitting on the bank with the boys waiting for the lorry. Now it stopped in the lane for them and blew its horn. More often that not it seemed to be raining and they ran to it with sacks over their heads. It was depressing weather, light late and dark early.

There had of course been a full inquiry into Peter's death. The camp had swarmed with uniformed police, both military and civil, and a verdict of murder had been reached. At the end of it all no one spoke and no one was charged. Middleton was obviously under a cloud as a result and things became disciplined and less relaxed. Peter had been buried in the local

226

churchyard after an Anglican service. All his friends from the camp had been allowed to attend. Middleton was there, grey and grave, and so were Robert, Margaret and the children. Ingleton came, for he had known the man, and so did Tom and George, dressed in their best. Schneider and Waldenburg attended, clicking their heels, appearing to consider a Nazi salute. A grim look from Middleton dissuaded them. Peter was buried beside weathered stones that time had erased, and was given a black slate slab.

The stone said:

PETER STUCK
OGEFR
4.2.21   +12.10.45

It was what the War Department usually provided.

When the men had a rare break from working on the house they fed the animals or gathered fuel. The big open fireplace was kept alight most of the time and consumed wood inexorably. Robert had had no idea that wood burned so fast and sent the men on parties to scour the spinney and raid the woods adjoining. It was dead, wet wood for the most part and Heinz cut it into cord with the saw. It was stacked in the open sheds to dry but for the most part as much steam as smoke seemed to go up the farm chimney. They discovered how inefficient the fine fireplace was.

The first frosts followed. They were hard and vicious, crackling the puddles through and through and even freezing a crust in the depths of the well. It was bitter work in the morning for the boys, pumping in turn while their breath froze. They did not have enough clothes and no coats. What wore out or what they outgrew could not now be replaced. They held on to the pump handle by a swathe of sacking wound round the cold iron and secured with twine. Birds came to the house for food and sat near them. They got little and took themselves off to the pigsties to try to steal from them. The grass was white and brittle until late in the day, and when it thawed was a sickly yellowy green without goodness. The cows were in, feeding off hay and chopped straw already, snuffling in it discontentedly.

'We're going to have to start feeding them mangolds,' Robert said to Margaret. They were sitting at breakfast. The table had been pulled as close to the fireplace as was safe and a log flickered sulkily. An oil lamp with a single wick burnt between them as it was not yet light enough to see properly in the house although it was nearly nine. The boys and Helen had all left for school at a quarter past eight.

'Shouldn't we keep them?' She knew little enough about it, but she had seen the dwindling stack of hay and was aware it was only December and January was a cruel month.

'There's a good clamp. We should have enough.'

'What do we do if we haven't?'

Robert looked at her sharply. His first reaction was annoyance, but he contained that. Perhaps her interest was real.

'I don't know. We can't afford to buy foodstuffs. Not until we have chickens to sell. Or eggs. Or until harvest.'

'Harvest is over half a year away.'

'Did you have to say that?'

'Robert, it's true . . .'

'You must understand, Margaret, that winter is always the hardest time. Everything is in the ground. Everything is spent out. We can do nothing but wait.'

When Wolfgang, Heinz, Ehrich and Wilhelm arrived, they approached the house beating their arms under their armpits and stamping their feet. They wore greatcoats and had pulled their forage caps down as far as they could over their ears. They stood uncertainly outside the house, waiting to be asked in. Margaret did not come out to welcome them these days because it would have meant having to greet Heinz in front of the others and she could not trust herself to display no interest. She was in love with Heinz.

Robert came out, his breath white in the air. He shut the door behind him. The men looked gloomy.

'All right,' he announced, 'we must get some mangolds from that clamp you built to feed the cattle. We'll get that done first thing. They need feeding now, and once it's over you will be working indoors for the rest of the day. We must get on with the plumbing and the carpentry. We must try to finish it.'

Wolfgang still translated everything, although the others now understood well what he said. Ehrich snorted and looked

228

glum. He had been looking forward to a hot cup of tea, even without sugar. It had been bitterly cold in the lorry and the driver had been slow because the roads were covered with morning ice. He had amused himself by shouting out to them, 'Must be cold in the backs there, lads!' or 'Any more for frost bite!' and they had replied with rude noises and sworn at him in German.

'Tea when you've finished,' said Robert, interpreting correctly the crestfallen expressions. 'I'll get the tractor and trailer. Wolfgang, come and help me put the sides and tail on and hitch up.'

Wolfgang followed him to the tractor shed. They lifted the long wooden sides of the trailer and dropped them into place, engaging the hinges. They secured them with pins. The trailer was painted like a farm wagon and the woodwork had been carved and painted red and blue and yellow. Next they lifted the tailboard and secured it. Robert turned to Wolfgang.

'Wolfgang, I would like you and Heinz to join us for Christmas Day. You have both worked very hard and we are allowed to invite two prisoners. Will you please tell Heinz.'

Wolfgang at first stared, unable to grapple with what he had heard, then a smile spread over his face.

'You are very kind. I will ask Heinz. I would very much like to come.'

'Fine.' Robert had already swung the starting handle of the tractor until it was hanging vertically downwards. He did not look up or catch Wolfgang's eye. He jerked the engine into life.

They paused to collect two forks to strip off the straw covering on the clamp, and then the rest of the men clambered on board the trailer. It was a bone-shaking ride because of the hardness of the ruts. The trailer had iron-shod wooden wheels and no suspension and the men held on to the sides, unable to speak, hardly able to breathe. Robert brought the tractor to a halt alongside the clamp. It stretched beside the hedge for one hundred and fifty feet, looking like the long-house of some ancient civilisation. The men got down with relief. Robert took one fork, Heinz the other. Robert started to clear the earth. Immediately a thin haze of steam started to appear from the cleared area. Robert pulled the straw back with his hands, scrabbling rapidly. A gentle pillar of white drifted upwards before the breeze caught it. He pulled out first one, then another mangold, throwing them to the field in front of the prisoners. They hit the ground wetly, mush flying off, the skin bursting. A smell of vegetable rot began to spread.

'Help me quickly!' he shouted, 'Get off the straw. They're fermenting.'

His urging was unnecessary. The men had lifted and topped and stacked these with the labour of their hands. They were their mangolds. They rushed to the clamp, Wolfgang lifting the earth in clods with the fork, the other men scrabbling like Robert at the straw beneath, then at the mangolds themselves. The clamp was warm, even hot in places. A disgusting stench rose from it. Whole stretches were mounds of hot blackened pulp with occasional pieces of yellow flesh. Short areas were partially rotted with some roots firm and good. They picked these out by hand, ignoring the mess and laid them aside. It was impossible to walk the clamp without plunging in. It had to be opened in the middle by standing on the ground and moving forward into the heart of it, spreading the mess to right and left. The steam rose continually in the cold air, as though they walked two corridors of burning ash. Robert was pale and distraught.

'They have the roots on them!' he shouted to Wolfgang, brandishing a rotten shell. 'There's nothing wrong with the roots! Tell me why they've rotted!'

'We stacked them carefully,' said Wolfgang. 'You saw we stacked them carefully. We did it well!'

'I know, I know!' He went to the tractor and sat down on the seat, viewing the ruin, lowering his head onto the back of his hands which clutched the wheel.

'This is bad,' said Ehrich.

'You can certainly say that,' said Wolfgang. 'It was not our fault. We treat them like children.'

'It has to be something else,' said Heinz. 'He told us to leave the roots on. They all have roots on. It must be the frost. Or the rain. The clamp is damp.'

'This is like digging into a corpse!' said Wilhelm.

'In a way it is a corpse,' said Heinz. He did not want to look at the smashed flesh or think of corpses. Unbidden memories were already attacking him in short flashes. The pulp disgusted

230

him. He was sorry for Robert. Ehrich on the other hand was more generous with his pity.

'Do you think this will finish him?'

They still worked down the centre. They were filthy now, coated with slime. Some of the roots were so hot they could not pick them up, but rolled them aside with the fork.

'Not just a thing like this,' said Wolfgang.

'He looks desperate,' said Wilhelm.

'Perhaps he is not a very strong man,' said Heinz. He had hardened his heart to take the man's wife and had no intention of allowing remorse to intrude. 'There is no reason for him to collapse.'

The others stopped. This was not at all like Heinz. Wolfgang looked at him sharply.

'What's the matter? He's always been good to us and treated us well. You watch yourself with his wife. That's the cause of this.'

Heinz's fists clenched and his face reddened. Ehrich was quickly to the rescue.

'Are you mad? In front of him? I want to get home sometime.'

Robert looked up, saw the men in a tight group although he could not see their expressions, the tenseness of Heinz.

'You carry on opening the clamp,' he shouted, trying to sound firm and unconcerned. 'I'll be back.' He climbed down from the tractor, unhitched the trailer and drove off at speed from the field, bounding and bucking. Turning into the lane he set off for Bargets, as fast as the tractor would move, slewing round the icy corners in his haste. Ingleton's wife, a wiry dark woman with concerned eyes, sensed that there was trouble.

'He's in the milking shed,' she said, 'I hope nothing's wrong . . .' But Robert had already gone. Ingleton looked up from where he sat beside a cow on a three-legged milking stool. He was tenderly washing her teats. The cow turned round to look at him in surprise, eyes rolling.

'Steady!' said Ingleton to the animal, which immediately relaxed.

'What can I do for you, Robert. You seem in a hurry.'

Ingleton had been wearing his cap sideways as he pressed his

231

head against the cow's flank. Now he straightened it and got to his feet from the low wooden stool.

'My mangolds have rotted. The whole clamp is steaming, yet I left all the root on. Why? I can't understand why!'

Robert's voice still contained a high note of panic. Ingleton paused, characteristically lifted his cap to scratch his scalp with his little finger, replaced it.

'That's bad news. Many gone?'

'Damned near the whole lot. Why would they rot? They were stacked with care. I know they were. They were properly covered with straw and earth. Have yours gone?'

'No.' The answer was even, almost apologetic. 'Mine are all right. Do you want me to have a look at them?'

'Looking won't bring them back.' Ingleton ignored the ungraciousness of this. He understood how Robert must feel.

'Well, the only thing I can think of is that they weren't sweated long enough before you clamped 'em. You raised them fairly early.'

Robert stared at him. His heart had began to race uncomfortably. He battled with his pride.

'What do you mean, sweat them?'

'It's only a guess, mind.' Ingleton was careful to be effacing. He knew immediately that he had been right. 'You see, when you pull old mangold, he sweats. Especially when he hasn't entirely stopped growing. Then you leave 'im out in the field for a day or two, just giving him a light cover of his own leaves until the leaves dry off. Old mangold, he breaks out in quite a sweat at the shock o' being pulled, wouldn't you, and if he isn't sweated first then he can ferment in the clamp. It's only an idea, mind, but if the roots were whole, I'd say that might be it.'

'What can I do? With the ones I can rescue.'

'Get them out of that clamp and into a barn to dry. And, when you've got them there, spread them thin, keep them well covered from frost, and keep an eye on 'em.'

'Thank you,' said Robert. 'I just thought I'd ask. I suppose that must be it.' He stood silent, not knowing what to say. Ingleton stood for a while aware of what the other man was thinking, sensing the calculations he was making and the decisions. Only Robert could now decide.

'Do you need a hand?' he asked.

232

'No, I'm all right.'

'I suppose I'd best get back to this old cow. She don't like being kept waiting.'

Ingleton gently seated himself again. Robert returned to the tractor and drove back to the field. The men had split the best part of the clamp now, but the numbers salvaged were no more than five per cent of the whole. He told them to load the trailer, carefully, to treat them like eggs. His immediate concern was for the cows. He drove back to the farm. The animals were hungry and letting the world know it.

'What's happened?' asked Margaret, coming to the back door as he hurried past. He was unreasonably angry with the question, and brushed it aside.

'Nothing. Absolutely nothing!'

'Something's the matter.'

'The damned mangolds are rotten. That's my winter feed gone, that's all!'

The frost had cleared from the ground and a wintry sun produced some warmth. He released the animals from the stalls and drove them out into the stockyard and from there up the lane to the top meadow where the grass was best. He needed time to think, to calculate. Just how much hay had he? He had to visit the stack. How much chaff and straw? How much feed could he get from the Ministry? He had relied on the mangolds. He would put the cows back out to grass for a day or two to make the best of what was left while he thought it out. He needed money for feed, but had none. It was the same at every turn, he was defeated by shortage of money. He cursed and hit out with a stick at the hedgerow, chopped at the last flowers of honeysuckle that survived the cold, stabbed at the crust of ice on puddles untouched by warmth. A pair of coots ran across the track in front of the cows, angular and crouching. Goldfinches dangled from the thistles. It was the time for scavenging. The cows were hungry and pulled at tussocks. Robert knew he would have to return to the bank yet again, and wondered what there was left to say that he had not already said many times before. What could he offer that he had not already offered? Was there some value in the seed in the ground? The cows had value, surely the bank would not let them starve? They were in calf and would double his herd in the spring, if only he could buy the time. He shut the animals in the field. Normally they would have cavorted into the centre of it but today, aware the grass was wan and thin, they hung about by the gate and looked after him for their food. On his return to the house Robert disturbed a flock of fieldfares stripping a holly. He thought bitterly that soon there would be nothing left to eat.

Outside the farm stood a Wolseley he did not recognize. Trying to calm himself he strode in to find Margaret in the inglenook with a new-looking tin bath in her hands. The visitor was Taylor. He leaned on the brickwork of the breast chatting to her, hat on head.

'Hello, Robert,' said Margaret. 'Mr Taylor's come to see you. He's brought me a new bath.'

'What do you want that for?'

'The old one had a leak. You said so yourself. I want to bath the children tonight. They haven't had one for ages . . .'

'Why now?' he demanded unfairly. He didn't want to see Taylor. He suspected he knew what the men wanted.

'Shan't charge for the bath,' said Taylor. He made no attempt to straighten himself up off the chimney and this made Robert angry.

'What are you doing lounging here?' he demanded. Taylor rocked onto his feet, thumbs still tucked into the top pockets of his dungarees, trilby still jammed on his head.

'Not a good day, Mr Ellis?'

Robert was tempted to tell him to go to hell, but controlled himself. He was in no position for such indulgences.

'Not a good day.'

'Ah well, these things happen from time to time. I was just saying to your wife that I bet she'd be glad to see the last of tin baths. Won't be long now, I hear. Just the plumbing. Just the pump. Just the electricity.'

'That's right.'

'Have you heard when we shall get electricity?' asked Margaret. 'What I can't imagine is not filling oil lamps.'

'Won't be to spring now. No chance before March. So much for promises.'

'They promised it before Christmas!' Margaret protested. Taylor shrugged and smiled.

'People are always making promises. It's a sad fact of life.'

He shifted slightly, moved his plump body nearer the flame in the hearth.

'Anyway, I'm sorry if I've caught you at a bad time, Mr Ellis, but I just called about the money for the extra pipe and the pump. Seeing as it's coming up to Christmas, a little cash comes in handy at the festive season!'

Robert's suspicions had been correct. He had not paid cash for these when he had collected them, claiming to have left his wallet at home. Taylor had waited three weeks.

'I haven't got that sort of cash in the house, Mr Taylor. I shall have to go to the bank. I'm going there this afternoon. Will that do?'

'Of course that'll do. I wouldn't have come here if I'd known it would be any sort of trouble at all . . .'

'It's no trouble.'

Taylor was watching him closely. He hoped he displayed unconcern. After a moment the man lifted his hat.

'Good day, Mrs Ellis, Mr Ellis. See you this afternoon no doubt!' Robert remained motionless. He made no attempt to show Taylor out, leaving it to Margaret. He took himself upstairs to the bedroom to change into his demob suit, wondering why. It had made no difference before. He looked at himself in the mirror and in doing so he could not help comparing himself with his army photograph. If anything he was thinner than when in the Army. He was still fit and tanned-looking, although the moustache had grown and was a little less military. He rubbed haircream into his hair and brushed it flat, then picked up a comb and split it neatly into a parting, brushing each section again. Just right, he thought. He wished he was still in the Army. He wished he did not have to deal with the Taylors of this world and with bank managers. And with Margaret. The thought was brief, but it was there. He straightened his tie and combed at his moustache.

William opened the battered rear door that led out to the bicycle sheds. Most of the town children left by the front and walked. He automatically squinted up at the sky. It was dark already. He had no coat and he hoped it wouldn't rain.

'William, here a moment.'

He paused, returned indoors to the lit, wood-smelling,

chalk-smelling corridor. It was Mr Gilbert, the deputy head, adding his pungent smell of tobacco and sweat, who sometimes taught them mathematics; Mr Gilbert who had observed William's plight when he had been forgotten at the gates. The girls filed past in a group. Sally and Mary lingered near the doorway, consumed with curiosity, nudging each other and looking back.

'Off you go home!' Gilbert called after them, and they held their hands to their mouths, giggled and ran away.

'Do you have a coat?' Gilbert asked William.

'No, sir.'

'Aren't you cold?' William shrugged. He had never thought about it. The weather was whatever it was and he accepted it.

'Would you like to earn some extra money by cleaning a motor bike?' He saw a flash of excitement in the dark eyes. It reminded him of himself as a boy.

'You must tell your mother though,' he continued, 'and I shall pay you sixpence.'

'Yes, sir!'

'Do you get pocket money, William?'

'No, sir.' He felt ashamed as soon as he had answered. 'I don't need any,' he added too quickly. Gilbert nodded gravely. Accustomed to farm boys he had watched William and John and had listened to rumour. In a small place, he heard almost everything. He had watched the wearing of their clothes, the elongation of their shorts until there was no more hem to let down. He had noted the holes in their shoes and the darns in their socks that gradually crept higher and higher up their legs. He had noted the absence of coats.

'You haven't joined the savings scheme.'

'No, sir.'

'Shall I write a letter to your mother on that as well?'

All children were being encouraged to put sixpence a week into National Savings stamps.

'I don't know.' William didn't know if they had sixpence a week. Everyone seemed to have a card except him. He was teased about it. He was unaware that Gilbert had noticed. He was frightened by the prospect of handing over such a letter, because Pa was bound to demand what it was for and why he needed it. Perhaps he could simply tear up the letter.

'I don't mind.'

'I shall be asking for a written reply.'

William's heart sank.

Gilbert led him through to where the machine was kept. Gilbert and his wife lived in a small house that had by extension of the school become attached. The motor bicycle was in a small room by itself. It looked beautifully clean and gleaming. Gilbert gave him a selection of dusters, a can of thin oil, and a tin of polish.

'Have you ever cleaned one of these before?' William shook his head.

'Then just go over everything. Look.' Gilbert showed him. 'It will take about half an hour.'

William set to. Half an hour for sixpence was an undreamed-of wage. He thought the motor bike was a very clean thing for something that needed more cleaning.

'Have you an appointment?' the girl at the bank said. He had to go to the trading counter and wait his place in the queue of depositors and withdrawers. Those behind him stared. They knew why men asked to see bank managers.

'No. We have no telephone yet. You know how it is . . .'

He tried his charming smile, but the girl only responded with a mechanical movement of her very red lips. Her hair stood up behind her like Betty Grable's. It had cost her a lot.

'I don't know if he'll see you without an appointment. Who shall I say it is?'

'Mr Ellis.' He spoke too low and immediately regretted it.

'*Who*?' she immediately demanded loudly in broadest Suffolk. She enjoyed this bit.

'Mr Robert Ellis, he knows who I am!' he replied fiercely. She gave him a top-to-toe look that was less than flattering, but went into the inner sanctum. She was gone some time.

'Mr Prewitt can see you.'

He sat down in front of the manager. Prewitt had half-risen to his feet, no more. Robert automatically glanced out of the windows towards the mulberry tree. It was black and twiggy. The courtyard looked dank and unhealthy. Prewitt was looking at him inquiringly. His hair seemed even thinner than Robert remembered, his cheeks like maroon morocco leather.

237

'What can I do for you?' he asked as if he did not know. Robert began with the mangolds, he explained about the clamp, he explained about the cows and the pigs and the chickens and the foodstuffs required and the seed in the ground.

'Would you like a sherry?' said Prewitt.

'Yes,' said Robert. The whole bottle, he thought. He noticed how much the manager's hands shook when he poured, striking a crystal tune from the glasses.

The men had carted in all the sound mangolds, leaving anything dubious to one side for immediate consumption. They had been laid out in a double layer interlaced with straw on the floor of the main barn and covered with more straw which they had split from the bales and laid loosely over them. Wolfgang had driven the tractor and had enjoyed himself. Now they were back to fuel, the other essential. Ehrich had claimed his right to drive the tractor this time, and he and Ehrich had set off to load and cart sections of a fallen elm, armed with a crosscut saw and axes. Wolfgang had gone with them for the first trip. He and Heinz would alternate at the circular saw, reducing the timber to manageable size. The gas engine fired its customary blue smoke rings into the cold air where they were slow to disperse and hung inside each other like Saturn's rings. The saw was silent, for, as soon as the tractor and trailer had left, Heinz had gone into the house.

Margaret allowed Heinz to help undress her. They sat together on the side of the bed and he smiled at her, his shirt and hair brown with sawdust.

'You'll leave it everywhere,' she said but he kissed her into silence and took off his clothes, standing in front of her naked and erect. She was embarrassed. She had hardly ever seen Robert like this and never another man. He lay beside her, kissing her mouth and breasts hard, stroking her thighs, caressing her vulva, spreading her legs and gently arousing her with searching fingers. He changed position suddenly and entered her immediately and with ease, thrusting again and again, urgently, then taking her with one arm around the waist and another round the shoulders rolled over so that she lay on top of him, head buried in his shoulder. He raised her head gently.

'Open your eyes,' he whispered. Her eyes were tight shut, out of shyness, out of pleasure, out of concentration on his penis within her, out of confusion at what she was doing. She opened them slowly. Heinz smiled up at her.

'You see, you *can* look at me. You are beautiful. You feel good, you have a beautiful body.' He moved his hips, moved within her so that she was caught unaware by pleasure, then as suddenly rolled back again so that he was upon her and thrusting into her violently and passionately. She heard herself uttering cries and noises, clutched at him, was overwhelmed, then lay still under his weight, wanting him to stay where he was but aware, with passion spent, of the dangers of his being there, of time passing, of someone returning. Heinz rolled off and lay on his back, one arm around her, still. She felt no guilt. She examined this fact with surprise. She had betrayed her husband, she had betrayed her upbringing, her Jewishness. Her body had betrayed her most of all because it had responded as it had not responded since she first met Robert, but that was only because body followed mind. There was no future in it. Heinz would return to Germany, she to her inevitability with Robert. She wondered if he had a wife, a girlfriend. She would never ask because she did not want to be told.

Heinz sat up, kissed her body from lips to toes.

'I must go now. I have to go back to the saw. They will be back soon with more wood. I love you. Can we do this again? Soon?'

She saw the face of an earnest boy attached to this body of a man and could not refuse it.

'We must find more time if we do,' she said. 'You have to go so soon. And, next time, no sawdust!'

He laughed.

'You must dust the bed! You even have sawdust down there!'

He dusted at her pubic hair, and she pulled the bedclothes over herself, watching him as he dressed. He kissed her once more, gently, and left her. It was only the second time they had made love and it had been much better than the first. She got out of bed and tidied the room. There *was* sawdust in the sheets. She walked naked up and down in front of Robert's photograph, getting a ridiculous sense of pleasure out of it. She could not forgive him for the way he brushed aside any attempt she made to care or find out what was happening. Whatever was wrong, she was in the wrong. If she failed to express interest, he punished her with scorn. If she expressed it, she was unworthy of explanation.

She examined herself in the mirror, at first her face and then her breasts, then standing up, facing it, turning sideways. She was still slim and attractive. For a woman who had had three children her child-bearing hardly showed. Her breasts were firm, stomach flat.

How could she love a German? She knew nothing of what he had done or where he had been. She knew he was a carpenter, she knew he was from Magdeburg but she hardly knew where Magdeburg was. She was not even sure that she did love him. She loved his need and hunger and body and boldness. She loved his unashamed nakedness and the way he looked at her. She loved the fact it could not last. She refused to think of what she would do when that time came.

Robert had been holding his empty sherry glass for some time now. It was warm in his grasp but no more seemed forthcoming. He was angry, desperate but trying to sound calm and confident.

'Even with a moderate yield, with the current price of barley and beans I am bound to be in surplus come harvest. You must see that.'

Prewitt sighed.

'I have to say, Mr Ellis, that every farmer that comes to see me says the same thing and, quite simply, they don't all make it. You owe the bank a very great deal already. The only security I have for what you *already* owe is next year's harvest.'

'I have to feed the cattle. They're in calf. Those calves will be worth a bit. They're security as well.'

'Yes, but if you sold them now wouldn't that answer all the problems you currently face? It would give you some capital and you wouldn't have to find the price of feed . . .'

They had been round to this position twice already. Prewitt was not giving in. No, he had said, and he meant no. He could not extend more credit. Yes, he had consulted head office. They had said no as well.

He didn't know what Robert was supposed to feed them on,

he wasn't a farmer. Robert should have thought of that before he bought them. Perhaps he would like to sell the chick brooders instead. Or dispose of the pigs. He was trying to do too much too fast without the necessary capital. He had put down his empty sherry glass at that point and pushed the bottle away from him.

The two men eyed each other in silence. Robert had hay for perhaps a month.

'I won't sell them, damn it! You won't make me! I'll find something!'

Prewitt bridled.

'Don't get angry with me, Mr Ellis. I have helped you considerably already. I can quite understand that you may be upset, but it's hardly my fault. You are responsible for managing your own affairs.'

Prewitt was eyeing the sherry bottle. As soon as Robert left he was going to pour himself about three glasses. He wished the man would clear out, go now while the going was good. He had seen it all before and this had the scent of disaster about it.

'You are ruining my chances for the sake of a few pounds!'

Robert stormed out. As he left, the girl looked up from her job at the counter and permitted herself a smug smile. She had seen it all before as well.

Mary Merrow called on Margaret at about four. The two women had seen each other only a few times, always promising to make it more often.

'Where's your husband? In the fields?'

'No, he's gone to town. To see the bank manager, I'm afraid.' Mary made a face.

'I know the feeling.'

They were sitting together on opposite sides of the inglenook. The wind feathered gently in the top of the chimney. The fire was barely alight.

'I see you're getting plenty of wood in.'

'This thing consumes it by the cartload.'

'I've blocked up mine. I use a paraffin heater.'

'The children like it. Perhaps we shall do the same when we get the electricity. The children can't wait for a radio either. We've been promising them one since we got here. All the town children rush home and listen to Dick Barton.' Mary nodded.

'It's a big divide, but no distance in miles.'

Mary looked at Margaret covertly. They were drinking tea and she was able to see her slenderness, the thin clothes. Nevertheless she seemed well, even excited.

'How do you find the German prisoners?' she asked. She noted that Margaret looked up at her sharply.

'In what way?'

'Are they all good workers. Can you trust them?'

'Yes. We've been very lucky, I don't know how we would have managed without them. We had one incident, someone trying to take a piece of leather, but nothing.'

'They say they're going to let them fraternize more. Let them go out to shops, even cinemas in the new year. I don't know how I feel about that. I think some people have mixed feelings.'

'They're only prisoners of war, not criminals. Ordinary people called up. Like our army.'

Mary made another face.

'Not all of them. Not the Nazis.'

Margaret wondered why the conversation was centring on prisoners.

'Were you just passing or did you call for anything in particular?' She felt she could address Mary with the same candour that the older woman was accustomed to using with others.

'It's the Germans I've come to talk about. I thought I'd better.'

'What?'

'Well, here's an example. You're a woman alone here, aren't you. Your husband's off out somewhere, and you've got four men on the premises.'

Margaret felt herself colouring.

'You'd better tell me what that all means.'

'It means that I've heard some talk, that's all, and thought I'd better tell you before you hear it from someone else. Don't get alarmed, it's nothing terrible.'

Margaret studied the other woman's weatherbeaten face, her lumpy clothes. Was this an attack of spinsterish frustration? Who had produced this 'talk' she said she had heard?

'What is it then?'

'Oh, just to do with being friendly with the Germans.'

'No, it isn't. I don't believe you've come to tell me that. It must be something more specific. Who are we talking about?'

Mary sipped her tea. The soles of her shoes were steaming slightly with the heat from the remaining log.

'Look, you do realise there is no reason why I should get myself into trouble with you by even mentioning these rumours. You should treat me more kindly.'

'I'm sorry. Of course I should.' Margaret was immediately contrite. Her guilt was showing.

'They say you find them attractive, or one of them.'

'Who is "they"?'

'I don't know. I heard it in the village. I heard it from Tom Baxter.'

'I see.'

'He is not a man I'd trust.'

'Thank you. I know.'

As they sat there she could hear the popping of the gas engine and the whine of Heinz sawing wood. Sound travelled easily down the huge flue. Mary Merrow must hear it too. She had a brief image of Heinz, his hair full of sawdust, of Heinz brushing at her. She smiled because the image was so intimate. Mary Merrow cocked her head.

'Well?'

'Nothing really. I was just thinking that people must talk.'

'The prisoners will be gone soon anyway. So I hear. They will start to repatriate them in the spring.'

'Will they?'

Margaret tried to stop the surge of pain that this produced. She knew it would happen at one level but could not accept it at another. Heinz had mentioned staying in England to her but she had not believed him and did not want it. How could she explain to him that perfection existed in their present relationship? She wanted snatched hours, she wanted urgency, sawdust not permanence. But spring was so near.

'Anyway,' said Mary awkwardly. 'I thought I ought to be neighbourly and let you know. They talk about me, you know, because I'm a woman alone.' She had risen to her feet and now she put the tea cup down on the table. 'This is East Anglia. Long on criticism, short on praise and hard as flint. Take care of Baxter. Steer wide.'

'I shall.'

When Mary Merrow had left in her car, Margaret returned to the bedroom and lifted the blankets. She ran the palms of her hands over the sheet again and again, smoothing them out, assuring herself no dust remained. Lifting the pillows to shake them she found the slightest scatter, a few grains of white wood, and picked them up individually, cradling them in her left palm. Separating the pillow case from the pillow on her side of the bed, she slipped them inside.

When Robert returned to the farm he was so obviously in a black mood that no one dared approach him. He seemed to notice nothing that the men had been doing and stood blindly in front of the mangolds that Wolfgang and the others had packed as lovingly as apples. Good, he nodded, good, but they knew he had not seen.

William returned later across the yard after leaving his bicycle in its place. The cockerel had fled immediately it saw him, running up the pile of bales, flapping and falling in its haste until it was within the very roof. From there it dipped and bobbed, making throaty noises. William felt triumphant. His enemy was defeated. He had sixpence. He did not dare give the letter to his mother about the savings scheme. Not now. The house was in gloom. Tomorrow was the end of term, then it was Christmas. He had no idea what it would be, he had never had his father home for Christmas as far as he could remember, but he was looking forward to it. Ma had said they would eat a chicken, maybe even two. Ma had said that two of the Germans would join them. Wolfgang and the one she had kissed. He wondered what Pa would make of it if he knew. It was too frightening even to think about. It was already dark and the men were waiting to hear the horn of the lorry. He saw that Helen stood near Wilhelm as they all waited in front of the open fire and grinned at her. She ignored him completely.

They tried to sing on the way back to raise their spirits because the atmosphere of the day had depressed them.

'So what,' said the practical Ehrich. 'We will find another farm.'

'We have been asked for Christmas,' said Wolfgang. 'Heinz and me. Sorry.'

'You lucky devils!' Ehrich was genuinely envious. 'Why not me?'

'He is only allowed two prisoners. That's the rules. Anyway, I'm not sure it's such a treat.'

Ehrich was not to be deflected.

'But why not me? I've worked there as long as you.'

'Don't ask me, I don't know!'

'I know why Heinz is asked!' said Ehrich.

'You shut up!' said Heinz.

'I wonder what we'll get for camp dinner?' asked Ehrich. 'I think it's unfair.'

Their words jolted about in the darkness in the back of the truck. It *was* unfair on Ehrich and the other two knew it. Wilhelm had not been with them from the beginning. He was younger too.

'We'll bring you what we can,' said Heinz.

'If there is anything,' said Wolfgang. 'That farm is in a bad way. He has no money. They talk about it all the time. He's been to the bank manager for a loan, but he can't get any more. It's all the same, just as it was at home. It's the bankers that ruin the world.'

Heinz was wrapped tight in his greatcoat in a corner, scarcely listening. He was trying to recall Inga, to test how he felt about her, to compare how he felt about Margaret. He saw her body, he saw himself brushing her, an image that returned and returned. He asked himself why he wanted to go to Magdeburg. What was there? Only memories. The realities would all have fled, or died or be rubble and broken glass. He had seen so many towns that had become anonymous heaps without meaning. Another mound of stone, another mound of bricks. Timber shattered and charred. They had all had names, people, familiar bars, trees, railings, the smell of bread, dogs that stole from the butcher, girls who sold themselves against some quiet wall.

He was not sure that he wanted Inga. At first they had been crazed with the exploration of each other's bodies. She wanted sex urgently, always, until he almost begged for mercy while she laughed at him, caressing herself. But she was avaricious and there was no doubt that her tastes were very different from his. She had no time for his carpentry for a start, wanting him immediately to open a shop, to sell not make. She could not understand the pleasure of making. She could make nothing herself, not even a cake, not even a dress. Was that what he was going back for? That and the Russians and the hate.

Wilhelm lit a cigarette with difficulty, holding it inside the collar of his coat. He had taken up smoking now that he was earning some real money, the tiny amount they earned on the farm. His face was young and cheerful in the brief flare of light. Catching Heinz's eye in that moment before it went out, he winked.

'What do you think of my girl friend then?' he asked. Heinz said nothing although he knew the remark was addressed to him. Wolfgang responded in the darkness.

'She's pretty but she's too young. She's only a schoolgirl. You leave her alone if you don't want trouble.

'She doesn't want to be left alone. Anyway, she's a well-developed girl.'

'You'll get her into real trouble if her parents find out.'

'If he gets her into real trouble,' said Ehrich drily. 'I should think he'll get himself shot!'

'I don't care!'

Heinz only half-listened to them arguing, the older men trying to talk sense into the younger. He was in no position to say anything. His moral position was no better and he relied on their discretion and silence. He wondered if Wilhelm would decide to stay in England as well, but decided he was too young. Heinz reminded himself, as he did daily, that someone, some fellow German, had murdered Peter Stuck. Friendly Peter, affable Peter, Peter with the grin, Peter fond of food. Why? Because he had fought back in the first attack? Because he knew something, because he had stumbled upon something? They were all very cautious now, all afraid they might be next. Whoever had done it was still at large, still watching them. Mohnke? Muller? Waldenburg? Kunkel? He had no doubt it was one of the Nazis or their homosexual ring. Was this going to be the foundation of the new Germany?

'You know, Ehrich, I could not live in Germany controlled by a Fourth Reich,' he said, 'I can't believe in our moral right and in the sacred defence of the Fatherland and that the whole world was wrong and all that claptrap.'

His words fell in a lull. He felt all the men become alert.

'Nor could I,' said Ehrich. 'What brought that remark on?'

'Thoughts of Christmas maybe. Thoughts of Peter and going home. How could anyone kill Peter?'

'There won't be any Fourth Reich,' said Wolfgang. 'Some fools may want it but there is no one to listen. Germany will lie fallow for a hundred years.'

'The younger men don't all think Germany was wrong!' said Wilhelm. They sat in silence after that, listening to the roar of the engine, watching the receding road. The night sky was still not as black as the enclosing hedgerows which seemed to try to clasp the lorry as it passed, rattling on the canvas. The same night sky as we have over Germany, Wolfgang was thinking. Their gloom was deep.

When he returned to his bunk, Heinz took out his diary. He kept no more than notes in it, knowing that it was not private property. Today he wrote:

'Farm. Seems out of money. Logs, mangolds bad. With M. Weather cold. Decision needed.'

CHAPTER ELEVEN

Christmas Eve. The cockerel knew its time had come. It had never displayed any particular fear of Robert despite its terror of William. When he approached it with a handful of corn in his left hand and a billhook in his right hand, however, it had no illusions and fled. William and John were parties to the murder. They were to head him off, but the bird eluded their flapping arms. Helen looked on, ready to flee herself when they caught it. She felt no love for the bird but could not watch what was planned. Margaret hid in the kitchen saying it was bad enough having to pluck and stuff it. For Christmas dinner they were to have the cockerel and one plump non-laying fowl which could be plucked from its pen. Robert had decided on beheading because he had never wrung a bird's neck. He dreaded the whole business. The meal was to be completed by a piece of ham that Ingleton had given them.

Eventually the cockerel cornered itself. It tried to hide in the pig pen, but the pigs attacked, snapping their teeth. From there it flew and tumbled into the shed, perching on the tractor seat. Robert and the boys closed in. The bird panicked, jumped from the seat and wedged itself between one of the wheels and the wall. From there Robert drew it after being thoroughly pecked. He held its body under his left arm to pin its wings, and its neck and head bobbed wildly, beak open and eyes wide. Robert's one ambition was to get the execution over as quickly as possible. He carried it to the wood shed where there was a chopping block, transferred the bird to a position between his knees and held out its head with his left hand. In this awkward position he struck off its head with two quick blows, but it slipped and he was left clutching the head.

'Catch it!' he shouted.

'No!' they replied.

It was off. They watched it, both horrified and fascinated as it ran headless across the yard until it careered into the side of the barn and fell over kicking. The boys rushed indoors. Helen was already there, hands over her eyes. Robert went to pick it up, disgusted by what he had achieved. The kicking reminded him of Paterson. He pushed back the memories and grasped its scaly legs.

Christmas morning was seasonably white with a light dusting of overnight snow. Margaret had made up Christmas stockings for the children the evening before and laid them on the ends of their beds while they were asleep. Helen joined the boys in the early near-light and they explored them carefully, finding the small things their mother had been able to acquire and comparing them. Pencils with marbled paint, a bar of chocolate obtained from somewhere, a rubber, a comic, sweets, an orange in the toe, a pair of socks. They had always had a stocking on Christmas morning, with or without Pa. It was reassuring. They took a long time, savouring each object, eating only one of the sweets, saving everything.

'Let's go outside in the snow,' John said. 'We have to do the pumping anyway. Let's get up early before they're about. The Germans are coming at midday.'

The sun was trying to struggle over the horizon. It made a low streak of strange yellow murk, heavy with snow. Overhead the sky was clear and iron-grey. They ran out into the field in front of the house, delighted with their footsteps, delighted with the tracks of rabbits, hares, a cat and countless mice and shrews. When they felt they were safely clear they pelted each other with snowballs, Helen first on William's side then on John's, then pursued by both of them. The boys had pulled on only their shorts and trousers and a jumper, and Helen wore her school blouse and a cardigan handed on by her mother. It was cold and their breath hung in puffs. They all wore shoes because they had no boots and these were soon wet. Helen enjoyed the wild indulgence of it. She felt she had not played with the boys since they had come to this place, perhaps since Pa returned home. She felt she was being propelled into another stage of her life, a stage she was uncertain of, where Ann Baxter was knowing and she knew nothing. Where Wilhelm embarrassed her with demands, with knowing hands.

'There's more snow on the way,' said Helen, looking at the sky. 'I hope it falls. I'd like to make a snowman. A proper one.'

'Ma said there would be a surprise for us later on,' said William. They had paused to blow on their hands and stamp their feet. 'I wonder what it is? My hands hurt!' He tucked them under his armpits, shivering slightly. They were all looking back towards the farmhouse. They could see a light in their parents' room, a light downstairs in the living room. Preparations were beginning but they felt reluctant to abandon the solidarity of their play.

'I don't think we have any money, anyway,' said William. 'I don't suppose we shall get anything much. I asked for books.'

'So did I,' said John. 'I wanted a football.'

'Do you think they really are broke?' William asked Helen. She was touched by his trust and his earnestness.

'They don't tell me anything more than you.'

'No, but you're bigger. You might know.'

'I think there's nothing to spare.' She pulled the cardigan about her.

'Anyway, it's Christmas and we aren't going to talk about that!'

She started to trudge back towards the house, knowing she must help her mother, protect her from the irritation of Pa.

'Are you going to eat the chicken?' asked William, walking fast to keep up with her. He was concerned that the magic of their play had been broken. He wanted to prolong the conversation, talk to her properly as they had on that day long ago when they first visited the farm in the heady heat of summer. He felt that Helen had changed since then, becoming more distant from them. She was growing rounder, changing. It alarmed him.

'I will!' declared John who had heard the question. 'I don't care.'

'I think I will,' said William.

'I'm not sure,' said Helen. It was a tactful reply. She had already decided she would eat the ham.

They reached the pump and began their work, accustomed to the rhythm of the clanking, counting quietly between speech. Helen watched the two boys, clutching herself against the cold. They were thin, wiry, pale. She wondered what Wilhelm was doing this Christmas Day, what was happening in the camp that he had tried to describe. She was ashamed to think of him, of how he had slid his hand between her legs. He had wanted them to make love. He had met her one day after school and they had gone into the barn and sat down behind the straw bales, surrounded by the peaceful noises of the hens. They had talked. Wilhelm had talked about Ann Baxter, telling her things they had done, and his hand had moved confidently. She had jumped away.

'No. Not that. Don't you understand!'

'*Ja*.' Wilhelm had grinned at her. He didn't sound convincing. It had been a shock to her although she knew she should have expected it.

'Let me pump,' she said, to dispel her thoughts, 'I'm cold.' She was pleased to be with her brothers. William smiled at her happily.

The house had been decorated with the abundant holly from their hedges and with paper lanterns that the boys had made at school. The fire was especially bright and Robert had carried in a large stock of logs. Smells of cooking started as soon as it was fully light. Margaret had dressed in one of her two best frocks and was determined to make an occasion of it despite their financial situation. She was particularly determined that Robert's gloom should not be allowed to blight their first real Christmas together.

'This is the first proper one you've had with all your family,' she reminded him. He looked surprised, then agreed it probably was. After breakfast the children opened their main presents — books for the boys and a book and a jumper for Helen.

'Here is the surprise!' said Margaret.

From behind her back she produced two parcels the children had never seen. They stared at them as if they were treasure chests.

'One is from your Aunt Sarah in the Bahamas and one from Uncle Bill and Aunt Ruth in America.'

But the children were not listening, they were examining. The parcels smelled of travel and jute string and sealing wax. Each knot was bright red and glossy with drops like new wet blood. They examined the customs label, the writing, the stamps. They had never seen foreign stamps before. From the Bahamas were some with the King's head and scenes and some green with black roundels with a ship in sail. From America, Presidents and American troops raising a flag. They would have been present enough. When the parcel from the Bahamas was opened, unimaginable treats spilled out — a packet of moist sultanas, a packet of glossy raisins, dates, chocolate, a book for each of them, a letter. Margaret shared the sultanas out into five piles and they ate them slowly. William soaked each one in spit in his mouth until it was large and squashy before biting the fruit. They would make them last for days. Robert said they were for cooking and took his and Margaret's into the kitchen. John made a face at William.

The parcel from America was a disaster. Inside were two heavy boxes of chewing gum. They stared at them in dismay. It couldn't be eaten. They couldn't comprehend.

'What *is* it?' William kept asking.

They liked the stamps.

Heinz and Wolfgang were dropped off at the lane at midday. In the farmhouse they heard the driver honk twice to give them warning. Flakes of snow were swirling down thinly and the sky remained yellow. Both men wore their greatcoats over their best clothes. Their hair was flattened with cream and their trousers had creases. Robert opened the door to them, shook their hands and stepped aside. The men entered the room awkwardly, looking about it as if they had never seen it before, enjoying the sight of the fire, the smell of cooking.

'Take your coats off,' said Margaret. 'Hang them up in the hall . . .'

Heinz looked at her quickly, looked her over, took in her good dress. Robert had retreated to throw a log on the fire and Heinz winked and gave her a slight nod of approval. She found herself smiling back helplessly. Wolfgang coughed, straightened his jacket pockets ostentatiously.

'My *Anstandsdame*!' said Heinz. Margaret looked at him blankly.

'Chaperon,' Wolfgang supplied. He looked so solemn that she nearly laughed and had to flee into the living room. Both men carried brown paper bundles which they clutched under their left arms. Robert ushered them to a position in front of the fire where they solemnly shook hands with the children, wishing them a happy Christmas. Robert gave them each a glass of sherry, which they held uncertainly until he and Margaret had one.

'Happy Christmas,' said Margaret, and when she drank they all did. Neither Heinz nor Wolfgang recognised the taste of this strange brown wine, but it warmed them and the fire was roaring. They were very touched, realizing that it must be scarce and that this was an act of friendship.

Margaret still did not understand Robert's motives for asking the men for Christmas. It was uncharacteristically generous and seemed too idealistic. She had pondered, then decided that it was probably an act of reconciliation or even guilt rather than sympathy. Or perhaps he simply missed the company of men now that he was bereft of his army career. These men had after all been soldiers and they shared a common past. He had never discussed it with her or offered an explanation and she was upset by this exclusion. She wished she could believe it was a simple act of generosity.

'We have made something for the boys,' said Heinz. He and Wolfgang proffered the wrapped bundles. She gestured to John and William to step forward.

'This is for William,' said Heinz. He was watching Margaret, but she was uninterested, distant. William took the package, John took his. They tore at the cheap paper when they should have been saving it. William exposed a stubby tugboat, made of wood and painted in bright colours; John a train with elephant ears and raised piping painted silver. The carvings were solid, heavy and seemed to be of one piece. The boys were enchanted. They turned the pieces around, smelled them. They reeked of linseed oil and fresh paint. They felt them, noting that the surfaces still had that slight sticky feeling when they dragged their fingertips over them. They were the first toys they had ever possessed.

'Heinz made them both,' said Wolfgang. 'I can't take credit for them.'

'Say, "thank you", boys,' said Robert unnecessarily. Their silence and concentration were thanks enough.

'Something for Helen,' said Wolfgang. Helen was surprised, she was expecting nothing, especially not a carving, but Wolfgang produced a wooden box which had undoubtedly once been for cigars. He opened it and showed it to her. Inside nestled two sets of chess men, carved and burned and strangely foreign, creatures of the Black Forest. Helen hesitated, then took them in wonder, picking up one piece at a time. A piece of material, some sort of red plush, had been used to line the box. It looked like a section of upholstery and probably was.

'I made these,' said Wolfgang. 'You will tell English people that we are not so bad? That Germans are not all barbarians?'

Later, when they ate the fowls, the boys swallowed their nausea and tried some, then some more. William refused a leg, feeling this was an act of cannibalism. Helen ate only the ham. Heinz and Wolfgang were alert, all eyes, picking up their knives and forks when the others did, careful to jump to their feet to help on every occasion. They ate slowly when their bellies urged them on. The fire was kept ablaze until even the brick floor glowed with heat. Robert had bought bottles of beer and they drank these as if they were nectar, sipping and declaring it was wonderful. William's cat patrolled beneath the table for scraps and William dropped bits surreptitiously. Conversation was polite and a little stilted.

Heinz and Wolfgang entertained them to a description of their towns in Germany, of the farms, the vines, the cattle, the hard winters, the hot summers. The war was not mentioned.

Robert asked Heinz if he had a wife, a girl friend.

Heinz froze. He had been raising his fork to his lips. Now he put it down on his plate again. He glanced up to meet Robert's eyes.

'No.'

Robert nodded, chewing. There was a thoughtful look in his eyes. Under the table, Heinz straightened his leg with infinite care and with his foot tapped Wolfgang a warning on his ankle. Wolfgang did not move a muscle.

'You must have a girlfriend back home,' Robert insisted. 'I don't believe that!'

He laughed what Margaret called his officer's laugh, full of false heartiness, jarring and intrusive.

'No.'

Heinz glanced rapidly sideways at Margaret. Her face was composed and rigid. He had no doubt she was tuned in to every nuance. Heinz felt he had to expand if he did not want this enquiry to continue.

'Not since I was a boy. Nothing serious. There was no time before . . . this.'

Robert nodded, still chewing, still looking at Heinz, still looking thoughtful. Heinz felt suddenly vulnerable. His position as a prisoner in this country had been dispersed with contact and with labour but at that moment he felt he was staring at a hostile officer again. The sort of man who had interrogated him at Kempton Park. Men without pity because they were controlling high passions. Although he was not particularly hot he felt himself break out in a sweat. He made himself raise his fork to his mouth, put in the food and chew. In his nervousness he gagged on it and could not for a moment swallow. Still Robert watched him, interested.

'Plenty of time when you get home, eh?'

'Yes, of course. Plenty of time.'

Heinz made himself smile, producing a grimace. He wondered what Robert knew or guessed. He was sure he had just had a warning. It could not be his imagination and could not just be accident. He dared not for a moment even look at Margaret who had sat as still as a mouse. He kept his eyes on his plate and concentrated on chewing everything very small, rolling it around until it was moist and easy to eat. Robert suddenly turned to Wolfgang and began a determined conversation about plumbing and the pump and what they would do in the new year when the electricity arrived. Heinz washed down his food with a gulp of beer. The incident had shaken him. He looked up to see if Robert was still watching him. He was. Even as he spoke to Wolfgang his eyes slid sideways from time to time, keeping him under surveillance. He ventured a glance at the children, who smiled at him. He worked round them all, feeling cheered by their open friendliness, touched by the thin, pinched faces and skinny wrists of the boys. His eyes briefly caught Margaret's.

'Happy Christmas, Heinz,' she said, and with the faintest pause, 'and Wolfgang.' She picked up her glass and drank from it. 'Thank you for all your work. Here's to 1946!'

'And may it be prosperous!' said Wolfgang, energetically injecting just the right note of joviality.

'And may it be prosperous,' echoed Robert. The words sounded hollow from him and fell like the well-wishes of a man on the gallows. Margaret got to her feet and poured out more beer. The moment passed.

As they were leaving, feeling fuller than they had for four years, Heinz and Wolfgang shook hands formally at the door with each of the children, then Margaret then finally Robert. They all stood in a row in the hall, watched by the driver who had come up to the house and been given the beer he had expected. He was disappointed there was none of the whisky he had hoped for, but you had to be in the know to get whisky. The man had a lorry full of Germans. He also had a belly full of beer. He knew he shouldn't really be driving.

'Good evening,' they all said to one another, 'and Merry Christmas!'

Margaret contrived to hold his hand for just a moment and squeeze it gently. Her eyes were kind but troubled. Heinz knew he had thinking to do. They crunched out into a white landscape with half a moon. Robert shut the door quickly behind them. Down on the road they could hear the other Germans singing. The driver trudged in front with his hands thrust in his pockets.

'Getting cold, lads,' he observed.

'*Ja*,' said Heinz.

'I like it,' observed Wolfgang.

When they reached the lorry, Heinz felt an enormous sense of relief. It was as if he had escaped from England. They climbed up over the tailboard, were hauled up by the men inside.

'You'll have to wait,' said the driver and stamped off a few yards to the hedge where he relieved himself at length. Two of the Germans jumped out to do the same, choosing their own place. The driver, not noticing, swung himself up into the driving seat and had started off before they realised what he was doing.

'Stop!' they shouted, beating on the back of his cab. The two men were already running and stumbling down the road behind the truck. One of them slipped on ice and fell sprawling. The lorry stopped abruptly. The driver opened his door and swung himself half out.

'What the hell is it?' he demanded. From behind them they could hear the two men laughing and yelling. A snowball hit the lorry then another.

'They were having a piss,' shouted Wolfgang. 'You nearly left them behind!' Another snowball hurtled inside the lorry, hitting one of the men.

'Let's get them!' urged a tall thin man Heinz knew only as Kurt. He swung himself over the tailboard and dropped softly into the snow at the roadside. He immediately started to scoop it up in his hands, rolling a snowball and hurling it back. Another man followed. Then another until half had gone.

'Get back in, you beggars!' shouted the driver. He could only open his door so far because it touched the bank and hedge in the narrow lane. 'Get back in or I'll leave you here!'

The men weren't listening and they didn't believe the driver. They ran up and down the road in the half moonlight as mad as hares, pelting each other, slipping and falling, hurling snowballs until their hands hurt as if they had been crushed. Heinz and the others watched. The improbability of the moment entranced them.

There was the sound of a door. The guard who travelled with the driver climbed down, unhitching his rifle from his shoulder, but when he reached the level of the tailgate he stood, holding it in his hands, and watched. He was a young man, pale and vigilant as a heron. Whooping, the men rushed for the lorry with the same concerted impulse with which they had left it. They scrambled back in, clumsy with cold. The guard shook his head at them. He was grinning slightly although he tried to look stern.

'Happy Christmas!' the miscreants shouted at him. He nodded, wagging a long finger at them as you would at a naughty dog, and climbed back into his cab. The driver shut his door again, the lorry moved on.

'This is a funny prison,' said Wolfgang. 'We have Christmas dinner out and a snowball fight and now we can't wait to get our bus home. What children we are.'

'There's nothing wrong in it.' said Heinz. Wolfgang could be too solemn at times.

'If we stay here, we will become too dependent. That is the trouble with it.' He paused, lowered his voice although he could not have been easily audible against the grinding of the lorry's engine. 'I thought you were in real trouble with Mr Ellis. You know, when he asked about your girl friend. I think he's on to something.'

'I don't think so.' Heinz tried to sound casual. He could see the way that Wolfgang was ponderously working.

'Maybe you should give her up,' said Wolfgang. 'It would be sensible.' Heinz did not reply. He watched the retreating countryside through the frame of the tail opening. In the half-moonlight it was black and grey and white like an old film. He knew he could not give Margaret up.

That evening the camp had a relaxed air. Animosities had been set aside although there was a certain curiosity coupled with jealousy for those who had spent the day with an English host. At nine o'clock when everyone had returned the men gathered in the open to sing carols to music provided by the camp band. The weather had cleared again and the mass of men steamed, the white drift of their breaths caught in the arc lights.

Middleton and Schneider stood on a raised dais, listening. Schneider kept his hands behind his back and stood stiffly as though on parade at ease. Middleton had his arms folded and wore a thick grey sweater against the cold. They appreciated his lack of uniform. Middleton sang some of the words although they were in German, and they could see he managed them well. When they had finished singing he spoke, about Christmas, about the meaning of Christ's sacrifice, about reconciliation and the love of man for man. It was sad and solemn and none among the men seemed unaffected although many pretended to be. Throughout his speech, whenever there was a break in the tannoy, they could hear the clear tumbling sound of English church bells, unlike anything any of them had heard in Germany, ringing complex rounds that swayed in the air.

Middleton stopped at the end of his speech and held up his hand, asking them to listen. In concentrated silence they strained to catch the weaving music. They listened for perhaps half a minute.

'You see,' said Middleton, 'that is the first time that we in England have been able to ring the bells for Christmas since the war began. Things are returning to normal here and all over Europe.' They ended by singing *Silent Night* to the stars.

When they returned to their huts, Wolfgang came briefly to pay Heinz a visit. 'Lights out' had been delayed until eleven. Ehrich had been sent a packet of biscuits by his mother, with a letter. Neither Heinz nor Wolfgang received any post. Ehrich shared out the biscuits with his friends in the hut. There were three each and they were German biscuits of the sort that were common before the war. They each made their biscuits last half an hour, nibbling at them like mice and savouring every morsel. When they had finished they passed the wrapper from hand to hand so that each man could read every word.

'Well, are we going home in 1946?' asked Ehrich, voicing what no one wanted to consider.

'Who knows.' It was Walther, dry, enigmatic. From elsewhere in the camp they could hear voices raised in song. Heinz thought of Peter, dead and murdered by a German and buried in an English churchyard. When he was free he would plant flowers on Peter's grave. He thought of the men throwing snowballs and the thin young English guard, alert but sympathetic. He had watched. He had not tried to intervene. He thought of Margaret, of his first glimpse of her in the summer meadow that was already so far away. Of George and Tom, the 'Walnuts'. There was nothing to go back for in Magdeburg. There would not even be biscuits from before the war.

CHAPTER TWELVE

Winter lingered like a disease on the land, not clearing up until late February. The boys saw it in terms of blackness — black mud, black puddles and ditches, black shoes and clothes. The farm yards were treacherous, deep with mire and the confined cattle lowed with discontent in their yard. The pigsty was a place of fluids and soft squalor. The days were perceptibly longer when the sun shone.

Margaret walked round the fields with Helen. The boys had their own amusements and Helen was no part of them. There seemed to be nothing else to do at weekends in this lull between seasons. Margaret compared it to a dead water between tides. They were walking round the far fields in wellingtons one Saturday trying to discern some change in the trees. Young oaks still rattled with tobacco-brown leaves. The drays of squirrels formed untidy clumps in trees. Their occupants were nowhere to be seen. Roving fieldfares and redwings sprinted from field to field in mixed bands. The two women stood at the edge of the woodland watching these intent birds as they stripped hollies and rowans, gulping the berries with unashamed gluttony. Soon they would go and that would be spring. They watched a family of goldfinches dangling from teazles and discovered wild snowdrops in bloom at the perimeter of the woods. They watched busy blue tits destroying young lamb's-tails which showed only the first hint of dirty yellow. 'They peck them to pieces,' said Helen. 'They'll never have a chance.'
  'There's plenty.'

From the woodland somewhere in the distance they could hear sawing and chopping. This was the time of the woodmen. Hedges should be cut back, hurdles should be made, coppice chestnut felled, stripped and worked. Somewhere Robert had engaged George and Tom to keep the roadside hedges subdued. He had only done this because he had to. He had received a letter from the local Council complaining about how they overleaned the road and threatening all sorts of powers. They could fine him, they could compel him or they could even have them trimmed and charge him. This last had spurred Robert on.

'I like these walks,' said Helen. 'I like watching all the living things.'

'I know you do. I know you get bored and lonely too.' Helen looked slightly embarrassed. She always wondered what her mother knew about Wilhelm and herself. They had never discussed it.

'A bit,' said Helen. 'I've grown to think of this as home now. When we first visited the farm, before we had bought it, I found it terrifying.

'And is it all right now?'

Helen stopped.

'The last time you asked me that was when we were polishing lamps. I remember it, you see. It was the privy I didn't like. It still is.'

'Do I talk to you so little that you remember every occasion?' Margaret was anxious.

'We don't talk a great deal,' said Helen. 'I suppose there isn't really a lot of time,' she paused, 'except that we seem to have plenty of it. I suppose what I mean is that Pa fills up all the moments. Either by being there or because you're worried. Either way we have no time.'

'It isn't as bad as that, is it?' Margaret could not disguise her hurt. She saw Helen's face withdraw, close down immediately and cursed herself for being so vulnerable and for expressing it.

'Of course it isn't,' said Helen and the moment was lost. They walked on again. A light mist was forming although it was only two in the afternoon. It smelled sweet and felt slightly warm, trapping the faint concealed heat of the sun. They paused at a huge chestnut, examining it. Buds had formed on every twig and each was dewed with a drop of sticky essence. Helen touched the buds with her finger tips, rubbing them together, then stooping to wipe her fingers in the beaded grass.

'Are we really broke?' she asked. 'I'm old enough to be told, you know. I won't tell the boys. And, if we are, what are we going to do?'

Margaret thrust her hands into the pockets of the old jacket she was wearing, drawing it around herself as if for protection. Helen noted the unconscious movement.

'We certainly do have financial problems. I hadn't really realised that in a farm you plough everything into the ground, even your hopes, and then have to wait. It never occurred to me. This is a bad time. Everything is spent and nothing's coming back. It's all in the hands of nature. The mangolds just about did it.'

'What will we do if we have to sell?'

'That depends on your father.'

'Why does it depend on Pa?' Helen's voice was sharp and impatient. Margaret flushed.

'Who else can it depend on?' She walked on quickly, in case Helen answered.

Towards the end of the month Mr Dudley from the Electricity Board arrived in a small black car. He brought a manila folder and a collection of forms printed on yellowed economy paper. He was a small man with a shiny bald spot which he scratched occasionally. His manner was very self-important, as of an aid worker bringing relief to the natives. He had dead-fish eyes and looked mistrustfully around the living room as though to judge if they were worthy of what was in his benefice to give. Robert had bristled at the sight of him and Margaret was left to do most of the talking.

'It will be an end to filling your oil lamps,' the man said, gesturing to the lamp on a hook on the ceiling. 'And you can get your bathroom finished and have some modern amenities. I expect you're looking forward to that.'

'Yes.' Margaret could not elaborate because Robert was scowling in the background. The man from the Electricity Board had told them how much the connection charge would be and had explained the tariff. He had made it plain that he wanted the connection charge paid sooner rather than later or there would be no electricity. Margaret knew they could not pay. Not now. She had seen their bank statement. It was overdrawn every month and every month the overdraft grew higher. They had forgotten the man from the Electricity Board. They had made his appointment last November.

'Just leave the forms,' said Robert.

'Does this mean you don't want a supply? When people ask me to leave the forms it generally means that. When people want a supply it's my experience they are so pleased to see me they sign on the spot!'

'No, it *doesn't* mean we don't want a supply!' Robert's voice was angry. 'I don't like your method of pushing us. We want a little time to read them properly.' He had on his military voice. He might have added "my man" at the end of each sentence. Dudley was unabashed.

'Of course if you don't have your supply put in now with everyone else it will cost you more. We will have to return for you alone, and you will have to pay the full cost of the visit instead of it being split. As long as you understand that.'

'I'm sure we understand that, Mr Dudley,' said Robert, 'but you must understand that paraffin is cheap to us and the oil lamps give a good light. There's all the interior wiring to consider before we see if it's such a bargain.'

Mr Dudley got to his feet, sensing defeat.

'Just think of machine milking,' he said, playing his last card. 'I hear you've the beginnings of a herd, Mr Ellis.' He could not place Robert as a die-hard Gabriel. He had met many of those, men who had never used an oil lamp in their lives let alone electricity. They were a dying breed but the East Anglian sense of economy was still about, as hard as an east wind off the fens. He picked up his folder and replaced the forms, then changed his mind and laid them out again.

'I'll call back in about a week.' He said good-day and left. Margaret looked at her hands and said nothing.

'It's the cows or the electricity,' said Robert. The words sounded like pebbles dropping on a tin tray. Margaret knew perfectly well what he meant but snatched anxiously at his chance to speak about it. 'What do you mean?' she asked, wishing immediately it did not make her sound so stupid. She was so easily disadvantaged.

'We can't afford the electricity,' said Robert crossly. 'Of course you understood that. You can't have been living in an entire vacuum all this time. Do you want to see the feed bill for those cows? I told you we couldn't afford to keep them without the mangolds.'

'I know, I know.'

'Well, don't ask what I mean.'

'I'm sorry.'

Robert was drumming on the dining-table with his fingers. His air of suppressed violence was alarming.

'I don't mind about the electricity,' said Margaret. 'I can keep filling oil lamps. It doesn't matter . . .'

'Don't be the brave wife,' snapped Robert. 'I can't bear that. This farm is a bloody disaster. Can't you see that? I can't feed the bloody animals anyway so what difference does it make. There isn't a choice. If we fold tomorrow this house will be worth much more with electricity and no one will give a damn about a few cows. With electricity someone else can put in a milking parlour, chick brooders . . .'

'But we aren't folding.' Margaret tried again, knowing in her heart that he would only hurt her for her sympathy.

'I've planted all the wrong things. Do you realise that?'

Margaret was puzzled.

'You talked it through with Clutton . . .'

'Clutton told me to plant what the Government wanted and I listened. He took me for a fool, and I am. Oats and beans. Now there's going to be a glut. Ingleton didn't plant oats and beans. West didn't plant oats and beans. Thousands of others did. So the bathroom and the house have to be finished and the cows must go.'

Then what? she wondered. Robert got to his feet with jerky energy.

'I'll arrange it right away. They'll go within the week. The longer they stay the more they eat and the more we get into debt. They can settle in somewhere else before calving.'

He turned and left. She looked round the room. The red bricks and dark beams oppressed her. The lamp on the hook was badly polished and she hated the oil lamps despite what she had said. The glass of the lamp was blackened and neglected. Last year they had been cleaned daily. Already this year she cleaned them once a week. Helen had become impatient with the chores too and anxious to have more time by herself or with Anne Baxter. She was moody and growing up fast. Margaret had seen Heinz look at Helen on two occasions and had felt a pang of fear and jealousy. Heinz had looked at her as a woman.

She was taken by surprise when Robert returned with Heinz and Wolfgang in his car. It was typical of the nervous and impetuous mood he was in, she supposed. He had driven straight to the camp in Braintree, seen Middleton and picked them up.

'We must get on with finishing the house,' he said by way of explanation, walking past her with the men, heading upstairs to the work. Wolfgang lifted his forage cap to her as he passed. Heinz gave her a quick smile and made a droll face. She could hear them clumping about upstairs, objects being dragged about on the floor. Robert reappeared quickly and would have walked straight past her and out of the door again if she had not called after him.

'Robert, where are you going?'

'I'm going to put the cows out on the back field while it's fine, to get some grass, then I'm going back to Braintree. Or maybe in to Colchester. I have to find out where the sales are. I have to see Kitton.'

'Is he the right man?'

'Why not? Do we know anyone else?'

He went. Margaret was left hovering, disconcerted by the sudden arrival of Heinz and not knowing what to do. There were largely decorations to complete now and a few bits of carpentry. She was forced to consider if she wanted to leave the farm, even though she had never wanted to come to it in the first place. Her feelings were very confused. She enjoyed the countryside, the freedom of her walks and the fields. She knew that she was trapped by it at the same time. She now saw that they were all prisoners of the time scale of nature and the annual rotation of the harvest. The slowness and magnitude of that terrified her. Things could no longer be measured by appreciable time, by months or weeks. They would be measured in years. How many *years* would it take for them to find their feet, how many *years* to breed a herd? But that was all over. The herd might restart in two or three years' time. Until then it would be only field crops and chickens and pigs unless Robert thought of something else. She was fond of the young cows. Unlike the chickens or pigs they had personalities. They enjoyed life, kicked up their heels and appeared to have a sense of fun. She would miss them.

She thought of Heinz. It had become natural to have him in the house with Wolfgang. It had become natural to wait for him, to wait for some time to become available for the two of them. He had become part of her life. She knew that like the farm itself it would have to come to an end. She had not contemplated that it might be so soon.

Robert had begun to talk wistfully of the colonies, of how the climate made all the difference in farming or anything else. He had not explained what he had in mind, but she thought that she understood. It was a theme that she had heard before the war. That somewhere there must be a place with a living for him because he was white, middle-class and well-spoken. Robert had never been able to deal well with people. He wanted a world that was free from Taylors and Testers and bank managers and Cluttons. Since his career in the Army this view had become more pronounced. He wanted obedience without question. From her, from everyone, because he was what he was. If she could have viewed it from a dispassionate distance it would have seemed desperately sad. Now he seemed to be contemplating some more distant prison for them all where he could rule as a white man.

She made up her mind to walk round the fields and visit the cows while she sorted out her thoughts; then she heard a car approach. She moved to the window and saw it splashing through the puddles. She had expected Robert again but was surprised and annoyed to see Baxter. He was intruding upon her private plans of solitude. Nevertheless she felt ashamed of her appearance and immediately ran to the hall to comb her hair in the mirror there. She looked at herself critically. The woman looking back had an anxious face which made her seem even thinner. She tried relaxing her expression and rubbed her cheeks to heighten their colour. She never felt like this in front of Heinz. Baxter created a sense of panic. He would be well dressed of course. She was angry with him for calling when Heinz was in the house. She knew without Mary Merrow's warning that he was a dangerous man. Take care of Baxter she had said, steer wide. Yet he flustered her into these absurd preenings.

He knocked on the door with irritating vigour. She paused deliberately before opening it.

'You were expecting me.' It was a statement, not a question. She was sufficiently taken aback to be unable to conceal it. 'Surely you knew I would be back? I thought of calling at Christmas but decided that wouldn't be a good idea.'

'What do you want?' she found herself hanging on to the door to bar his progress. He was dressed in cavalry twill and sports jacket with a canary-yellow waistcoat. His eyes were already past her and into the house.

'Who's that working?'

'Two of the German prisoners. They're decorating.'

'Let me guess. Wolfgang and Heinz.'

She ignored the irritating smile he permitted himself.

'I know you're here alone,' he continued, 'apart from our friends upstairs. I passed Robert on the road. He was on his way to Braintree. Have you been avoiding me, or have I been avoiding you?'

'That's a ridiculous sort of question.'

'Will you ask me in?'

She moved to one side to stop this exchange on the step.

'You can't stay long. The children will be home from school soon.'

'You *are* avoiding me. That's a terrible excuse!'

Margaret felt herself colouring.

'Don't be ridiculous. It's a statement of fact.'

Baxter's eyes were roving round the room. Margaret realised that this was only the second time that he had visited the house.

'Things not going too well, I gather. Having to sell the cows.'

'Please come to the point. What do you want here?'

He looked at her gravely, then as if making a decision sat in an armchair. Everything he did seemed studied. He now had his back to the window so that she could only partly see his face. In response she picked up the iron poker and jabbed at the sulking fire so that it sent a column of orange sparks up the chimney. Baxter stretched his legs out in front of him to emphasise his relaxed calm. Margaret continued to play with the fire, balancing another piece of wood across the centre of it and levering up the logs. She was pleased to see a small flame lick out, then become steady.

'You will have to light the lamps soon,' said Baxter. 'I should think they'll need light upstairs to work.' He indicated the big lamp on the hook on the beam. 'But all that will change, won't it, when the electricity is installed?'

She said nothing, wondering what he knew. She wanted to tell him to leave but did not dare provoke him. She moved from the insipid flicker of firelight and deliberately sat where it was most dark.

'You're short of money, aren't you?' he said. Margaret sat still and said nothing. 'I know,' he continued. 'I know Prewitt. If God was just, Prewitt would be turned to stone. Winter's bad for farmers. January and February are the worst months. How's the dictator taking it?'

Margaret could not control her anger.

'You mustn't talk like that about Robert. Leave this house!'

'You don't really mean that, Margaret. You know you're lonely. When the evenings have drawn in and there's nothing but worries to see in the firelight. I don't want you to leave. For entirely selfish reasons, I hasten to add. We started off well together. Have you had any fun, any real laughing fun since our Grand Prix in the field?'

'Your conceit amazes me. Of course I have.'

'Tell me what it was, then. What was fun?'

'Teaching the boys to ride bikes on a gusty day, watching them succeed. Making bread. Watching the young cows chase each other. Gathering holly, seeing the corn grow, seeing the birds in flocks on a frosty morning. Do you want me to go on?'

'But none of that is with Robert.'

'I wish you would leave.'

It was true that she had not summoned up a single shared thing but she had not meant to be disloyal.

'I have the money you need,' he said. She moved as if about to leap up but he raised his hands rapidly, palms towards her, willing her to silence. 'I would like to help. No interest. Except perhaps in you.' She did leap up.

'We don't need your money. Now go away.'

'You don't want it, but you need it.' His even features and smooth manner infuriated Margaret to an extent she thought she had never experienced before. 'Think about it,' he continued, 'life is all a deal. My marriage is nothing at all, not a piece of chaff in the wind. What's yours to you? I'm a realist, you see. And what's this German to you? You know it can't last. Think about my offer.'

He was on his feet, smoothly, and had reached the door and gone before she could gather her wits. She watched him back the car out. He waved to her cheerfully from the open window, then wound it up and drove off. She sat back in the chair, angry at her incompetence and shaky with anger. Upstairs she heard something being dragged — they were working with trestles — then the rumble of voices. It was comforting after Baxter's visit. The lick of flames had died, perhaps when Baxter had opened the door.

House dark, mind empty, heart empty, she thought. Baxter's horrific honesty should not shake her. She should laugh at it. She determined to continue with the walk she had planned and not to allow him to wipe everything from her mind. She got up and pulled on her wellington boots and coat, letting herself out quietly so that Heinz upstairs should not know that she had slipped away. She did not want anyone to know where she was.

Outside, the wind gusted fitfully, breaking up patches of cloud. She walked across the mud of the yard and followed the hedges of the six-acre and the nine-acre in a long sweep, making for the cows in their grazing. The loss of their vitality would sap the life-force of the farm, she was sure of it. She entered the bean field, inspecting the beans and realising that she had not seen them since they first appeared with seedling vigour. Then they had been pale knuckles of vegetation, punching through the cracking earth. Now the plants were high enough to hide a dog, but she could see there was something wrong. They were dark green, almost black, and the leaves hung downwards. They looked as though the frost had nipped them. Moving forwards she saw that some lay horizontal and that the stems looked pulpy. She picked up a stalk and it collapsed, bending in half, then folding over completely with a soft noise. She could smell rot. Her fingers were wet with slime. She retraced her steps to the hedgerow and wiped her hands on a tussock of long grass. Now that she could see further into the field she realised that whole areas of it lay flat. A lark rose singing from the decay, triggered by a shaft of sunlight that burst from the cloud. It spiralled higher and higher, answered by another in a distant field. The rays of the sun formed themselves into a dramatic fan. Margaret watched the scene of beauty, feeling she might never see it again. She was struck by the same overwhelming sadness she had felt when she had seen her dead father.

'Are you sure you really want to see him?'

Judith, magnificent in black, projecting strength and love for them all.

'Yes, Mum, just a peep.'

'All right, now hold my hand.'

He was very white and his lips had been coloured. The shape of his face had changed. Margaret thought, I shall never see him again, ever, and had looked, then squeezed her eyes, looked, then squeezed her eyes, trying in this way to imprint the sight for eternity. Now she could no longer really remember what she saw.

She had felt the same at the end of their holidays by the sea. She had walked with Judith and one of her sisters along the beach somewhere. The sun was setting and the blaze was cataclysmic. The other two said it was getting cold and wanted to go back but Margaret sat on a wet dark rock staring into the blaze until her senses were confused and numb.

Judith had to shake her.

'Come along, Margaret, are you all right. Now you've fallen. You're tired. It's bed for you, right away. We have an early start tomorrow.'

Her eyes were swamped with clouds of colour. How could she explain.

The yellow of the sun caught echoes in banks of rose hips in the hedge around her, in yellow coltsfoot blazing on the bank. She moved on past woodland where celandines and wood anemones littered the floor with the wasteful abundance of nature. Birds sang in the secret glades, chattering in alarm as she passed. She wanted the children to grow on this farm, despite the loneliness and the isolation.

She was terrified by how much Baxter seemed to know.

She hurried to the far field to look at the young cows. They saw her immediately and sidled towards her, snorting and bobbing. They were dribbling from the pleasures of real grass. She wished them well, wherever they were going.

The boys soon established that only Heinz and Wolfgang were in the house and it gave them the opportunity they had been awaiting. They returned to the barn where they had stored their bikes and climbed to the very top of the straw bales. In a recess between them and the wooden wall John pulled out a paint tin. The lid was firmly hammered on and the tin had been bound lengthways with four strands of stout fence wire, with a further hoop of it around the middle. The wires had been twisted taut with pliers. In the very edge of the lid was a small hole with a piece of straw in it. John set the tin on a bale and both boys sat back and looked at it with satisfaction.

'It's a big tin,' said William. There was excitement and awe in his voice. He was afraid of the tin. 'What if Pa finds out?'

'Why should he?' John was dismissive. 'Anyway, I don't care. No one will ever know what happened. How could they?

'Won't it bring the police?'

'So what.' He paused, picking up a straw to chew. 'There won't be anything to find. Not with an explosion like that.' He looked at William. 'What do you think of Pa anyway?'

'What do you mean?'

'You know what I mean. Ma and him don't get on, do they? He doesn't really like us either. There's no money. We're the poorest kids at school, I reckon.'

'I don't want to talk about it.'

'Why not?' John was relentless, his voice demanding.

'I just don't.'

'You're afraid to think about it, aren't you? You should do. What's going to happen if this farm goes bust?'

William's immediate reaction was to deny it, but he knew that if he did John would pursue him.

'Yes, I am,' he said. 'So what? I can be afraid if I want to.'

John was satisfied with the admission.

'I'm not afraid,' he said. 'Let's go.' He got up and picked up the tin. 'Bring the cordite.'

William fished down between the bales and brought out a two-pound jam jar full of short black grains. He was thinking of Ma and Heinz. He could not discuss it with John. He could discuss nothing with John. Would Ma leave Pa? He liked Heinz but he didn't want him as a new father. He imagined telling his classmates at school that his mother had married a German. The notion filled him with horror. What would they do to him? What would other people do to them? He wanted desperately to love Pa and he longed for Margaret to love him too. He wanted Pa to change. His powerlessness made tears rise to his eyes. Luckily John had already climbed down from the bales and was shouting at him impatiently to hurry up. He wiped his eyes on his shirt sleeve and jumped down from bale to bale.

They took the dog with them and made their way carefully through the mulch carpet of the woods. Without leaves it was no longer a hiding place. William saw it as a huge stubble, bare and open. They moved almost noiselessly. Sometimes a rotten branch snapped softly and they paused to listen for a moment. Small birds flitted above them in high branches, disturbed by their progress. The dog chased scents this way and that, excited but finding nothing.

They crossed the clearing at a crouch. There were no signs of fresh vehicle tracks. Fallen leaves had drifted into every rut. The encampment among the trees was derelict. The boxes lay on their sides and the winter winds and snow had shredded the canvas of the walls. The Americans had not been here for months.

They advanced boldly now. It was their wood. The pile of grey bombs was monstrous and they walked to them with awe. John was ahead and stroked one of them, running his hands down its cold steel flank.

'Feel it!' he urged. 'Go on!'

William did as he was bid to prove he was not afraid of them, but his heart was pounding and he could not speak for fear. He nodded instead. The fins on the bulbous tubes seemed improbably small and, now they were beside them, William could see markings on the side and mysterious ports and countersunk screws. The bombs were chocked up on huge blocks of rough-sawn wood bolted to a wooden frame. John held a finger to his lips and they listened for a long time. Far far away they heard the sound of chopping, shots as some farmer fired at pigeons. John placed the bound tin underneath the lowest bomb in the stack, adjusting it so that it lay on its side with the hole and projecting straw touching the ground. He put out his hand to William, who automatically passed him the glass jar of cordite. John began to pour a thin trail away from the straw and the tin.

'Maybe we shouldn't be doing this,' said William, finding his voice at last. 'Maybe we'll kill someone. What about the size of the bang?'

'You're scared,' said John, continuing to lay the trail. 'There's no one here. This should wake the place up a bit. I expect they'll hear it in Braintree or even Colchester!'

'Let's not do it . . .'

'You run away then. We can't stop now.'

The trail of the fuse was extended into the woodland. John was tipping the thin line of cordite out with the greatest of care, knowing that any break in it would mean failure. He cleared away stray leaves and twigs as he went. William walked alongside him, watching and holding the dog who wanted to stick his nose in the trail, consumed with curiosity. When the powder finally ran out the fuse extended about a hundred yards.

'We'll have to run for it,' said John. 'Don't fall, don't look back and when you get to the field go straight across and don't stop until we get home. Then sneak into the house to our room.'

'Is it long enough?' asked William doubtfully. 'Will we have enough time?'

'Of course we will.' He took a box of matches from his pocket and without further comment lit the fuse. It fizzed immediately, giving off a white glare and grey smoke. They ran like hares, clearing the woods in moments, crashed through the hedge and tore across the wheat field. They stumbled over furrows and clods, arms and legs flying. Patch the dog barked with excitement and hurtled ahead.

The explosion was not what they expected. It was a dull and disappointing thud, not an earth-shattering, earth-moving, tree-flattening roar. They stopped. The dog pointed towards the source of the noise.

'They didn't go off!' said John.

'Run,' urged William. His relief made him feel sick. Saliva seemed to have lodged in his throat. John reluctantly agreed. They hurried back to the house.

William glanced at John as they ran. There was something wild about him that worried him. John seemed to hate Pa, while William didn't. John seemed to want to destroy and to have no fear. John shared nothing of himself with him. William was accustomed to blurt out his feelings but John said nothing. William wished he had someone to share with, that Pa would show some weakness or some humour, but Pa was as remote as John.

When they reached the house they managed to get to their room unseen. William took his cat with him for comfort while John was excited and began planning another explosion. William didn't listen. His eyes were turned to his Rhineland tug. It was his only toy. He felt desperately unhappy.

Robert drove back from Braintree in a black mood. Kitton the auctioneer had received him briefly but quickly passed him on to a Mr Wethered who, he said, dealt with animals. Wethered, about fifty, smelled strongly of beer and was off-hand about the cows. It was hardly a great number to get excited about. He managed to convey the impression to Robert that he was really doing him a favour to put them in the stock sale at all. Wethered had bleary eyes and wrote down the particulars in a dog-eared note pad he kept in his jacket pocket. It did not inspire confidence.

'Are you sure you've got that down?' demanded Robert brusquely. 'These are fine animals, you know. They should fetch a good price.'

Wethered sighed. It conveyed the impression of a deep and weary distrust of the opinions of mere farmers.

'I don't want to sound impolite, Mr Ellis, but you will understand that I shall have to be the judge of that. I never met a man yet who didn't believe his own beasts were fit to win at Smithfield.'

He would come and look at them tomorrow and they would go in the sale next Tuesday. He showed Robert the catalogue of the last sale. They agreed terms. The deed was done.

The glittering shafts of sunlight made him angry. What use

were they now? They signalled the turn of the year, but they were too weak to green up the grass, useless to save him. They only reminded Robert that it would be late April or May before that. He had had no conception of how slowly the seasons dragged.

He stopped the car on the road when he came within sight of the house. He could see it clearly through the wind-stripped hedges. He tried to envisage in his mind's eye how it could look. The external plasterwork needed repair and it needed painting. The massive chimney needed re-pointing. The front garden should be converted from vegetable patch to orchard. He could see it all if he only had the money and if he was allowed the time. He began to think ahead. Turning off to the farm he drove round to the back yard instead of approaching the house in the normal way. He got out and went over to the pigs, treading carefully from one drier island to another in the mess. He was wearing his good suit and shoes. The pigs snorted and grunted at him, raising their heads so that their noses stuck over the sty. He scratched the top of their heads. Perhaps this was where his future lay, not cows. Pigs and chickens. One of the animals managed to jump up so that its forelegs overhung the sty. While he was scratching the other animal it nipped his arm painfully. Robert let out an exclamation and hit it sharply on the nose with the back of his hand. The animal grunted and dropped back into the sty. There was nothing beautiful about pigs as there was about cows.

Depressed, he returned to the house by the back door. From the kitchen he saw Margaret and Heinz in the living room. They were embracing and her arms were locked around his shoulders. As he watched they moved back from each other without releasing their embrace. They talked to each other, gently.

Robert turned and retreated like a thief. In the yard he ran through the mud, ignoring his suit, ignoring his shoes. He flattened nettles and briars and ran into the adjoining field of young oats, straight for the middle, not caring about his direction or the damage, running until his lungs hurt with gasping and he had to stop. He was in the middle of it, a tilled flat plate of infant greenery with hedges around its horizons. The crop rows seemed to radiate from him as if he was in a vortex. Running had made him giddy and the plate of green seemed to tilt. He closed his eyes. He wanted to shout and yell and curse at God, at Margaret, at Germany, at himself. Instead he said nothing.

After some time he opened his eyes. He looked round the field, followed the hedgerow right around the perimeter, turning slowly on the spot. He tried to recover from the field and the sky and the air that feeling that had possessed a small boy. The liberty beyond dreaming. He could not.

He walked carefully back the way he had come, retracing his footsteps through the damaged crop. A pair of lapwings sprang up and ran before him, then rose screaming to drive him off.

He returned to the car and steered it quietly back to the road. From there he drove noisily to the front of the house, rattling over ruts. He slammed the door noisily and fiddled needlessly with the windscreen wipers.

When Margaret opened the door to him he could hear the noise of the work upstairs.

'Was it all right in Braintree?' she asked. He looked at her as if this was an unexpected remark. She was struck by his whiteness and grimness. His moustache was like a wipe of charcoal on white paper.

'I've arranged the sale.'

He still looked at her, not moving.

'Did you hear that loud bang?' she asked. 'There was an explosion.'

'No. Not in Braintree.'

He felt exhausted.

'Let me make you some tea?' said Margaret.

'Yes,' said Robert. He sat down in an armchair, feeling this was no longer his room.

Heinz was astonished to be given two letters by Ehrich on his return to camp. They both carried the Allied occupation stamps, but one was clearly from his mother. The other was from Hamburg. He knew immediately it was from Inga and he lay down on his bunk as casually as he could to hide his emotions.

'You're a lucky fellow!' called Ehrich. 'Two letters, eh? From the girlfriend?'

'Mind your own business!' He heard Ehrich chuckle. Heinz debated which to open first. The thought of news from Inga alarmed him. He opened his mother's letter. Another sheet of coarse brownish paper. She must have been eating before writing it, or perhaps it was the careless hands of the censor, because there were fingerprints upon it, slightly greasy.

'Dearest Heinz,

How are things with you? We received your letter safely and are very glad that you are now allowed to write a letter a month. We hope you will try to. I am glad that you are fed well in England. We have very little food here and things are quite difficult.'

Across the next two lines the censor had used obliterating ink. Heinz tried holding the sheet to the light but could make out nothing. The Soviet authorities clearly did not want details broadcast.

'I have managed to contact Inga and she says she will write to you. Her letter to me was very short so I cannot tell you any news. How was the winter in England? It was very cold here.'

The next two lines were obliterated.

'However, we made a small celebration for Christmas. The Spring is with us early and perhaps it will be a good summer. We hope to see you during it as we hear there is talk of repatriation. It may only be rumour.

'Please write as often as you can. All our love,

Mum and Dad.'

He wondered how he could ever tell them that he was thinking of staying in England. Perhaps he could get them out of Germany? He did not like the look of the censorship ink. How much of what he was writing was getting through? He read it again, imagining what was unsaid and what had been deleted. He knew from the English papers and from the B.B.C. news that parts of Germany were starving. He felt sick at heart. What continuing retribution would the Allies and particularly the Russians take?

He turned Inga's letter round in his hands, reading the Hamburg postmark. She had posted it in Wandsbeck. Her writing was stiff and childlike, the letters scarcely joined. He leaned over to his locker and took his carving knife, carefully slitting the top of the envelope, then lay back on his bunk and sniffed inside it to catch some scent of her. He thought that for just a moment there was a faint perfume, then he was aware only of the fish glue that secured the flap. He removed the letter cautiously. The paper was thin but whiter than his mother's. She had written in purple ink for some reason. Perhaps it was all she could obtain.

'Dearest Heinz,

Your mother has written to me and given me your address at Camp 78, England. As you can see I am in Hamburg. I hope you are well and are being well looked after. Things in Hamburg are not good. The city is badly damaged from bombing and most of it is in piles of ruins. Still, the trams are running again and shops are open.

I am living in Wandsbeck which is not much damaged. I have to tell you, Heinz, that since you went away I have become engaged to be married here. I know this will be bad news for you, but we did not think it fair to keep you in the dark. We hope you will understand. I have not told your mother as I did not want to upset her.

Best regards and fond memories,

Inga.'

Heinz stared at it, speechless. He looked at the head of the letter. There was no address. There was no explanation of who 'we' were. The breathtaking ease with which she had disposed of him began to sink home and he began to laugh, at first quietly to himself, then louder so that Ehrich leaned over his head hanging upside down.

'Something good?' he asked.

'Yes, yes, it's good. It shouldn't be but it's good.'

Ehrich still hung there.

'Going to tell me?'

'No, not now. Another time. Something personal, you understand.'

'Lucky man!' Ehrich disappeared.

So that was that. His stay in England was confirmed. That afternoon he had told Margaret of his intentions. She had seemed pleased. It would all be difficult but it was a new life. He got on well with the boys. He must see the Commandant to discuss the situation. He would have to wait, to get his timing right.

Margaret and Robert lay silently in bed. Neither was asleep. The gusty wind had dropped after clearing the sky and there was a moon. Margaret was considering again and again what Heinz had said. He declared he loved her and that he was going to stay in England. He had said no more but he made his inference plain. She had smiled and nodded because she was too full of mixed emotions to think. She supposed she did love him. Listening to Robert breathing beside her she knew that she did not love Robert whatever else she felt for him.

Robert suddenly sat up, alert. He swung his legs out of the bed and pulled back the curtains, letting moonlight flood in. He opened the window.

'What is it?' she asked, alarmed.

'Shh!'

He leaned out as far as he could. In a moment he was inside again, slamming the window shut. He pulled off his night clothes and started to dress.

'There's a cow in trouble out there. I can hear it. Get dressed.' She got up without argument.

'I'll fetch the lanterns and a torch,' he said. He was already clothed while she still struggled. 'You'd better get the children as well. If they're straying we'll have to search.'

The search was brief. Guided by the lowing and bellowing of the animals they quickly traced them to the pond. Robert shone the torch at the far side where a hedge separated it from the pasture. The hedge was broken and two animals were in the water. Robert swore. They had sunk so that only head and shoulders were above water. As they all watched the creatures started to struggle in the cone of light, wallowing and sinking further. Robert turned it off. His voice was hard and clipped with anxiety.

'If they struggle, they'll drown. William, go round to the field and make sure none of the others is near that hole. Block it. John, go to Ingleton and apologise. Tell him what has happened and ask him if he would be good enough to bring his tractor round. It has headlamps and he can light the whole place. I'll get the tractor and the rope. We shall have to get a rope around them to help pull them out.'

Margaret and Helen were given no tasks. They stood beside

the pond in the moonlight and made encouraging noises to the bellowing animals. They could hear them struggling and splashing.

'We're supposed to be selling them,' said Helen. 'I suppose this is terrible.'

'I don't know. We have to get them out. We have to have the money.'

'I hate this farm,' said Helen. 'It's almost as if it wants to harm us.'

'That's nonsense. Farming is just like this, animals are just like this. You can't predict these things . . .'

She thought of the field of beans. She had not dared to ask Robert if he had noticed.

A barn owl flew over the pond and hooted from a large tree. Helen shivered, clutching herself.

'Go and get more clothes on.'

'No, I don't want to be alone in the house while this is going on.'

'Robert arrived with the tractor. Its lights were yellow and inadequate to light the far side. He had two lengths of rope that he joined together. From the other side of the pond they could hear William shooing the cows.

'There's nothing here to block it with,' he called.

'Then stay there.'

Robert had put on boots. He picked up one end of the rope and walked into the pond, steadily, heading towards the cows. The water reached his knees, then his waist, and was soon up to his armpits. He moved slowly, holding the end of the rope aloft. He had offered no explanation to the two women and they watched impotently. They heard him talking to the cows.

'Easy, easy. Steady now, stay . . .'

Robert was alongside the first animal. Its eyes were rolling wildly, showing huge white rims. He put his hands on its neck feeling it quiver at his touch, but at least it stood still. He looped the rope over its neck and tied a noose that was just tight enough to slide up its head. The animal rocked to and fro, trying to extract a leg from the enclosing mud. Robert knew he must keep their heads up. If they knelt down they would go under. He backed slowly away from the animal, holding the rope and waded back to where the tractor stood. He was soaked from head to foot and black up to his shoulders. He wrapped the other end of the rope around his waist and then over a shoulder and moved back until it was taut and pulled. The cow's head turned towards them and it roared. The noose caught and its neck stretched out. The bellowing increased. They could hear splashing.

'Help!' shouted Robert. 'Pull!' Margaret and Helen took hold of the rope as best they could but the pond edge was wet and was becoming slippery. They stumbled and dragged Robert forward.

'Stop.'

His face was almost expressionless, his commands were delivered in monotone. He unwound the end of the rope from his body and ducked beneath the front of the tractor, pulling it taut and knotting it around the front axles. He climbed on the machine, roaring the engine, and began to back it slowly. The animal's head was pulled towards them again. The rope tautened and it let out a frantic roar. Somehow it managed to plunge free for a moment then fell in again, nearer the shallows. Robert backed off and repeated the process. The rope snapped out in the pond.

Robert drove the tractor forward and was about to wade back into the foul-smelling water when they saw bright lights approaching and almost immediately heard the sound of Ingleton's tractor. John was riding on it. It parked alongside Robert's elderly Fordson and Ingleton jumped down, quickly assessing the situation. Both animals were now clearly visible.

'You need a rope around the near one's body,' he said, 'if you keep pulling her by the head you'll break her neck or pull her head off!'

'All right. The rope's just snapped.'

'I brought one.'

Ingleton produced a substantial coil from the back of the tractor. Robert picked it up and before anyone else could move had waded back in, carrying it.

'I'll help!' called Ingleton.

'Stay there.'

They watched him lay a hand on the animal again, talk to it until it was still, then slowly lower himself into the water until he was completely under. He emerged and moved slowly round the animal's head until he was alongside its other flank. There he slowly sank again, to emerge with the other end of the rope. They saw him tie it above the animal's shoulders. He waded back, shaking with cold.

'Try that,' he said. Ingleton turned his tractor quickly, its lights catching distant trees and disturbing the owl. He tied the rope to the tow bar and began to move forward cautiously. His powerful machine had a deep roar that drowned out the noise of the animal. A cloud of blue smoke rose in the lights. They watched anxiously as the rope tautened, rose horizontal from the water, then finally slackened as the animal gave a huge heave and fell sideways, splashing. It was free. Robert dashed forward to take the slack rope and, pulling by hand, drew in the floundering beast. It lay in the shallow water shivering, refusing to rise. Robert stood beside it, shaking even more. His teeth were chattering so that he could not speak. He felt around its shoulders and neck to see if the rope had done any damage and then tried in vain to undo the knots with cold incompetent hands. Ingleton waded in beside him, took him by the shoulders and propelled him to the bank.

'Get something warm on, man, you'll die out here!'

'What about the other one!'

'It'll come out, now get something on.'

'Not till it's out!' Ingleton undid the tightened knot and slipped the rope from under the cow. It looked at him with mad eyes. Ingleton stooped over it, pulled back an ear and shouted.

'Get up, you beast!'

The cow's head shot up and it struggled to its feet, shaking. Ingleton seized its tail, bent it up tight and shoved. The cow walked out.

'That has to go in the barn.'

They heard voices and a car approached slowly. West was driving and Jempson walked in front, giving directions to avoid the ruts. Margaret went to Robert and tried to put her jacket around him, but he brushed her impatiently away.

'What are you doing here?' he asked.

'John Ingleton called me,' said West. 'You'll need more pairs of hands.'

Robert turned to Jempson. His teeth were chattering again and he was only able to stare at him in astonishment.

282

'Bill said to me, you know the place, and I said, I do. So I came. I see you've got one out. Get one of the boys to take her back to the barn and rub her down with straw. Rub her all over, but be gentle, mind. You'll need the vet for her, she's heavy with calf. Keep her quiet and still.'

Ingleton produced a rope halter from the back of the tractor. It seemed he had thought of everything.

'I'll take her,' said Helen quickly. It was something she could do and she was cold. Ingleton quickly slipped the halter over the animal's head. When Helen led on, the cow lurched unsteadily but moved forward.

'Take care,' said Ingleton. 'Take her slowly. Let her stop when she wants. If she lies down on you, come back to us right away.'

'What about the other cow . . .' stammered Robert.

'Faggots,' said Jempson. 'It's deep out there. She won't be able to get a foot on anything. We must make a raft for her. If we get bundles of faggots under her feet we can haul her upright and she'll stand. You did well, Mr Ellis, to get the first one out. We must get a rope to this one's head to keep her from drowning.'

Before he could finish Robert had taken the rope again and started to trudge into the pond. Ingleton and Jempson shouted at him to stop but he paid no attention.

'It's my cow!'

Ingleton turned to Margaret.

'He'll get his death of cold. How long has he been in there?'

'Half an hour.'

'Can't you stop him. We'll take over.' She called to him.

'Robert, let Mr Ingleton and Mr Jempson take over!'

He shook his head. Reaching the animal, he held out his hand towards it then laid it comfortingly on its neck. It strained and moaned. He made a loop of rope and tied it around its neck. Ingleton on the bank took up a gentle strain and tied the rope to his tractor. Robert half swam, half waded back.

'These faggots . . .' he asked.

'Sit down!' commanded Ingleton.

'But where are the faggots?'

'Under the hedge there,' said Jempson simply, 'in case they should ever be needed.' He pointed to an overgrown mass of

283

brambles under the hedge to one side. They were stoutly wired and seemed perfectly preserved.

'Good faggots don't rot,' said Jempson with satisfaction.

The men and John formed a heap of them at the water's edge. Robert seemed dazed.

'I didn't even know they were there . . .'

'Why should you?' said Jempson. 'Never burn 'em. It's a labour to bind 'em, I should say it is. But they last.'

'I'll get them out there,' said Ingleton hoisting a bundle on his shoulders.

'No!' shouted Robert. 'You've all got your good clothes on. I'm filthy. Pass them to me!'

He ran into the water again like a man possessed, clapping his hands together and extending them.

'Come out of the water, man!' shouted West.

'Pass them, hurry!' shouted Robert. Ingleton shrugged threw his bundle to Robert. Robert waded out to the cow.

'Leave it there,' said Jempson. 'Put them all round old cow. They'll settle themselves, just you see, because they're wet.'

'Make a chain,' said Ingleton.

They passed the dense bundles out one at a time. Robert moved round the animal, making a mat that radiated from it and slowly sank. The cow was groaning now, a hoarse noise like snoring but coming from deep in its throat. Its chin touched the water and the rope that held its head up was tight. Its eyes were turned upwards.

'We need another rope under its body,' said Ingleton.

'I'll do that,' said West. He took a second rope from Ingleton's tractor and waded out to join Robert. Together they fed the rope under the animal and tied it behind its shoulders. Ingleton hitched it to the tractor, giving Jempson the head rope.

'We'll try and get her onto the faggots!'

He engaged the gears and let in the clutch slowly. The rope became taut. The animal groaned and moved its head from side to side. The tractor stopped.

'I'll put it on the winch!' shouted Ingleton. 'It will be slower and give me more power.'

He transferred the rope. Robert and West grappled in the mud, hauling and pushing at the animal. They could feel its legs and were trying to work them free, to get its knees or feet on the sunken faggots. Ingleton engaged the winch. The drum turned with infinite slowness. Margaret, oblivious of her own coldness, watched the rope strain, shedding droplets of water in the dirty yellow light. The tractor began to move slowly towards the pond, wound in by winch. Ingleton stopped it.

'We'll have to strap it to a tree,' said Jempson. Ingleton nodded. The thin man was moving confidently. His knotted hands took more rope, passed it around and under the front axles of the tractor. Ingleton sat and watched. He had the utmost confidence in Jempson as one farmer in another. He watched Jempson pass the rope around the trunk of a tree and repeat the lashing so that he had a double thickness. He tied knots calmly and firmly, checking each one with a tug to see it was right.

William, watching from the hedge, could see the struggle beneath him most clearly. Robert and West were both pulling at one of the animal's legs together. They seemed to get it up, for the animal started to move its body. The water slapped about like oil in the mixture of light from the headlamps and moon. They moved to another leg. Robert was completely under water, scrabbling and splashing. He was like a madman, without feelings or concern, teeth rattling whenever he tried to say a few words.

They shoved at the cow together and then pulled another leg up.

'She's floating on her forelegs!' shouted West. 'You might be able to drag her in now!'

The tractor growled noisily and spewed blue smoke. The winch turned and the tractor moved until the lashing restrained it. Ingleton gave the engine more power. The ropes creaked, the bark on the tree cracked, making them start. The rope began to slowly wind in. West yelled excitedly.

'She's moving! Easy!'

It seemed to them all to take an infinite time. An inch at a time the cow and the raft of faggots was drawn across the pond. West waded behind it, exhausted.

'Look after Mr Ellis!' shouted Ingleton. West turned in time to see Robert collapsing into the water. He had him quickly and dragged him to the bank. The cow was trying to struggle to its feet in the shallows but was ignored. Margaret held Robert's head. William left his post on the far side of the pond and ran round.

'I think he's just passed out,' said Ingleton. 'He's very cold. Put him in the car, Bill, and get him to the house and into a bed as fast as you can. Mrs Ellis, he needs a warm drink. Never mind the cow. We'll see to it and get the vet.' His thin terrier face was pale and showed the strain he had hidden until now. He went to the car and opened the door. Bill West helped Robert up, almost carrying him to it. Margaret got in beside him, putting her arm round his shoulders. He slumped against her, shivering violently.

Shutting the door on them, Ingleton stooped. The yellow light made his teeth look more yellow. She tried to stutter thanks to him but he held up a hand.

'He fought for them cows like a good 'un,' he said and turned away as West drove off.

'What do you think?'

The three men and the boys stood in the barn looking at the cows lying in the straw from a split bale. They had been joined by the vet who had just finished examining them. A Tilley lamp was hooked on a nail and hissed gently, producing a round pool of light.

'This one will lose its calf, that's certain, and I'm not too happy about the mother. She's about thirty months, and I guess the calf is about two hundred and forty days. We'd better not move her to a stall. The other may lose hers as well, but the cow seems all right.'

'Poor beggars,' said Ingleton. 'And Mr Ellis was hoping to sell them on Tuesday.'

'I thought he was building up a herd?' said the vet. Ingleton shot a warning glance towards the two boys.

'No. He wanted to sell them.' Ingleton turned to the boys. 'You two had best go. There's nothing more here. Your Pa did a good job in that pond. You should be proud of him.'

'You should,' said Jempson.

When Jempson told his wife what had happened, she laughed harshly. Jempson scowled at her.

'Seeing as he can't get mangolds,' she said, 'he's better off without cows. It fits, don't it!'

'Shut up!' said Jempson. 'You always was a hater. I want that farm to do good, so just you shut up!'

Margaret sat at the side of the bed, watching Robert. He was asleep peacefully, his face more relaxed than she had seen it since before he went away to the war. She felt tenderness towards him. She had watched his frantic persistence with admiration and respect. She could have loved him for it once, but it was all too late. She felt deep sorrow for him. No more.

CHAPTER THIRTEEN

Four days later the police arrived on their bicycles. The Sergeant was a tall florid man and the Constable was white-haired, lined and weatherbeaten. They both looked very hot. They were not pleased at the length of the journey and the up-hill shoves.

John and William sat together on the sofa, William clutching the cat for comfort. The policemen confronted them and Margaret and Robert stood at each end of the sofa. Helen had pretended to leave but was listening outside the door.

'We know you've been making explosions in the meadow,' the Sergeant said. 'Everyone has heard them. We've been down there and had a look. You can't fool anyone, my lads. There's tins and burn marks all over the place, and what are these we found in a rabbit hole?'

He delved in his trouser pocket and pulled out a handful of opened brass cartridges. The boys were white as paper. They stared at the floor.

'And we followed your tracks across the field. You two boys aren't very clever, are you? You ought to know better than to run across a growing crop. Don't you know you can see it for days? We know where you've been breaking in, we've seen it all. It's a miracle you're still alive.'

He turned to Margaret.

'This is a very serious matter, Mrs Ellis. I expect we shall have to report it to the Chief Constable, seeing as what was involved. If they had set those things off they could have flattened everything for miles. There wouldn't have been a window left in this house for a start. You should keep a better eye on them with things like that around.'

Margaret looked angry but said nothing.

'Surely they're not fused?' said Robert. 'There was hardly any chance of them setting anything off!'

'Now then, sir, I don't see as that's any defence . . .' The Sergeant was inclined to be belligerent.

'I'm not offering a defence, Sergeant. I'm asking a question.'

'No, they ain't fused.'

'They shouldn't be in the woods at all. Nor should the ammunition. And it should be properly guarded.' Margaret was letting her annoyance show. 'Who is responsible for guarding it?'

'All that's as may be but these boys should be taught a good lesson. They've been stealing and causing explosions and running wild and are lucky to be alive in my books. If they was grown-up they would be going for trial.' He stooped down to the boys. 'As like as not they would be spending some time in Chelmsford Jail. I expect the Magistrate will want a word with you.'

When he had left, Margaret fled from the room and Robert thrashed them in a towering rage. They knew he would but still hoped against hope that he wouldn't. John struggled and fought, but William just accepted it.

Much later that night Margaret came to see them in their room. She slid in quietly holding a finger to her lips and sat on John's bed.

'Why did you do it?' she asked quietly. William sniffed. She repeated the question. John stared at the ceiling. Their lamp was turned low and the draught created by the opening and shutting of the door made the circle of light from the funnel revolve on the ceiling.

'To make a big bang,' sniffed William. Both boys were resentful not penitent.

'But why?'

'To show Pa!' said John, vehemently.

'Show him what? I don't understand.'

'Just show him.'

'He doesn't need any more worries. It was a dreadful thing to do.'

289

'It's about time he worried about us!' said John. He turned over so that his face was away from her and pulled his blankets over him. Margaret kissed William on the forehead. John would not allow her. When she had left them, John turned to face William.

'I hate him and it serves him right!'

William said nothing. He didn't hate him, he just wanted him to be different.

CHAPTER FOURTEEN

Robert stood in front of the house with Wolfgang, Heinz, Wilhelm and Ehrich. He was in a cheerful mood and seemed excited by the work ahead. It was clear and warm at last and they squinted, holding hands up to see what he was talking about.

'You see that area of plaster,' he was saying, pointing high up on the pink-wash front of the building, 'you can see it is detached. Can you translate that, Wolfgang?'

'*Ja.*'

'Well, it must be cut back. Behind, there are wooden laths on a timber frame filled with brick. The plaster is lime and sand mixed with horse-hair. We have no horse-hair so it will have to go back in lime and sand only. You will add just a touch of cement. It's important that it is no more than one part to ten parts of the lime.'

Ehrich was nodding. He was the plasterer. He understood what Robert was driving at.

'It must not be too strong,' he said. 'If you had an old mattress, we could get the horse-hair.'

Robert smiled.

'You're absolutely right, but we don't have a mattress.' To the others he said, 'Ehrich is in charge of the plastering.'

Ehrich grinned and looked pleased. Robert pointed to the front again.

'The rest of it must be inspected, tapped lightly with a hammer. If any of it is loose, cut it out. Then the whole front needs repainting in the same pink. It is a Suffolk colour. The chimney needs repointing and the ridge tiles must be taken off carefully and reset in cement mortar.'

He paused while Wolfgang translated the more technical bits for Wilhelm and Heinz. The sky above the ancient tiles was blue as Bristol glass. They stood behind the old well-head. It had been sealed now with a lid made by Heinz from thick planks. The shaft of the pump still poked through it and the handle was there wrapped in cloth, but the pump was an electric one down in the depths.

Against the front wall of the house lay the long thatching ladders that Robert had purchased at the sale. He thought that he had never yet had the chance to use them for their purpose and now never would. It already seemed so long ago since that day in the meadow. The ladders were gaunt and bleached and the rungs had become slack from being dried out in the barn. Heinz had laid them out on the ground when he saw them and doused them with buckets of water to make them swell.

'You will have to make one into a roof ladder to get to the ridge,' said Robert. It was Heinz's turn to nod.

'I will do that. I will strap on timbers . . .'

'You have enough sand, lime, water, tools . . .?

The men looked about them, at the pile of yellow sand, bags of lime, two buckets, two shovels, two plasterer's trowels. Heinz saw they needed a board to mix on and that they needed two hawks. He would make these easily. He said so in German.

'What was that?' asked Robert.

'Heinz will make boards. To hold the plaster.'

'Good. I'll leave you to it then.' They could hear the tractor running in the old orchard beyond the walnut tree. Robert left them.

'He's in a good mood,' said Wolfgang. 'I've never seen him so cheerful. Considering he's had to sell the cows, I'm surprised.'

'The house seems to be his pride and joy.' said Heinz. 'It must be old.'

He lowered one of the ladders and hoisted it onto his shoulder. 'I'll make this one up for the roof, it won't take long.'

'We'll start on the loose stuff on the front,' said Wolfgang. 'Ehrich is in charge of mixing plaster.'

Ehrich threw a ball of yellow sand at him, laughing. They were going to enjoy the sun and the work.

Robert walked to the Fordson White Spot. It was emitting a hot haze of smoke. It had been transformed by the addition of a bulldozer shovel that he had hired from Taylor and Tester. He had paid their outstanding bills with the mortgage to get it.

He climbed onto the tractor and roared the engine, delighting in the sound of it, pulled the lever that lifted the shovel and backed the tractor. Starting forward, he lowered it and began to push, rocking it back and forwards as Taylor had advised him until it bit into the soil of the orchard. In front of him his objective was the old privy shed. Pushing a brown bow-wave of earth before him, he demolished it with one shove, backing off again and again to fill the pit until he had obliterated all traces of the thing. He sat and looked at the brown bald patch. Taylor's 'internal sanitation' was complete. It was an end to that chapter. He leaned on the wheel of the tractor, watching the dust settle. It was hot now and he was wearing only a vest. The machine and the dust and the sun reminded him momentarily of Africa and he felt a great pang for the place and the simplicity of things. England, Europe, was nothing but a minefield of problems and poverty and rules. He knew he must escape. The farm was a trap. He watched the Germans tapping at the plaster on the front of the house. He wondered if they realised, if Margaret truly realised that it was being prepared for sale. As the vet had predicted, the two cows that had fallen in the pond had both lost their calves and one of the cows had died from internal injuries, perhaps caused by being dragged out. For whatever reason a massive infection had developed and the vet was powerless. They had all stood in the barn — the animal had never been moved — and watched the vet perform his desperate rituals that turned out to be last rites.

'I'm sorry,' he had said eventually, 'she's in a bad way, in pain, I must give her a shot of something. You understand . . .?

'All right.'

Margaret had fled but the boys had stood and watched. He wasn't talking to the boys after their behaviour and they weren't talking to him, but kept apart, pale but interested. There was nothing to see. The animal's head dropped after the injection and then it lay on its side. There was a quiver in its flanks, then nothing.

Robert had sold one pig and had the other killed. Ingleton said the butcher was his man. When Robert told him what he wanted, the butcher asked if it was to be done up at the farm, and did he have a big enough copper to scrub it? Robert had blenched at all this.

'Don't you have a slaughter house?'

'Certainly I do, but most farmers hereabouts don't bother with that. We just put him in a frame and cut his throat and it's all over. Nothing to it. You know old George, don't you? He's the best man for that. Let him have the innards and he's happy . . .?

Robert had arranged for the butcher to take it away. The butcher had smiled, thinking his own thoughts, but Robert didn't care. The animal had been starved for a day then left in the back of the butcher's van. It came back in the back of the butcher's van, but this time was split in half, dismembered, shaved and pickled. George came with it and supervised while it was hung up the chimney for smoking on the chains and pulleys. Now when the boys looked up to the sky they could see the two sides in the flicker of firelight with the ribs glinting like piano keys. They lived off bacon.

Robert turned off the tractor. It was an act that returned him to the reality of the present. He climbed down and set off round the fields. He had to think and plan and he had to get away from the house to do it.

Margaret hid in the house, not knowing what to do. She had been surprised by Robert's insistence that they should have the whole gang of men.

'We can't afford all of them,' she had insisted.

'We can't afford not to,' was all Robert had said.

Since their last conversation on crops, Robert had said nothing about his plans. The chickens were their only source of income. Every morning the children collected the eggs before school, a task to replace the pumping. They brought them into the back kitchen in baskets and buckets and she stood there and scrubbed the fouled ones, then packed them all in layers in pressed card containers for collection.

She hovered in the living room, longing to see Heinz alone, but knowing that this was going to be difficult. She wondered if Robert had hired so many for that reason. She was crucified by anxiety that Baxter or Mary Merrow or someone might have said something to him. Robert would never give a sign. In all respects he seemed to become more of a blank book to her. They no longer made love, they no longer argued. Robert treated the children like lodgers and her like a housekeeper. She stared out at the bright day and began to cry, remembering Mary Merrow's sternness when she had hoped for an ally. It was true that a woman here was utterly alone. How could she leave Robert for Heinz? Even if they waited until the climate was better towards Germans. He said he wanted it, was arranging to stay. He was forcing her into it slowly but surely. What was the alternative?

A life with Robert.

With his photograph of himself.

Of duty.

She remembered all three children playing in the snow on Christmas morning. She had watched them run out early, understanding that she was seeing a fragile moment that might never be repeated and that for Helen at least it might mark the passing of childhood. Her own had slipped away with no huge milestones.

She could hear the men chopping at the plasterwork outside and hear voices. Heinz was talking in German. She tried to find comfort in listening to them. They were laughing and enjoying themselves. She could see Ehrich shovelling away and hear the ring of the shovel on a stone slab as he struck it to clean it. She must make them tea. It had become such a habit that they would wonder why not.

Robert walked the fields to kill time. His plan could only be put into operation when they went back in the lorry. He decided he would go to Braintree for the afternoon, leave the farm alone, leave Margaret too.

In the distance he could see the house and the ladders propped against it. Heinz must have succeeded in making up some sort of bracket, for one of the ladders also lay up the slope of the roof. Someone — it looked like Wilhelm — was sitting astride the ridge. Listening carefully, he could just make out the sounds of chopping and scraping.

He walked round the empty upper meadow. With the cows

gone it was growing well and would give a crop of hay in July. To bale for others. He would sell that too.

He was able to think more clearly in the open. The house filled him with irritations. Things not done, the children, untidiness. He had told Margaret nothing of his real plans. Nairobi or Salisbury or Fiji. The choices seemed limitless. He might return to a job for a bit until he discovered where the best farms were. In the end he must get back to farming. But how different it would be from all this. He recognised it had been a mistake. England was exhausted, Europe was exhausted. In the colonies there would be real space, real manpower and room for growth, a decent respect for things, no Taylors, no Testers with their watchful impertinence.

Perhaps the children could be sent away to school or even left in England although he could not see how he could afford that. He could not comprehend what Margaret could have done with them while he was away. Helen he could tolerate, but the boys did not even seem to be his anymore. They resented him. They resented discipline or control. And Margaret. She must be made to see. Could he forgive her? Not yet, it was all too soon, but away from this place where she could see him properly things would be different. She would be able to earn that forgiveness and they would both put it behind them as something that had arisen from confusion. From poverty.

He had walked round now to the largest bean field. Nine tenths of the crop were black. It wasn't worth harvesting. Ingleton had said to plough the lot in. He had not said to Ingleton that it would be a waste of fuel because he was leaving. He would cut the hay, but sell the corn still standing.

'You aren't going to spend it?' demanded Sally, eyes flashing. She had one arm round William's neck in case he changed his mind and was propelling him along the hot pavement. Behind her trailed her friend Mary with the dark hair, and three others. They all wanted a share.

'Yes, I am.' said William as bravely as he could. He had his National Savings book clutched firmly in his right hand. 'It's mine, so why shouldn't I?'

'Won't your Pa give you a belting?' Sally's eyes rolled with pleasurable awe.

'I don't care. Anyway we have plenty of money.'

'No, you don't, that's a lie, you haven't got *any* money, you never do!'

Her arm was withdrawn from his shoulder, she danced in front of him, blonde pigtail bouncing.

'I do, I just don't bring it to school. You don't know everything!'

'Buy me some liquorice sticks!' demanded Mary, practical, not interested in scoring points. 'That's what I want.'

'I want a lead bomb,' said one of the boys, 'and caps. He's got those. And he's got those sherbets that fizz up your nose. You don't need coupons for them!'

'We're taking it all down to the river,' said Sally. 'We're going swimming.'

School was over and they were walking to the Post Office. William had two shillings and sixpence in his savings. At the door of the Post Office the other children drew back, standing in the alley at the side where the postman entered. William felt sick.

'Go on then!' hissed Sally. William walked in as bravely as he could. There was no queue. A lady in spectacles looked down at him and smiled.

'Yes?'

'I want to draw out my money.' His voice sounded mangled and strained to him. He hoped the woman wouldn't notice. She took the book from him and turned the pages to look at the stamps.

'You have two shillings and sixpence in this book. Do you want to take it all out?'

'Yes.'

'Are you sure? Shouldn't you leave sixpence in to keep it open?'

'Yes.'

'Do you know what you want?'

'Yes, I'll leave sixpence in.'

The woman leaned over towards him, fixing him with a gimlet eye.

'What do you want the money for?'

'My mother is buying me some new shoes.' The woman smiled.

'That's nice. I hope you get good shoes.' She stamped the pages of the book, handed him two shillings and returned it. William walked out as slowly as he could.

On the river bank they spread themselves out where the children usually went to swim. William had never been and was enchanted. They all stripped down to their underpants and knickers and paddled and splashed. Sally could swim and did so. They were impressed. Sally sat next to William. He was very shy of looking at her in her knickers. He was relieved to see she didn't have a chest that was any different from his. Her friend Mary had little bumps. He kept his eyes averted.

'Why are you doing this all of a sudden?' asked Sally. 'You never came swimming before.' They were sitting on a large stone watching the water rush between their toes. The bottom of the river was of very fine gravel and the water was clear. Streamers of bright green weed had secured a hold here and there.

'I might be leaving soon.'

'How do you mean?'

'My Pa talked to Robert's dad about it.'

'Robert Kitton?'

'Yes.'

They both looked round. Robert Kitton was skinny with large ears and always knew too much. At the moment he was trying to persuade Mary to look down his underpants. Seeing he was watched he let them go with a snap and blushed.

'What are you all looking at?'

'We know what you're showing her! What did William's dad say to your dad about their farm?'

'He said he was selling it. He said he was going abroad. To Africa.'

Sally turned to William.

'He never told you this?'

'No.'

'I wonder what it's like in Africa? Do you want to go?'

'No.'

They had a bottle of lemonade which they were keeping cool in the water. William took it out, undid the stopper and passed it to her. It was deliciously cold.

'Robert Kitton tried to get *me* to look down his front,' she said confidentially. 'He does it to all the girls. He says he's got a big willie!'

They roared with laughter, throwing themselves down on the grass of the bank. It was a secluded spot, partially concealed from the bridge by a willow and a bed of balsam.

'I don't want to go to Africa,' said William presently. 'I want to stay here.'

'What will you do?'

What could he answer to that? A swallow swept down the river, dipped into the water and was gone.

'If I go to Africa, I shall come back. Have another sherbet . . .'

William was right in his assessment of Sally. She was immediately distracted and sucked vigorously at the paper straw. What would he do about Africa? It seemed a very large problem.

Robert had managed to kill time. First the walk round the fields, then a trip to Braintree, then back to the pub for lunch and a drink. It was something he was not used to and he felt awkward. Clara, the pale girl, had not been able to place him although she recognised him and watched as he drank. There was no one else in the place because he was late and it was a working day for men on the land. He asked her if she would like a drink but this embarrassed her and she refused.

He drank heavily, feeling he needed it. It was something else he had not done for a long time. He wanted to talk to the girl, to tell her he was sorry about what had happened to her, but did not know how to do it. The fireplace was stacked with wood and the interior that had seemed warm and bright before was cold and dark. The worn linoleum and buttoned furniture depressed him. Clara depressed him. He was relieved to get back into the sunlight. Nothing seemed to hold any pleasure for him.

He took the drive back to the farm very slowly, through the back lanes edged with pink roses and a froth of cow-parsley. He looked at the crops of other farmers, at barley that shone with the gloss of groomed hair, at the soft green of oats. He watched other men's cows grazing in meadows confused with butter-cups. The grass was tall now and pink with its crop of seed. The animals stood in the shade, swinging their tails at flies. He could hear a tractor working, perhaps taking the first cut of hay. He was confused by his love and hate of it all, by his desperation at what should have been.

He pulled up the car in front of the house. The men stopped and looked down, then continued with their work. A substantial area of plaster had been cut away and replaced with the first rough coat. Small patches had been cut away here and there. Ehrich and Wilhelm were both on the ridge and he could see a line of rebedded tiles. Wolfgang and Heinz were on the ladders. He continued round to the back of the house, parking there. He walked to the shed with the gas engine, noting new sawdust. Heinz had been making the brackets for the ladders or cutting new laths. He was out of sight of Ehrich and Wilhelm on the ridge, but they would have seen him cross the yard and enter. He turned the pulley of the gas engine by hand, pulling at the hard black belt. It shone like dull steel and the leather would not stretch. He picked up a length of wood and used it as a lever, forcing it between the belt and the pulley with one hand while he turned it with the other. The gas engine sighed as its pistons slid in the cylinders. The belt had moved. Robert repeated the operation, clawing at it in his haste and breaking a nail. He must be as quick as possible.

Suddenly it was free and fell with a smack onto the bench. He took the other end off the drive to the saw and folded the object. The stiff leather refused to bend and as soon as he doubled it one way it sprang out another. Looking round desperately he found a length of twine and tied the thing into a bundle, doubling it over and over and tying one knot after another. It was still larger than he had anticipated, but he was able to conceal it under his jacket. Looking round the building his eye was taken by a set of chisels stuck in a rack. He had bought them with the handsaws, squares and other carpenter's tools at the sale. He took them out one by one and put them in his jacket pockets. As rapidly as he could move, he was at the door. From there he strode purposely to the car, his arm pressed to his side trapping the bundle against his ribs. Getting in carefully, he drove back towards the front of the house, pausing at the gable wall. There he was out of sight. He pulled the belt out from his jacket and stuffed it under the front passenger seat of the car. He disposed of the chisels under the floor matting in the rear.

He continued round to the front where he braked noisily and got out briskly. He slammed the door behind him. The men looked down at him. Robert addressed Wolfgang from the floor of his ladder, ignoring Heinz.

'Tell the men to come down. Immediately. I want everyone now.'

Wolfgang looked puzzled.

'This coat of plaster is not quite finished. I think Ehrich should . . .'

'Just tell them to come down!' Robert commanded. Wolfgang shouted to the others in German.

'We are to come down. Now!'

'Why?' asked Ehrich.

'I don't know.'

Robert waited, scowling until all four men were standing on the ground. He couldn't see Margaret at any of the windows but had already noticed a tray with four tea mugs neatly placed on the well cover. She must be in and she must know they had been called down from the roof. Perhaps she was in the hall. He hoped she was listening.

'Something serious has happened,' he snapped, 'I want you all to stand up straight. Make a line!'

Wolfgang and Heinz exchanged glances expressing bewilderment. Ehrich and Wilhelm obeyed, puzzled.

'This is a total breach of trust, and I intend to get to the bottom of it. Wolfgang, you will translate if you think I say anything that cannot be understood.'

'*Ja*.'

'Mr Ellis.'

'*Ja*, Mr Ellis.' Wolfgang's face was expressive of hurt. Robert seemed beside himself. It was like a slap in the face.

Robert walked up and down in front of them, looking them in the face one by one. They looked back, looked away. Robert lingered in front of Heinz, but after returning his stare evenly Heinz straightened up and stared into the blue sky.

'Someone has stolen the belt from the gas engine and a set of chisels as well. After the matter with the belt from the threshing machine, I view this with the utmost seriousness. Translate that.'

He paused while Wolfgang tried to put it into German. The men stood more upright, their faces became wooden.

'Without that belt nothing can be driven. Belts are unobtainable since the war. Chisels are unobtainable. This is a serious theft and will have to be reported. I want the articles back. Last time I gave you three minutes to return them. I will do the same again. I am going indoors.'

He marched past them and entered the house. As he thought, Margaret was in the hall and had been listening.

'This is disgraceful!' he said. 'I can't leave the farm for a few hours without things being stolen. The first time I could overlook, but not this!'

'It couldn't be Wolfgang or Heinz . . .' Margaret was agitated, 'you can't believe it was either of them . . .'

'Why not? I don't know who took the other belt.'

'But we know them.'

'Do we?' He swung on her with an iciness that made her step back from him. She wondered if it *was* possible that either could steal. What did she really know about Heinz? She felt sick in her stomach.

'Where have you been all afternoon?' he demanded.

'In the house. Except when I made them tea. I was baking.'

'Then how would you know where anyone has been? Someone must have been to the shed. There's sawdust there.'

'I think Heinz was sawing . . .'

As soon as she uttered the words she clutched her mouth with her hand.

'I see,' said Robert gravely as if this was a revelation.

'All right,' said Heinz, 'get this clear. I didn't take the belt or the chisels. You don't really think that, do you? Where would I put them? Do I look as if I've got them?'

'We aren't accusing you,' said Wolfgang. 'But we have to ask. No one else has been to the saw.'

'So someone else has stolen the belt. While we were all up on the house some thief has nipped in and taken it. And the chisels. It's the only explanation.'

'We're in a spot,' said Ehrich. 'If we can't produce the things we'll be in real trouble. He's not going to believe someone else took them.'

'We can't produce what we don't have,' said Wolfgang.

302

'He'll think we've hidden them. Or someone has,' said Wilhelm. 'We'll get solitary for this.'

'I'll try to tell him that none of us has touched the things,' said Wolfgang.

Heinz wondered if the things had really gone. He could not voice his thought in front of the others but he would have liked to have said it to Wolfgang.

Robert re-emerged from the house. He stood outside the door and looked first down to the ground in front of the men, then along the row they made in the elaborate slow motion of army inspection. He halted in front of Wolfgang.

'Where are they then?'

'We do not have them, sir. None of the men has taken them.'

'I see. So where have they gone?'

Wolfgang shrugged.

'We think someone else must have stolen them while we were all up on the house, sir. Some thief who was passing.'

'Did anyone see this thief?'

'No, sir. We have all been busy working.'

'Do you want to think about your reply a bit longer?' Robert was deadly calm. His face matched theirs for woodenness.

'We do not have them, sir.'

'Get yourselves ready to go back to camp. Take those ladders down and clear up the plaster. When you have done that, march to the road and wait there for the transport.'

Heinz was cutting whistles when William came upon the men at the roadside. They were all sitting down and looked moody and preoccupied. William had not quite dried out and he was uncomfortable. He was also late. He called out a cheerful hello.

'Hello,' Heinz replied, pausing in his whittling. 'How are you?'

'I think you should not talk to us,' said Wolfgang. 'We are in trouble and you will get into trouble too.'

'What trouble?'

'Your father thinks we took the belt from the gas engine but we didn't.'

To William it meant little. He was hurt that he had not received their usual warm greeting.

'Can I have a whistle, Heinz?'

'Sure. I have made enough.'

He passed one to William who climbed back onto his bicycle. They watched him push along the road, wobbling slightly, then heard the thin reedy notes as he blew a warble. William turned slightly in his saddle and waved. The men waved back, mechanically.

'This makes me sick at heart,' protested Wolfgang, 'this is not the same man as at Christmas. What does he think we are? We've worked, we've done everything right, I thought he trusted us.'

Heinz said nothing. He cut another length of ash, rolled it between his palms, notched it, prepared to make another whistle.

'Sit down, take that chair.' Robert sat. The two men had met before so there was no need of further formalities. 'You asked to see me and I gather you have a rather serious charge to make.'

'I'm afraid so.'

'Heinz Geisseler.'

'Yes.'

'I will have to make a formal report. Can you give me the details?'

Robert repeated what he had already told a junior officer. His absence from the farm, the discovery of the theft, the opportunity that he gave them for replacing the stolen goods. He explained about the previous incident that he had not reported. He explained that only Heinz had been to the outbuilding, that this was confirmed by the other men. Middleton listened with a minimum of interruption, writing everything down carefully in a neat sloping hand. When Robert had finished he pushed back his own chair and stretched his legs.

'Do you smoke?'

'I used to smoke a pipe. Not now.'

'Me too. You were in Africa, weren't you?'

'Yes. How did you guess?'

'It wasn't a guess. I knew Paterson, you know.' Robert stared at him. His mouth had suddenly gone dry and he coughed. Middleton seemed to be watching him. The conversation had taken a different turn from what he had envisaged. 'He was your lieutenant, wasn't he? When he was killed. I was at school with his older brother. I heard about it from him and knew you must be the same Robert Ellis. You were with him at the time, weren't you?'

'Yes.' It emerged more as a noise than a word. What had happened in that crater in the desert had seemed to be in a past life. It was intensely personal, it was his own cowardice and shame. No other individual could or should know anything about it. What was Middleton driving at?

Paterson's bloodied head, the hole in his back. 'Help me.'

'A mortar, wasn't it?'

'Yes.'

'It made a bit of a mess of him.' Middleton looked absently at his notes.

'He was killed right away.'

The answer fell from his mouth too fast. Middleton's gaze flicked over him again.

'It sounds brutal to say it, but that's the best way to go. I've seen too many men mangled. I expect you have . . .'

Robert could only nod.

'You don't hate the Germans, do you?'

The question was so unexpected that Robert found his voice.

'Of course not. What an extraordinary question. I can't say I like it!'

'All right, all right, I have to ask that. You have to understand my job here. These prisoners are in my charge. There is nothing to support what you say, it's your word against this man's. There are some men who bear a hatred from the war. I don't think you're one of them. In fact I know you've had them in your house doing up the place and you invited two of them for dinner on Christmas day, didn't you? One of them was this Heinz Geisseler too. You must have thought he was an honest enough chap . . .'

'I suppose I did. What does that alter?'

Middleton's response was casual. 'Oh, nothing of course. I just like to have the facts and the background.'

'This isn't at all what I expected. I have come here to report

305

continued theft by one of your prisoners and it has become some sort of inquisition!'

'I'm sorry if it seems like that. That's just my incompetence.'

This man is far too competent, thought Robert. He must be watched at all times. He has been picked for this.

'I have to keep an eye and an ear open about fraternisation you know, however harmless. You know it's still officially frowned upon in some circles. Some camps won't allow men on the land yet. We are liberal here at Braintree.' He seemed to notice something wrong with his shoelace, but from where Robert sat he couldn't tell whether there was or not. Middleton spent about half a minute fiddling with it, stooping.

'How did your wife get on with the Germans?'

Robert told himself to keep calm. He controlled his facial expression well and managed a shrug.

'Well, I think. She made them tea and bread, the usual things . . .'

'I am going to put Geisseler on a transfer to another camp, and then on the first list for repatriation. That will be in the first week of October. Do you understand? He will go back to Magdeburg in the first eight thousand. He will leave this camp tomorrow. You don't need to know where he's going. A long time from now, in four, six months, you will get a postcard if the Russians let it through. You will reply, and it will probably never get there. That seems to me best in the circumstances.'

Robert stared. His face was reddening and he felt sweat forming round his collar. Middleton was looking into his eyes like a hypnotist. His face was closed in, unsmiling. There was a finality about his delivery that made it a judgement and prediction in one. Robert managed to say that he agreed. Middleton stood up and Robert realised that he was being released. He got to his feet. Middleton had opened the door, and held it there for him.

'I think it would be better if you didn't have *any* prisoners on the farm for the time being, don't you?'

'Yes. You're quite right.'

'I shall remember you to Paterson's brother if I may.'

'Please do,' stammered Robert. Middleton shook his hand

with courtesy and no warmth. Robert was glad to escape. He wondered just how much Middleton knew.

Margaret was waiting for him when he returned. He could see her grief and anxiety and could find no room in his heart for any pity, for any feeling at all except anger that she had exposed him to the whole thing.

'What is going to happen?' she asked. 'What did the Commandant say?'

'Heinz Geisseler is going to be repatriated. In view of the previous incident as well, he is of the view that he must be the thief. That is that.'

Margaret could contain herself no more. She burst into tears and fled upstairs to the bedroom, crying and crying. Helen appeared, alarmed, followed by the boys.

'What was that?' asked Helen. 'What's the matter?'

'Just a rather nasty business with one of the prisoners. He was stealing. I had to report it and he will be punished.'

'Who?' asked William.

'Heinz.'

William nodded. He knew to say nothing, give nothing away. After a few minutes he walked out to the barn by himself and sat on a straw bale watching the chickens. Unbidden tears squeezed from his eyes but he sniffed and wiped them away with a cuff. From his pocket he took the ash whistle that Heinz had given him and played it. It made three notes and he could make them tremble. He knew that Heinz did not steal. He knew why Ma was crying too. He wished that he was grown-up.

CHAPTER FIFTEEN

It was a warm July day, perfect for hay-making. A breeze stirred in the hedgerows and flowed across the uncut grass. It was a time for white butterflies that moved jerkily about from scabious to sow-thistle. Swifts already seemed restless and their screaming was urgent. Robert drove the tractor and mower round and round the perimeter, working slowly in towards the centre. He had never cut hay before but it was easy compared with most other tasks and he was enjoying it. It was a last act, as he would be sold up and gone before harvest. Their furniture was mostly packed and Kitton had sent his men round to catalogue everything. He had already overcome his regrets and was looking forward again. He planned and booked his first steps. Nairobi as he had said, then north-west or north-east to find a farm. It would give him the solitude that he yearned for. Margaret would stay with her brother until he sent for her. The children would remain in England. Margaret's brother had said he would pay for that for a year until they had found their feet. It was all satisfactory.

He glanced down behind and to the side, watching the swath-board and knives. Across the field he saw Jempson. The man was standing waiting for him. It was strange how the man had never been able to stay away. When he reached him he stopped the tractor. The chattering din of the mower ceased. Jempson was carrying a gun. He seemed shy.

'What are you doing here, Mr Jempson?'

'Don't mind, do you?'

'Not at all. Brought your gun, I see.'

'This old field was always crawling with rabbits. I've had up to thirty out of her at mowing. I don't make any promises, mind, but I reckoned you might like something for the pot, and I certainly would. They should start coming out of there when you get about halfway to the middle and they heads for the wood just over there . . .' He pointed.

'That's fine,' said Robert. He was not sure how to leave the man. Jempson instinctively understood.

'Don't you bother about me. I shall keep myself out of the way.'

'Are you going to come to the sale?' asked Robert, curious.

'No, I shan't do that. One sale is enough for me. I don't want to see all them things sold all over again so soon. Anyway, I should be right upset if you make more than I did!' Jempson summoned a dry chuckle. Robert started the engine and continued on his way.

On his next circuit of the field he saw a familiar car through the hedge. Taylor and Tester stood in the field in the shade of an oak. They were watching as always, apparently content to do no more. Robert found them very distracting. He was angry at their casual ways. It was still his land.

He stopped the tractor, expecting them to come forward, but they still stood, looking. Like vultures, he thought, sitting on a branch. He owed them nothing. They had been paid out of the mortgage as well. He climbed down and walked over to them.

'Good morning, gentlemen, what can I do for you?'

'Mornin' Mr Ellis,' said Taylor, 'I hope you don't mind us just standing here.'

'What do you want?' asked Robert sharply. Taylor wore his uniform of trilby, dungarees and army boots. He was sweating slightly in the heat. Tester looked as black as a coalman and was unshaven. Taylor glanced at Tester and raised an eyebrow.

'I hope we aren't going to part on bad terms, Mr Ellis. I think you should be pleased, what with going to Africa. We always sold you things at a good price, you know. We never pressed too hard for payment.'

Robert ignored this lie.

'All right, I'm sorry, what do you want?'

'We were just looking over the old tractor and mower, weren't we.' Tester nodded and shifted the position of his feet. 'Then I wondered what you was going to do with all this hay. Now we're prepared to buy it off you, loose or baled if the price is right. Then we were thinking that there might be other things you would like to dispose of, remembering that we don't charge a fee.'

'I've already sold the hay to Ingleton.' Taylor shrugged.

'Well, that's a shame. You know, Mr Ellis, I don't think you've ever really liked me and Tester, which is a shame as well. Sometimes people doesn't, but we get by. It's strange how a little thing can bring a man down, isn't it. With William the Third it was the gentleman in black velvet, with you it was them mangolds that started it all, and just for the want of sweating.'

Robert could not contain his anger. He was appalled again by how much of everyone's business they knew.

'I don't need your advice,' he shouted, 'just get off my bloody land!' Jempson had been approaching quietly. Taylor nodded to him, nodded to Tester and the two of them left.

'Don't you worry, Mr Ellis,' called Taylor as they departed through a hole in the hedge, 'it don't bother us. We get most of it in the end. See you at the sale!' He raised his hat derisively.

The two boys watched the mowing from just within the field gate. Here ragwort grew and it was swarming with yellow-and-black caterpillars. Margaret would not come. She was not interested in last acts of agriculture. She and Robert were civil to each other and she kept house for him but no more. She had listened to all his plans and agreed. She had agreed what a good idea Kenya was, what a wonderful place it must be to farm, how good it would be to get away from England, how good it would be for them both to start all over again without the children, because she was not going. She had no precise plans but would work at whatever she could. The children would go to state school in London. There was no question of paying for education. Her brother might be able to find her a secretarial job. It wouldn't pay much but she was accustomed to a poor living. All she had to do was keep up the pretence. She did not know if she always succeeded. Perhaps Robert knew in his heart that she would never join him and was glad.

'I'm looking forward to London,' said John. They were lying

on their stomachs trying to race two caterpillars up a blade of grass.

One would not move at all, the other was inclined to climb down.

'I think I am,' said Wiliam. 'Pa will be gone.'

'Are you pleased about that?'

William took a long time to answer.

'Yes. But we've had some fun here. I'm going to miss it. When I grow up, I'm coming back. I'm going to be a farmer.'

'Bet you won't!'

'You'll see.'

The mower was returning around the uncut sward towards them. There was a sudden commotion in the grass, a flash of black and white and the tractor stopped with a jerk. Robert jumped off it with a yell. William shouted and ran forward.

'Get back!' Robert bellowed. 'Stay away!' But William was not to be stopped. His cat lay in the grass with its legs cut off, hissing and screaming. Robert shouted for Jempson. No one seemed able to move. Jempson ran up, wheezing. He was an old man and could not be quick. He summed up the situation immediately and William turned away with his fingers in his ears as two shots rang out. He ran from the field to the road and up the road to the house and flung himself on his bed. It was the end to everything. From the farm he would take two things, his wooden tugboat carved by Heinz and the ash whistle.

CHAPTER SIXTEEN

Nairobi. December 7, 1946.

'Dear Margaret,

I think I have found the right farm. It is quite remote and very much in the heart of real Africa.

I am making the arrangements to purchase. It has almost five thousand acres of land for crops and I don't know how many thousand acres of grazing. There isn't a house on it that we would care to live in but I have been told how to go about getting a decent bungalow built. I am told, incidentally, that the farm has some of the best land in the district. Our neighbours will be the de Hoops. I have met them and I think you will like them. I will write again as soon as arrangements have been completed.

Your husband,
Robert.'

Magdeburg. December 10, 1946.

'Dear Mrs Ellis,

I am in Magdeburg as you can see and I want to thank you. I want you to know that I did not steal the belt or anything. That is true, you must believe me. Things here are quite difficult.'

The next lines had been obliterated entirely in the censor's ink.

'You are to write to me at this address if you would be so kind.

Yours sincerely,
Heinz Geisseler.'

The letters had arrived together by coincidence. Margaret put them on the fire together.

C